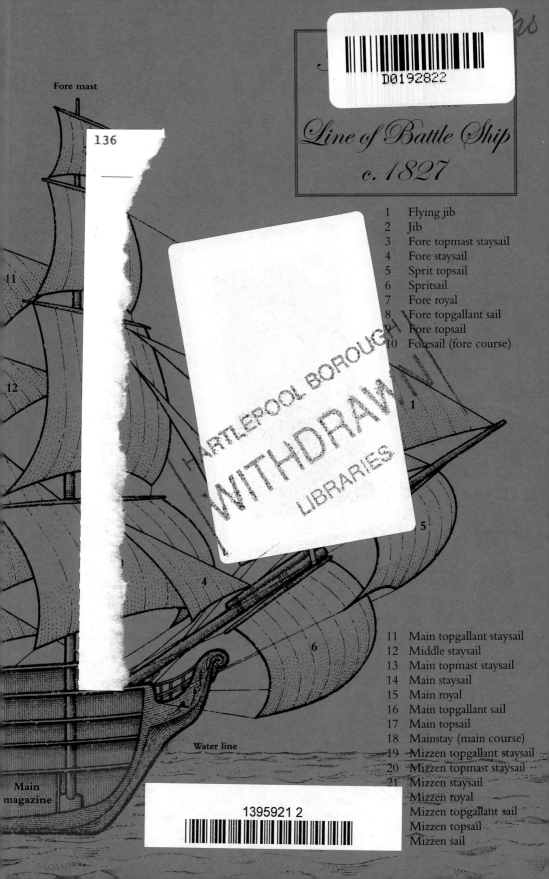

Fore mast

136

Line of Battle Ship
c. 1827

1	Flying jib
2	Jib
3	Fore topmast staysail
4	Fore staysail
5	Sprit topsail
6	Spritsail
7	Fore royal
8	Fore topgallant sail
9	Fore topsail
10	Foresail (fore course)

11

12

4

1

5

6

Water line

Main
magazine

11	Main topgallant staysail
12	Middle staysail
13	Main topmast staysail
14	Main staysail
15	Main royal
16	Main topgallant sail
17	Main topsail
18	Mainstay (main course)
19	Mizzen topgallant staysail
20	Mizzen topmast staysail
21	Mizzen staysail
	Mizzen royal
	Mizzen topgallant sail
	Mizzen topsail
	Mizzen sail

MAN OF WAR

www.booksattransworld.co.uk

MAN OF WAR

ALLAN MALLINSON

BANTAM PRESS

LONDON · TORONTO · SYDNEY · AUCKLAND · JOHANNESBURG

TRANSWORLD PUBLISHERS
61–63 Uxbridge Road, London W5 5SA
a division of The Random House Group Ltd
www.booksattransworld.co.uk

First published in Great Britain
in 2007 by Bantam Press
a division of Transworld Publishers

Copyright © Allan Mallinson 2007

Allan Mallinson has asserted his right under the Copyright, Designs
and Patents Act 1988 to be identified as the author of this work.

A CIP catalogue record for this book
is available from the British Library.

ISBN 9780593053423

Addresses for Random House Group Ltd companies outside the UK
can be found at www.randomhouse.co.uk
The Random House Group Ltd Reg. No. 954009

The Random House Group Ltd makes every effort to ensure that the
papers used in its books are made from trees that have been legally
sourced from well-managed and credibly certified forests. Our paper
procurement policy can be found at: www.randomhouse.co.uk/paper.htm

Typeset in 11/14.75pt Times by
Falcon Oast Graphic Art Ltd

Printed and bound in Great Britain by
Clays Ltd, Bungay, Suffolk

2 4 6 8 10 9 7 5 3 1

CONTENTS

MAPS

The Mediterranean and the course of HMS Prince Rupert, *1827 (page xii).*

The Allied Squadrons and the Turkish Fleet at Navarino, October 20th, 1827 (page 276).

FOREWORD

1827

'Soldiers and sailors are always acceptable in society,' says Mary Crawford in *Mansfield Park*. But, says Kipling a century later:

> *In times of war, and not before,*
> *God and the soldier men adore;*
> *When the war is o'er and all things righted,*
> *The Lord's forgot and the soldier slighted.*

Certainly army *officers*, especially when in regimentals, remained acceptable in society after Bonaparte had ceased his great disturbing. It was the rank and file who all too quickly regained their status as 'the brutal and licentious'. Sailors were spared this ignominy to some extent, for when they were not at sea they did not greatly trouble the country – at least not beyond a few ports. Their officers may have lost a little status (in the opinion of Sir Walter Elliot of Kellynch Hall they had, of course, possessed little in the first place), but the relative fortunes of the army and the Royal Navy were anyway changing. Traditionally, Britain had entrusted her prosperity and safety to her 'wooden walls', the ships that kept the seas safe for her merchantmen, and saw off the periodic threats of invasion. There was a hearty fear of a standing army and the expense and hazard of continental campaigns. And this was no less so, to begin with, in the war with revolutionary France. The death of Nelson had moved the fleet and the nation; the 'band of brothers' – Nelson's captains – and their younger siblings had not imagined, however, that their service would soon be eclipsed by men in red coats ashore. After 1808, when Bonaparte's invasion of the Iberian Peninsula gave Britain her chance to come to grips with the real Napoleonic engine of war, the Grande Armée, Trafalgar became rather a distant, if hallowed, memory; Salamanca, Talavera, Vitoria – these and others were the names that thrilled an Englishman in the decade that followed. And then the greatest of them all – Waterloo, the Iron Duke's culminating victory, which sent Bonaparte to his distant, fatal exile, and ushered in the concert of Europe on which an everlasting peace was to be built.

Now, however, in 1827, two decades after Trafalgar, the pendulum of military fortune was swinging back: it was His Majesty's ships that would again make war in the cause of peace and of liberty; the slave trade was being vigorously suppressed, and a triple alliance of Britain, France and Russia would oblige the Turks to quit Greek waters – the very cause for which Byron had died in the Peloponnese, and which philhellenes throughout Europe had long promoted. The Royal Navy was at last resurgent. Men like Matthew Hervey's friend Captain Sir Laughton Peto, who had thought themselves beached, would have their chance once more.

But what of those in red coats? There were certainly far fewer of them than at any time in the life of all but the most grey-haired. Many were gaining a good dusting in far-flung corners of the growing empire; Hervey's own uniform, though blue not red, had had a good dusting in India, and of late in the Cape Colony. But the growing use of the army to police the nation's agrarian, industrial and political unrest made the cavalry unwelcome in some quarters ('Peterloo' was on the lips of many a rabble-rouser yet, and in the pages of the radical press). And when the explosive element of Catholic emancipation was added, coupled inextricably as it was with the condition of Ireland, society at times looked distinctly brittle. The old order was changing; the statesmen and soldiers who had brought Bonaparte to his knees and had managed to keep a lid on the unrest during the economic depression that followed were passing. New men gilded the ancient games.

This, then, is Matthew Hervey's world, simple soldiering no longer his refuge. Family and friends are become equally a source of comfort and of disquiet. His future is on the one hand settled and propitious; on the other, uncertain and discouraging:

> *Thoughts of great deeds were mine, dear Friends, when first*
> *The clouds which wrap this world from youth did pass . . .*
> *And from that hour did I with earnest thought*
> *Heap knowledge from forbidden mines of lore.*

> Shelley

MAN OF WAR

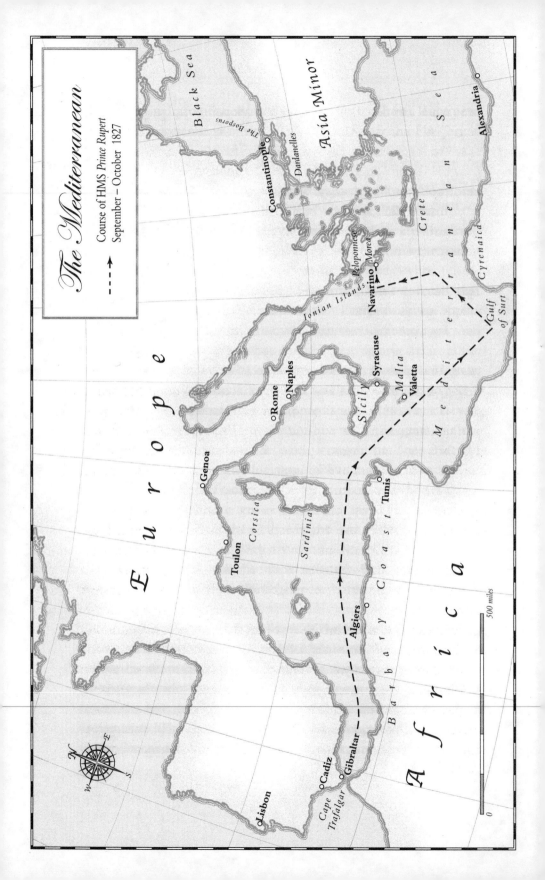

The Mediterranean

Course of HMS Prince Rupert
September – October 1827

I

A FIRST-RATE COMMAND

Gibraltar, 28 September 1827

The barge cut through the swell with scarcely a motion but head-way – testament to the determination with which her crew was bending oars. In the stern sat Captain Sir Laughton Peto RN, his eyes fixed on their objective, His Majesty's Ship *Prince Rupert* – glorious sight against the backdrop of the Rock. To Peto's mind *Rupert* was in no measure diminished by the towering crag; her three decks, her lofty masts, somehow outsoared the shadow of that Pillar of Hercules. Neither were her batteries belittled by those of the massive Montague Bastion, which Peto himself had only lately quit. Impregnable as was the citadel-Rock, *Rupert* was yet the most powerful of His Majesty's ships at sea, a floating fortress able to send any of the King's enemies to the bottom, as her forebears had done two decades earlier (and not many leagues to westward).

Any ship of the Royal Navy would look admirable at anchor in Gibraltar Bay, reckoned Peto: the Rock and the 'Nelson chequer' were as perfect a unity as any he could think of. As perfect as if they had been in Plymouth Sound, at Spithead, the Nore, or at Portsmouth. And Peto had been intent on nothing but the great three-decker from the moment he stepped into his barge.

She was an arresting picture, to be sure, but neither did it do for a captain, especially one of his seniority, to have eyes for so mere a thing as a boat's crew; his attention must be on more elevated affairs than a midshipman and a dozen ratings. Above all, though, it was opportunity to study his new command as an enemy might. Peto was acquainted by reputation with her sailing qualities, but how might another, impudent, man-of-war's captain judge her capability? He fancied he might know what a Frenchman would think. That mattered not these days, however; it was what a Turk thought that counted, for a year ago the Duke of Wellington, on the instructions of the foreign secretary, Mr Canning, had signed a protocol in St Petersburg by which Russia, France and Great Britain would mediate in the Greeks' struggle for independence; and increasingly that protocol looked like a declaration of war on the Ottoman Turks.

What a mazy business it all was too: the prime minister, Lord Liverpool, on his sickbed for months, and in April the King sending for Canning to form a government, in which many including the 'Iron Duke' then refused to serve; and now Canning himself dead and the feeble Goderich in his place. Peto did not envy Admiral Codrington, the commander-in-chief in the Mediterranean, whose squadron he was to join: how might the admiral do the government's will in Greek waters when the government itself scarcely knew what was its will? He could not carp, however, for he was the beneficiary of that uncertainty: soon after *Rupert* had left Portsmouth, where formerly she had been laid up in Ordinary, their lordships at the Admiralty had sent a signal of recall to her captain (and promotion to flag rank), followed by an order for him, Peto, to proceed at once to Gibraltar to take command in his stead.

The wind was strengthening. Peto did not have to take his eyes off his ship to perceive it. Nor did he need to crane his neck to mark the frigate-bird that accompanied them, tempting a prospect though such an infrequent visitor was – and sure weather vane too, for he had frequently observed how the bird preceded changeable weather, as if borne by some herald of new air. With a freshening westerly it would not be long before *Rupert* could make sail; and he willed, unspoken, for hands to pull even smarter for their wooden world – *his* wooden world.

He had waited a long age for this moment, for command of a first-rate; waited in fading expectation. Well, it were better come late than never. And so now he sat silent, perhaps even inscrutable (he could hope), in undress uniform beneath his boatcloak: closed double-breasted coat with fall-down collar, double epaulettes for his post seniority, with his India sword hanging short on his left side in a black-leather scabbard; and within a couple of cables' length of another great milestone of his nautical life.

At their dinner at the United Service Club (when was it – all of six months ago?) he had told his old friend Major Matthew Hervey of the 6th Light Dragoons that he was certain another command would not come: 'There will be no more commissions. I shan't get another ship. They're being laid up as we speak in every creek between Yarmouth and the Isle of Wight. I shan't even gain the yellow squadron. Certainly not now that Clarence is Lord High Admiral.' For yes, he had been commodore of a flotilla that had overpowered Rangoon (he could not – nor ever would – claim it a great victory, but it had served), and he had subsequently helped the wretched armies of Bengal and Madras struggle up the Irawadi, eventually to subdue Ava and its bestial king; but it had seemed to bring him not a very great deal of reward. The prize-money had been next to nothing (the Burmans had no ships to speak of, and the land-booty had not amounted to much by the time its share came to the navy), and KCB did not change his place on the seniority list. Their lordships not so many months before had told him they doubted they could give him any further active command, and would he not consider having the hospital at Greenwich?

But having been, in words that his old friend might have used, 'in the ditch', he was up again and seeing the road cocked atop a good horse. The milestones would come in altogether quicker succession now.

And what a sight, indeed, was *Rupert*! Even with sail furled she was the picture of admiralty: yellow-sided, gunports black – the 'Nelson chequer'; and the ports open, too, of which he much approved, letting fresh air circulate below deck; and the crew assembling for his boarding (he could hear the boatswain's mates quite plainly). What could make a man more content than such a thing? He breathed to himself the noble words: *gentlemen in England, now abed, will think themselves accurs'd they were not here*.

There was *one* thing, of course, that could make a man thus content: the love, the companionship at least, of a good woman (he knew well enough that the love of the other sort of woman was all too easy to be had, and the contentment very transitory). And now he had that too, for in his pocket was Miss Hervey's letter.

Why had he not asked for her hand years ago? That was his only regret. He felt a sudden and most unusual impulse: he wished Elizabeth Hervey were with him now. Yes, in this very place, at this very moment; to see his ship as he did, to appreciate her lines and her possibilities – *their* possibilities, captain and his lady. Oh, happy thought; happy, happy thought!

They closed astern of *Rupert* – Peto could make out her name on the counter quite clearly now – and he fancied how he might see Elizabeth's face at the upper lights in years to come. When first he had gone to sea, a lady might have stood at the gallery rail, but galleries had fallen from fashion. A pity: he had always loved their airy seclusion. The Navy Board was now building ships with rounded sterns, and sternchasers on the upper decks (Admiral Codrington flew his flag in one of these, the *Asia*). And about time, too, was Peto's opinion, for a stronger stern and a decent weight of shot to answer with made raking fire a lesser threat. But in his heart he was glad to have command of a three-decker of the old framing: she was much the finer looking (in truth, his own quarters would be the more commodious too); and he certainly had no intention of allowing any ship to cross his stern.

His cloak fell open, and in pulling it about himself again he noticed his cuff: Flowerdew would be darning it within the month. But that should be of no concern to him. He was not – never had been – a dressy man. If the officers and crew of His Majesty's Ship *Prince Rupert* did not know of his character and capability then that was their lookout: no amount of gold braid could make up for reputation. His service with Admiral Hoste, his command of the frigate *Nisus*, his time as commodore of the frigate squadron in the Mediterranean, and lately his command of *Liffey* while commodore of the flotilla for the Burmese war – these things were warranty enough of his fitness for command of the *Rupert*.

Not that it was any business of the officers and crew: he, Sir Laughton Peto KCB, held his commission from the Lord High Admiral himself. These things were not to be questioned, on pain of flogging or the yard-arm. Except that he considered himself to be an enlightened captain, convinced that having a man do his bidding willingly meant that the man did it twice as well as he would if he were merely driven to it. Though, of course, it was one thing to have a crew follow willingly a captain who was everywhere, as he might be in a frigate, but quite another when his station was the quarterdeck, as it must be with a line-of-battle

5

ship. *Nisus* had but one gun-deck; in action the captain might see all. *Rupert* had three, of which the two that hurled the greatest weight of shot were the lower ones, where the gun-crews worked in semi-darkness, and for whom in action the captain was as remote a figure as the Almighty Himself. The art of such a command, he knew full well, was in all that went before, so that the gun-crews had as perfect a fear of their captain's wrath – and even better a desire for his love – as indeed they had for their heavenly maker. If that truly required the lash, he would not shrink from it, but at heart he was one with Hervey in this: more men were flattered into virtue than were bullied out of vice. Besides, in these days of peace, the press gang and assize men were no more: the crew were volunteers. The old ways had gone.

A huge blue ensign hung from the stern flagstaff (Sir Edward Codrington was Vice Admiral of the Blue), the onshore breeze merely ruffling its points. Peto could see the smaller Union flag billowing a little more from the jackstaff on the bowsprit: it would have been hoist as soon as the anchor was dropped, and would be hauled down again as they got under weigh, for it would otherwise foul the jibs and fore-staysails. The familiar and reassuring routine! Yes, it was good to be drawing near one of His Majesty's warships again – the only three-decker in Codrington's combined fleet: 120 guns – thirty-six more than the biggest line-of-battle ship the Turks could dispose, one whole deck of eighteen-pounders. The expense of taking a first-rate to sea was prodigious: their lordships at the Admiralty were always reluctant, therefore, to bring a three-decker out of the Ordinary. And soon his own pendant would be streaming from the main mast! He was most conscious of the investment in his charge.

'I could not find better hands on the Post List,' the Duke of Clarence had said when he told him he was to have her. The compliment had startled Peto, for he had been of the decided conviction that the new Lord High Admiral had no very high

6

opinion of him (because, he had told his old friend Hervey, he himself had no very high opinion of Clarence); but, advanced as he was on the Post List, and having served – he trusted he did not flatter himself – with distinction and honours in the late war with Ava, why should he *not* have command of this wooden fortress, whose broadsides were the equal and more of Bonaparte's grand battery at Waterloo?

'Boat your oars!' came the reedy voice of the young midshipman as the barge neared the gangway on *Rupert*'s starboard, lee, side, recalling Peto to the lonely state of captain of a first-rate.

Peto glanced at him, studied him for the first time – a mere boy still, not yet sixteen perhaps, but confident in his words of command and boat handling. He had blond curls and fine features – so different from the Norfolk lad of fourteen that he himself had been as midshipman in the early years of the 'never-ending war'. *He* had never possessed such looks, as would delight fellow officers and females alike or earn the seaman's habitual esteem of the patrician. Big-boned he was: 'hardy-handsome' his mother had called him, which was not handsome at all in her reckoning (or so he had supposed). But Elizabeth Hervey had not rejected him. *No*; not at all. Indeed he thought that Miss Hervey had once actually made eyes at him – in Rome, many years ago. Oh, how he wished he had recognized that look (if look indeed it had been – preposterous notion!).

He snapped to. Belay the thought! For he could hear the boatswain's call.

In *Rupert*'s lee the water merely lapped at the towering wooden walls. With oars now vertical the midshipman steered the barge deftly to the side, and Peto stepped confidently onto the lowered gangway as yet she ran in. He would have been content to scramble up the ladder to the entry port on the middle deck, as many a time he had, for he fancied himself as agile still as when he had been a midshipman; but he was pleased nevertheless to come aboard this way, with less chance of missing a footing or losing his hat in a sudden gust of wind. He glanced at the decoration above the port, handsomely carved dolphins gilded as freshly as the ship's name had been whitened. The lieutenant had evidently been active since they had put in to port three days before. Peto marked it with some satisfaction. He did not know the lieutenant, Lambe, except that he had a good reputation. A bit of sea-greening on the stern counter and dulling of the carving gilt he could have endured (who knew what repairs the Biscay weather had occasioned?), but Lambe had chosen to smarten these presents. If they were not meant merely to distract, it augured well.

And now the piping aboard, the shaking hands with officers and warrant officers – he had done the same before, several times; but never on a first-rate. To be sure, he had hardly set foot on a three-decker since he was a young lieutenant. He had decided not to address the crew, as he had when taking command of *Nisus*, for whereas his frigate's complement had been but two hundred (and he could know every man by name and character), *Rupert*'s was in excess of eight – far too many to assemble decently for the sort of thing he would wish to say. Command of a first-rate was perforce a rather more distant business. Strictly speaking, command even of *Nisus* was properly exercised through his executive officer, the lieutenant, and to some degree by the master, but in a ship of two hundred souls the captain's face was daily – at times hourly – known to all. His own quarters were on the upper deck: he had to climb the companion to the quarter-deck, and in doing so he might routinely see half the crew. As captain of *Rupert* he would merely step from his cabin under the poop: descending to any of the gun-decks was an 'occasion'. His world was changing even if he were not. He could no longer be the frigate-thruster. But his nature was by no means aloof, and he now must find some happy middle channel between his own inclination and the customs of the service. He did not expect it to take long, or even to try him; but meanwhile – as any prudent captain – he would take up the command firmly yet judiciously. He passed the assemblage of officers with but a nod here and there.

In an hour or so His Majesty's governor of Gibraltar would pay a call on him, and then, if the westerly continued to freshen, *Rupert* would make sail for Syracuse to take on the pure water of the Arethusa spring, just as Nelson had before the Nile. Peto knew that a long blockade of the Peloponnese – if blockade were what Codrington intended – would be thirsty work. He knew it from long experience, though not perhaps as much in the eastern as the western Mediterranean, and also from recourse to that most faithful of teachers, history. For he had with him – and had been reading most assiduously since leaving England – Thucydides, *The Peloponnesian War*. And in that latest edition of Dean Smith's translation he was reminded of the necessaries of such a course, for the Athenians at Pylos, blockading the Spartans on the island of Sphacteria, had been reduced to scraping away the shingle on the beach to get relief for their thirst. He could at least make sure *his* men had the sweetest water (and there was none sweeter or more plentiful than from the spring of that patron-goddess). Thence, from Syracuse, he would set a course for Codrington's squadron in the Ionian. For the time being, however, he would withdraw to his quarters, hear the reports, read the signals, sign the returns.

Flowerdew, his steward of a dozen years and more, was waiting. The sentry presented arms – more sharply, thought Peto, than even the well-drilled marines on *Nisus*. The red coat, the black lacquered hat, the white breeches and pipeclay – Peto suddenly felt himself a little shabby by comparison in his sea coat. But that, he reminded himself, was how it should be: a marine sentry was by his very turnout a powerful aid to discipline, whereas a captain's attire must be weather-seasoned. He might put on his best coat for His Majesty's envoy (his dunnage Flowerdew had brought aboard earlier in the day); there again he might not.

He took his first, portentous steps aft of the sentry, followed by his executive officer and Flowerdew. At once he saw how much bigger were his quarters – appreciably bigger than any he had occupied before. He saw the little oils on the bulkheads which he had had on *Nisus*, and the furniture, over and above what their lordships provided, which he had bought from the previous captain (who had been only too happy to strike a bargain and thus save himself the expense of shipping home). He could be confident, too, that his cherished silver, china and glass would be safely stowed.

'Coffee, sir?'

'Thank you, yes, Flowerdew.'

'With your leave, sir,' said the first lieutenant.

Peto took off his hat and placed it on the dining table (Cuban mahogany reflecting the sun through the stern lights like a mirror). 'By all means, Mr Lambe. A half-hour's recollection, and then, if you please, you may give me the ship's states.'

'Shall I assemble the old hands too, sir?'

It was the custom of the service for a new captain to 'read himself in' – to read his commission before the caretakers and old seamen aboard the ship.

'By all means.'

The executive officer replaced his hat, touched the point and withdrew. 'Ay-ay, sir.'

When Flowerdew came with coffee he found his captain sitting in his favourite leather chair. Peto had had it made many years before in Madeira, with pouches fixed on each arm: the left side for his clerk to place papers for attention, and the other for Peto himself to place them after his attention. But rather than attending to his clerk's papers, Peto was staring out of the stern gallery, and with a look of considerable contentment. Flowerdew could not be surprised at this: if his captain mayn't have a moment or two's satisfaction in his new command then what did it profit a man to be in the King's service?

'Coffee, sir.'

Peto nodded, and raised his hand in thanks.

Flowerdew had no wish to intrude on the moment; there would be time enough to get back into the old routine. He placed the cup and saucer in Peto's hand, and left the cabin quietly.

Peto reached inside his coat and took out Elizabeth's letter. He had placed it within the leather binding of an old copy of Steel's *Mastmaking, Sailmaking and Rigging* from which he had removed the pages, and wrapped it in an oilskin. Even thus preserved, the letter bore the signs of much consultation.

Horningsham
28th March 1827

My dear Captain Peto,

Let me at once say that I accept your offer of marriage with the very greatest delight. I perfectly understand that you were not able to travel to Wiltshire, and I am only content that you did not delay until you were able to do so. For my part, I should have wished at once to accept, but you will understand that I felt a certain obligation to my brother, though I could never have doubted his approval.

I am so very happy too at your news of command, though I shall confess also that my happiness is tempered considerably by the thought that H.M.S. Prince Rupert is taking you so very distant. But that is the way of things, and you may be assured that I shall never be a jealous wife where your ship is concerned!

I am so very proud, too, that your command is to be in the
Mediterranean, not only for its healthiness and beauty but
because I believe it a very noble thing that we should assist the
Greeks in their endeavours to shake off the Ottoman yoke. You
will, of course, be now daily in my prayers – I think I may say
constantly – and they will be for your safe and speedy return.
    My father will make the usual arrangements for the notice of
our betrothal, which I must trust shall be to your liking.
    I hasten to close this, though I would write so very much
more were there the time, for the express boy is come even now,
and trust that you shall receive it before you sail.

Your ever affectionate
Elizabeth Hervey

Peto read it a second time, and then a third. It was the first letter in a female hand that he had ever received. He had no certainty of the tone or convention, but he considered it the warmest expression of esteem. How different it felt – strangely different – taking to sea with a wife awaiting his return (for he already imagined her in the Norfolk drawing room, wed): his world was no longer wholly wooden, sea-girt and male.

He folded the letter, replaced it between the bindings, wrapped it in the oilskin and put it back into his pocket. As he did so he thought again of Elizabeth's sisterly duty – so admirable a thing – and then the object of that duty, and wondered how was his friend in southern waters. Perhaps – his own new command notwithstanding – he might even envy Hervey a little, for would not his friend have more prospect of the smell of black powder than would he himself in the Ionian? The native tribes of the Cape Colony would know no better than to chance against His Majesty's land forces; but the Turk must know that he could have no fight at sea with a first-class naval power. And certainly not with *three*.

12

He drained his cup, and glanced about his new quarters – new, but entirely familiar, for the difference between these and his earlier quarters was more of scale than design, or even luxury. He looked at the painting of *Nisus*, his first command – Flowerdew had fixed it on the starboard bulkhead exactly as it had been on *Liffey*, his last. He had loved *Nisus* – a frigate of, to his mind, most excellent proportions – to the exclusion of all else. Next to the painting – *portrait* – of her, Flowerdew had fixed the oil of his Norfolk home, in which he had yet truly to take residence. Never, indeed, had he thought he would prize it so much as now he did, for no longer was it an unlooked-for refuge ashore, more wreckers' yard than haven: Elizabeth Hervey – Elizabeth Peto – would one day, soon, occupy it. Truly, he told himself, he was at this moment possessed of the very best of *both* worlds.

II

A SIGHT SO TOUCHING IN ITS MAJESTY

London, seven months later, 22 April 1828

Acting Lieutenant-Colonel Matthew Hervey, officer commanding the detached troop of His Majesty's 6th Light Dragoons in the Cape Colony, and acting commanding officer of the Corps of Cape Mounted Riflemen, rearranged his bones as he got down from the Rochester mail. The Canterbury turnpike was a fine, fast road, which served only to make the occasional pothole more jarring, though from Deptford, where it became a mere municipal affair, not evenly made or mended, the jolts had come with greater frequency and severity. His travelling companion, Captain Edward Fairbrother, also of the Mounted Rifles (the lieutenant-governor at the Cape, his old friend Sir Eyre Somervile, had insisted that Fairbrother should accompany him on account of his wound and the remittent fever), looked distinctly qualmish, for the coach's rolling action had at times been pronounced – though not as bad as the packet's rolling off the Azores, when even Hervey, whose sailing-stomach was strong, had been prostrated for two days. Yet despite heavy seas they had made the passage from Cape Town to the Medway in just short of six weeks.

Fairbrother, his indisposition notwithstanding, was as arrested by the sights and sounds of the metropolis as Hervey had been that day, thirteen years before, when first *he* had come to London – and by this same route. Southwark High Street, narrow, towering, inn-lined, had been all mid-morning bustle, so that the captain of Mounted Rifles had fancied he might be in Shakespeare's London; or even Chaucer's, for Hervey had pointed out The Tabard (though nowadays it was called The Talbot). And London Bridge, no wider than that high street but just as teeming and looking every bit as antique, had afforded him two sights as inspiring as might be: downstream the Tower of London, and all the evidence of the capital's maritime commerce; upstream, but a stone's throw from the mail, the new London Bridge, its massive, graceful arches not yet complete but already as sure and solid as anything he had seen – certainly these late years in Africa. Here was security, confidence, investment, and increasing wealth. Here was the future.

'We may take a paddle steamer down the river later this week, if there's time,' Hervey had said in answer to his wide-eyed enquiries.

Fairbrother had liked that. And then in Lombard Street, where the mails drew up at the General Post Office, he was wholly taken by the crowded, purposeful activity, both wheeled and pedestrian. Never had he seen its like, not even in Kingston when a slaver filled the wharves with its black cattle. He shook his head slowly. 'I begin to understand, my friend.'

'Understand what?' replied Hervey absently, seeing down what little baggage the mail would carry for them (Private Johnson would bring the bulk of it by stage later in the day).

'The great enterprise.'

Hervey thought he understood, but elucidation he would leave until another time. He had his own preoccupations for the moment. He wanted above all to know the particulars of the Royal Navy's engagement in the Ionian, what *The Times* was calling the Battle of Navarino Bay. The first report – the only one he had seen, and that in South Africa – spoke of a great many ships and a great many casualties. He had not the least idea whether his old friend Sir Laughton Peto's ship had been engaged, however, for he knew that Peto had first to make passage to Gibraltar to take up his command, and that the journey thither, and thence to Greek waters, was with sail an unpredictable business.

It was his intention therefore, as soon as he and Fairbrother were established in the United Service Club, to go – this very afternoon – to the Horse Guards and ask his friend Lieutenant-Colonel Lord John Howard, assistant quartermaster-general, to give him sight of the official despatches (a month's worth of mail and *Gazette*s had been adrift still when he left Cape Town). He might even learn something about the wretched board of inquiry. That was the true imperative for his recall to London. He did not relish it – far from it – but it were better that he grasp the nettle than be stung with it at the hands of some malefactor. There were always those who would see the army as a cruel instrument of repression. He had rather liked Shelley – admired him, even – when they had spent those days together in Rome a decade before (God rest his soul – for Shelley most assuredly possessed one, whatever he himself had professed . . .), but he abhorred the poet's disliking of the army, and bridled even now at his invention of that word 'liberticide' and its appellation to the unlooked-for, and thankless, duty of aid to the civil power.

He had thought there would be no inquiry. That had been his understanding when Lord John Howard had prevailed on him to withdraw his report on the incident at Waltham Abbey. Before the Africa commission, while in temporary command of his regiment, the 6th Light Dragoons, he had found himself embroiled in a savage little affair at the royal gunpowder mills. Home Office spies had discovered a plot in which an armed body of Irishmen working on a nearby navigation were to break into the mills and carry off a quantity of powder. Hervey's dragoons had foiled the attempt, and with considerable execution, but the business had troubled him, for the actions of the Irishmen – drunk, most of them – had not suggested any serious enterprise. He had smelled fish (a parliamentary bill for Catholic 'emancipation' was the cause of much agitation in certain Tory quarters), and he had submitted a report implying as much. However, his friend had persuaded him to withdraw it, for an inquiry would have required Hervey's presence in London, and the appointment at the Cape therefore would not have been his.

This compromising had further troubled him, and still did. It had not been his habit to temporize, although these days he knew that stiff-back honour rarely profited anyone – or for that matter the cause of honour itself. But in the week before leaving the Cape for what his old friend the lieutenant-governor called convalescent and matrimonial leave, a summons had arrived from the Horse Guards to attend a court of inquiry into the whole affair of Waltham Abbey. Hervey feared not that such an inquiry would heap opprobrium upon him (except, did *any* soldier emerge from aiding the civil power with an unblemished record?), rather that the affair would detain him in London and bring him unwelcome attention. The first he did not want, for entirely personal and family reasons, and the second he could most definitely do without, for his aspirations to command of the 6th Light Dragoons remained, even if the odds grew longer by the day, and any less-than-entirely favourable findings would do nothing to advance his suit.

The strangest intelligence had come with that summons too: the Duke of Wellington was now prime minister. Following the death of Mr Canning, and the resignation of his successor Lord Goderich, the King had asked the duke to form a government, which he had done, dutifully though not without difficulty.

Hervey had learned all this on the Rochester mail from a pair of particularly loquacious attorney clerks. His informants had been unable to tell him, however, who had taken the duke's reins at the Horse Guards, though they were able to confirm that Lord Palmerston – for all his support of Canning and his contrary stance now to the 'high Tories' – remained at the War Office, which news pleased and troubled Hervey in turn since thanks to Lord John Howard he had some acquaintance with the minister. But it was Palmerston who had ordered the court of inquiry.

There was a line of hackney carriages outside the post office. Hervey engaged one, tipped a boy to transfer their baggage, and bid the driver take them to the United Service Club.

Fairbrother at last fell silent as they drove along Poultry and Cheapside, and then by way of St Paul's, Fleet Street and the Strand to St James's, wholly transfixed by what he saw, a juxta-position of grandeur (new and old alternating – conjoined, indeed) with dereliction of a kind he had not seen; yet a lively dereliction, not a waste, the noise and the vigour of it all beyond his former imagining.

'So much is torn down and built each time I come,' said Hervey as they passed yet another demolition site, scene of scaffolding and cranes straining to replace with new before the old was even wholly reduced. 'The new London Bridge was nothing when last I crossed the old one. And downriver they are driving a tunnel from one side to the other.'

Fairbrother shook his head in amazement.

'I must tell you again, though, the United Service you will not find more than passing comfortable. A new club is being built,' (Hervey smiled as he realized Fairbrother must picture all London abuild) 'and the committee has spent very little on the existing premises as a consequence. It is a pity we shan't be able to try the new ones.'

Fairbrother turned to him but momentarily. 'My dear fellow,

it is excessively good of you to put me up at your club, no matter what its condition. I hope it occasions *you* no discomfort.'

Hervey frowned. 'As I have told you before, you mistake matters if you once think otherwise.'

Fairbrother turned his gaze once more to the building work on the Strand. He did not think that he did mistake matters; he rather thought that Hervey did. He admired the lieutenant-colonel – *his* lieutenant-colonel, indeed – of mounted rifles (and major of light dragoons); in truth he had not met his like. But his previous association with British officers did not predispose him to believe that Hervey was at all typical of his caste. Oh, to be sure, the officers of his former corps, the Royal African Regiment, were not out of the top drawer; half of them could not have passed for gentlemen save for the badges of rank which proclaimed them to be so. But it was not merely they: Lord Charles Somerset, the previous lieutenant-governor at the Cape, had never deigned to receive him, and his son, Colonel Henry Somerset, had never troubled to disguise his contempt – except, of course, of late (saving a fellow's life put even a Somerset under a powerful obligation to be civil). It was true that the present governor, Hervey's old friend Sir Eyre (and Lady Somervile), had received him at the Castle with the greatest courtesy; no, with the greatest *warmth* – but this he was inclined to attribute to the Somerviles' time in India, where a dark skin (not that his own could be accurately described as dark) was no impediment to society if the native were a gentleman. For the rest, he would reserve his judgement.

'See here,' said Hervey in an effort to be aptly cheery as they passed Charing Cross. 'This part is called the Bermuda and Caribbee Islands, though I'm not sure why. They say it is all to be pulled down, and a vast *piazza* made of it in memory of Nelson.'

Fairbrother peered indifferently at the slum-jumble about St

Martin's church. No decent planter in Jamaica (in which category he firmly placed his father) would thus house his slaves (in which category he could not deny had been his mother). But then, he imagined that the inhabitants of these crowding tenements were not so gainfully employed as plantation slaves.

'They are what you call rookeries?'

'I don't know that they are rookeries – I think the term is applied more to the tenements in the old city – but they are noisome, for sure. Over here,' (Hervey smiled ruefully) 'not so very far away, is where the King lived when he was regent.'

Fairbrother turned his attention to the other window. In a minute or so the building site that was the old Carlton House came into view.

'And there is the new United Service Club. Or *will* be. Not long now by the look of things; the glaziers have made a beginning.'

The hackney swung into Regent Street, and Fairbrother could only marvel at the change that a mere hundred yards brought: from dereliction to royal palace, and now to a street as graceful as any he expected to see. The carriage turned right into Charles Street and pulled up in front of four Corinthian columns, which marked the entrance of the United Service Club.

A red-waistcoated porter whom Hervey did not recognize advanced at once to the kerbside. Hervey paid the driver, nodded to the club servant, who began taking the baggage from the hackney's boot, and then he and his friend made their long-looked-for entry to 'the Duke's Own'.

'Good morning, Thomas,' he said quietly at the lodge.

The hall porter looked up. 'Why, Colonel Hervey, sir! It *is* good to see you. We are expecting you, of course, sir.'

Hervey was relieved, though he did not show it. The United Service's servants, loyal and delightful as they were, had no more reputation for efficiency than any other club's staff. And although he had sent an express immediately on disembarking, the day before, he could not then be certain that rooms would be available. 'And my guest, Captain Fairbrother.'

The hall porter glanced at Fairbrother, and perfectly maintained his smile of welcome. 'Of course, sir. There are two excellent rooms on the west side.'

'Capital, Thomas. Are there letters for me?'

'I will look, sir.'

Hervey nodded. 'We shall take coffee the while.'

'Very good, sir. Mr Peter is on duty.'

Hervey gave Fairbrother a look of 'I told you it would be thus' as they made their way to the United Service's principal public room.

In the coffee room they met Major-General Sir Francis Evans, who had been the general officer commanding the Northern District when the Sixth had been sent to the Midlands to suppress the Luddite violence (where Hervey had distinguished himself in the most trying of circumstances). That had been a decade and more ago, and the intervening years had made him even more crabbed in his aspect.

Hervey bowed. 'Good morning, Sir Francis.'

The old general narrowed his eyes. 'Hervey?'

'Yes, General.'

'Hah! By God, sir, I must say your exploits are vastly entertaining.'

Hervey's brow furrowed. 'General?'

'Can't open *The Times* these days without reading your name – castles in Spain, powder-mills in Hertfordshire, wilds of Africa . . .' (Hervey shifted a shade awkwardly.) 'How are you, my boy?'

Hervey smiled. 'I am excessively well, General. May I present my good friend Captain Fairbrother of the Cape Mounted Rifles . . .'

The general turned to Fairbrother and scowled. 'You're the

officer who rescued Somerset's nephew, are you not? You and Hervey here.'

Fairbrother returned the well-meaning scowl with a smile, and bowed. 'Just so, Sir Francis.'

'Desperate affair, by all accounts,' said the general, turning back to Hervey. 'And young Somerset appears to have fought quite a battle with these Zulu. I imagine you had a good view of things?'

Hervey was at first puzzled by the question, for it suggested that he and Fairbrother had had a somewhat peripheral involvement, until he realized what might be the game. *The Times*'s report, if it had been based on the official despatches, which were in essence Colonel Henry Somerset's own (and on what else could it be based?), and undoubtedly further coloured by letters to Somerset's father and uncle, men of no little influence, would for certain exalt the name of Somerset. Well, so things went. 'We did indeed, General.'

'A man to watch, eh, Hervey?'

Sir Francis Evans was a shrewd old bird. There was just something in his tone . . .

'I do watch him, sir.'

The general nodded, knowingly. 'Sit you down, gentlemen.'

Hervey glanced at Fairbrother and raised his eyebrows a fraction to signal that their quiet half-hour's coffee was not to be had. But Hervey knew too that the general would oblige them with all the club crack, of which he was more in want than peace and quiet at this time, no matter how rattling their morning had been.

Hervey cleared his throat. He wondered how much his own report on the incident at Waltham Abbey – which was meant to be the most confidential of documents – had to do with the general's invitation. 'Thank you, Sir Francis.'

The hall porter interrupted. 'Excuse me, gentlemen. Sir Francis, there is a messenger from the Horse Guards for you. Colonel Hervey, sir, these are the letters for you.'

The general rose, complaining. 'By God, sir, I wait half the day and then the deuced word comes at the least convenient moment. I had more peace when I was in harness. See you, Hervey: when this is done I would speak on the Africa business more – and Waltham Abbey. Lord Hill is displeased with the notion of an inquiry, to say the least.'

'Lord Hill? How so?'

'You don't know? Hill is the new commander-in-chief.'

Hervey was vastly pleased to hear it. *Everyone* had a high opinion of Lord Hill. 'I look forward to speaking with you about Waltham Abbey, General.' (Sir Francis might no longer be serving, but he undoubtedly had the ear of the commander-in-chief.) He bid his old supporter good day.

'Will you allow me a few minutes?' he said to Fairbrother as he sat down again, holding up his post.

'By all means, as long as there is coffee ... and this most excellent publication.' Fairbrother in his turn held up a copy of the *Edinburgh Review* which he had remarked lying by itself on a side table.

Peter brought them each a cup of the strongest bean, and Hervey turned his attention to the little package of letters. The regimental agents, in Craig's Court, forwarded routine correspondence and that of affairs, but a fortnight before leaving the Cape, Hervey had sent word of his imminent return to a number of addresses, asking that any reply should be made to his club. There were half a dozen letters, three in hands he recognized, and a small package. He read the three in unfamiliar hands – they contained nothing disquieting nor pressing – and then turned to the others.

The first he opened was from Kat – Lady Katherine Greville – who wrote that she would be in Warwickshire until the middle of

April (the present month) and that she looked forward to receiving him at Holland Park as soon as she returned. Hervey had fully expected such an invitation, which he would not be able to accept (the circumstances of their former acquaintance, and his betrothal to Kezia Lankester, made it improvident to say the least), but he had felt obliged to write since for Kat to learn that he was in England without his having told her would only occasion . . . difficulty.

The letter from the Reverend John Keble expressed delight at the news of his betrothal, and hearty agreement to preach at the wedding, as he had done on the first instance of his friend's marriage. In truth Hervey was not greatly troubled by the question of a sermon, nor, indeed, about the wedding arrangements in general, for the situation was vastly different from that first; but it had somehow seemed meet that it should be Keble, and, as he well recalled, the curate of Coln St Aldwin's possessed the gift of brevity in these things. Keble's letter also referred to his book of devotional poetry recently published, a copy of which he was sending under separate cover – which Hervey saw was the package. This he opened, more out of curiosity than zeal for poetry. The title page proclaimed *The Christian Year*. It did not urgently command his attention, though he was touched by the sentiment expressed in such a gift, the continuing kindness of this fine scholar-churchman towards him, especially since they had hardly been intimates. 'See you, Fairbrother,' he said, breaking his companion's intense study of the *Edinburgh Review*: 'a book of poetry by the man who's to preach at my wedding. I fancy it will be good, but more to your taste than mine at the present.'

Fairbrother took it with a somewhat wry look.

Last, Hervey opened Kezia's letter. It was written from Hertfordshire, her father's house, on the fifteenth, and it began, as had those he had received at the Cape, 'My dear Colonel

24

Hervey'. The salutation was beginning to vex him rather. He knew well enough that it was entirely correct, but Henrietta had always been so . . . unrestrained in her correspondence (Kat too, though that was different). But, as he frequently reminded himself, the circumstances of his engagement to Lady Lankester were by no means the same as those of his marriage to Henrietta – nor even, truly, similar. They had been so much younger (it was all of thirteen years ago); except, by his reckoning, Kezia Lankester could not be more than a year or so older than had been Henrietta then . . .

The rest of his affianced's letter, in the substance of its contents, was encouraging. Kezia looked forward to his coming to Hertfordshire, and she was content to be married in the summer from her aunt's house in Mayfair. There were other details, and Hervey read over the letter again to be certain of them; and, too, for some intimation of sentiment. Just as in the earlier letters, though, he found none. His own to her, he would admit, could claim not a deal more (how might he write of the desire he increasingly felt?), but it pained him nevertheless. Did she not at least *admire* him enough for there to be some intimation of *her* expectation? Yes, for his part he had proposed to her after a very reasoned deliberation; it was neither romance nor passion in the conventional sense. And he supposed she had accepted him on the same terms, for she had had but a moment or two for reflection before doing so (he could hardly imagine that she had, before, entertained hopes, since they had met so infrequently). But even so . . .

There was no letter from Elizabeth, which surprised him, for his sister was a most dutiful correspondent. But he had no cause for anxiety at this lack of intelligence from Wiltshire: if necessary, evil news could ride post from Horningsham to London in a day, and the absence of an assurance that all was well did not trouble him therefore. All the same, he had expected *some* news, even if only an inconsequential report of his daughter's progress in the schoolroom. He would be down to see them in a fortnight, though, or perhaps three weeks ... These things could wait; especially now that he had made proper arrangements for the future.

III

FRIENDS AT COURT

Later

After a lunch of veal pie and hock, Hervey set out for the Horse Guards with Fairbrother, leaving him at the arch to walk to Westminster Abbey to see Nelson's tomb. At the commander-in-chief's headquarters he found the assistant quartermaster-general writing with particular concentration.

'I trust I do not disturb urgent business?'

Lord John Howard looked up with some surprise. 'My dear fellow!'

They shook hands.

'I said I trust I don't disturb urgent business.'

Howard shook his head. 'Not so urgent as to detain me on such an occasion – the arrangements for Clinton's force: the duke's recalled them.'

'I did not know it,' said Hervey, with some caution: mention of the expeditionary force in Portugal, which was supposed to keep the peace between the rival factions for the throne, made him feel awkward still, for his own sojourn there in advance of the force's arrival had almost been the end of him – the death of him, even. 'Affairs there have evidently quietened?'

'A reasonable deduction, but not necessarily true. The duke believes we should not be entangled, especially since now the Spaniards show no appetite to intervene. The duke is of the opinion that these matters are best settled by the Portuguese themselves.'

Hervey was not surprised to hear it: the Duke of Wellington had been opposed to the expedition in the first place, believing it to be another of Mr Canning's wild adventures in what was the business of other states. He wondered now if his own tribulations – notably his incarceration at Badajoz – had been without point, for withdrawing the force only sixteen months from sending it seemed hardly propitious as far as peace in Portugal was concerned. Except, of course, that at Badajoz he had forced himself to consider his condition, and thence to amend it. Without Badajoz there was no betrothal to Lady Lankester, no mother for his daughter.

Howard rang for a messenger to bring tea. 'By the by, your last letter was most welcome. It gave the official account a little colour, shall we say.'

'Somerset's account? I fancy it was accurate, but ... incomplete.'

Howard smiled. 'The duke was of the same opinion.'

Hervey was content again. He held that virtue, if not entirely its own reward, would certainly speak for itself, but he was ever grateful to have such a friend at court as John Howard. They had known each other these dozen years and more, never intimately but with the highest mutual regard. 'Rather a wild place, the Cape Colony. At least, that is, the eastern frontier; the Cape itself is a most delightful place. The east will increasingly be like trying to erect defences against the sea, for I can't suppose there can be a settled frontier for as long as there are untold millions wandering the interior.'

Howard looked not exactly sceptical, but his enquiry

suggested he had supposed it otherwise. 'Do you believe it of any greater order of apprehension than was, say, India, or the Americas?'

Hervey nodded slowly. 'You have to stand in that country to get a true sense of it. I never had so powerful a feeling of being in deep waters – never in America, nor India. I mean ... of waters that ran so deep.' Lord John Howard could only imagine. He had rarely served beyond Whitehall and had never heard a shot fired in anger except very distantly. But Hervey both liked and respected him for his diligence as a staff officer and his absence of pretentiousness and conceit.

'Is that the lieutenant-governor's opinion too?'

'It is. I sent on Sir Eyre's opinion and the estimates to the Colonies Office this morning.'

The messenger returned with tea.

Howard let him pour two cups and withdraw before cutting to the subject that he knew must preoccupy his friend. 'The court of inquiry for Waltham Abbey: you will not know what is decided as to the evidence, I imagine?'

Hervey shook his head: he had heard nothing; but this was not in truth his preoccupation. 'Howard, if we may, before the inquiry, I should very much like to ask you of this affair at Navarino. You know that Peto was under orders to join Codrington's fleet: it would be good to hear confirmation that he's well.'

Howard looked surprised: the battle had been six months ago (although its consequences were almost daily a matter of speculation). And then he nodded. 'I have to remind myself of the distance you have been from the centre of affairs. Do you not, though, receive the *Gazette* regularly?'

'We were several in arrears when I left the Cape.'

'Well, Peto's name was not on the list. That, I may assure you. I would most certainly have noticed – and, indeed, have remarked on it at once on seeing you, for I know what a friend he is. I myself would count him so. When my clerk is returned this evening I shall have him hunt out the relevant *Gazette* with Codrington's despatch and all. I confess I read its detail but cursorily. It was an affair of much pounding, as far as I could tell.'

'I'm relieved to hear he's not on the list at any rate. I'd be indeed obliged if your man could hunt out the despatch. There ought to be copies in the United Service, but the imminent move seems to have disordered things somewhat.'

Howard nodded, wrote a short memorandum and placed it in his tray.

Hervey could now turn with a clearer mind to his own concerns. 'I saw Sir Francis Evans in the United Service this morning. He said the new commander-in-chief is unhappy with the inquiry.'

'Well, it vexes Lord Hill, certainly,' said Howard, pouring them both more tea. 'Though it's not a matter of pre-eminent urgency exactly. What to do with the Militia is the question of the moment – and, of course, where to find troops for every scheme the government has dreamed up. That, though, is a good deal less of a business now with the duke in the saddle. No, Lord Hill is of the opinion that the court of inquiry will end up all of a piece with the others we've been suffering these several past years, principally that we're bound to have the radicals calling for even more retrenchment. But that is beside the point. The inquiry's to take written evidence to begin with and then assemble to decide what they will. Your returning now is most apt: they make a beginning towards the end of May.'

Hervey sighed ruefully. 'Who is to be president?'

'It is not yet decided.'

There was just a note of evasion in the reply. Hervey narrowed his eyes and inclined his head.

Howard in turn sighed. 'See, I may as well tell you as not. Hill wants Sir Peregrine Greville to do it.'

'*What?*'

Howard looked distinctly uncomfortable. 'It is not decided absolutely.'

'But why Greville? The old fool's—'

Howard held up a hand. 'Lord Hill believes that it is Sir Peregrine's very ... seclusion in the Channel Islands, his immunity from the condition of affairs here, that makes it apt for him to preside.'

Hervey struggled to suppress his rising panic. His indiscretions so far with Lady Katherine Greville had gone unremarked publicly, but such a state could not survive long once a court of inquiry were convened: every tattler and budding Gillray in London would be peddling the connection. 'When will it be decided?'

'Soon, I hope. The War Office has asked for a convening order by the month's end.' Howard rose. 'I know it's the very devil, but ... Stay if you will for the moment; I must have words with Lord Hill.'

Hervey tried to compose himself. He exaggerated the danger, no doubt. But try as he might, he could not dismiss the image of exposure – and all that would follow: breaking-off of the engagement, an end to his hopes for command, perhaps even resignation of his commission. In truth, oblivion.

In a minute or so his friend returned. 'Lord Hill wishes to see you.'

Hervey looked astonished. 'Wishes to see me?'

'I told him you were here, and he wishes you to tell him at first hand of the affair with the Zulu.'

Hervey breathed a sigh of profound relief, for he had supposed the worst, that the commander-in-chief wished to interrogate him on the business at Waltham Abbey – and by extension, though it were no logical progression, nor even likely that Lord Hill knew, about his connection with the wife of the Governor of Alderney and Sark.

'He recalls you very well from Talavera, you know.' Howard said it in just such a manner as gave away his admiration for a record of service as active as his own had been desk-bound.

'Upon my word . . . It will not matter that I wear a plain coat?'

'Not in the least.' Howard smiled. 'If you cannot wear scarlet it is infinitely better that you wear plain!'

Hervey rallied. '*Nulli secundus*, Howard. Don't I recall that right?'

'So say the Coldstream.'

Hervey's interview with Lord Hill lasted a full half-hour. It was entirely agreeable. The general was not called 'Daddy' Hill by the army for nothing, and his appreciation of Hervey's service that day at Talavera had not diminished with the years. At the close the commander-in-chief said simply that he, Hervey, was not to worry over the business of Waltham Abbey: he felt certain the Sixth had acted with all proper and unavoidable severity. 'Indeed, I may go as far as to say that as soon as the consequences of *inaction* that night are understood by the more radical sections of parliament and the press your gallant regiment's standing will be even greater. Make no mistake, though, Hervey: the inquiry'll be a deuced tiresome thing. There'll be mischief.'

Afterwards, Hervey took his leave of the Horse Guards without ceremony, conscious that Lord John Howard had pressing business to be about (the sooner the Lisbon five thousand were back on these shores, or at Gibraltar, the sooner, quite evidently, would the new commander-in-chief and the new prime minister be content). The two friends made an appointment to dine at Howard's club – White's – later in the week, and Howard assured

Hervey that he would send any news of the inquiry to the United Service with the greatest promptness.

Hervey now hurried to Westminster Abbey. He had never been inside before, an admission which Fairbrother had found at once extraordinary and engaging. He wondered if indeed Fairbrother would still be at the abbey, for he had stayed twice as long at the Horse Guards as expected. The abbey had been their rendezvous, however, and its being empty of any other life save a candle trimmer, Hervey found his friend easily enough, by a marble monument to naval prowess, though not to 'the immortal memory'.

'Lord Nelson's was as fine, I trust?'

Fairbrother looked resigned. 'It is not here, but in the cathedral.'

Hervey frowned. 'I should have known that. I don't believe I did.'

'This one is to Charles Holmes, rear-admiral of the Blue, commander-in-chief Jamaica . . . my father's godfather. I did not know his memorial was here.'

'You have more illustrious connections than do I,' said Hervey, taking a closer look at the inscription. 'It must give a man a powerful sense of obligation to have such a connection memorialized in the nation's parish church.'

Fairbrother turned his head to him and smiled ironically. 'You think me English, do you?'

Hervey pondered on it for a moment. He was not sure *what* he had thought. 'I believe I do!'

'Well, I may tell you one thing. I am less drawn to the appellation by monuments such as this, than by those yonder.' He nodded to a jumble of busts and plaques across the nave. 'You honour your men of letters as much as your men of war. There's Chaucer's grave there, and so many poets as to lift the weariest of spirits.'

'I shall bear it in mind when next mine are low.'

33

'And do recollect, if you will, my friend, that Admiral Holmes may have been my father's godfather, but my mother's – if such a thing there had been – was some heathen savage.'

Hervey put his hand on Fairbrother's shoulder, and smiled warmly. 'You do not suppose that I think so much of that? And I tell you once more that you quite mistake the matter if you imagine anything but the same of my brother officers at Hounslow.'

Fairbrother looked at him in evident disbelief. 'Hervey, you astonish me.'

Hervey smiled. 'Perhaps I do make somewhat light of it . . .' In truth, he knew that acceptance by one's fellow officers was a deuced tricky business. There were any number of things to which they might take exception, and which varied between regiments with no very great predictability. He himself, for all his un-remarkable complexion, had found it to be so. He could still recollect how disapproving of Jessye, his 'cob-charger', his 'covert-hack', the mess had been at first; and how his name, because of its presumed connection, had brought him approval in certain quarters, and then, when clerical impoverishment had revealed itself, how that approval quickly disappeared. It had ceased to trouble him, however. Or rather, he had increasingly managed to confine it to a place of isolation. He was determined that his friend should have no fears on that account: 'Perhaps I am *inclined* to dismiss these things for their unworthiness, but I sincerely trust that I judge it faithfully. You saw how were my troop at the Cape?'

'I saw, of course.' Indeed, Fairbrother had seen nothing but to admire. Therein lay the problem, though, for so excellent a body of men and such admirable officers were surely so elevated above what had been his own murky purlieus – the Royal Africans – that he could never hope to be received with more than plain civility.

34

But Hervey did not catch the nuance. 'I tell you, you will find my regiment the more intrigued by an acquaintance with Chaucer than with illustrious family monuments.'

Fairbrother shook his head, returning the smile with faux weariness. 'I do think *you* believe it to be so!'

'I am certain of it,' he said, resolute. 'Now, shall we take a turn about the green lanes? I must tell you of my interview with the commander-in-chief . . .'

They left by way of the Dean's Yard, and Hervey realized he must be walking the same cobbles as had his old friend Eyre Somervile, as an ink-fingered schoolboy. How perfect a nursery for affairs of state, it appeared to him, for the great enterprise that was India, and for the regulation of a dozen other places about the globe whose allegiance was to the Crown: the school stood in the shadow of the very place of coronation, within sight of parliament, a stone's throw from the office that controlled the greatest navy the world had seen, and from the headquarters of the army that had done the most to bring about the destruction of the 'Great Disturber'.

Somervile: it reminded him – he must present his compliments at the office of the Secretary for War and the Colonies before too long in case there was anything in the lieutenant-governor's despatch that required, as Somervile himself had said, not elucidation but elaboration. But all that could wait a day or two, probably more, knowing how distracted was that office at present. No, there was indeed a more pressing concern, one which no amount of good-humoured banter with his friend could quite put from his mind. The court of inquiry was no longer a nuisance to him; it threatened his all.

'Fairbrother, I beg you would forgive me, but something has come up and I must needs attend to it at once.'

'By all means. It is not serious, I hope. May I be of help?'

Hervey smiled thinly and shook his head. 'It is something

requiring urgent attention, else . . . but no, thank you. I fear it is lonely business. You will be content to see the sights?'

'I am no more strange to London than were you on first visiting.'

Hervey's smile grew broader. 'A very philosophical answer. The generality of advice is, I understand, not to venture the other side of the river on foot, though I think that extreme counsel. I shall be back in time for us to dine together, but if for any reason I am delayed – the streets can become nigh impassable of an early evening – then you must call for dinner yourself. You will be quite at your liberty to do so.'

'I think I shall first visit with your parliament,' said Fairbrother brightly.

'Your parliament too,' said Hervey, with mock reproach. 'She is just yonder, as you see. Now, if you will excuse me, I must find a hansom cab.'

It then occurred to him that he would most likely find one outside parliament itself, so they walked there together through St Margaret's churchyard. No fewer than six cabs were drawn up outside, as well as a good many private carriages. Fairbrother insisted on seeing his friend into one.

Hervey hesitated to give his destination to the driver. 'Hyde Park,' he said, sounding uncertain.

'Which end, sir?'

'Kensington Palace.'

Fairbrother raised his hat as the cab rolled away.

At Holland Park, Hervey dismissed the cabman for an hour. It was the deucedest expense, engaging a hansom for such a time, but he needed some independent means of getting back to the United Service Club, and he did not suppose that these new-found conveniences ranged very far west of the Piccadilly bar.

A familiar face answered the door. 'Good afternoon, George,' said Hervey.

The footman admitted him and showed him into the library. 'Lady Katherine is engaged at the present, Colonel. Shall I bring you tea, sir?'

Hervey shook his head. 'No, George, thank you. I fear I have not a great deal of time.'

'*The Standard* is there at the table, sir, new-arrived.'

Hervey thanked him again, took up the newspaper and sought to divert himself for as long as Kat was engaged.

In the pages of *The Standard* he found much gossip, which might as a rule have served, but in the circumstances it merely aggravated his own misgivings about the inquiry. Only news that the Duke of Wellington was appointing a committee to consider raising a police force for London diverted him sufficiently to have the half-hour pass moderately quickly.

The doors of Kat's drawing room opened. Hervey heard, and rose unseen. Kat was all smiles, and her caller likewise, an officer in the uniform of the Second Foot Guards, some half-dozen years Hervey's junior.

Kat now saw him in the library: 'Matthew!' She advanced on him unselfconsciously and kissed his cheek. 'Do you know Captain Darbishire?'

'I do not.' He trusted that he hid his wholly unreasonable – indeed, inexplicable – resentment at finding another officer calling.

'Colonel Hervey,' said Kat to her caller.

'Sir!' Captain Darbishire braced, and bowed.

Hervey returned the bow, but Kat disobliged him from the duty of conversation. 'Captain Darbishire has brought me an invitation from his general, to attend a ball at Almack's.'

Hervey nodded. 'Let me not detain you, Captain Darbishire,' he said, a shade brusquely.

Captain Darbishire's confident air was fast changing. He knew very well who was Colonel Hervey: a man who had seen off revolutionaries on a dark night at Waltham Abbey, and who had worsted African warriors on their own ground. He imagined that an aide-de-camp from the London District headquarters would be given no quarter, stuttered his apologies and took his leave.

When he was gone, Kat led Hervey into the drawing room. 'I am delighted you are come, Matthew. When did you arrive in London?'

'This morning. I—'

Kat was overjoyed by this evidence of her lover's eagerness, and when the footman had closed the doors, she embraced him. 'How long shall you stay?'

Hervey was dismayed by how rapidly he was losing command of things (as always seemed the case when he came to Holland Park, no matter how resolutely). 'Kat, there is something urgent I must speak with you about.'

'Indeed? Must we speak of it at once, or may I ring for tea?'

'I . . . I'm not sure that I can stay at all long. I have an engagement this evening . . . with a brother officer.'

'Oh,' declared Kat in a tone of mild affront. 'I might have known your regiment would have first call on you.'

He chose not to rise to the challenge. 'Kat, the devil of a thing has come about. I was at the Horse Guards today and I learned that there's to be a court of inquiry into the affair at Waltham Abbey, and that . . . Sir Peregrine is likely as not to be president.'

Kat looked perplexed. 'Is that such a cause for alarm? He is generally the most agreeable of men.'

Hervey shifted awkwardly. 'The point is, Kat . . . the inquiry will attract public attention – it's bound to. And that is sure to occasion comment. Do you not see?'

Kat saw, and also that the comment would hardly be to her

advantage either (she supposed that Hervey's concern was not principally for *her* reputation). But it suited her to be obtuse. 'Do you really think it likely?'

'Yes, Kat: I consider it *very* likely.'

'What would you have me *do*?'

Hervey had not imagined he would have to suggest it. He was staunch nonetheless. 'Ask Sir Peregrine to decline the presidency.'

Kat looked bewildered. 'How shall I manage that? I cannot interfere with military matters in that way!'

Hervey was astonished. She had interfered several times before on his behalf – and to secure preferment rather than so simple a thing as this (he imagined that persuading her husband to decline an invitation would not be too difficult). 'Kat, I—'

'Matthew, it is evidently troubling you greatly. Let us sit and talk of it, and see if there is anything I might do.' She rang for tea.

Hervey sat.

It was after midnight when he returned to the United Service Club. He was surprised to find Fairbrother in the coffee room still, reading Southey's *Life of Nelson*.

'My dear friend, I am so very sorry I did not keep my appointment. I was detained against my better judgement, if not in truth my will. But I think the trouble may be soon resolved.'

'I am very glad of it,' replied Fairbrother equably. 'In truth, too, I have been glad of an evening with Southey. I confess to having felt excessively tired after leaving Westminster.'

Hervey smiled ruefully. 'I have heard that parliament has that effect.'

'No, parliament was invigorating in the extreme. There was a debate on reform of the franchise. Feelings ran unconscionably high. I never heard such a bear house!'

'I dare say. Have you dined?'

'Yes, and very agreeably – at the club table with two officers not long returned from the Indies.'

'I'm glad of it. I—'

'I did not say: the debate was in the House of Peers. I heard Lord Palmerston speak. He is a most engaging man, I think. Exactly as I had imagined him.'

Hervey kept his peace. He too had liked Palmerston when they had met briefly, a year or so before; but he did wish the Secretary at War would not now persist with this inquiry.

The night porter came into the room to turn down the lamps. Hervey ordered brandy. 'And then to bed. While there is time – before I am taken up with clerks at the Colonies Office, and attorneys – I would show you things, tomorrow.'

'I should be excessively grateful to you, Hervey. Excessively. But I am minded that I am meant to be a salutary companion: you are sure you do not overtax your constitution – the fever, the wound?'

Hervey knew his constitution had proved serviceable, and tried not to look sheepish. 'I assure you I am perfectly well.'

Fairbrother laid aside his Southey, as if to convey that the matter was settled. 'Did the porter tell you there is a letter? He said he would place it in the rack.'

Hervey rose and went to the hall to retrieve it. He saw at once that it was in his mother's hand, which immediately disquietened him, for she scarcely ever wrote. He broke the seal, and read:

Horningsham
14th April 1828

My dear Matthew,
I trust this finds you well and timely. I hardly know where to begin, but there has been a most unlooked-for development, a

most disagreeable thing has occurred (trouble not, for we are all in good health) and I am at my wits' end to know how to deal with it. I would that you come here as soon as you are able, for I think that only you have it in your power to put things aright. I cannot put the matter into words but beg you would believe me when I say that it is of the greatest moment to our happiness and standing. Please therefore come with haste, for it is not a matter that can bide without grave consequence to our reputation and position.

     Your ever loving Mother.

IV

A PASSAGE TO MALTA

Gibraltar, the same day, 28 September 1827

'Sir Laughton?' The first lieutenant had returned very carefully upon his half-hour.

'Just "Captain", if you please, Mr Lambe.'

'Ay-ay, sir. I have the old hands assembled.'

Peto nodded. He would read them his commission, as was the tradition, and address a few words to them. But he thought first to address the question of the admiral's quarters, about which he had given no instructions. By custom when the admiral flew his flag elsewhere the captain of a first-rate had the use of the cabin on the upper deck, but since Peto expected Sir Edward Codrington to transfer his flag to *Rupert* as soon as she joined his squadron, he had no intention of putting himself to the inconvenience – and, indeed, the indignity – of vacating his accommodation within so short a time.

'The admiral's apartments, I trust, are in serviceable condition? I had better take a look at them before beginning on general rounds.'

Lieutenant Lambe looked at him quizzically. 'They are, sir. I believe Miss Codrington is most comfortable.'

Peto's expression of indifference turned to one of thunder. '*What?*'

'Miss Codrington, sir. She came aboard this morning. She is, I believe, comfortable. And her maid.'

'*Maid?*'

'Yes, sir; her maid,' replied Lambe, even more puzzled by his captain's inability to grasp what were after all mere domestic details. 'They are both quite comfortable.'

Peto's eyes narrowed, and his hands gripped the sides of his chair. 'Mr Lambe, of what are you speaking?'

Only now did the first lieutenant perceive that his captain might be unaware of their passenger – and that the intelligence was not welcome. He cleared his throat. 'Admiral Codrington's daughter, sir: she is on board for the passage to Malta. The orders came when we put in. Forgive me, sir, but I assumed that you had been told of it ashore. Miss Codrington travelled by packet here, but the admiral wished for her to be conveyed on board one of His Majesty's ships on account of the piracy still off the Barbary Coast. I thought it expedient to accommodate her in the admiral's quarters.'

Peto boiled, though without (he thought) showing it. 'Very well.' He rose. 'You did right, Mr Lambe. That, I take it, is the reason for the sentry I saw there.'

'I thought it only proper, sir. We have an ample enough complement of marines.'

'Mm.' Peto thought it only proper too – eminently proper. Two women on the upper gun-deck: it was like putting a couple of ripe peaches next to a wasp's nest. 'I had better pay my respects. Perhaps you and she will dine with me this evening?'

Lambe hesitated. But a request from his captain was to be taken always as an order. 'I'd be honoured, sir.'

'Flowerdew!'

The captain's steward scuffled in.

'Three for dinner, one a lady: hock and a light burgundy.'

'Oh, very refined,' muttered Flowerdew as he knuckled his forehead and scuffled out again.

'He's been with me a good age,' said Peto by way of explanation, though not as a rule given to explaining himself.

'Sir, Miss Codrington, she—'

'Enough of Miss Codrington for the time being, Mr Lambe. But I will say now that we are not putting in at Malta; she will have to transfer to the sloop.'

HMS *Archer*, sloop-of-war, was to convoy with them for Admiral Codrington's squadron.

'Ay-ay, sir.'

'Very well; let's to the old hands. And then afterwards I'll see Miss Codrington while you assemble the standing officers.'

Peto's tone, though not meant to be peremptory, nevertheless stayed his lieutenant in the inevitable protest. Indeed, Peto had decided that although he would have to exercise command rather more formally through his executive officer and his sailing-master than had hitherto been his practice, there could be no part of the ship he would consider himself denied – except, of course, the wardroom. He would be prudent, naturally, in choosing his time of visiting certain quarters: the midshipmen's berth was nothing like the bear garden of *his* day, but of an evening it were better steered clear of so as to avoid taking unintended offence. Likewise the gun-decks when dinner was served up: the rum ration was half of what it had been in the French war (a quarter of a pint only, mixed with water), but it was still enough to loosen a man's tongue, and it did not do to give unnecessary occasion for a flogging. No, prudential judgement were his watchwords. It was the first time in more than a decade that one of His Majesty's first-rates was being sent to sea in the expectation – in the *possibility*, at least – of a general action: the hand was heavy on his shoulders.

And yet it troubled Peto not in the least. The bad old days – the *glorious* days, so the nation had it (and as well let them believe it!) – were gone; the press gang was no more, the drafts from the assizes there were none; nor even were there the county ballots. Now the crews were volunteers, for whatever reason a man joined – for the bounty, for the abundance of grog and plenty of prize-money, which the placards in the sea ports still promised, and against all the advice of those of earlier generations who had been deceived. Some still joined as boys, having no other family, and remained in the service all their lives: 'once a sailor, always a sailor'. And some, though without his, Peto's, schooling or means, joined because they were agitated by the same instinct as his. The true man-of-war's man, so the saying went, was begotten in the galley and born under a gun, his every hair rope-yarn, every tooth a marlinspike, every finger a fishhook, and his blood right good Stockhollum tar. These volunteers did not need the lash and the starter. In truth, the starter had been proscribed by the Admiralty for the best part of twenty years (well, to drive them to work, at any rate: Peto had known it to be admirable summary justice in the hands of a good boatswain). And here he had a full crew, not many landsmen at all said the watch bill – all come from half a dozen guardships at Portsmouth. They would be handy enough with sail, he could rely on it; though how handy was their gunnery he would not know until they exercised tomorrow.

The Royal Marines sentry presented arms as the captain emerged from his cabin.

Peto touched the point of his bicorn, and turned to look him in the eye. 'What is your name, sir?'

'Frost, sir.'

'And where is your home?'

The marine looked puzzled. 'Corporal Figgis's mess, sir. I'm berthed aft on the orlop, sir, I am.'

'Where were you *born*, man; where is your family?'

45

The marine, his face now the colour of his jacket, took an even tighter grip of his musket. 'Fak'nam, sir.'

Peto nodded, with studied satisfaction. Fakenham was a good distance inland; it was a wonder the 9th Foot had not 'listed him, though the army was not so recruit-hungry these days. 'I myself am a Norfolk-man. I shall count most especially on you.'

'Yes, sir.'

Peto turned away, imagining that the man might be a degree more inspired by such an exchange, but supposing in truth that the discipline of the marines made equal machines of them all.

'Off hats!' barked the boatswain.

Some two dozen veteran seamen were gathered aft on the upper deck, all in their best. Peto decided to address them from the foot of the companion ladder rather than from the quarterdeck – much less of a business, and much the more intimate, almost as if he had been aboard *Nisus*.

He descended the ladder very sure-footed, took the folded paper from his pocket, and read with due gravity but not too solemnly: 'Admiralty orders to Captain Sir Laughton Peto. You are to proceed at once to take command of His Majesty's Ship *Prince Rupert*, wheresoever she be found, and thence to join the fleet under the command of Sir Edward Codrington, Vice Admiral of the Blue.'

This much they knew already, to be sure – the entire crew indeed, for the previous captain's orders had been the same – but it was indeed the custom, and it did no harm to make the connection in men's minds between the Admiralty in its exalted remoteness and their ship and her commanding officer; and it gave the older hands a certain standing when they went back to their messes to report to their shipmates what the new captain was like.

'Have any of you men served with me before?' Peto's voice was that of a seasoned officer hailing against the wind.

He did not expect any to answer 'Ay'; nor did any.

'Then I shall tell you that I have been a frigate man for long years, and will have *Rupert* answer as if she were a frigate too. It *can* be done, for you are all *professional* seamen – not men taken from their homes, or assize men – and therefore you can cut about the tops a deal better than many a crew I had when we fought Bonaparte.'

He paused for dramatic effect. There was a murmur of what sounded like approval.

'Pipe down,' snapped the boatswain.

Peto judged it the time: he had begun by reading them the Admiralty's authority; he had told them of his service and flattered them by reminding them of their own status and capacity; now he would tell them what the enemy demanded. 'I do not require this for my own amusement, mark you. I shall not send you running aloft to make sport, or hold you at gun drill for the accolade of fastest in the fleet. No, I shall do these things whenever it is necessary because our adversary the Turkish devil, being sober and vigilant, will otherwise cause His Britannic Majesty's Ship *Prince Rupert*, and those who sail in her, untoward damage. Sailors, we have the habit of victory to preserve!'

Peto waited for the approving buzz, then set his jaw, turned confidently and stepped off aft.

The knot of men parted to let him through. 'Three cheers for Captain Sir Laughton Peto! Hip-hip!'

'Hurragh!'

'Hip-hip!'

'Hurragh!'

'Hip-hip!'

'Hurragh!'

It had gone well, he told himself as he made for the admiral's quarters. These things were not *always* done well: it was not always possible to judge the words aptly if the crew's humour was not known.

A few eavesdroppers knuckled their foreheads sharply as he passed, and the sentry presented arms.

He rapped smartly at the door on the larboard side (both doors opened on the steerage, which served as dining room and office, but to starboard was the state room, where the cot would be, and he counted it indelicate to present himself thus). As a rule after knocking he would have entered, but the admiral's daughter was not the admiral.

The lady's maid answered.

Peto at once took charge. 'I am the captain, come to pay respects to Miss Codrington.'

The maid (Peto thought she looked more like a governess, for she was closer his age and wore spectacles) curtsied. 'Good afternoon, sir.'

Peto stepped into the steerage and glanced about with an inspecting eye. A cover lay on the table, and the chairs were likewise shrouded. The bulkheads were fresh painted – eau de nil – and the deck sailcloth gleamed in its black and white chequer; all evidence of Lambe's percipience and industry. He waited for the maid to lead him to the admiral's day apartment.

'The captain, Miss Rebecca.'

Peto entered, stooping slightly to remove his hat. It was the first time he had been in such quarters in more years than he cared to remember, and he did not wish to collide with a beam. But if a beam were occasionally intrusive, the admiral's apartments were otherwise of some dimension, near twice the size of his own cabin, which was itself commodious by any nautical standard. At a writing table facing the stern lights was the daughter of the man who would soon take possession. She rose and turned, and curtsied.

'Good afternoon, Captain.'

Peto could scarce believe what he saw, nor at first could he quite reply. The admiral's daughter was but thirteen or fourteen. He cleared his throat. 'You are very welcome on board, Miss Codrington,' he said uneasily, making a brisk bow.

'Thank you, Captain,' she replied, smiling. 'But I cannot answer to "Miss Codrington" for I have two elder sisters unwed. My name is Rebecca.'

Peto cleared his throat again. He was unused to such self-possession in the ablest midshipman, let alone a slip of a girl. 'Well then, Miss Rebecca, my name is Peto, and I should be honoured if you would join my lieutenant and me at dinner.'

'Thank you, Captain Peto; it is I who should be honoured.'

Peto cast his inspecting eye about the apartment as best he could, a shade awkwardly, for it was the first time he had visited female quarters, however temporary they were. He cleared his throat once more. 'Very well; very well. I bid you good day then, Miss Co—, Miss Rebecca.' And he turned and took his leave, gathering up his authority again as he did so.

He took the rungs of the companion ladder purposefully, but scowling. The occupants of the quarterdeck saluted. Those merely taking their ease moved at once to the lee side, while the officer of the watch – a midshipman, since *Rupert* lay at anchor – presented himself.

'Elphinstone, sir. Signal from the port admiral: the governor's compliments; he will not now come aboard.'

Peto studied the youth in whose charge was his ship. Seventeen, eighteen years? Grandson, grandnephew perhaps? Lord Keith had died but five years ago . . . 'Thank you, Mr Elphinstone,' he said thoughtfully.

Lieutenant Lambe had returned on deck.

'The governor is not coming aboard, it seems,' said Peto, returning his salute.

'Your pleasure, then, sir?'

It was an old-fashioned locution, but it seemed apt: they stood on the quarterdeck of a first-rate, within hailing of that brave Rock, as if waiting to step onto the stage – and a great stage at that. The wind was freshening; Peto clasped his hands decisively behind his back, and gave the order to begin the great undertaking: 'Weigh anchor; make sail!'

Lambe smiled with that knowing pride that properly passed between a lieutenant and his captain. 'Ay-ay, sir!'

It was six bells of the afternoon watch, one hour before the supper time. Hands knew they must be doubly sharp about it, and the officers that their new captain would be watching like a hawk. Peto adjusted his watch to the ship's time – three o'clock – clasped his hands more tightly behind his back and affected all the detachment he could. He would hope to speak not at all until sail was set (and here he would learn what sort of a sailing-master he had in Shand, a warrant officer he had not before encountered), and then he would tell Lambe to set a course for Syracuse.

At once the little boats – the girls and 'Jews' – were all of a bob as the trade were bustled off ship unceremoniously, with or without their earnings, and the merchants with or without their credit. Boatswain's mates did the bustling, while the officers did their best at placating. But this was one of His Majesty's ships of war, and there was no room for argument once the captain had given an order: everywhere was activity, and all directed to the execution of that command.

On the middle gun-deck eight dozen men, marines mainly, began bearing on the capstan bars – donkey work if ever there was – while on the lower deck, the ship's boys stood ready to lash the messenger rope, which the capstan turned, to the anchor cable as it came through the hawse hole, and then to follow it aft to the hatchway and unclip the 'nipper' so that the cable passed down to the orlop deck, where as many men again stood by to stow it. Weighing anchor was the least popular of all the dangerous

and gruelling work of a ship's routine, as noisome on the orlop (the cable was invariably rank after any time in the water) as it was backbreaking at the capstan. Only the nippers enjoyed it, as well they might, for they had to be agile and dextrous rather than mere substitutes for horsepower.

Had he been aboard *Nisus*, Peto could have observed this work; from *Rupert*'s quarterdeck he would see only the forecastle gang, mustered ready to cat and fish the anchor. They would be all he saw of the industry required to raise it (or *them* if the current required more than one anchor: there were two at the bow, eighty hundredweight apiece, and the burden of the sodden cable on top of that). He could not judge with what effort and skill the crew worked, only by the result – which, in the end, was all that must concern him.

Meanwhile, all hands not bent to weighing anchor – the starboard watch and the idlers – fell in to their stations, the topmen confidently climbing the shrouds and edging along the yards, ready. The master had ordered all sail set. Peto approved. The wind was quite decidedly freshening, but it would be as well to get decent steerage-way to round the point of the Rock without having to stand too much out to sea. They would have to get the topgallants in once they were in open water if the wind continued to blow up like this, but in all probability that would be a couple of hours more – time at least for the larboard watch to have something hot inside them.

'Signal to *Archer*: Take station to windward.'

'Ay-ay, sir!' The signal midshipman scuttled off to the poop deck and his flag lockers. An easy signal: Peto noted that he had it run up in under the minute.

'Anchor aweigh, sir!' came the call from the hawse hole not long after, repeated up the hatchways until the quarterdeck had it.

Peto nodded, if barely perceptibly. An efficient signal officer, and the anchor off the seabed sharply: it was as it should be, but he had known it otherwise. The master made no move, however. Peto wondered, but then thought him right: with a full set of sail and a lee anchor there was every chance of fouling. Better to wait until the ring broke surface and the hook of the cat tackle had been put through.

In a few minutes more, 'Hooked!' came the cry, and at once the master raised his speaking-trumpet: 'Halyards!'

Peto checked his watch. Fifteen minutes: not *too* bad in twenty fathoms. But it was the topmen he wanted to see. They had gone up the shrouds smartly enough – but a ship at anchor and nothing but a breeze . . .

The foremast topmen had the gaskets off the fastest, then the main and mizzen at one and the same time, topgallant yards first, then tops and then lower – just as should be, a sight to please the most critical gaze. Peto screwed up his eyes in the sudden glare as the chalk-white canvas unfurled evenly, like rolls of haber-dasher's calico on a show-frame, the sail trimmers so deft with the sheets that the light wind at once caught sail full and braced. Off came the topmen smartly, and then the master's mates barked at the trimmers to haul on the ties and halyards to raise the yards.

Rupert was under weigh. Peto checked his watch again: five more minutes.

Lambe saw, and was certain they were deserving of praise. 'They were good topmen we had out of Portsmouth, sir, and they had a fair go of it in Biscay.'

'Very gratifying, Mr Lambe,' agreed Peto, with just enough of a note of encouragement while reserving his final judgement. He would want to see them shorten sail in a squall before pro-nouncing himself entirely satisfied. 'The gun-crews?'

'Not so practised, I'm afraid, sir. Guns were double lashed for most of the passage.'

'Mm.' Peto was not so sure. A frigate was tossed about a good deal more than a three-decker, and he had not had occasion to run more than a couple of days without drilling the gun-crews. 'Could they not have exercised on the upper deck?' The lightest guns of the main battery were naturally on the upper deck (he had been glad to find the eighteen-pounder – which had served him so well in *Nisus* – on *Rupert*'s upper deck, rather than the twenty-four as had lately been fashionable).

'They could have, yes, sir.'

Peto would not press him. It was the captain's business to exercise the crew, and he suspected Lambe had done his best. 'Well, we had better clear for action tomorrow and have a thorough go.'

Lambe had expected it. Peto's reputation assuredly sailed before him. But it was one thing to exercise the crews by gun or even deck, and quite another by broadside. He knew it would be a not altogether happy affair: the standing officers and mates would know their business well enough, but the landsmen ... There would be shouting, cursing and a good deal of bruising; perhaps a case or two for the surgeon, or even for the chaplain. But if they *were* to see action they must needs learn soon how to clear quickly and completely – and the lieutenants how to command their gun-decks. There was nothing quite like a man-of-war broadsiding. 'Ay-ay, sir!' he rasped.

Peto returned to his attitude of studied silence. It was strange, he marked, how the sounds of the ship – the creaking of timber, the groaning of rigging and sail – he heard, but at the back of his mind. Hear them he must, for they told him how his new ship handled, but he did not have to *listen*; long years at sea had some-how accustomed his ear to effortless attention. Yet the screaming of the gulls above the promising wake commanded his notice just as if they had been his crew speaking, for they seemed to be welcoming him back to their world. He had been ashore some time, after all. On the beach indeed.

And what a world it was, his as much as theirs, the prospect restorative, the sun on his back, so that he felt as some basking amphibian warming on a stone to invigorate its colder blood. Soon he would be entirely in his element again. Unless he looked aft, the sun he now saw only in effect and reflection – the lengthening shadows on the deck, the glinting white horses as the sea heaped at the bows – but it was the sun of the Mediterranean, of the south: it touched him differently; it touched the water differently. And although there was not yet the taste of salt on his lips, the air was the briny pure of the ocean, as different from that on land as country air from town.

He breathed it deep but hid his contentment. For the moment he must observe how *Rupert* answered, how she ran. Her master knew best her sailing qualities, and he would watch without words (if that were possible, strange as it felt) as Mr Shand conned her beyond the Punta de Europa and into the Mediterranean true. Then, with sea space enough for *Rupert* to make headway in any wind, he could retire to his cabin to read more of her papers while the boatswain piped hands to supper: a half-hour's solitude perhaps, until at five o'clock, an hour or so before dark, Lambe would call the crew to their stations, the guns would be cast loose, the pumps rigged, the lifebuoys placed in position, and the quarterdeck officers – the lieutenants and midshipmen – would make their inspection and report to him, and thence to the captain, that the ship was in good order for the night. After that – and not before – he, Peto, could retire, bathe, change his linen and ... (he sighed) entertain Miss Rebecca Codrington.

The very devil of it! His first evening he would as a rule have had his lieutenant and two or three of the others, the master perhaps, and the chaplain (being a son of the parsonage, despite some distinctly unreligious views, he did favour a chaplain when there was one, which was not often on a frigate, and certainly never in his experience one of any profound learning – 'the Reverend Mr Lack-Latin'). Why in heaven's name was Codrington's daughter going to Malta? He sighed again, and shrugged: fool of a question; why should she *not* be going to Malta? That was what daughters did, he supposed – go to see their fathers. He shook his head; it was extraordinary how little he knew of what young ladies did. Except that Miss Rebecca Codrington was but a child. He shook his head again. No, that would not do. She was by his own reckoning thirteen or fourteen: no longer, as the rascals of the midshipmen's berth would have it, 'jail-bait'. But as far as he was concerned Miss Rebecca Codrington was a minor – whatever the law said – and he would not have her subjected to any familiarity. Then came further doubts: he supposed she ate the same food as a grown-up woman . . .

With the wind now abeam and freshening by the minute (he pulled his hat on a fraction tighter), they were beginning to make leeway. There was more than enough sea space to tack clear of the point, however, or even to wear it, especially with the sea running so calm. Peto was beginning to wonder when the master would take in sail, or brace them round, but Mr Shand merely turned *Rupert* another point into the wind. Still he would not interfere: the ship was in no danger. Shand was just risking having to call all hands on deck to shorten sail quickly.

In five more minutes Peto saw for certain that *Rupert*'s line of movement through the water would take her well clear of the point, and with the wind veering if anything she would probably only increase the clearing distance. *Nisus* would not have answered like that, he knew; she would be making more leeway, and running perhaps two knots faster. He had told the old hands that a three-decker could handle as well as a frigate, and he knew it – as long as the captain gave his orders five knots faster. He would, anyway, have to learn *Rupert*'s handling keenly, and he

55

was glad of Shand's no doubt unintended demonstration of how she ran in light airs.

Half an hour later, Shand ordered the helm to starboard, and sail braced square. *Rupert*'s bow began turning away from the wind and the fast-falling sun, and the smiles on the faces of trimmers and topmen alike said it all. The screaming of the gulls fell away to the growing noise of timber and rope, the assurance that the ship was straining – *working*.

'Carry on, Mr Lambe,' said Peto, satisfied, quitting his chosen place aft of the wheel and to weather, touching his hat to acknowledge the salute he did not see but knew had been given. He could now at least leave the quarterdeck, entirely content, and with that face the prospect of dinner with some equanimity.

He went to his cabin. Flowerdew had laid the table already. The glasses, flatware and cutlery were well set, with not the slightest disturbance as *Rupert* continued to gather speed. He wondered if Miss Rebecca Codrington suffered at all from sea-sickness, for if she did she was fortunate indeed that there was such weather at this time of year; the change of seasons could bring the severest of storms in the western Mediterranean. Seasickness had never troubled him, no matter how heavy the weather. He fancied he could at least in that respect claim superiority to Nelson; and to countless others, for that matter – seasoned hands – who would cast up for days in the lightest swell at the start of a voyage, until they found their sea legs, to remain untroubled by the worst of things thereafter. It would, of course, be more convenient if his passenger confined herself to her cabin (though the crew would not be able to clear so fully for practice-action tomorrow), but he would wish seasickness on no one save the King's enemies.

He sat in his 'Madeira chair' and shuffled a few papers. None of them detained him (the purser, and his clerk, had done their work well). He laid them aside, and took out Elizabeth's letter once more. He unwrapped it and gazed at those delighting words again: *My dear Captain Peto*, and *Your ever affectionate Elizabeth Hervey*. Such words as he had never seen, or heard! And, oh, how he wished she were here now, in this fine place, his cabin, on the finest of ships. He did not recollect that, before, when he had been at sea, he had ever had a thought of anything *but* being at sea; he left the shore behind him, and with it all land-bound thoughts. Until now. It was the strangest thing. Neither did he think it unseamanlike, as once undoubtedly he would have done. But, he warned himself, he had better have a care: it would not do to moon – certainly not to be *seen* to moon. He supposed that married officers somehow attained a sort of ... equipoise. Perhaps he would, too, a few days out from Gibraltar. It undoubtedly did not serve, sitting unoccupied in his cabin, thus. Better that he be on deck, even though there was no need. And why *should* there be need? He might enjoy the last of the sun.

The sun, indeed, was fast nearing the horizon, and the words of Milton came to mind. They did so frequently. He had first heard them a dozen years before, aboard his beloved *Nisus* on her passage east, to India. His new acquaintance, Captain Hervey, ADC to the first soldier of Europe, had several times recited them, since when Peto had read all of Milton's work, and some of it twice and three times over. *And the gilded Car of Day / His glowing Axle doth allay / In the steep Atlantick stream.*

What a fortunate encounter his with Hervey had been; though not at all propitious at first. Yet now he was possessed of a fine friend, who would indeed be soon connected to him by marriage. He wondered how his friend fared at the extremity of that dark continent to starboard. And although he was not in the habit of regular prayer (other than the seaman's need of comfort in the storm) he found himself asking for a blessing for his friend – and for his friend's family.

The bell sounded the hour. Peto snapped to, and addressed himself to the present – the evening muster. He did not intend going about the ship on this first day at sea (he must leave his lieutenant a little space so soon out and under a new captain), but he would walk the gangboard to the forecastle, casting an eye over as much as he could, animate and otherwise, without too much appearance of inspection.

Marines stood by the carronades, their fighting quarters. It was not unusual, but on the whole he preferred the jollies to be under small arms: they did more service in picking off an enemy's sharpshooters aloft than raking the decks with grape. He would speak of it to Lambe before tomorrow's exercise. But what else he saw he approved of – and it was all so different from his own time in a ship of the Line, in Nelson's day: at evening muster, with the second rum issue not two hours before (and twice the ration it was today) there would be many a man fumbling and stumbling in his stupor, thrashed by the petty officers with a knotted rope end, until some wretched word of insubordination saw him clapped in irons for captain's punishment – the cat at the grating – next morning. But that had perforce been the way; what other was there with men brought and kept aboard against their will?

He had disliked it, of course; none but a captain predisposed to cruelty could have liked it (there were such men, he would admit). Without the rum few men would have transgressed so; but how could a crew be kept content without grog? Yes, there had been some temperance men – by conviction or through poor constitution – who would drink cocoa or tea instead, trading their tots for coin or credit, but the great majority lived for their rum. It was only the rum ration that had made life bearable. Peto wondered, deep down, if it could be otherwise today were it to come to war with the Turk. He turned and made his way back along the gangboard on the opposite side, passed the guns on the quarterdeck with but a glance, and climbed the companion to the poop.

Two midshipmen stood smartly to attention, and two clerks behind them. Peto looked them up and down in an unofficial sort of way, before fixing on the one: 'Let me see your telescope, Mr Pelham.'

The signal midshipman handed it to him.

Peto trained it on *Archer* half a mile ahead and to larboard. 'You know what is parallax, Mr Pelham?'

'I do, sir.'

'Do you consider that your telescope has parallax error?'

Pelham hesitated. 'I had not, sir.'

'I very much fear that it does.' He handed back the instrument.

Pelham put it back under his arm and continued to stand at attention.

'Have a look, man!'

The unfortunate midshipman did as he was bid. 'Sir, I see it now.'

Peto turned and stalked away. There was little to be served by telling the man (if man were truly the right word; boy seemed more apt) that he ought to have discovered the error for himself before they left Gibraltar, so that he might have had it rectified – or have found a new one. Neither did Peto want abject humiliation for him in front of two of the crew. All the same, his signal midshipman … What did it portend, that below the surface of what he saw with approval – indeed, at his first look below that surface – there was inadequacy?

He had thoroughly vexed himself as he came up to the wheel. 'Mr Lambe, Mr Pelham's telescope has a pronounced parallax error. How in the name of heaven does he suppose he will read a signal at any distance?'

The lieutenant was not quite so dismayed. 'I am certain he would not suppose it, sir. He fell heavily as we beat to. I suspect that is when the damage was done.'

Peto looked at him, uncomprehending: the deck was motionless.

'He lost his footing coming down from the main mast. He had gone aloft to see if there were any last signals ashore.'

Peto scowled. It could happen to anybody, though more was the pity young Pelham hadn't thought to discover the injury to his telescope . . .

Lambe would not absolve himself, however. 'I should have insisted he went to the surgeon. But he's plucky, and wouldn't surrender the poop to Gardiner. I will have him and the telescope replaced.'

By now the lieutenants were coming on the quarterdeck to report that all was in good order. Peto took a few paces to the rear to let Lambe work things his way. At length, with the last report made, Lambe was able to turn to him and report that the ship was ready to change to the night routine.

'Very good, Mr Lambe. Secure guns and pipe down hammocks.'

'Ay-ay, sir!'

Peto cast his eye about one more time. 'And I would see Mr Pelham back in his place as soon as may be.'

'Ay-ay, sir.'

'And you will join me at dinner?'

'With great pleasure, sir.'

Peto nodded, his look softening to something approaching a smile, and turned for his cabin.

An hour later, in fresh linen and his second-best coat, Peto stood looking out of the stern windows, the brilliant red twilight a picture he thought the finest of artists would never be able to capture faithfully, for it was more than mere colour. It would not be long before the moon was up – a good moon, he expected – and they ought to be able to keep a fair rate of sailing throughout the silent hours (the wake was whitening – no doubt of it).

He ducked into the starboard quarter gallery to observe the set of the sails for a last time before dinner. Hands were already taking in the topgallants; he could want no more of his lieutenant and the master. But then, with but a handful of three-deckers in commission, why should it be other? There was many an able officer who would no more go to sea, for all his capability.

Things had certainly changed, he mused. Except the ships themselves. *Rupert* was built a little stronger, perhaps, but in essence – in detail indeed – she was just as *Victory*. And at Trafalgar *Victory* had been forty years old. In his time in the East, and lately beached in Norfolk, he had given these matters much thought. He had seen steam manoeuvring to advantage at Rangoon – and, indeed, he had come to Gibraltar by steam packet (though sail had, in truth, conveyed him for much of that journey) – and although he could not imagine how a paddle wheel might move a ship of the Line, he thought it not improbable that some keen-witted engineer would find a way. And if somehow the army's Shrapnel shell might be adapted, or even one that might explode and rupture a ship's side, would that not spell the end of the wooden walls? The Navy Board would have to clad its ships in iron, like the knights of old. And had not the knights then become immobile?

He sighed. Would it come in his time? It was strange: in one breath he longed for the innovation, for the capability was there and others might seize it (the Americans for sure would be think-ing of it: they held the old ways in little regard. And the French, of course. None but a fool doubted they were the better shipbuilders; it had been as well they were not the better sailors!). And was not *any* advantage to be taken to defeat the King's enemies? Yet in another breath he wished for not one jot of change, for it was the old world that had served so well, and he had mastered it.

If ever he got his flag and it ended up being soot-specked at the mizzen ... Well, it would at least be a flag. He had always reckoned that had he been born twenty years earlier he would have made Vice; but now he would be content to retire a rear admiral, and doubtless he would fly his flag ashore rather than at the mizzen mast of a line-of-battle ship.

A confident knock at the cabin door brought him back to the present.

'Come in!' he roared (though with the ship under weigh it would have sounded fainter to whoever knocked).

The door opened and Admiral Codrington's youngest daughter stepped inside, escorted by Lambe.

Her appearance gave Peto some surprise. She had put her hair up. She wore a white, long-sleeved muslin dress, embroidered and satin-trimmed, with a gathered bodice and pointed lapels. About her neck were coral and pearls. She looked nearer sixteen than thirteen.

Peto shifted awkwardly. 'Miss ... Rebecca: good evening.'

She curtsied. 'Good evening, Captain Peto. This is a very pleasant apartment.'

He cleared his throat. 'Indeed, yes, though in the service we call it a cabin. Only the admiral's is called *apartment*. Your father will install himself there as soon as we ... that is, *Prince Rupert*, joins his squadron.' He thought for a moment: did he dismay her by such a notion? 'You are aware, are you not, Miss Codrington, that your father is at sea with the fleet?'

'Oh yes, Captain Peto; I know he is to fight the Turk.'

He had certainly not expected her to be so particularly informed ... or so matter of fact. He cleared his throat rather noisily. 'Well, that is not quite as they would have it in London, though it may come to it, which is why we make haste now for the Peloponnese.' He smiled. 'Not that I mean, of course, that *you* go to the Peloponnese, Miss Codrington. The sloop accompanying us will take you into Malta as we pass the island.'

Rebecca frowned. 'I wish I *could* go to Greece. I have read Thucydides, you know.'

Peto saw Lambe's eyes widening. He hoped his own were not doing so. 'Indeed, indeed. Do you read the Hobbes or the Smith?'

Rebecca looked mildly put out. 'No, Captain Peto, I read from the Greek. I have been taught it since I was ten.'

Flowerdew, who had been standing in the corkscrew fashion that he invariably adopted when there were guests of whom he did not wholly approve – or, as in this case, simply could not fathom – stepped forward to his captain's rescue. 'Wine, sir?'

'Ah, yes,' said Peto, grateful yet again for his steward's sense of occasion and timing. 'Will you take a little ... wine, Miss Co—, Miss Rebecca?'

'Thank you, Captain Peto, I shall.'

'Hock?' He enquired as if she might not know the word, let alone its suitability.

'Hock would be very agreeable,' she replied, with a bright smile.

Peto looked at his lieutenant, who wore an expression of suppressed mirth. 'Mr Lambe?'

'Thank you, Captain: *most* agreeable.'

Flowerdew already had the bottle uncorked and in a cooler – and two more, and three of burgundy (his hands were a shade rheumaticky these days, and he liked to have plenty of time with corks).

'How long shall it take us to reach Malta, Captain Peto?' asked Rebecca, taking her glass and smiling at Flowerdew, who merely frowned, if rather sweetly.

'If this wind freshens a little more, as I expect it to do, a week, six days perhaps.'

Rebecca looked pleased at the prospect. 'But you will not confine me to my cabin for that time, Captain Peto?'

'By no means. You may have the freedom of the quarterdeck,

your maid too, of course. But I would that you did not leave your quarters unless accompanied . . . by a steward, or the like.'

Rebecca nodded. 'Where is the quarterdeck to be found?' she asked, sipping at her hock.

Peto, though startled somewhat by the lack of knowledge, was nevertheless pleased that conversation was not inhibited by the disparity of age. 'It is the deck you walked hither. It is reserved for the officers.'

'But may I see the guns? I saw a very little of them when I came on board.'

Peto hesitated. 'If there is opportunity.' There would be opportunity enough to *hear* them; that was certain. 'Tomorrow we shall exercise the guns. If the weather is fine you may observe from the quarterdeck, but you will have to fill your ears with lint. I'll have the surgeon give you some.'

'Thank you, Captain Peto!'

It was extraordinary. He could not determine whether she was a child who periodically sounded like an adult, or vice versa; but she was engaging company for sure. 'What say you, Lambe?' he tried, thinking to con the subject away from gunnery.

His lieutenant was uncertain what he was asked: the matter was evidently decided. And then he realized that his captain was in need of a tow. 'I say, sir, that I believe we shall have a fair day for it' (the weather was always a safe subject). 'A red sky at evening muster, and high cloud.'

'Just so,' agreed Peto.

Flowerdew took a step forward. 'Cook says not to be long about the wine, sir, else the lobster'll go leatherlike.'

Peto thanked him, and took note. His cook had been with him these dozen years and more, and he was not inclined to try his devotion too much – especially not on his first night at sea in twelve months.

They moved to the fine old table in the steerage, Peto at the head, Rebecca on his right. It was not his custom to say grace privately, or at such a gathering as this, and so he tucked his napkin into the open-front of his coat and picked up knife and fork. He was about to comment upon the fine appearance of the lobster, by way of opening, but Rebecca spoke first.

'Mama says that now Lord Goderich is prime minister there will be no war. Mama says that it was only Mr Canning who wished for war. What is your opinion, Captain Peto?'

Flowerdew poured more hock, giving his captain a glance, eyebrows raised.

'My opinion, Miss Rebecca? In truth I should not be in the least surprised to find that your father has had communication from Constantinople instructing him to withdraw from the Ionian. I believe it is true that Mr Canning was the principal architect of the treaty by which we now intervene in the Greek war, and that by all accounts Goderich is a mild sort of fellow, but the treaty obliges us to act, and it is certain that France – and most certainly the Tsar – will not rest until the Ottoman Porte is humbled in this. I must say that Canning's dying in all this is deuced inconvenient.' He looked at Lambe in a manner that invited comment.

'I would say, sir, that the Tsar will not be content until the Turk is well and truly humbled, and he can sail his ships through the Bosporus when he will.'

'You are surely in the right there, Mr Lambe.'

'This treaty, Captain Peto: have you seen it?'

Peto smiled, a shade indulgently (it was endearing that she should think him elevated enough to be given sight of the Treaty of London), but also wryly, for although in large part the treaty was secret, *The Times* had published the salient clauses within a week of its signing. 'I have not read the treaty in its entirety, Miss Rebecca. There was – you may know – a protocol' (he paused; she nodded her familiarity with the word) 'made last year between the Tsar and the King, and this provided for us to take steps to persuade the Turks to leave Greek waters – which is why the Mediterranean fleet was despatched to the Peloponnese, and your father made commander-in-chief.'

Rebecca nodded again, without the slightest sign of girlish pride in a father's position, rather with an intensity for understanding what she might.

'It was only in July, when the French joined the alliance, that a formal treaty was signed.' Peto took a sip of his wine, rather feeling the need of it suddenly. 'And that treaty, I understand, was based largely upon the earlier protocol, but with a secret clause, which was that if the Porte would not accept mediation within one month, the three allies would send consuls to Greece – which, of course, is but a short step from recognizing the country – and that if the Porte, or for that matter the Greeks, refused an armistice,' (he looked at her again for assurance that she understood, and she again nodded) 'then the allies would interpose between them in order to prevent hostilities.'

Flowerdew coughed, and Peto began wolfing his lobster.

Lambe came to the relief. 'I think you will see, Miss Rebecca, what a responsibility your father bears. He has a fine fleet, and the Turks know they cannot prevail against the Royal Navy. And when *Rupert* joins him it will be manifest to them that there is no other way than an armistice, for she is certainly the biggest ship in the Mediterranean.'

Rebecca's face lit up. 'I would so very much like to be there when my father's ships make the Turks turn away!'

'Ah,' said Lambe, without perhaps thinking. 'What if they should *not* turn away; what if they were to fight from a feeling of indignation?'

Peto, his mouth unfortunately full, was unable to protest, and so the conversation was not diverted from the alarming prospect of bloodshed.

'If my father were to come on board this ship, Mr Lambe, I should want to stand beside him, *especially* if it came to a fight!'

Peto, managing to swallow a prodigious mouthful with the aid of half the contents of his wine glass, cleared his throat pointedly. 'Miss Rebecca, your spirit is admirable, as I would have imagined it to be in the daughter of Sir Edward Codrington, but I would counsel against too bellicose a stance. I do not believe His Majesty intends that we go to war with the Turk!' Except that he, Peto, was of the opinion that placing themselves between Greek and Turk could lead to one thing only, for the Turks were too proud a people, and the Greeks too devious (rather try steering a middle course between Scylla and Charybdis than these two!).

When the remains of the lobsters were cleared, and the finger bowls, Flowerdew brought a rack of lamb.

'You may be lucky, Miss Rebecca; you may yet eat fresh meat the while to Valetta,' tried Peto, intending to lighten the table talk (he had bought two near-full-grown lambs at Gibraltar, though scraggy specimens by English measure). 'Otherwise it will be the salting barrels.'

'Oh, I think I should be happy on salt beef, Captain Peto, if that is what you would eat.'

Truth was, Peto was never at all happy on the damnable ship's ration – a binding regime ten days out of port once all the fresh leaf was gone, and which no quantity of apples could quite relieve. But evidently Miss Rebecca Codrington was determined to be a worthy admiral's daughter, and he must take care not to appear too dismissive of her purpose, however naive it was. He smiled. 'Your attitude does you credit. Now, may I enquire why you travel to Malta? Shall you stay there long?'

Flowerdew poured the burgundy, which Peto first tasted and approved.

Rebecca sipped hers with confidence. 'I am to take up residence with my family, Captain Peto. I imagine I shall stay for as long as Mama is there. She has engaged a governess.'

Peto nodded, but rather to say that within a couple of years she would need a guard not a governess. She was a pretty thing. Every midshipman and lieutenant would soon be taking soundings. He had observed how his fellow midshipman had made love to Admiral Tryon's daughter at Portsmouth, and to Griffin's at Gibraltar, and they not a deal older. Not he, though; the wild Norfolk coast had taught him many things, but not how to present himself with advantage to a female.

Conversation turned to Malta, its history and people. Peto knew the island well, and Lambe had once spent the best part of a year there when his ship had been laid up in repair. Rebecca was eager to hear everything.

A fruit compote followed the roast. It tasted strongly of rum, but Rebecca appeared to enjoy it, with copious cream. When they were finished, Flowerdew brought a Stilton cheese, but before they could begin there was a knock at the door. Flowerdew answered it.

'Lieutenant of the watch presents 'is compliments, sir. Unlit sail to southward.'

'I will go if you wish, sir,' said Lambe, pushing his chair back.

'Very good, Mr Lambe.' Peto had no intention of turning out on so sketchy a report (he had no intention of doing anything in such circumstances that he would not have done aboard *Nisus*: it was not his way to make any false show of address).

When Lambe was gone, Rebecca asked what was the nature of the report. Peto explained that standing orders required the officer of the watch to send word to the captain if there were unidentified sail to windward, and that it was then the captain's discretion. The report was of an unlit (or, as likely, ill-lit) ship on the weather gage. A three-decker had nothing to fear, but a darkened ship off the Barbary Coast was worth attention.

Rebecca declined the Stilton (Peto wondered if it were on account of the maggots: two or three had, most insolently, wriggled out). 'Will your wife come to Malta, Captain Peto?' she asked, with what sounded like hopefulness.

Peto's hand almost miscarried the decanter of port. 'I do not have a wife, Miss Rebecca. That is, I do not have a wife *yet* . . .' (he cleared his throat) 'I mean that I *shall* have a wife . . . I am to be married.'

Rebecca's face lit up once more. 'Oh, Captain Peto, that is very delightful!'

Peto struggled to conceal his own absolute pleasure in the subject. It *was* delightful; it was the most delightful thing ever to have happened to him (for delight was not the appropriate word to describe taking command of a ship). This child – this young woman indeed – had a way with directness that was altogether disarming. He bowed, obliged.

'May I enquire who is the lady, Captain Peto?'

'You may indeed!' he replied, seizing the decanter again, this time with great firmness, and recharging his glass (Flowerdew then discreetly replaced the stopper and removed the remainder of the port, to Peto's faint discomfiture). 'She is the sister of a very dear friend of mine; an officer of light dragoons, however, not a naval officer.'

'But you both wear a blue coat!' she said brightly.

Peto smiled, and nodded slowly, acknowledging the aptness of the observation. 'We do indeed, Miss Rebecca Codrington; we do indeed. You are evidently a keen student of uniform.' He was surprised by how easily he teased. It was all on account of that letter – that astonishing letter: 'the world turned upside down', as went the song he had once sung in the midshipmen's berth.

'What is her name?'

'Elizabeth.'

'I like "Elizabeth". Is she "Lizzie", or "Eliza"? Oh, she is not "Bess" is she? Or "Beth"? I am not so partial to those.'

Peto was wholly taken aback; it was not merely by Rebecca's decided expression but by his own uncertainty as to the answer. 'I . . . I have only heard her answer to "Elizabeth".'

'*Please* don't call her "Beth", or "Bess", for I should not like it.'

'Miss Codrington,' (he wondered if it were the wine speaking, and felt suddenly negligent) 'you will allow me to please myself in this regard! She will answer very properly to "Lady Peto".'

Rebecca smiled broadly, draining the contents of her water glass. Peto sighed inwardly: this slip of a girl appeared to be gaining something of the measure of him. And it was deuced unfair, for he had not the slightest experience of her sex – not of the sensibility at least – other than of Miss Hervey; and that, perforce, was of a somewhat restricted nature. But what manner of excuse was that? What experience did this . . . *girl* have? He almost shook his head in despair – and wished, indeed, that Lambe would return to say the unlit ship was a pirate with hostile intent.

V

THE REVERSE OF THE MEDAL

Wiltshire, 23 April 1828

'D'ye know, Fairbrother, I had quite forgot: what is the day today?'

The chaise, engaged at short notice and therefore prodigious expense, was bowling comfortably along the downs towards the valley of the Wylye, which Hervey always thought of as the home stretch. In half an hour they would be at his father's vicarage in Horningsham. It had been a most pleasant drive. Breakfasting early, they had left London at seven o'clock, and it was now approaching five of the evening (he would be ready to adjust his watch, for Warminster time was a half-hour or so behind London's). They had stopped but once, except to change horses, and then for the briefest of meals, and they had talked for every mile of the way.

Hervey had racked his brain but could think of no likely cause for his mother's alarm. In the end he had concluded that very likely it was another fit of the vapours, occasioned no doubt by some dispute of his father's with the bishop (he remembered well enough the tumult of 'popery in Horningsham' before he went to India). But if his mother wrote to him, she was by her own reckoning in need of him, and he could do no other but come at once, although there was pressing business in London – and perhaps even more in Hertfordshire. The compensation was, of course, that he would see his daughter. It had been almost eleven months – another birthday, which again he had been absent from. She was now ten years old.

Fairbrother glanced inboard briefly at his questioner. 'It is a Wednesday, but those are legion; it is the twenty-third of April, and therefore St George's Day, as I have observed from the flags on the churches – which evidently you have not.' He had enjoyed the day as much as any he could remember. He wondered what made it special in his friend's mind.

'It is the regimental day.'

'Ah. There will be revelries in Hounslow?'

Hervey smiled. 'I hope so. Tea and rum is taken to the dragoons by the officers and serjeant-majors at reveille, and then before morning stables the senior officer presents a red rose to each man.'

'Why red?'

'That is a good question. Nobody knows, really. Quite prob- ably because there were once not enough white ones. And after duties everyone gives their rose to a female of his favouring, on account of the commanding officer's giving his to an old nun in the convent where we were lodging in Spain ... or France; I forget which.'

'I wonder where they will be bestowed in Cape-town,' said Fairbrother, with a wryish smile.

'I wonder too.'

Cape Town: it had been but nine months since his landing there, and yet it seemed an age. Fairbrother was today as agree- able a travelling consort as any he could wish for, and yet when first they had met, in the indolent comfort of his 'retirement quarters', he had been aloof, resentful, querulous even. Only by degrees, subdued by the charm of what he perceived to be a most

72

peculiar attachment of the dragoons to each other – more especially of those immediately about Hervey – and by the re-kindling of an extraordinary talent for the soldier's art (and indeed exemplary courage), had Fairbrother mellowed and become Hervey's boon companion.

'Well, I am glad to be seeing "God's country" at last.'

Hervey leaned forward to look out of the window as they joined the turnpike at Heytesbury, off the wind-blown Salisbury Plain at last and into the gentle valley of the Wylye, with its villages strung like pearls between the episcopacies of Sarum and Bath. 'Did I describe it thus?' He smiled; he knew he had the habit of doing so. 'Not long now.'

Fairbrother nodded. 'You have never spoken much of your sister. Might you tell me a little of her before we meet?'

'Have I not? I have told you she is to marry my good friend Laughton Peto. *Sir* Laughton, indeed.'

'Oh, just so; and you mention her name with regularity, but I am not enlightened ever.'

Hervey frowned at the challenge. 'As you well know, she is to marry Peto. They met many years ago, I believe when he came to Wiltshire for my wedding, and then later in Rome when Elizabeth and I had gone there for . . . to see Italy' (he did not feel it expedient still to disclose to Fairbrother the extent of his melancholy after Henrietta's death, though that was some . . . ten years ago). 'They became engaged last summer, just before Peto joined his ship.' He suddenly looked askance. 'That is, I *assume* he received Elizabeth's acceptance before putting to sea. By heavens, what a business is courtship in uniform!'

'Quite.'

'My father has been vicar of his parish for many years, and lately Archdeacon of Sarum, and Elizabeth has done good works in the parish – or I should say parishes, for my father has had the additional cure of several when they had no clerk. And she has always been active with the workhouse in the town. You know, it was she who found Serjeant Wainwright.'

'Indeed?'

'Yes. He comes from an indigent family hereabouts. Though I say "family", he doesn't know his father; Elizabeth knew of their situation and urged me to enlist him.'

'In that alone she has done you the greatest service.'

Hervey sighed. 'That, and a hundred other things.' He turned to look at his friend direct. 'I could not measure my gratitude to her. Such sound sense and compassion.'

'I look forward to making her acquaintance.'

'You must not alarm her, Fairbrother, or any of the family.'

His friend looked bemused. 'I have left my animal skins at the United Service Club, Hervey.'

'Don't be an ass. I meant you are not to alarm them with stories of the Cape.'

'As you wish. Though it was not my intention.'

'No, but Georgiana might wheedle it out of you, or it might come out casually at dinner on account of some unintended line.'

'I understand, though do you not think they might have some inkling of events from the newspapers?'

'That is possible. But by and large I keep these things to myself.'

Fairbrother said nothing. He was a guest, even though he accompanied his friend on the orders of the lieutenant-governor – 'captain-nursemaid', Hervey had ribbed – and since he was not on intimate terms with the manners of the English gentry, he was content to take counsel and observe. But how *stiff* it all sounded compared with the way things were in his own country!

The joy of the last mile to Horningsham was to him undiminished by such thoughts, however. The prospect of Archdeacon Hervey's church, when it came, was especially pleasing, and then the parsonage was all charm (Hervey had told him that it was but a modest house and establishment – 'my father did not have benefit of Queen Anne's Bounty'), a hotch-pot of building covered in ivy and moss and vines. They had been hourly expected, for Hervey had increased his expenses by sending an express, and as soon as the chaise's wheels growled into the drive, the household came outside to greet them.

Fairbrother was wholly intrigued by the ceremony. Whenever he had returned to his father's house the greeting had been with him alone, and at his mother's cabin it had been all exuberance, with no precedence but that gained by the agility of any number of aunts, uncles and cousins. He descended from the chaise and watched as his friend greeted his father with an easy smile, but with a bow rather than a handshake (or kisses, as he himself would have in Jamaica). The Venerable Thomas Hervey did indeed look as his title, a kindly old gentleman, an Englishman of proper sentiment and loyalties, and just as his friend had described him. Mrs Hervey, on the other hand, of whom her son had spoken little, looked less at ease, a woman, he imagined, of indifferent sensibilities and limited comprehension. He did not think she would care much for his intrusion on the household. Hervey greeted her with kisses and a sort of indulging frown, as much as to say 'I am here, and I am sure all will be well'.

His sister now came forward, with a look that he, Fairbrother, could not quite recognize. It seemed to carry at once both deference and superiority, defiance even – but certainly the strongest affection. There was no doubting their kinship: the shape of the face, the eyes, the . . . assumption of authority. It was really most striking. They embraced, and Hervey stood back and smiled in a way that said how prodigiously proud he was of her. And then, last in line, standing with perfect composure, was the child of whom Fairbrother had heard his friend speak so much, yet without once imparting any appreciable knowledge. She advanced, curtsied – which he surmised was the culmination of a morning's practice – and then burst into excited greeting, throwing her arms wide and hugging her father about his waist before he was able to bend, or to lift her up to embrace. She was her father's daughter – the likeness was clear – yet so unlike her aunt as to remind Fairbrother that there had been a mother too.

When he had untangled Georgiana's arms for the moment, Hervey turned. 'Father, may I present Captain Fairbrother.'

Fairbrother, his hat already in his hand, bowed formally. 'Good evening, sir.'

Archdeacon Hervey held out his hand, and a warmth suffused his face, so that Fairbrother was certain of his welcome.

'And my mother,' (Mrs Hervey curtsied) 'my sister,' (Elizabeth both curtsied and smiled with complete naturalness) 'and . . . Miss Georgiana Hervey, my daughter.'

Georgiana's forehead and the inclination of her head betrayed curiosity: Fairbrother's complexion was by no means as dark as some of the sable servants in Bath, or even as some of the Horningsham farm hands at the end of a fierce summer; but neither were his features those of the county. Fairbrother observed, however, that it was curiosity not alarm, nor any measure of distaste. And he could never find himself able to condemn a child of barely ten years, especially one who was able to greet her father formally and then throw off that formality without leave.

She curtsied. 'Good afternoon, Captain Fairbrother.' Then she turned to her father again. 'Where is Private Johnson, Papa?'

'In London. There are things there for which I had need of him.'

She looked disappointed.

When the chaise, its driver and horses had been attended to – in which the entire assemblage appeared to play a part – they went inside to tea. And then Elizabeth and the housemaid showed them to their rooms (though Hervey's had been the same since his brother had died), where hot water was brought, and word that they would dine at eight o'clock. The family was all politeness, Fairbrother concluded.

'I will come for you in an hour,' said Hervey, when he had satisfied himself that his friend had every requisite, before descending discreetly to enquire of Elizabeth what was the 'untoward event' which so disturbed the peace of the parsonage at Horningsham.

To his surprise, however, he found his mother at the bottom of the stairs. She took him into the little sitting room reserved for her. He rarely entered it, and found himself staring at its contents – china figures, samplers, a vast box of sewing, and but one book, whose title he could not make out from where he stood.

'I am glad you are come, Matthew, and hope it is of no inconvenience, but I am at my wits' end, and your father is of no use in it whatsoever.' Mrs Hervey shook her head, sat down and looked at him as if some response were already required.

Hervey, in the circumstances not wanting to smile, yet feeling it necessary to make light of the inconvenience, managed something he reckoned appropriate. 'I had not any fixed arrangements, Mama.'

Mrs Hervey nodded, satisfied. 'By the way, your friend – a very gentlemanlike man.'

'Indeed he is. And a brave officer too.'

'It is very distasteful that he should be exposed to all this. As exposed he must be.'

Hervey's brow furrowed. 'Exposed to what, exactly, Mama? What is the cause of my hastening here?'

Mrs Hervey looked distressed again. 'I cannot know how to begin, for it is too shameful . . .'

Hervey decided there was no course but to sit in silence until she could bear it no longer: any attempt to coax it from her seemed likely only to occasion more procrastinating.

She began dabbing at her eyes (though he saw no actual tears), and sighing with such rapidity that he thought he must reach for the smelling salts. 'Oh, I have had such palpitations as no person should have to endure!'

'Mama!'

His exasperation – which Mrs Hervey took to be a very proper alarm – did the trick. She took a deep and expressive breath. 'Elizabeth says she will not marry Captain Peto.'

'What? But she has *said* so. She wrote and accepted his proposal.'

'I mean that she has changed her mind. She no longer wishes to marry him.'

Hervey was all but dumbstruck. How could it be so? 'But she has accepted his proposal.'

'Matthew, I know she has accepted, but now she intends . . . renouncing her acceptance. That is why I wrote to you. I have tried everything with her but she will not have a word of it.' She produced a second handkerchief, and pitiable sobs.

Hervey's brow was more thoroughly furrowed than ever his mother had seen it – had she but the capacity to notice. 'What reason does she give? What reason *can* she give?'

Mrs Hervey looked out of the window. It was still daylight enough to see the distant elms, and the rooks settling to the nest – in just the manner, it had seemed to her, that at last *both* her offspring were about to settle. 'She says' (sob) 'she does not love him.' She began shaking her head again, as if asserting that there was no future to be had for Elizabeth or, indeed, for herself.

Hervey was reduced to uncomprehending silence. A few moments ago he had thought his sister the most wonderful of women, about to become wife to the most wonderful of men.

But now ... And what, indeed, of Peto? He had still no news of his situation: he might be in a chaise from Portsmouth this very minute, returning from battle – that second Trafalgar – in the expectation of the loyal greeting which was rightfully his. *It is not a matter that can bide without grave consequence to our reputation and position*, his mother had written. He had been inclined to imagine her mistaken in whatever it was. But not now.

'What is Father's opinion in this? Has he forbidden it?'

Mrs Hervey's look was of even more abject despair. 'I have not had occasion to tell him. He has not been at all well this past month.'

'And Elizabeth has not told him?'

'I begged she would not.'

They sat for some time in a state of incapability, Mrs Hervey's sobs subdued but continuing, until her son found himself able to ask, 'Has anything ... *particular* induced this determination on Elizabeth's part?'

Mrs Hervey let out such a sigh, as if she might wholly expire. When she spoke it was almost in a whisper. 'I wish I could say there was not. It is all on account of ... a certain person.'

Hervey's frustration with this most disconnected way of proceeding almost got the better of him. 'Mama, you really must compose yourself and tell me all there is to know, for how otherwise am I to prevail on Elizabeth to change her mind?'

Mrs Hervey began searching about her pockets for smelling salts, but to no avail. She sighed deeply once more, and waved her hands as if in submission. 'It is all on account of ... a Mr Heinrici. She met him not two months ago ... and now she believes she is in love with him and intends marrying him.'

'*Heinrici?*' Hervey could scarcely credit it, not least that Elizabeth should have her head turned by someone with so outlandish a name.

79

His mother nodded. 'Or *Baron* Heinrici, I should call him.'

'He is German then? Or Dutch?'

'Yes. He took the lease on the Heytesbury estate last year. Elizabeth went to the house to buy hangings or some such, which he did not wish for.'

His mother's concern for precise domestic detail, while she remained indifferent to that of real significance, almost deflected Hervey from a right judgement: not only was his sister's inclination to break off the engagement deeply dismaying, he now saw that she acted in it quite recklessly. It was not in the least like her, and he concluded that there must be some strange imbalance in her humours – not in the old sense, of course (that was so much quackery), but something must very definitely have disturbed her equilibrium. To throw over his old friend, the very finest of men, for . . . who? A new-come German? (Hervey was sure, now, the name was not Dutch.) Who, indeed, was this Baron Heinrici, with his new lease on the agreeable Heytesbury estate? Why, indeed, was he come to Wiltshire at all? What could possibly have turned Elizabeth's head so, for in everything he had known her undertake she had shown matchless judgement (better, even, than his own)? He must observe her closely at dinner for some sign of what disturbed her.

No, that would not do; it smacked of deceit. He must speak with her *before* dinner. Let them have it out, and then if she did not see where sense and duty lay (he could hardly conceive that possible, but then in her present state of evident . . . derangement, *anything* was possible) – if she could not see the proper course, then she would have the whole of their dinner to reflect on the situation, the whole unhappy, untoward business!

In consequence of the shocking family news, Hervey was able to afford Georgiana only a brief interview, promising to spend the morning with her instead. She told him of her pony – the one he had bought her when he had come back from India – and the Broadwood piano (which he had sent her for her . . . he did not remember quite *which* birthday). She wanted to play for him there and then. But he had to protest that it was a pleasure he must suspend until the morning too.

Georgiana was disappointed, but not excessively so, for she understood that her father had travelled a very great distance and would wish to rest. And there was his friend Captain Fairbrother to be looked after, and Aunt Elizabeth too . . .

Hervey professed himself grateful to Georgiana for her patience, and accompanied her to her bedroom, where he saw that the housemaid had already brought a bowl of hot water. 'I retire myself without assistance, Papa,' she said, matter of fact rather than proud.

'Very well,' he replied, kissing her forehead. 'Until the morning.'

Elizabeth was in their father's book room when Hervey sought her out. She had put on an evening dress, quite formal, and she looked perfectly composed when he entered.

'Well, brother, you have spoken with Mama and will know my news. That is why you are come, is it not? Mama sent for you?'

Hervey was thrown disconcerted onto the defensive. 'I should anyway have come at the first opportunity.'

Elizabeth raised her eyebrows challengingly.

'But Elizabeth, this is a sorry affair. I—'

'Sorry? *Sorry*, Matthew? I see no cause for sorrow. I had hoped you might take pleasure in my happiness!'

Hervey now raised *his* eyebrows. 'I did. I most certainly did – last year when you accepted Peto's offer of marriage.'

Elizabeth looked away momentarily. 'I am very sorry, of course, to disappoint so good a man as Captain Peto.' She looked directly at him again. 'But I took advantage of that same good nature. I should never have accepted the offer, for I did not love him.'

Hervey looked at her, astonished, incredulous. 'But you would have come to love him. He is so fine a man. What else could you wish for?'

Elizabeth smiled benignly, almost indulgently. 'I cannot marry a man I do not love, Matthew, no matter how much I admire him.'

Hervey shook his head, lowered his voice and spoke slowly. 'How can you go back on your promise? And why was I not to know until now, and from Mama?'

Elizabeth returned the challenge in his eyes, calmly defiant. 'I did not promise. That would have been for the marriage ceremony itself.'

Hervey bridled at what he perceived as casuistry. 'Elizabeth! You gave your answer to a man who was sailing to face the King's enemies. Is that not of some moment?'

Elizabeth almost smiled in her exasperation. 'You mean it mightn't be so bad if he were merely on a guardship at Portsmouth?'

Hervey was positively angering. 'I mean, is Peto not due some especial consideration thereby?'

Elizabeth sighed. 'He is, *of course*. And I shall write to him in the most considerative terms, I assure you.'

'You have not written to him?'

'I have written to him, yes. I have written several letters to him – why would not you think that I had? But . . . I am only lately come to the certainty that I cannot marry him, and therefore to the resolve to write to him in those terms. Do you know how long it takes a letter to reach him?'

Hervey was puzzled by the turn. 'No?'

'Well nor do I! I have not received a single letter since he sailed, and that the better part of a year ago. I know, of course, that he

82

will have written, but I don't suppose the mails are obliging at sea.'

'Elizabeth, there is an irreverence in your tone which I find incomprehensible. Do you not understand that Peto commands the most powerful of His Majesty's ships presently at sea, or that he has held that command in the greatest of sea battles since Trafalgar?'

A note of pleading replaced the wholly defiant: 'But Matthew, I cannot be obliged to marry a man against my inclinations on account of his gallantry . . . or on account of my previous error of judgement.'

Hervey found no answer.

'Besides, I love Major Heinrici.'

'I cannot believe it!'

'That I love someone? Whyever not, Matthew? You knew him once indeed: you must admit that he too is a fine man.'

'I? *Knew* him once?'

'In Spain, and at Waterloo.'

Hervey was beginning a very distant recollection . . .

'In the King's German Legion.'

Hervey now recalled it – but a *Rittmeister*, a captain of cavalry, a man several years his senior. 'I don't understand . . . How . . .'

'He is a widower. His wife died three years ago. There are three children – three daughters.' Elizabeth's face brightened with a happy confidence that even Hervey could not fail to recognize. Indeed, he had never seen her face thus.

He turned away. He must not let such a consideration cloud his judgement.

Dinner was not a joyful event. Hervey had told Fairbrother what had transpired between Elizabeth and him, as much as anything to save his friend from any innocent but uncomfortable remark at table. Fairbrother, however, had registered bewilderment at Hervey's vehemence, and the following morning, while his friend walked with Georgiana and her pony in Longleat Park, he offered to accompany Elizabeth on an errand towards Warminster.

'I am sorry you have met us in these less than concordant circumstances, Captain Fairbrother,' Elizabeth began, forthright, before they were long left the parsonage.

Fairbrother was not in the least discomfited. Rather he welcomed the opportunity to address the matter. 'Do not trouble for my part, Miss Hervey; I am only sorry that there is any occasion for discord in so evidently close a family as yours, about which I have heard much.'

'You are very gracious, sir,' replied Elizabeth, and meaning it. 'I am gratified at least to know that we occupy some part of my brother's thoughts when he is at his duties.'

Fairbrother sensed the acerbity, for all Elizabeth's sweetness. 'Miss Hervey, forgive my interference, but I have spent much time of late in your brother's company, and I can certainly attest to his thoughts in that regard. He has been more occupied with what he perceives as his familial duty than I have observed in any man.'

Elizabeth smiled, conceding. 'I am sure it is so, Captain Fairbrother. Indeed, I wish at times he were not so very occupied.'

Fairbrother frowned. 'You think it ill suited to him in some way?'

Elizabeth sighed. 'In truth I do, for he cannot think . . . evenly. He is bound still by some sense of guilt in the loss of his wife, and I am sure that it clouds his judgement in all things.'

'I may certainly attest to the rawness of his feelings in regard to his late wife.'

Elizabeth's expression became pained. 'She was my good friend too, sir.'

She did not add 'Matthew forgets that', but there was no need. And Fairbrother began to perceive the extent of her solitude – only daughter of a poor country living, unwed, no longer on calling terms at Longleat. It was all too clear why she had been content – happy, even – to accept an offer of marriage from one as sure as Captain Sir Laughton Peto; and then so decided when that most extraordinary, unexpected, unlooked-for, disconcerting thing – *true* love – should befall her. At this very moment he wished to put a protecting, brotherly arm around her – as her own brother ought – and to assure her of his strenuous support. 'Miss Hervey, in this I would hope to be your good friend as well as your brother's too. I am gratified – forgive me – to see you are so solicitous of his well-being. May I ask you a question?'

'You may ask whatever you please, Captain Fairbrother, but I beg you would not try to divert me from the course I have chosen, for it would be both fruitless and disagreeable.'

'Miss Hervey, I would not dream of it. I wished only to ask of your brother's intended. I will be frank: he has not spoken of her in any terms but the most matter-of-fact – where they are to live and such like. Do you know the lady?'

Elizabeth again quickened her pace, as much as to say she was on safer ground and could proceed without circumspection. 'I have met Lady Lankester the once but could form no opinion of her. If Matthew has concluded that she will make him a good wife then I can have nothing more to do with it.'

Fairbrother noted the return of acerbity. He wondered if Elizabeth were making the point that in denying her brother the right to interfere in her own choice of partner in the marriage stakes, she must likewise forfeit that right. But he was inclined to proceed with a certain blitheness, if only to bring the matter to an amicable close. 'Well, I may judge for myself, for I believe we shall go to Hertfordshire soon.'

Elizabeth stopped suddenly, her ears pricked. The call of the cuckoo came again, clearly and not so very distant. 'The cuckoo, Captain Fairbrother.' She smiled, happily – the first he had seen her smile thus. 'I walk these lanes every day, and it is the first cuckoo I have heard this spring.'

'*Thrice welcome, darling of the Spring!*'

'Indeed, Captain Fairbrother! You like Wordsworth?'

'I do – very much so, Miss Hervey. He was a little contrary, though, was he not? A vile, unholy bird did he not call the cuckoo elsewhere?'

'I believe he did,' said Elizabeth, smiling, a little wry. 'But I believe a poet, at least, might be allowed some contrariness of opinion – as any man.'

Fairbrother smiled to himself.

'Where *does* the cuckoo go in winter? Or do they merely stay silent? Oh, I had not thought: are there cuckoos in Jamaica?'

Fairbrother returned her smile, which had now its usual sweetness. 'Oh, indeed yes, Miss Hervey. And very gay-painted they are – unlike, I imagine, your English birds!'

'I confess I have never seen one, in winter or in summer. And I may say, Captain Fairbrother, that never have I heard its call with such pleasure.'

She said it so decidedly, not a trace wistful.

Fairbrother fancied he understood, for both Elizabeth's face and manner were ever open and expressive. Many summers must have come and gone, and many a village wedding, yet his friend's sister had remained in her unwed state, every summer the same, but a year older – riper, as the Prayer Book so felicitously put it – until now, when there was the happy prospect before her of matrimony. And undoubtedly to a man she loved, and rather passionately it seemed. Perhaps there was even the prospect of children, for Elizabeth Hervey was surely not beyond the age of childbearing?

'Georgiana, you would do well to keep your heels lowered,' said Hervey, somewhat peremptorily.

His daughter, delighting in the sole attention (as she thought) of her father, was only too content to oblige him without demur;

and in any case, she was accustomed to a certain abruptness in his manner, for she knew that there was little time for pleasantries when speaking to his soldiers in the face of the King's enemies.

'It won't do, you know, Georgiana: you will have to begin riding side-saddle. Your aunt really should have insisted on it before now.'

'It is not Aunt Elizabeth's fault,' replied Georgiana pluckily. 'For I would not have it.'

Hervey was not inclined to let a child's insistence excuse the dereliction. 'That is as may be, but it does not alter things. You cannot go about astride now that you are' (he had to think for a moment) 'ten.' Nor, indeed, when she was about to leave the county for rather more polished society. That, however, he would not mention – for the time being.

'But I don't *want* to ride side-saddle,' she insisted, shaking her head.

Hervey had not begun the walk with the question of Georgiana's seat uppermost in his mind (or, indeed, in his mind at all). He had not been bent on some quarrel with her on account of the propriety of riding astride. Rather had he found himself continuing vexed by Elizabeth's defiant manner – as if she wilfully misunderstood his good intentions, and likewise failed to see the injury all this would do to the family; and not least to Peto, who even now might be making his way hither in the happy expectation of marriage – or at any rate doing further battle in the Mediterranean in the comfortable knowledge that Elizabeth waited for him decently at home. She had even had the audacity to ask if he – Peto's good friend at that – would go with her to meet this Heinrici! It was scarcely to be borne. It was as if their whole life to this day, the notion of duty on which they had been brought up in that Wiltshire parsonage, reinforced by the Scripture they had each of them heard in equal measure, counted for nothing. That a man (or a woman) might throw over what he knew to be the right course to secure that which was the more pleasant to him! And was not the pleasure a delusion too? How might any man (or woman) take pleasure with the awful prospect of being haunted by a failing in duty? It would come to gnaw at the vitals, would it not? Then there would be no more pleasure, only infinite pain to endure – much greater pain than a man might fancy he must bear on rejecting the course of pleasure in the first place.

He cursed himself. All this vexation was intruding on his time with his daughter – little enough as that always was. 'I—'

'I know why you are angry with Aunt Elizabeth.' (Hervey tried to protest but Georgiana would not be stayed.) 'It is because she wants to marry Major Heinrici and not Captain Peto!'

Hervey's mouth fell open. How did Georgiana know of it?

'I like Captain Peto, but I like Major Heinrici better. He is very jolly, and he has three daughters who are all very pretty and nice.'

Hervey checked himself. His first instinct was to chide Georgiana for speaking of that which she – a child – could not understand, for *daring* to presume to interfere in business that was so patently not hers. Except that there was nothing childlike in her evident powers of observation and discernment. And in truth he could scarcely deny that the business was as much hers as his, for although he essayed to act (at his mother's bidding) as paterfamilias, it was Georgiana whose daily living was to be affected until such time as he, her father, set up his own household. And when would that be, she might well ask.

He forced himself (the effort truly was not great) to smile, and he patted her thigh. 'I am sure Major Heinrici is an agreeable man, Georgiana, and that he has very agreeable daughters, but ... I think you will understand that your Aunt Elizabeth has given an undertaking – a promise, indeed – to marry Captain Peto, and that it is quite impossible now that she should ... default on that promise.' The pony was quickening its pace in the distraction that was the discussion of duty, and Hervey found himself having to stride out not wholly comfortably. 'Do try to keep your pony in hand,' he added, as pleasantly as he could. 'Else I shall be forced to conclude you should not be off the lead rein!'

Georgiana brought the little gelding back to collection without remark, intent as she was on the more important matter. 'But if you promise something and then you learn later that for some reason it cannot be as you had supposed, it is surely not right to continue as if nothing had happened?'

The unexpected requirement to explain himself was irksome, but Hervey was pleased nevertheless – proud even – of this evidence of his daughter's intelligence and sensibility. It boded well, for he had never, he hoped, been of the belief, as were many, that a woman ought to have no opinion on any matter of substance. Quite the opposite indeed. And besides, the females of his acquaintance had hardly been of a reticent persuasion either. He smiled again, perhaps a shade indulgently, but certainly warmly. 'You know, my dear Georgiana, these things – I trust you will not misunderstand me – will be so much the better addressed when you are older. But for the moment I believe I can say that there are many roads to marriage, and that after starting on one it is not necessarily the wiser to depart from it when the ways become heavy, for all roads have their difficulties. It was on the best road in the country that my good friend Major Strickland was killed, a road well made and fast – admitting of too *much* speed indeed.' He suddenly wondered if the morbid metaphor were entirely apt.

'I do not believe I agree with you, Papa, but I understand what it is that you say, and Aunt Elizabeth has always impressed on me that that is as it must be.'

Hervey could not have faulted his sister's regulation. He nodded.

'Aunt Elizabeth always says we must be especially attentive to what you say because we may not see things as do you, who moves in society.'

Hervey stifled an embarrassed cough. He reckoned he probably owed more to Elizabeth's sound sense, learned as it may have been very parochially, than to that of *elevated* society. 'Yes, well, that is very proper of your aunt.'

'Will you come with us to Major Heinrici's, then, this afternoon, Papa? The youngest Miss Heinrici has her birthday today – she is seven – and there is to be a party.'

In that instant, Hervey almost said that he would, not for his sister's sake (although he would have to admit to the merest softening in his attitude on account of Georgiana's advocacy), but because seeing his daughter's delight at the prospect was truly engaging. To do so, however, would be an implicit disloyalty to his friend Peto; and his scruple – and his stomach – would not permit it. Elizabeth had lost her way. These things happened while travelling. It was not always easy to tell that a road led nowhere. Even the best of guides could take the wrong turning in a storm. But he, Elizabeth's brother, could see things very well. He knew which was the right road, and what steps she must take to regain it. He would help her. That was his brotherly duty, unwelcome as first it might be.

VI

THE COMMON ROUND

HMS Prince Rupert, the first morning at sea

The unlit sail gave Peto a night of broken sleep.

A quarter of an hour after first sighting, the ship had turned east to steer the same course as *Rupert*, some half a mile off the starboard beam. Lieutenant Lambe reported this while Peto and Rebecca Codrington were still at table. Peto had listened with care but with no great concern. Sailing as they both now were before the wind, the other ship no longer had the advantage. He asked where was *Archer*: Lambe said she was eight or nine cables, a mile perhaps, ahead and to larboard still. It was where Peto would have expected her to be – pity, since intercepting an unknown ship was precisely the thing a sloop did well. He had a mind to order a warning shot across the unlit's bows, which would have the merit too of signalling to *Archer* to attend on new orders, but that would mean the sloop heaving to while *Rupert* came up within hailing distance. They could signal with lights, but Peto knew it was a hit and miss affair for all but the simplest of codes. If he were really troubled by having an unlit sail on his starboard beam he would clear for action, yet the likelihood of there being a Turkish man-of-war this far west was surely very slim; and he was not going to turn out the entire crew merely to demonstrate that he had the will to do so.

He therefore told Lambe to have the watch keep a sharp eye, to fire a warning gun if cloud covered the moon and the lookouts lost sight of her, and to report to him hourly. Then at first light the midshipman on the forecastle recognized her as a Genoan pinnace, and Lambe signalled *Archer* to intercept her and enquire why she sailed unlit – which by four bells of the morning watch she was able to do. *Archer* reported that the Genoan's captain claimed she had been shadowed by pirates since leaving Ceuta, and, darkened, had sought to shake them off while taking 'sanctuary' close on a man-of-war. Peto had no reason to doubt him, and wished the Genoan well by return, especially since her captain sent across a fair-sized parmijan and half a dozen flasks of Tuscan red.

Pirates: the very devil, the whole of the Barbary coast and beyond – Peto had given many of them a watery grave and had hanged almost as many more when he had been commodore of the frigate squadron; when, indeed, he had gone into their very nests with the Americans (fine fellows, Americans; he was glad he had never used powder against them in the late war). They would be plying in and out of Algiers no doubt, exactly as before. When the Turks were sent back to Constantinople he expected Codrington would turn his attention to them. Not that that would be a job for a three-decker; they might stand in at Malta for a week or so until their lordships recalled *Rupert* to home waters – back to being a guardship, with a skeleton crew and long days ashore. Or even back into the Ordinary, de-masted and ungunned. But why worry himself about that now? *Sufficient unto the day is the evil thereof.*

There would be evil today right enough: it was not possible to inspect a King's ship, no matter how diligent its lieutenant, without finding something amiss. All he could hope for when he made his first rounds was that the faults could be righted by sweat rather than blood, and from within the ship's own resources. His old friend the commissioner at Gibraltar had told him he believed *Rupert* to be well found, but he would only know for certain when he had seen for himself.

At eight o'clock Peto came onto the quarterdeck. For three hours the idlers and larboard watch had been holystoning the decks and swilling the dirty sand into the waterways and scuppers. The swabbers had flogged the decks until they were dry, and the trusted hands had brightened the brasswork about the rails and bitts. And when the sanding, holystoning, swabbing and polishing was done, other hands had flemished down the ropes and stowed the washdeck gear, so that by seven o'clock the work had been practically finished. When Lieutenant Lambe came back on deck after his morning shave he had professed himself pleased with things – as well he might, for this was but the day's routine (every day barring Sunday), although the boatswain's mates had known full well that a keener eye would be cast on their charges on this morning. At half past he had sent the mates below to pipe 'All hands. Up hammocks', and the entire crew – sleepers as well as watch – had scurried with their lashed-up bedding to the upper-deck nettings, where the quarter-masters and midshipmen supervised the stowing, after which Lambe had been able to dismiss them to breakfast.

'Good morning, sir,' he said brightly, touching his hat. 'Seven knots at present, five in the night.'

Peto nodded. It was a morning exactly as the evening's red light had promised – the shepherd's delight, but the sailor's even more so. He loved Norfolk as loyally as any man (his father, and his father before him, had been born next-the-sea) but the fairest day in Nelson's county could not compare with such a morning at sea, the sun on his face, the wind filling the sail, and the air as pure as the water of the Arethusa spring. He glanced at the rate-of-sailing board: a following wind and twenty miles during the middle watch (the calculation was simple enough). 'Thank you, Mr Lambe. Have the master set royals and t'gallants when I am finished my inspection, if the wind does not freshen by much. We ought to be making nine knots while the sea is favourable.'

'Ay-ay, sir.'

'Have you had your breakfast?'

'I have, sir.'

'Do you have any objection to a little more?'

Lambe looked faintly bemused. 'By no means, sir.'

Peto turned to his steward, who had come on deck with a coffee pot and cups. 'Would you bring us a plate apiece of the ship's burgoo?'

Flowerdew poured them coffee and then shuffled off in the stooping gait he adopted when asked to do something he found contrary to his own ideas of what was proper (or expedient).

'Is that Mr Pelham I observe on the poop?'

'It is, sir. He stood the middle watch, and came back on deck as soon as it was light enough to signal to *Archer*.'

'Call him, if you will.'

Lambe beckoned the midshipman, who sped down the companion ladder as if the drummer were beating to quarters.

'Sir!' he squeaked, a discernibly new telescope peeping from beneath his cloak.

Peto returned the salute. 'Mr Lambe informs me that you sustained an injury yesterday. Have you yet reported to the surgeon?'

'No, sir.'

'Why not?'

'I did not consider it serious enough, sir.'

'Indeed? Have you some medical qualification?'

'No, sir.'

'Then kindly give yourself the benefit of the surgeon's, else how am I to rely upon what you see through that telescope of yours ... It is a *new* telescope, is it not?'

'It is, sir. I bought it of Mr Adams.'

Peto wondered what Adams – whoever he was (another midshipman, he supposed) – would make do with instead, but that was not his direct concern; he could leave the discipline of the midshipmen to Lambe. 'Very well. Help yourself to coffee, Mr Pelham,' he said, and with a measure of warmth, indicating the tray which Flowerdew had placed on the gallery locker.

'Thank you, sir,' replied the midshipman, fairly taken aback.

Lambe smiled to himself. He had fair roasted Pelham after the business of the parallax, and was himself thinking of some magnanimous gesture. This more than saved him the effort.

'How old are you, Mr Pelham?'

'Seventeen come next month, sir.'

'And where are you from; where do your people live?'

'I was born in Plymouth, sir. My father was captain of *Repulse*. He is dead now, sir; my mother also.'

Peto rather wished he had not asked. He was sentimental enough to believe a man must have a home to return to. And even though his own parents were now gone, he had the prospect of a warm heart and hearth. A smile almost overcame him, indeed, at the thought of Miss Elizabeth Hervey – Lady Peto – in the hall of that handsome Norfolk manor, advancing smiling to greet him on his return from some commission or other ... He cleared his throat. 'I am sorry to hear it, Mr Pelham. I did not know your father, though I know *Repulse* to have had a fine reputation in her day.'

'He was killed off New Orleans, sir.'

Peto now dimly recalled the loss of the ship in that wretched and unnecessary campaign: Mr Midshipman Pelham had been semi-orphaned a long time ... 'And your mother?'

95

'She died as I was born, sir. I was brought up by an aunt until such time as I could go to sea.'

A full orphan – Peto almost groaned; he ought to have expected it.

'Mr Pelham was a volunteer at twelve, sir, on my last ship,' said Lambe.

It told Peto a good deal about them both. 'Then I trust you shall pass for lieutenant quickly, Mr Pelham. There is no time to lose even in these days of peace.'

'I intend doing so, sir.'

Peto nodded thoughtfully. 'Good. Capital, capital ... And I would that you dine with me and Mr Lambe this evening.'

Pelham's boyish but handsome face lit up like a signal lamp. 'Thank you kindly, sir.'

Flowerdew returned with two bowls of oat gruel. Peto took a spoonful, as gingerly as he felt he might in such company, and tasted the crew's breakfast.

Perhaps his memory – or his palate – played tricks on him, for he found it not nearly as repulsive as usual. In the East Indies, his former station, they had had a very decent porridge of corn and cinnamon, but the oatmeal cakes which the Victualling Board supplied were rough rations indeed, and boiled up in the galley copper, with water a month or more in the hold, the gruel was better fit for the sty under the forecastle. The Board held it to be a necessary corrective to the otherwise constipating ship's diet, but the majority of men, Peto recalled, thought it a far better emetic.

Lambe saw his surprise. 'We have an active purser. He sent back a good deal of the provender first offered.'

Peto nodded appreciatively. Time was when a captain appointed his own man, or rather put forward his clerk's name to the Admiralty, but of late there had been a fashion to place experience in the position, for too often the purser had been in truck with the merchants who supplied the ship (and, shame to relate, in truck with the captain as well). 'And real coffee to be had, you say, Mr Lambe? Remarkable.' The old 'Scotch coffee' of the mess decks had been a foul brew, burnt biscuit boiled up to a black paste in rank water, and sugared until it could hold no more. 'I shall expect to see contented faces and good constitutions at my inspection.'

'You may depend upon it, sir, as ever it has been,' replied Lambe, just as wryly.

At a half past eight o'clock, Peto descended the companion ladder to the upper deck and began his first inspection of *Prince Rupert*. Lambe accompanied him together with the boatswain, three mates, the master-at-arms and two corporals, the serjeant of marines and several midshipmen, whose job it would be to attend on any observation the captain made. He began with the larboard battery, walking slowly, hands clasped behind his back, here and there nodding to a salute, here and there bringing some fault, or something he would have done otherwise, to Lambe's attention, who at once delegated the business of correction to the appropriate member of the party, whence followed a good deal of barking and growling while Peto continued his advance along the line of eighteen-pounders. He then turned aft to walk the starboard battery, the routine as before. By and large he approved of what he found: so much of it was new made, and the men looked likely – and for all their sanding and swabbing, they were clean and serviceably dressed.

It took him but an hour to see over the gun-decks, though he fancied he missed nothing; long years inspecting and being inspected had given him an unfailing eye. But all this was merely preparation: the guns were lashed and the instruments of gunnery fastened up; he would see later what sharp work the gun-crews could make of it.

He descended to the magazine, taking off his shoes, as standing orders required, to have a good look about the inside. The gunner was a big, powerfully made man, who had to stoop at his station. He spoke softly, as if noise as well as sparks were a danger; Peto felt certain of him at once. As he did too of the carpenter, who conducted him along the hull walk – always a place for grazing the forehead and bruising the shoulders – with a running commentary on the state of the timbers, pumps, masts and spars. 'Not once above ten inches, sir, the well,' he reported with palpable pride.

Peto nodded appreciatively; maintaining the depth of water below the maximum permitted of fifteen inches (without excessive pumping) was remarkable in a ship of *Rupert*'s age, and not long re-commissioned. 'Very good, Mr Storr,' he said as they came to the cockpit, turning to him directly now and fixing him with a quizzical look: 'We have met before, I think.'

The carpenter's face shone as bright as had Midshipman Pelham's. 'We 'ave, sir – on *Amphion*.'

It was eighteen years ago. Peto nodded. 'Mate to that old dog Pollard, as I recall, Mr Storr?'

'Ay, sir. And many a good trick 'e taught me,' replied the carpenter, lapsing into broader Devon. '*Amphion* wor a good ship, sir.'

'That she was, and in what I have seen so far I believe we may say that *Rupert* follows her.'

'She does that, sir. As strong a framing as you'd see.'

Peto clapped his hand on the carpenter's shoulder – a perhaps familiar gesture, but one he felt entirely at ease with. 'I'm obliged to you, Mr Storr.'

Next was the midshipmen's berth, which was *not* likely to be so obliging. Peto was never inclined to be intrusive, for he remembered well enough the cherished sense of private space ('privacy' would be a wholly inapt word) when he himself had been a midshipman, but the berth – little more than an enclosure knocked up by Storr's mates – bore all too evidently the signs of late breakfasting.

'Mr Lambe, who is senior here?' (he knew the answer well enough, but there were ready ears to entertain).

'Lord Yarborough, sir.'

'Indeed? Then inform my Lord Yarborough, if you please, that he will have his fellow officers bestir themselves betimes.'

'Ay-ay, sir!'

'Mr Craig, have this berth turned out, if you will!'

'Ay-ay, sir,' replied the boatswain, with relish.

'Very well, and now last to the surgeon's. D'ye suppose *he* expects us?'

Peto's eyes were now accustomed to the orlop's gloom, but even so, he had to blink to believe them as he entered the cockpit. 'What in the name of God . . .'

The surgeon, a shortish, wiry man of about thirty, wearing a black Melton coat and a stock like a parson's, stepped forward. 'Good morning, sir.'

They had shaken hands the day before, but Peto had not been able to take much measure of him. He looked a capable sort – an intelligent face, high forehead, good hands, if perhaps his physique lacked the obvious power for the more strenuous of amputations. 'Mr Morrissey, what is the meaning of this?' He knew he ought by rights to be addressing the question to his lieutenant, but the affront was taking place in the surgeon's own part of ship.

Morrissey looked rather more puzzled by the captain's displeasure than dismayed. 'With respect, sir, I understand it to be the custom that a woman repairs to the cockpit when "Quarters" are sounded. That is what they do here.'

'I know what is the custom, Mr Morrissey, but . . . ' He turned to his lieutenant. 'Why are these women aboard, Mr Lambe?'

'They drew lots at Portsmouth, sir, and were to be put off at

Gibraltar for the first merchantman to Malta, but their husbands made representations, and since we had become obliged to convey Miss Codrington to Malta I considered that it would be inequitable to put them off.'

Peto huffed. Since when had equity any part in the customs of the service? But he was well aware of the Admiralty's new leniency towards women (the order now being simply that 'no ship is to be too much pestered with wives'). Lambe was right: it served no good to compel a sailor's wife – however loose the term – to leave her husband's ship while the admiral's daughter enjoyed the comforts of the admiral's apartments. No matter that the presence of the one would have no effect on the discipline of the ship, while the other could only tend in the very opposite direction.

'Very well,' he said, clearing his throat, and trying not to stare too much at the surgeon's temporary auxiliaries: there were a dozen of them, one or two distinctly matronly, clearly the true partners of a lifetime, but several of them (it was surely no trick of the light?) uncommonly pretty. How the times were changing!

He cleared his throat again, took out his hunter and held it to the lantern above the surgeon's table. A quarter before six bells – eleven o'clock; he could have an hour's practice at the guns before the watches changed. It would be enough to see how sharp was the crew. 'Very well, Mr Lambe, let us be about our business: we shall beat to quarters and clear for action!'

The order shrilled from hatch to hatch as the relay of midshipmen passed the word 'arsey-varsey' – from orlop to quarterdeck – until the drummer of marines caught it and began beating 'Hearts of Oak' in rapid time. Everywhere men sprang to their tasks like hounds to the scent. Peto had seen it so many times that it ought to have been a commonplace, but the thrill of the drumming, and the blood-lusting heaving on the guns never failed to set his own blood coursing, as if it would burst from his very veins. His hand twitched for the hilt of his sword (Flowerdew would be waiting with it on the quarterdeck, as he had always done): now they would see what the crew of His Majesty's Ship *Prince Rupert* were made of.

Giving the order on the orlop was not without its advantages, however unusual: it allowed Peto a fair impression of each gun-deck as he made his way to his own station. The carpenter and his mates had already made aft, like terriers, to the officers' quarters to unship the bulkheads – he had no fears on account of Mr Storr and his men – but other hands looked less capable, less ferocious in their clearing of comforts and the like. The boatswain knew it too: he was already among them flaying and lashing. In Nelson's day he would have used the knotted rope; now he could only use his tongue (at least when there were witnesses). But with what violence and volume did Craig assault the crewmen thus! And with most palpable effect as the mates hurled trenchers and pots through the gunports to speed the effort.

On the middle deck they were already casting guns loose from the lashings, though too gingerly, to Peto's mind – like men who still *feared* them as wild beasts rather than handling them as if tamed brutes. They seemed to know the working of their business, however, getting away the tackles neatly enough, and the breechings. Crows, handspikes, sponges and worm were all being laid out smartly, wads and shot garland too.

When he reached the upper deck the first of the gun captains were returning from the gunner's storerooms with their cartouches and gunlocks, and the powder-boys were struggling up the ladders with their 'salt-boxes', the charges for the first broad-side. Others were sprinkling wet sand on the decking, fetching buckets of drinking-water to each gun, and tubs of saltwater for the swabs. Above the waist and quarterdeck the netting was going up, if awkwardly, much to the consternation of the master's mates; but aloft, Peto observed the topmen stopping the sheets and slinging the lower yards with chain as ably as ever he had seen it.

As he took the ladder to the quarterdeck he noted the re-assuring red of the marines on the poop and forecastle. They were ever a steady and steadying sight – and some of them now armed with rifles, he was pleased to see (for practised as the marines were, the sea-pattern musket had as much windage as the land pattern, and was consequently no more accurate). He saw the fifers and drummers mustered in the waist, a dozen little fellows in oversize coats, younger even than the ship's boys. They would keep the marines well supplied with cartridge during the fight – and cheer them with a merry tune as they closed for action. Peto felt an uncharacteristic lump in his throat at the sight of them – and the powder-monkeys – as he went to his place of command.

Lambe was already at his post as Peto took his sword from Flowerdew and buckled it on. He touched his hat to his captain, perhaps a shade anxiously, for he knew the clearing was too slow (not a single lieutenant had yet reported his part of ship ready, save the captain of marines), but he would make no excuse. They had held but two exercises with the guns – each 'dry', without powder – and this Peto knew already. It mattered not a jot, though, that heavy weather in the Channel and Biscay had kept the gunports closed, for the enemy made no concessions.

Peto touched his hat by return and took out his watch, rubbing salt into the soreness that was the lieutenant's consternation. 'It will not do, Mr Lambe. Fifteen minutes gone and not a battery ready.'

'No indeed, sir.'

'And the boats still inboard.'

'Sir.'

The boats should by rights have been lowered – and with them the hen coops – but Peto had not wanted to risk breaking the tow and having to wear to recover them. All else he had ordered clear as for action. No, not quite all. In a line-of-battle ship they did not invariably cast the goats and the other livestock over the side, for the manger was a strong barricade and little likely to be destroyed. And in Peto's experience an animal when it was dismembered made much less noise than did a seaman.

He looked up at the full course: he would not shorten sail for the practice, as he would in action (he wanted *Rupert* to maintain her fair sailing rate). A dove walked along the main yard, and, all about, wheeled hopeful gulls, for once silent. He smiled grimly: they would scream and scatter in a few minutes more.

A great spout of water arched across the lee side of the quarterdeck, sending Rebecca and her maid scurrying to the weather rail. Peto suppressed a smile. The pump evidently worked – strong and powerful. If it came to it, if flame reached sail, the hose could play on the courses well. Then he cursed himself. Miss Codrington was a deuced distraction, for he found his thoughts wandering as a consequence to Elizabeth, imagining what impression his ship's industry would make on her. Good God, that it should come to this – at his age and seniority! He glowered at Rebecca, though at once thought mean of himself for doing so.

'You, sir! Yes, you!'

A startled midshipman by the lee companion ladder realized his captain meant him. He hurried to his side. 'Sir?'

'What is your name?'

'Burgess, sir.'

'And what do you do there?' Peto knew well enough what he did.

'Relay your orders below, sir.'

'Very well. Have Mr Pelham come here at once.'

It took but seconds to accomplish.

'Mr Pelham, I am surprised you are not at your station.'

It was a moot point. As signal midshipman, Pelham's place was by the captain until such time as he had a signal to hoist, but the previous captain had preferred the elevation of the poop to the more limited observation, but closer control, near the wheel. Pelham would certainly not argue the point, of course, but his captain *had* asked him a question . . .

Lambe decided to see if Pelham had the composure to answer on his own account, though he could easily have answered for him (he was already sensing that he knew his new captain's way).

'I was making ready to signal *Archer* that we were about to fire, sir.'

Peto was content. He was doubly content, for his signal midshipman was clearly not one to be cowed in the excitement of action. And his lieutenant, indeed, plainly had the capacity to think beyond the commotion on deck by ordering the signal.

'Very well. Signal *Archer* and then escort Miss Codrington to the poop and explain to her what we are about.'

'Ay-ay, sir!'

Peto could not tell what Pelham made of the order (neither was he in the least concerned). For all he knew, it might be as delightful to him to have the ear of the admiral's daughter as manifestly it had been to receive his captain's invitation to dinner. He could only think how mortified he himself would have been as a sixteen-year-old midshipman obliged to entertain a female aboard a man-of-war at such a moment. He smiled to himself almost mischievously.

The lieutenant of the middle-deck starboard battery reported ready, followed a few moments later by both of the upper deck's. In another two minutes all the batteries were accounted ready, and the carronades. Lambe held each officer on the quarterdeck until the last had come, and then formally reported to Peto that the ship was ready for action.

Peto, looking black, snapped closed his hunter with some force.

'Gentlemen, I have never before been aboard a ship of any rate that took so long to clear for action! I perfectly understand that *Prince Rupert* was re-commissioned but a month ago, but in that month I should have expected more of you.'

Lambe felt the rebuke keenly, for the discipline and working of the crew was essentially his business, no matter what the inclination of the captain or how foul the weather.

'You let down Mr Lambe, you let down your men, you let down yourselves.'

It was carefully calculated: the guilt was proven, the lieutenant's dignity was maintained – perhaps even enhanced – duty invoked, and the captain's assumption of confidence in his officers rehearsed.

The little assemblage of officers looked whipped.

There was another card yet to play, however, and Peto did not flinch from the clean sweep. 'And, gentlemen – how it grieves me to say it – you let down your King! It will not do, I say.' He waited until the silence was all but intolerable. 'I trust I shall not have occasion to say so again.'

'Ay-ay, sir,' came the unison response as Peto searched for eyes that preferred the deck to his.

'Gentlemen, only let me have your best. It will be good enough, I am sure of it . . . Very well, to your duties!'

He turned to his lieutenant as the others cut to their posts. 'I compliment you on the work of the topmen, Mr Lambe. Admirable; quite admirable.'

'I will tell the captains of the tops, sir,' replied Lambe, modestly but cheered.

Peto cleared his throat, as if to be done with what had gone before. 'Very well, Mr Lambe,' he began, in a voice intended to carry to each side of the quarterdeck. 'We shall exercise the batteries. Carry on if you please.'

He had conferred with Lambe the evening before. *Rupert*

would fire two broadsides, starboard first, and then by deck, gun by gun, as they were ready. This way he would gain a better impression of her gunnery since he would otherwise not know by how much the slowest crew impeded the rest. And they would fire full-charge with the quoins out so that he could see the reach of shot.

Lambe put the speaking-trumpet to his mouth. 'Sile-e-ence!'

The midshipmen at each of the hatches relayed the cautionary order.

'Starboard battery, stand-by . . . Ready . . . *Fire!*'

Even running in a calm sea at nine knots, *Rupert* shuddered like a tautened rope with the explosion of three hundredweight of black powder – and four hundred tons of iron jumping like crazed roughs. Smoke billowed through the hatches in the following wind, masking the waist, but Peto knew well enough the scene below, the guns at full recoil, muzzles inboard, worms scouring out the cartridge remnants, sponges dowsing the embers before the loaders ladled in the new cartridges, driving home the wads of rope yarn onto the charge with the rammer; then the roundshot and its containing wad; and the captain of the gun plunging his corkscrew into the touch hole to prick the cartridge, pushing in the quill primer-tube with its fine-mealed powder, and the rest of the crew heaving on the breeching tackle to run out the gun, lashing it secure, heaving with the handspikes so it was properly trained – until at last the gun captain could hold up his hand to show ready to the lieutenant.

Peto observed the face of his Prior hunter with the utmost concentration. It had been the best that money could buy (short of having one encrusted with precious stones) – the best time-keeping, the most reliable, the most able to withstand the rigours of the service. He had bought it with the prize-money from Lissa, and many had been the time he had watched intently its second hand, though never perhaps quite so fretfully as now. A frigate's gunnery was one thing – life or death when it came to action, as

106

any man-of-war, but action was not the primary business of a frigate: in frigate work navigation preceded gunnery. In a line-of-battle ship gunnery was everything. Her *raison d'être* was gunnery. She was nothing but a floating fortress – arsenal and battery combined; more weight of cannon than even Bonaparte had been able to mass at Waterloo. It was why their lordships had brought *Rupert* out of the Ordinary. Her gunnery would overawe the Turk; or if it did not, it would *overpower* him.

The second hand passed twelve for the second time, and then five . . .

The lead gun of the lower-deck battery fired, and then her others in a thunderous drum roll, the upper deck's beginning three seconds later, and the middle deck's a fraction after them. Peto shook his head. Every gun had fired: the gun-crews were doing their job faithfully at least; but so slowly that against another three-decker – or even a well-served 74 – half the guns might be put out of action by the return broadside. Even the French, in the late war, for all their time blockaded in Toulon or Cadiz, could fire a second broadside in two minutes! If this had been the *Nisus*'s gunnery he would have been laying into the crews from the top of the quarterdeck companion, and his voice would have carried to the forecastle even against the wind.

'Larboard battery, sir?'

Peto braced. 'Very well, Mr Lambe; larboard battery.'

'Larboard battery, stand-by . . . Ready . . . *Fire!*'

Rupert shook once more. Peto glanced at his hunter again and watched for the fall of shot – a good mile and a half (it might have been more; it was not easy to judge in open sea), great fountains of water, the thirty-two-pounders' reaching just beyond the upper deck's eighteens', but all in a satisfyingly regular fashion. Not that he would expect to engage a ship at such a range, unless it were trying to run from him, but it was well to know just how far he might stand off a shore battery, say.

Smoke billowed as before, so that once again the waist was soon hid, and he began pacing, fretfully again, until just as the second hand touched twelve the upper-deck battery thundered back into life, and the lower decks' seconds after. For a moment he contemplated summoning the lieutenants and midshipmen, but that he had done already, and he could scarcely add to what he had said. He could assemble all the gun captains – or get Lambe to berate them . . .

No, it was not the way. They knew what he wanted – what the service required: a full broadside in a minute and a half. At her best, *Nisus* managed a minute and fifteen, and it made no difference that her guns weren't as heavy, for a line-of-battle ship had extra men. No, he would repeat the exercises until they fired as they should. He had enough powder and shot to risk twenty broadsides at practice, and if they couldn't manage it by the end of that . . .

'Mr Lambe, have them fire by batteries. I'll see who is the first to ninety seconds – *and* who is last!'

'Ay-ay, sir!'

Lambe gave the order, and Peto's admonishment. When all the batteries reported ready, he glanced at his captain for the word.

Peto took out his hunter again, and nodded.

'Fire!'

Half an hour of smoke, flame, thunder and back-breaking work – both broadsides heaving as if they were in a general action: only the absence of the enemy's shot eased their labour. Peto fancied he could hear the officers' hoarse encouragement, and the mates'; until after ten minutes he could hear next to nothing unless it were bellowed in his ear. It was always the same: the whole of the crew would be shouting at each other for the rest of the day.

It was long past the dinner hour when the last battery – larboard upper deck – managed to reload and fire within the ninety seconds; and with only two rounds left for each gun. The lieutenants reported to the quarterdeck one by one as their batteries fell silent, and from each it was the same: the worm- and spongemen had gone about their work too gingerly to begin with, the loaders even more so, fearful of premature discharge; and the rest had been plain lubberly with the tackle. But they had warmed to it. They had all most definitely warmed to it.

Peto nodded: he had thought as much. They would get sharper with the tackle by daily practice, though the gunworkers would only get more confident if they used powder, and he could not afford to give them much of that. Once there was the enemy firing at their backs, too, they might be a deal less eager to sponge and ram and load. Perhaps he thought too meanly of them, but he had seen it all before. And there were but a couple of weeks only to get *Rupert* into the sort of trim that Admiral Codrington had a right to expect.

He turned to his lieutenant. 'Well, Mr Lambe, let us see how things stand below.'

VII

REFORM

27 April 1828

They took the mail back to London, four days after coming down. Without the urgency of a family summons Hervey could not justify to himself the expense of posting. It had the advantage, too, of limiting conversation, for in truth he felt a mite wearied by the business in Horningsham, the last day especially, when Elizabeth's defiance drove a wedge between them; and, he feared, between him and Georgiana.

He even felt its thin end edging between him and Fairbrother, for in the afternoon he and his friend had walked to Longleat, and Fairbrother had practised a deal of advocacy on Elizabeth's behalf. Hervey had tried to explain that however good a man was this Major Heinrici, he could be nothing compared with Peto. Fairbrother suggested that they go and meet him; indeed, he proposed that it was in honour the very least that Hervey could do if he were acting as paterfamilias. But Hervey had scorned the notion, suggesting it might then become an affair of pistols. To this Fairbrother had expressed himself perplexed by the ways of the English, and had fallen silent on the matter, although at dinner that evening he went out of his way to cheer Elizabeth.

Not that she appeared much in need of cheering (cool certainty, Fairbrother thought it; shamelessness was Hervey's opinion).

Hervey was inclined to ascribe his friend's solicitousness to the natural good manners of a guest, rather than believing he truly took her side. Nevertheless, he had not wished to spend a day in a post chaise in conversation upon the topic (which seemed inevitable if they had been placed in each other's exclusive company), and so the mail had served him well in terms of both economy and retreat.

What had saddened him most, besides the business itself, was Georgiana's opinion. Perhaps he ought to have known that she would side instinctively with Elizabeth, who had stood *in loco matris* for so long; at ten years she could hardly be expected to make any informed judgement of her own in these matters. Except that he had rather hoped she might. Was it really so very difficult to see? If his mother and he saw with perfect clarity, then why not Georgiana? He was angry that Elizabeth had taken her to meet this Heinrici in the first place: it was, to say the least, indelicate – disloyal, indeed. But he wondered, too, if there were not some other consideration – if Georgiana's attitude were not somehow connected with a reluctance to leave Horningsham for a new home. After all, he had not been able to tell her where that might be: Hounslow, he imagined, if he were to return to his regiment, or the Cape if he were not; perhaps, and worst of all, for even he saw that it might be uncomfortably alien, to Hertfordshire until the question was settled.

No, he must not allow that, Hertfordshire. Not, at least, without his company. It was time to follow the drum, though it had been Henrietta's determination to do so that had led to her death (but could they in truth have lived any other way?). Besides, had not Kezia Lankester gone to India with her new husband, when most wives did not? Was that not a sure sign of her true and doughty nature? Kezia Hervey would not be content to sit in

Hertfordshire, or even Hounslow, while her husband sailed abroad. Of that he was certain.

It was after nine when they got to the United Service Club, and the dining room had closed. There was no water for a hot bath (how Hervey was looking forward to the move to the new club house: he had become quite used to ready hot water in India), and so while bowls were got up for their rooms, the two friends sank into the leather tubs of the smoking room with brandy and soda. The porter brought Hervey his letters. One bore the stamp of the commander-in-chief's headquarters. He opened it at once.

The Horse Guards
23rd April

My dear Hervey,

I send you the briefest word to say that I have just seen the casualty lists for the battle at Navarin and may assure you that Captain Sir Laughton Peto's name is not contained therein. You will be saddened to know that Captain Bathurst of the Genoa was killed, for I believe you said you met him once, as well as several captains of Marines, which Service seems to have borne the most considerable losses, ten of them on the Genoa alone. I confess I had not perhaps given the affair the greatest attention before, for I saw the official returns only in the New Year, by which time other matters were pressing. I may direct your attention to a full account of the battle, by Codrington's own hand (whose own son, a midshipman on the flagship, was most grievously wounded), in the London Gazette Extraordinary of November 10, last, which, if not to be found in the United Service Club, you are at liberty to read here when you will.

112

*I hope this allays your very evident, and proper, apprehension
on account of your friend.*
Believe me &c,
Howard

Hervey sighed with deep satisfaction: allay his apprehension it most certainly did. He held up the letter as if it were material evidence in the case of Peto vs Heinrici. 'It is from John Howard. He confirms that Peto was unharmed in the affair at Navarino.'

'Deo gratias,' said Fairbrother, and looking as if he meant it (a jilted, *wounded* hero would have been too much for any of them to deal with).

'I must write to Elizabeth, express, tomorrow.'

'That it may bring her to her senses?' he asked, in a tone that suggested irony.

Hervey looked at his friend suspiciously. 'That she may know her affianced is well.'

Now Fairbrother sighed, and took a long measure of his brandy-soda. 'My dear friend, I do not even apologize for pressing this. We are by accident or otherwise close companions; but I counsel the greatest caution in all this. I know what I believe, though I cannot be certain: no woman of your sister's sensibility would do as she does without the utmost conviction. If you persist in . . . frankly, *hectoring* her, you risk both reinforcing her will and driving her from you.'

Hervey was tired. He had not slept much these past days, and his mind had been wholly active during the journey up. He was in no mood for dispute, even if he had had the inclination. He too took a long measure of his brandy-soda. 'Fairbrother, I confess that in Horningsham I wished you were not there; and now I'm only thankful you were. If there is some strange female madness in this, or wilfulness, the last thing I wish is that I make matters worse. If you believe that I serve my purpose better by

113

caution, then so be it. I confess I am at a loss to know how to bring Elizabeth to her senses, only that I must.' He drained his glass, placed it on the wine table between their tubs, and stood. 'Come; let us go and find a chop house.'

Fairbrother finished his glass and rose without a word. He must be content enough that he had achieved his immediate object, even if his friend entirely mistook his purpose.

Next day, Hervey took Fairbrother to watch the changing of the guard, before going to see Lord John Howard. He felt most particularly well. The remittent fever, the last bout of which had laid him so low at the Cape, was now wholly expelled, and he had back his colour and constitution in full measure. And the *iklwa* wound to his leg was but a neat scar. He felt ready for the saddle again, and watching the Life Guards only increased that certainty.

The business of Elizabeth occupied him, but by no means exclusively. On the drive back to London the matter of the court of inquiry had returned once more to the forefront of his mind. He knew that he ought by rights to be dealing with the matter by first applying to the Sixth's orderly room, and they in turn to the headquarters of the London District, but the disadvantages of following the 'chain of command' were all too obvious. Besides, who with a friend at court – the commander-in-chief's headquarters – would apply, so to speak, at the palace's back door? He was, indeed, almost shameless in this now. Where once he would have thought it beneath the dignity of a regimental officer to concern himself with anything but the regiment, he now knew otherwise: an officer must keep himself as much posted of affairs in Whitehall, in both military headquarters and civil ministries, as of events in the field. He despised the necessity, of course; but it did not follow that he must despise himself in the exercise of that necessity. Why should he leave the race open to lesser men who would not balk at chicanery? Even the Duke of Wellington had not risen by merit alone.

And with each chicane he found the business a little easier. Sometimes he did not at first recognize what he did. He wondered, indeed, if there were occasions when he did not *later* recognize it. And it troubled him. While he had been a prisoner in Badajoz – not eighteen months past – he had resolved to lead a new life, as the Prayer Book had it. His coming marriage had sprung from that very resolution. But soon the muddy business of the army in peacetime (what other way was there to describe the business of obtaining command?), and, he had to admit, his own weakness of will, had recalled him to the ways he had forsworn. It did indeed trouble him. But he took comfort in knowing in what cause it was: he wished only for a peaceful and settled state of matrimony, as once he had enjoyed (albeit briefly, and not without tempest, although passionate to a degree which the recollection of could discomfit him still). He wished above all for a proper and settled state of family for Georgiana. And he wished, and confided that the wish were not inimical to that cause, for command of the Sixth.

This latter he was never more sure of than now. The time at the Cape Colony with his troop, and with a half-colonel's brevet and command of the Cape Mounted Rifles, had convinced him that only the lieutenant-colonelcy of his own regiment, the regiment he had joined as a seventeen-year-old cornet and which had become his true family, could satisfy what it was inside him that remained after the death of Henrietta. It defied logic: he would be full colonel today if only he had accepted other offers (he chided himself for false modesty: he might be major general). It was not logic but something visceral. It began at Corunna, when the Sixth had stayed together and come through it together, where others had fallen apart. *And* in the years of Peninsular endurance that followed – the long, wearying years through

115

Portugal and Spain, siege after siege, battle after battle: so many comradely friendships forged, so many of those friends lost. And Waterloo, battle of battles, a day like no other, longer than any he could recall, where he had watched a serjeant go knowingly to his death so that he, Hervey, might escape to do his duty, and the good name of the Sixth be burnished ever the brighter. And the Armstrongs and the Collinses, the Wainwrights and the Johnsons, and the countless others – faithful witnesses, all; how could he rest as long as there was the possibility of holding the reins of His Majesty's 6th Light Dragoons?

He had sent a note in advance to Lord John Howard and was therefore admitted quickly, the assistant quartermaster-general receiving him with his customary warmth. Hervey marvelled as ever at his friend's ability to give the impression of having all the time in the world, though the business of the army came across his desk. It did not trouble him that Howard, by his own admission, had never heard a shot fired in anger: he knew how the army worked, and how to work it. But not only that: he had enjoyed the confidence of two very different commanders-in-chief – the Duke of Wellington and his predecessor, the Duke of York – and it looked very much as if he would gain that of a third. Hervey knew that whatever his own superiority at arms might be, he could never have filled his friend's boots. Lord John Howard was no mere military courtier, as once he had supposed him to be; he was a staff officer, and one with a rare imagination for the consequences for those at the disposal of his pen – *and* for those at whose disposal that pen was.

'My dear fellow, how very good it is to see you,' said his friend, smiling, shaking Hervey's hand almost boyishly, and indicating a chair. 'I have just learned the deucedest piece of news, which I would have sent to you at once had you not so felicitously presented yourself.'

A messenger brought in coffee. Hervey had to wait while the coffee was poured before learning what it was that so animated his friend (it was evidently of a sensitive nature, not merely confidential). He took the opportunity to thank him for sending the reassurance of Peto's absence from the Navarino casualty lists. As soon as the messenger was gone, he returned eagerly to the promised news. 'Deucedest?'

Howard nodded, leaned back in his chair and sipped his coffee. 'Have you heard of a place called Retford, in Nottinghamshire?'

Hervey recalled it well, and smiled ruefully. 'I do believe I led a cavalry charge there, or very close, these ten years past.'

His friend caught the smile. 'Ah yes; so you did. Rather like Waltham Abbey, was it not?'

It had been an affair of Luddites, 'blanketeers' or whatever banner they marched under. In any case, it had been machine-breaking and worse on a grand scale. 'I don't recall that we had cause to shoot so many.' Hervey's tone was decidedly sardonic.

Howard took note of the signal. 'Well, Retford – *East* Retford to be precise – returns a member of parliament, and since the place is no more now than a few farmhouses, there's a move to give the seat to a city; Birmingham, I think.'

Hervey evidently strained at the less-than-momentous news.

'Oh, it's no very great business, of course, but Palmerston believes it to be his opportunity for principle. There are other seats too for "reform". And all rather closer to home than the vexing affairs of Catholic voters in Ireland. He told me the other evening at White's that he was giving it his gravest consideration, that he could not rest until he had persuaded the cabinet of the urgent need of redistributing a great number of seats.'

'Is one of them Waltham Abbey?' asked Hervey caustically. 'If reform of parliament is truly to be had, I think it a pity that East Retford did not engage Palmerston sooner. I confess a growing detestation of such places!'

Howard raised an eyebrow sympathetically. 'What are we come to if such men as you speak thus? Well, the duke has the reins now, so we may hope for better times.'

Hervey finished his coffee and laid down the cup. 'But I don't see the import of East Retford. Frankly, my dear Howard, I am interested in but one thing at present, and that is the progress of the inquiry.'

'Of course, forgive me; I should have made it plain. Palmerston has asked that the inquiry be postponed until the question of East Retford is settled.'

Postponement was in some ways to Hervey's advantage (especially if it were to be until after the wedding), but he was uncertain. 'Why? I don't see the connection.'

'A public hearing on Waltham Abbey, with all the business of Irishmen and gunpowder, would serve only to strengthen the opposition to reform.'

'Astonishing!'

'That, it may be. But you and I wear uniform; I beg you would think as does a politician.'

Hervey sighed deeply. He did not envy the Duke of Wellington, who had worn uniform for three times as long as he, and yet now must deal with men who would change their coat for the price of . . . 'So what is to happen?'

'Sir Peregrine Greville comes to London in a fortnight or so and will begin taking depositions in camera.'

Hervey was further deflated. 'Then there is no change in that regard.'

'What regard?'

'Sir Peregrine's presiding.'

'No,' said Howard, sounding puzzled. 'Were you expecting some change?'

Hervey shook his head. 'I had . . . hoped . . .'

A clerk came in. 'It is close to the hour, my lord.'

Howard rose. 'Forgive me, Hervey, but I must attend on the commander-in-chief, now. As soon as I hear anything further to your advantage' (he cleared his throat slightly) 'or otherwise, I will of course send word at once. Do you wish, by the way, to see the *Gazette*, or were you able to find the United Service's copy?'

Hervey had not yet looked for it; neither had he the time this morning to read it at the Horse Guards. In any case, the urgency had passed: Peto was well. 'I thank you, no. I'll be sure to find the club's copy. I must not detain you any longer. I thought I might be required to make some deposition or other immediately, but if I am not then I think I shall leave London for Hounslow this afternoon, or tomorrow perhaps. And then,' (he brightened the more) 'for Hertfordshire.'

Howard returned the smile. 'Why do we not dine together this evening? Palmerston will be at White's, no doubt, even if but a short time.'

Other than the obvious pleasure of dining with his old friend, Hervey could see no merit in the invitation, and in the circumstances he could not be bent on mere pleasure. 'You are ever kind, Howard, but I have pressing business.' He thought to mention the vexations with Elizabeth (his friend had once had a *tendresse* in that direction, albeit very brief), and then thought better of it. Lord Hill could not be kept waiting, on any account. 'But I should like very much that we dine when I am returned. In a week or so.'

He rejoined Fairbrother outside, and they walked together across the Horse Guards' parade towards St James's Park, Hervey wondering if he might write to Kat to urge her to take urgent action to detain her husband in the Channel Islands.

Fairbrother said something, but did not have a reply. 'Hervey?'

'Oh, I beg pardon. I—'

'I said that the Guards were truly a most arresting sight.'

'Yes, yes indeed . . .' It was a useful observation by which to displace anxious thoughts of Sir Peregrine. 'And, you know, they're no mere dandies. I recall watching Sir John Moore's regiments marching into Sahagun through the snow, and at Corunna. The Guards stood like no others. I never saw anything as fine.'

It was not *entirely* true: he had seen many a thing as fine in the infantry of the Line, but in action, in the face of the enemy; at other times they could be incapable of comporting themselves as soldiers, especially if there were liquor to be had. Somehow the Guards were the same whatever the place. It was their very appearance of superiority that was so heartening in the field. Lord John Howard's boots had rarely touched other than a parade ground, but Hervey knew he would have served as well at Sahagun or Corunna – or Waterloo. 'I have a high regard for their officers. They have a saying: the serjeants show a guardsman how to fight, and the officers how to die.'

'I counted several black faces, too,' added Fairbrother, with mock wonder.

'Indeed?' Hervey knew it had been Lord Palmerston's desire to grant commissions to men from the Indies, but he had not supposed the initiative had borne such spectacular fruit.

'Clad in leopardskins, and crashing about with cymbals!'

Hervey returned Fairbrother's frown. 'Ah yes, the sable drummers. Something of a tradition with their bands.'

'Well, I cannot trouble over it. They are better housed and fed, by the look of them, than many a cousin of theirs.'

Hervey lifted his hat in return to a salute from a passing orderly.

'How do they know to do that?' asked his friend. 'He must have passed half a dozen in plain clothes, and not once did I see his hand rise.'

'It is a mystery to me, as you. And by the way, since you touch on the matter, I have been meaning to ask for some time: your

120

honoured father – he intends holding his slaves still, I imagine?'

Fairbrother looked discomfited, and for the first time since leaving the Cape. 'He does, and I profit from it. But in truth they are not slaves. They may not in law be free men, but they are not kept at the plantation by force. And they are well provided for, even in old age. My father employs as many hired hands as he has slaves – *more*, I think. He has not been able to buy these twenty years.'

Hervey wished he had not tilted at his friend. These were deeper waters than were safe to sport in – deeper, even, than the vexations of family. 'My dear fellow!' He put a hand to Fairbrother's arm.

'Think nothing of it. Where is it we go now?'

Hervey's face creased, uneasy. 'See, I fear I must desert you again. I have letters I must write. Could you bear to explore a little on your own once more – a couple of hours, say?'

Fairbrother looked entirely content with the suggestion. 'Perhaps I may go to parliament and call on Mr Wilberforce?'

Hervey smiled, rueful. 'You may indeed. I'm sure he would welcome it. But I think, from what I hear, you would find him poor company. He would but preach at you! Nor am I sure he still sits there. See, we shall dine early and then leave for Hounslow. I must pay my respects to the colonel and report on the state of things with my troop. And you may look about the barracks, and dine with the mess. You will be prodigiously delighted. Buy yourself a gay neckcloth!'

VIII

THE MESS GUEST

The cavalry barracks, Hounslow, next day

Hervey had been, if not in trepidation, then certainly wary of the return to Hounslow. He had, after all, absented himself, albeit entirely regularly, from the Sixth: as temporary commanding officer, he had taken the opportunity to post his own troop to the Cape, so that he would have a detached command. And he had done so when he might have supposed the new commanding officer – an 'extract', a man from another regiment – had most need of him. He fully expected a certain reserve, therefore, on that account. Fairbrother for his part was convinced that there would be some disdain of his colour, despite all the assurance of the past weeks. Lieutenant-Colonel the Lord Holderness, commanding officer of the 6th Light Dragoons, showed nothing but an entirely gentlemanlike disposition to both of them, however.

Hervey had long remarked the phenomenon of patrician command. Sir Edward Lankester had possessed it, his brother Ivo too – an easiness with all ranks, an assumption of equality in which the officer was yet *primus*, an effortless facility with the tools of the trade, which others acquired only with the greatest industry, a natural mastery of the situation – of ground and

122

events – which spoke of some connection almost otherworldly. Strangely, though, both Lankesters had died at the head of the Sixth and yet few men in the regiment spoke of them now, as if they had been of such pure fire, saintly soldiers even, that none could feel true kinship. Lord Holderness had the air of the Lankesters. And as a consequence the Sixth would be well found and happy, and favoured by senior officers, who liked the security of association with such a regiment. It was welcome too, for – heaven knew – the Sixth had had their share of hard times and villainy.

'I am glad you will stay to watch the beginning of the manoeuvres tomorrow,' said Lord Holderness as they came to the end of their long interview, turning an ear to the open window as the band on the square struck up 'Young May Moon'. Herr Schnatze had serenaded them a full hour, and the regimental march signalled the end of the practice. 'I understand the new general officer commanding intends putting his regiments through their paces, seeing of what they are made. And, you may hear, we had the most agreeable of visitors yesterday, the Duchess of Kent and her sister, and Princess Victoria.'

'Indeed, Colonel?' replied Hervey, mildly intrigued. 'Was their visit to any particular end?' It was always good for a regiment to receive royal visitors. The dragoons especially thought themselves better for it. There were some who remembered Princess Caroline still, when *she* had been colonel-in-chief: she would flirt quite outrageously, and many a hardened old NCO would become like a thrusting recruit again when she was gone.

'I believe the King is minded to give us a royal colonel.' (Lord Holderness showed no inclination to exclude Fairbrother from the intelligence, nor even to beg his discretion.) 'I wonder, though, what is your opinion in the matter, Hervey?'

'I cannot but think it a fine thing, Colonel.' Had he known Lord Holderness a little better he might have said that a royal

colonel would add several thousand to the value of their
commissions – as it had for the Tenth, whose colonel had for
many years been the Prince of Wales. 'Is it to be the Duchess, or
Princess Victoria?'

'Oh, neither of them. I do not think the Duchess would find
the appointment appealing, in her present situation,' (Hervey
supposed his self-imposed exile had deprived him of the Court
gossip) 'though she is the most charming of company. And
Princess Victoria is a mere child.'

Hervey frowned, and somewhat ruefully. His own mere child
was perfectly capable of arresting attention.

'Not nine years old, indeed.'

'I should have known.'

'No, I believe that His Majesty has it in mind to appoint the
Duchess's sister, Princess Augusta of Saxe-Coburg. She is her
brother Leopold's favourite, and Leopold is apparently of some
moment to the nation.'

Hervey turned to Fairbrother. 'You see what effect a regiment
of light dragoons may have on affairs of state, without even turning out.'

Lord Holderness appreciated the joke. 'Though our turnout
shall have to be all the smarter for it: the King will watch the
manoeuvres tomorrow.'

Hervey smiled again, more wryly still. 'I doubt he'll be content
merely to watch, Colonel. No doubt he would want to report to
the prime minister that he took the head of the army for a few
hours.'

'Oh, indeed,' said Lord Holderness, well acquainted with the
King's mild delusions (he was known to describe how he
personally was in the van of the cavalry at Waterloo). 'But I
rather think these manoeuvres are to be quite searching, not at all
the usual evolutions. In any event, I hope so. Lord Hill is to
attend.'

Hervey sat up. 'Lord Hill?' The King was one thing; the commander-in-chief quite another.

'As I said: quite searching.' Lord Holderness rose. 'I'm certain the regiment will acquit itself admirably. I found it in excellent condition when I took command.'

It was a compliment, and no doubt intended as one, but Hervey was too guarded, still, to acknowledge the honours. 'They will serve, Colonel; you may depend upon it. And,' (he cleared his throat: the time had come to grasp the nettle) 'I do indeed regret that I am not able to be in my proper place.'

Lord Holderness smiled doubtfully. 'Oh, come, Hervey. You must have no scruple on that account. I confess I was disappointed when I found you had posted yourself to the detached command, but I cannot condemn it. Indeed, I should have done the same myself. And in any case, I suspect that capering over the Berkshire countryside would be dull fare after all that I read of the Cape.'

'I am obliged to you, Colonel. But the opportunity for practising war is ever welcome. Truly, I am only sorry that business at the Horse Guards, and' (he coloured somewhat) 'in Hertfordshire, compels me to return to London the day following tomorrow. With your leave, though, I should like to observe as much of the manoeuvres as may be.'

'You are most welcome.'

As had been the custom for as many years as Hervey had worn blue, the officers dined together the night before the manoeuvres (in the late war they had done so before each battle). Fairbrother wore his uniform of captain in the Cape Mounted Rifles, but Hervey wore his Sixth regimentals rather than Rifles, for he was, after all, at home. The dinner was choice, the wine was a good vintage, the band was lively and the evening altogether merry. Fairbrother found himself most agreeably engaged in conversation

125

throughout: the officers around him at table were free and easy, solicitous and affable.

After dinner, in the ante-room as he drank brandy and soda, the senior cornet appeared at his side holding the reins of a compact-looking gelding, a handsome sorrel. None of the other officers affected to notice with the least surprise.

'Sir, would you care to try Albany? He's to be yours for tomorrow.'

Fairbrother had enjoyed a good measure of champagne and burgundy, but he saw nevertheless the challenge which the cornets were laying down. He glanced at Hervey, who smiled back at him sympathetically.

'I think that would be most helpful,' he replied, taking the reins with every appearance of ease. 'Whose charger is he?'

'Ashcroft's, sir; presently on furlough.'

'It is very generous of Mr Ashcroft.' Fairbrother put a hand to the gelding's face. The horse did not flinch – though that told him nothing certain about its temperament: he had known horses which stood as still as statues, but which turned into jumping jacks with a man in the saddle. He put his nose to the gelding's muzzle, and gently blew, as one horse to another. Then standing by the saddle on the nearside, he shortened the reins, and asked for a leg. The senior cornet obliged, and Fairbrother lay across the saddle for a few seconds before swinging his right leg over the gelding's quarters, sitting upright, ignoring the stirrups and letting his legs hang long.

The officers continued to affect indifference, as if a horse in the ante-room were an everyday thing.

Fairbrother braced himself for the inevitable invitation to jump a chair, or put out the candles in the dining room with a sabre, but instead the mess serjeant brought a silver tray on which was a bottle of champagne, and a gilt figurine, half the size of the bottle, of a woman, full-skirted, holding a basket above her head.

'The late colonel-in-chief, sir,' said the senior cornet, with a wry smile.

Hervey groaned. The figurine had been a leaving present from a mess wag: the saying had been that Princess Caroline could always be up-ended for a measure of champagne.

The senior cornet poured a good measure into the gilt basket. It pivoted at the raised hands, so that as he then slowly inverted the figure the basket remained upright. He then filled the skirt and handed it to the mess guest.

Fairbrother knew what he was supposed to do. He put the skirt to his lips and began drinking carefully, tilting the figurine gently so as not to spill from the basket, which he assumed would immediately invite replenishment. The gelding remained most obligingly still, and Fairbrother was able to drain the skirt and then the basket without spilling any of the champagne. There was a murmur of approbation from the officers, now disposed to acknowledge the jape.

'A bumper, sir?'

Hervey frowned, unseen however; the trouble was, Fairbrother had made it look all too easy. He wondered if he should claim guest's privileges for his friend, but somehow thought better of it. The japery was good-humoured enough, and a slightly heavier head in the morning was a small price to pay for comradely diversion.

'With pleasure,' replied Fairbrother, handing back the figurine.

Lord Holderness, no longer oblivious to the proceedings, turned to Hervey. 'A fine-looking man, your Captain Fairbrother. Who are his people?'

Hervey told him as much as he knew, which was a good deal on his father's side, much less on his mother's, as well as adding that in the field he was the best of men, that he owed his life to him several times over. Lord Holderness was intrigued, and said that he was much taken by Fairbrother's gentlemanlike mien. He would be pleased to receive him in Yorkshire when the manoeuvres were ended – as he would Hervey and his new bride, too.

'That is most handsome of you, Colonel.'

Lord Holderness's face now became more solemn. 'Tell me, Hervey: the Waltham Abbey business – it's the very devil of a thing that this inquiry be got up. Patent politicking. I have spoken to Lord Hill of it – you have a friend there, for certain – and I've a mind to raise the matter in the House.'

Hervey was somewhat abashed. 'I am grateful to you, Colonel, but to be frank I had hoped to avoid exposure. I was told at the Horse Guards yesterday that the inquiry would be delayed, and preliminary evidence taken in camera.'

Lord Holderness nodded, weighing the information. 'Peregrine Greville – he's an old fool. He'll do exactly as he's told.'

Hervey hoped indeed that he would. Or at least as Kat told him. 'I could have hoped for a more . . . *active* president, I must say.'

Lord Holderness eyed him directly. 'But in other respects his presiding gives you no cause for disquiet?'

Hervey swallowed. He wondered what were the rumours (Kat had not always been discreet). 'I am confident that what we did at Waltham Abbey will bear any scrutiny, Colonel.'

'I do not doubt it,' said Lord Holderness, though not entirely dismissive. And then he smiled again as he saw that Fairbrother was about to begin his second go.

All eyes were now firmly on Albany and his jockey as the senior cornet filled Princess Caroline's skirt and basket with more bubbles. Fairbrother pushed his leg forward and felt for the girth fastenings, tightening them as far as he could. Then he took the figurine and drained the skirt slowly as before, managing to spill not one drop from skirt or basket – to a now generous applause of 'bravo!' and 'huzzah!'

But instead of then simply finishing the modest contents of the basket, he proceeded to slide slowly out of the saddle on the off-side, and head first under the gelding's belly, holding out the figurine the while in his right hand, until, legs wrapped round the girth but now wholly inverted, he drained the basket. Then, changing hands, he proceeded to right himself on the nearside entirely by the strength of one arm.

The mess erupted. Fairbrother dismounted, and stood (remarkably steadily, thought Hervey) with the most contented of smiles, acknowledging the ovation.

'Well,' said Lord Holderness, shaking his head. 'I never saw the like. I confess before he mounted I wondered whether he would be able to keep the horse between himself and the floor. What a very singular fellow. And his conversation so diverting too. I do see your attachment to him.'

'Except that he has set a devilish precedent for every new cornet!'

Lord Holderness smiled ruefully. 'I cannot mislike him for that. You and I were inducted into a hard school; I fear sometimes a young man favours too comfortable a billet in peacetime.'

Hervey was disposed to think him right. He was faintly surprised, however, that patrician command was sensible of such a thing. And he chided himself for that surprise, for both Lankesters might have said precisely the same.

Lord Holderness gave his glass to an orderly and made to leave. 'I hope for a good rousting about by the general these next few days. It shall do us no end of good.'

IX

THE HABIT OF COMMAND

Hounslow, the following morning

At precisely eight o'clock, by the striking of the bell on the guard-house clock, Lord Holderness rode onto the parade square to take command from the senior captain, under whose orders the squadrons had formed up. The Sixth prided themselves on their speed of forming, disdaining the regiments of foot, whose serjeants would have had them fall-in on the square an hour ahead of their time, and with show parades for good measure before that. In the Sixth, 'boot and saddle' was blown but an hour before 'general parade', the serjeant-majors presented their troops five minutes after the orderly trumpeter's second call, and the regimental serjeant-major would require only the muster states before handing over the parade to the senior major (except that this morning the senior major – Hervey – was off parade, his place taken by Second Squadron Leader). Then it would be 'march on, officers', and within the minute all would be ready for the commanding officer.

'Most admirable,' agreed Fairbrother, watching with Hervey from beneath the trees adjacent to the parade ground. 'They have the bearing of an altogether different stamp of man than I was privileged to command in the Royal Africans.'

Sometimes, the way Fairbrother mixed sincerity with irony could be quite trying, but Hervey was confident, now, that he was able to discern the one from the other. 'We do flatter ourselves that a better sort of man finds his way into the cavalry, but I assure you it is by no means the rule.'

'Then it is greater to the credit of the NCOs and officers.'

A wasp danced about the nose of Hervey's gelding, which appeared to be increasingly suspicious of its intentions. He hoped the animal was more at ease with other elements of the countryside: he had taken a horse that no one seemed to know anything of. He must trust that it was not one of the kind that knew only the stable and the pavestone (Fairbrother's charger looked an altogether better prospect for the field).

'I am glad you are disposed to think so. It was partly my design in bringing you here.'

Indeed it was, but to what purpose, he would not reveal. The visit of an officer from one corps to another was usual enough, a simple affair of pride and courtesy. But Hervey had a mind to test his own high opinion of his regiment. In one respect it was tested often enough: there was no end of inspections, and occasionally more searching trials such as Waltham Abbey. But to see the regiment put through its paces by the district commander, as Fairbrother would, must surely expose all that he, Hervey, realized that he took for granted. He did not know – he did not dare trust any longer – if he would ever attain command of the Sixth, but he had determined on knowing whatever there was to know of the regiment, knowledge for its own sake, even. And Fairbrother was the one man whose opinion he could bear to seek, as well as count on.

Lord Holderness was every inch the cavalry commanding officer. His frame was lean, his face had the features to distinguish him as a considerable gentleman whether in shako or forage cap, and to this was added – besides a uniform that

appeared as though it were from the tailor that very morning –
that air of easy, natural authority which in others Hervey had so
admired, and yet without wholly comprehending.

'Yes,' said Fairbrother, nodding as if confirming a previous
opinion: 'Lord Holderness is a man whom all would wish to
follow.' He did not try his friend's loyalty by adding 'Let us see
what he would lead them into'.

Private Johnson edged his trooper up alongside Hervey's
gelding. 'Shall I go wi' t'baggage, then, sir?'

'No,' replied Hervey, perfectly aware of his groom's reasons for
seeking the anonymity of the quartermaster's train: Johnson had
spent the last hour trying to avoid the attention of the serjeant-
majors, any one of whom would have found fault with something
or other (at least when Hervey had been acting commanding
officer Johnson had enjoyed a measure of immunity . . .). 'I may
need you to gallop for me.'

'Right, sir,' he said wearily. He had feared as much, but now
reconciled himself to twenty-four hours' 'trouble'.

The regiment formed into column of route, the trumpeter
sounded 'walk-march', and the band struck up 'Early One
Morning'. Hervey's gelding had taken three steps before
he could reassert the bit. 'The devil of this horse's manners!' he
spluttered.

Fairbrother smiled. 'I am but a foot soldier, irregularly mounted.
I would not dare to sit without the curb applied!'

Hervey smiled back; Fairbrother was indeed one of the few
men who might speak his mind thus (and aptly: Hervey knew he
had loosed the reins all too readily). He pointedly changed the
subject. 'Do you think we shall have rain?'

Hervey's mock enquiry as to the weather had not been wholly
without proper cause. Two days before, when they had driven to
Hounslow, the weather had been execrable, the rain pelting so

hard on the roof of the chaise that it had frequently been too trying to maintain any conversation. Neither had the rain served the useful purpose of washing the turnpike clear of traffic, so the drive had taken a good deal longer than usual, the coachmen all having brailed themselves up in their cloaks, content with a pace that did not increase the flow of water against them. It had continued intermittently all the next day, and all through the night. But this morning it was as fine a day as they could wish for, the sun already warm and the air scrubbed clean.

They marched mounted to Windsor: it was no distance, and Lord Holderness was intent on presenting his regiment to the sovereign in perfect order. Otherwise they would have led for the first half-hour, and boots would have borne the evidence. And a fair sight the Sixth looked, though a mere three hundred, the turrets of Windsor Castle a perfect backdrop to the martial line of blue in the home park, sun glinting on shako plates as the dragoons waited at ease for the King. When the inspection was done they would remove the shako plumes and put on black oil-skin covers, the rule for field service.

It was strange how such a simple amendment transformed the look of a dragoon, thought Hervey as he watched from the serrefile. Rather like a woman gathering up her hair and weaving in a feather. The plume made a dragoon peacock-proud; it was a fact. When he removed it he became more the bird of prey: no gaudy plumage, not so much given to display. Not that the Sixth ought to have been plumed for the inspection, for they were not in review order. They wore overalls and plain boots instead of breeches and Hessians: the King was to see his soldiers *almost* as they appeared to his enemies – serviceable, not showy. Hervey was one with Lord Holderness, however, on the demands of smartness before the former Regent: those woollen plumes of white and red drew the eye, and most favourably.

'When did you last see His Majesty?'

Hervey turned to Fairbrother and frowned, a shade apologetic. 'I have never seen him.'

'Is that not quite astonishing?' replied Fairbrother, his face suggesting that it was.

But Hervey looked just as surprised. 'I don't think so, not in a regiment of the Line, though I confess I nearly saw him last year, at the Duke of York's funeral, except that it was in the middle of the night. Do I disappoint you?'

Fairbrother shook his head in his formerly habitual, airy manner. 'I confess I am more disappointed for you than for myself. I had supposed that cavalry officers might enjoy a certain favour with the King since he is of so martial a bent.'

Hervey smiled. 'He was colonel of the Tenth a good many years, but I don't think his interest amounted to more than embroidering their uniforms lavishly.'

'And how might he enjoy reviewing his estranged wife's regiment?'

The Sixth had once been 'Princess Caroline's Own', as the Tenth had been 'The Prince of Wales's Own', but the distinction had in later years, with the royal estrangement and the Princess's indiscretions, brought them as much derision as prestige. 'I confess I had not thought of it,' said Hervey lightly, and truthfully, for even Caroline's portrait had been removed from the officers' mess, as well as her name from their title. He smiled, wryly: 'Perhaps that is his design in exposing Princess Augusta to us: an act of oblivion rather than of diplomacy.'

'And how did *you* like Princess Caroline, Colonel-Major Hervey?'

'I confess I never met her either, though I did see her once.'

'Then you have nothing with which to compare the attractions of your colonel presumptive?'

'I have seen her likeness often enough, as I told you: we had rather a fine Romney. It's the devil of a thing to say, but she was not the greatest beauty of the court.'

'And *that* taking account of the portraitist's art too, no doubt.'

'Flattery? Well, the Romney was, shall we say, gay.'

Fairbrother smiled knowingly. 'Ah yes. And appropriate she should be remembered thus. A woman more sinning than sinned against.'

Hervey laughed. 'Her guilts were not close pent up, that is sure.'

Lord Holderness's voice recalled them: 'Dragoons!' That cautionary word of command, the familiar 'Dragoons' rather than 'Regiment' – by which the Sixth, standing or sitting easy, was brought to a more uniform position of 'at ease' – was the privilege of the commanding officer. Hervey wondered whether it would ever be his. He turned his head forward, the time for chat over.

'Dragoons, atte-e-enshun!'

Hervey braced.

'Dra-a-aw swords!'

Out rasped three hundred blades. Hervey saw from the corner of an eye the procession of carriages. So did Fairbrother: 'I thought he would be mounted,' he whispered.

'*Sic transit gloria . . .*'

The carriage procession and its escort of Life Guards drew up in front of the regiment.

'Dragoons, royal salute, prese-e-ent arms!'

The officers' sabres rose and then lowered, and the Sixth's trumpeters sounded the stuttering middle Cs and Gs of the royal salute.

'Recov-e-e-r swords!'

Back came the sabres to the carry.

Lord Holderness rode forward, saluted and presented his regiment to the occupant of the foremost carriage. 'Your Majesty's Sixth Light Dragoons, three hundred sabres, are ready and awaiting Your Majesty's inspection.'

135

The King raised an ornamented walking stick in acknowledgement, as a field marshal raised his baton, and the phaeton began its drive along the double line of dragoons. When it passed the supernumeraries of the serrefile Hervey was at last able to observe his sovereign at close hand, the man who as Regent had been second only to Bonaparte in the life of the fashionable young officer. Bonaparte was dead, however, and the Regent was King, but it would be difficult to picture this sad, bloated man, immobile though by no means ancient, as victor. Hervey felt repelled. He had expected better. He had detested what his poet-friend had once written of the prince – *the dregs of their dull race ... mud from a muddy spring* – but oh, what a falling away there had been, what decay since Waterloo. What decay in the army, indeed. So many regiments disbanded, so many reduced. There were a hundred dragoons at the Cape, but even so ... The regiment mustered a mere three hundred sabres now, scarce enough to see off the mob. '*Sic transit*, to be sure,' he lamented.

The trumpeter blew the officers' call. 'You, too,' said Hervey, nodding to Fairbrother as he pressed his gelding forward.

When, the day before, Lord Holderness had said he must meet the King, Fairbrother had protested that it did not seem fitting, though he was eager enough to be presented. He had wondered if the graciousness were not somehow a means of subordination, a display of effortless ease in welcoming the outsider, as if nothing could touch the superiority of the 6th Light Dragoons; but as the day and then the evening had worn on, the graciousness had seemed wholly genuine, so that he told himself he was bewaring of shadows once more (as Hervey had told him more than once at the Cape). 'A king and two princesses in the one day: can any officer of the Royal Africans before have boasted such a thing?'

Hervey smiled. 'You made the whole Ashanti royal family prisoner, did you not?'

Fairbrother acknowledged the wit: 'I am hoist with my own petard.'

'I have observed that powder is a most indiscriminating commodity . . . Just smile at them all: they will be vastly charmed. We "proper" officers shall have to be more formal.'

Hervey, as senior major, though not on parade as such, was presented first. 'Major and Brevet Lieutenant-Colonel Hervey, Your Majesty.'

He saluted. 'Your Majesty.'

The King bowed (or rather, nodded) – a somewhat peeved return, thought Hervey, almost disapproving, as if there were a smell beneath his nose. However, the royal eyes fell on the Bath ribbon worn inconspicuously about his neck inside the tunic collar (Hervey was sure he detected some flicker of regard).

'Hervey,' said the King, nodding slowly, as if weighing the name and what he saw.

Hervey regarded it as entirely rhetorical, yet silence by reply would have seemed inadequate. 'Yes, sir.'

There was what seemed a long pause, and then: 'Waltham Abbey.'

Hervey, though taken by surprise, and not knowing whether the recognition was by way of approval or otherwise, answered clearly (and some thought a shade defiantly), 'Your Majesty.'

After a further interminable moment, the King made an un-mistakable bow of dismissal. Hervey saluted, reined back three steps, turned to the right and began his return to the rear. As he passed the first of the two carriages – a pony phaeton – drawn forward of the rest, he turned his head left and saluted. Its occupant, a child of about Georgiana's age, with long ringlets and a large velvet cap, smiled. Hervey, taken by pleasant surprise (a relief following the King's uncongeniality), returned the smile with a will, which he then found himself embarrassed by when turning his salute to the occupant of the second carriage, Princess

137

Augusta of Saxe-Coburg. She looked at him with amusement, having seen the smile which Princess Victoria had drawn, as if in some conspiracy of indiscipline. It was a look he might have seen in the face of Henrietta.

When all the officers had been presented, and had retaken their places – Fairbrother the last – the King and his party began taking their leave.

'Dragoons, three cheers for His Majesty the King: hip, hip, hip!'

'Huzzah! Huzzah! Huzzah!'

The carriages wheeled right, the King raised his hat, and the trumpeters sounded the royal salute.

'Not an especially happy king, I should say,' suggested Hervey, recovering his sabre.

'I do not suppose I would know,' replied Fairbrother, a little archly. 'Was the "Merry Monarch" so very cheery?'

'You are at times very contrary.'

'I could not admit it. But I *would* say that Princess Augusta will be an adornment to you all.'

When the formal dismissals were made, Lord Holderness assembled his principal officers under one of the many great elms in the home park, and read them the general's orders for the manoeuvres:

Information. The enemy is in possession of the whole of the country to the North of the R. Thames, and has a lodgement to the depth of half of one mile to the South of the bridge at Dorney. All other bridges up and downstream to a distance of thirty miles are destroyed.

Intention. 6th Lt Dgns accompanied by section of 1st (Chestnut) Trp RHA are to seize the bridge at Dorney by first light tomorrow and hold it until relieved. In the event that the

bridge cannot be held against superior forces, it is to be
destroyed . . .

He continued through the various special instructions, the
method of communicating with the divisional headquarters (as
the general's orderly room was to be known), the limits of
manoeuvre, paroles and the like. Hervey could not but mark how
different was the scene from the old days, in the Peninsula and
Belgium, for every officer was studying his map, and a good map
too – one of the Ordnance Survey's admirable new sheets. They
had had nothing its like in the French war.

'How great an obstacle is the river?' whispered Fairbrother.
The two sat to the rear of the active officers (his friend already
beginning to fret at his status as a mere observer).

'You saw it as we crossed at Eton, though not so wide as
there,' whispered Hervey in reply. 'But the rain will have swelled
it to some consequence.'

Lord Holderness now laid aside the orders. 'Well, gentlemen,
as you perceive, a straightforward enough assignment, though by
no means easy – which, I conclude, is the general's purpose. We
have a bridge to capture, three or so leagues upstream, and by
five o'clock tomorrow morning. That is the long and the short of
it. I would hear your opinion in the matter.'

It was not unknown for a commanding officer to consult with
his troop leaders before action; nevertheless Hervey thought
such candour augured well, for many a new man (and this
was Lord Holderness's first manoeuvres with the regiment)
would have wished to display early his own mind and will.

Captain Myles Vanneck, in temporary command of First
Squadron, spoke at once to the essence of the matter. 'Colonel,
do we believe the "enemy" is of a mind that the river is impassable? Since if he does, he will expect that we have no option
but to make a direct assault on the bridge.'

Lord Holderness nodded. 'As soon as I learned the general scheme of things this morning I sent the riding-master and his staff to reconnoitre the river as far as they might, and to look for boats. They report that every one has been tied up on the far bank or else placed in bond, so to speak, by the general's staff. The riding-master believes that swimming is too perilous an undertaking: the river is swelled to a great speed. He likens it to the Esla.'

There were few in that gathering who had been at the near-disastrous crossing of the Esla that day, fifteen years ago, when the Duke of Wellington began his final push to evict the French from Spain, but 'Esla' was seared deep in the collective memory of the regiment. And it was not, after all, a true enemy that was to be attacked: was the enterprise worth a single dragoon's life? Hervey was keen to hear the verdict.

'It seems to me,' said Captain Christopher Worsley, in temporary command of Second Squadron, 'that it is above all a test of our powers of *éclairage* in the dark, if such a word is not thereby inappropriate.'

Lord Holderness smiled. 'I think, in a way, the word is really most apposite. Shall we say *au clair de la lune*?'

There was polite laughter.

Fairbrother was intrigued by the jousting; but Christopher Worsley, he knew, had been with Hervey at Waltham Abbey – had been shot down, indeed – and by comparison, a ride through the night in peaceable Berkshire must be nothing. 'There *is* a moon, I take it?' he whispered.

They had not seen it in a week, but the tables declared there to be one. 'Yes; and fullish,' replied Hervey.

Myles Vanneck spoke again. 'But we may expect for sure that the Grenadiers will be picketing every approach to the bridge. One of their company officers told me they would be nine-hundred strong in the field.' The First Guards, the Grenadiers,

140

were the principal element of the opposing forces, and Vanneck did not underestimate them, for all that their days were tied to parades in the capital. 'Do we know where the rest of the GOC's force is, Colonel?'

'Yes,' said Lord Holderness assuredly. 'They do not march from their barracks until tomorrow morning. These are preliminary trials for us and the Grenadiers, since we had no field inspection last year. It is, in truth, a contest of horse and foot. We and the Guards shall have the general's undivided attention for a full twenty-four hours.'

'Do we have any information regarding what else the Grenadiers may be doing, or are they entirely disposed to keeping us from the bridge?'

'I am proceeding on that assumption,' replied Holderness. 'If they have other assignments then that is to our advantage. But the ratio, as you perceive, is three-to-one against us, and we the attacking force. Not what the strategian would call favourable.'

'But we have the initiative,' suggested Vanneck.

'We do,' agreed Worsley. 'But we need more of it. Do they have any guns?'

'I don't know,' said Holderness. 'But we may learn more when we meet with the Chestnuts in one hour.'

The little group fell silent.

'What is *your* opinion, Hervey?' asked Lord Holderness, raising his voice slightly to include his erstwhile second in command.

Hervey could see no immediate course but the application of ruthless logic. A direct assault was impossible: the odds were too strongly against them, even (perhaps especially) at night. Yet if there were nine hundred Grenadiers within half an hour's forced march of the bridge (as must be assumed), then it would avail the regiment nothing to capture it too early by, as the French called it, *coup de main*, for a determined counter-attack would hurl any but the strongest force from the bridge. If, however, the *coup de main* were left until the last minute – until just before first light – there would be no time for a secondary plan to be put into action if that were to fail. The only conclusion possible was that *coup de main* must be combined with *ruse de guerre*. But how, he could not yet fathom.

'I see no alternative to getting across the river between here and Dorney, Colonel, and making a surprise attack from the rear with a small number of men, say a dozen, and then to employ some ruse – which I cannot yet conceive – to persuade the Grenadiers that a counter-attack would be futile.'

Lord Holderness nodded, intrigued.

'I am not proposing we disguise ourselves and try one of the bridges; the general will have them well posted with sentries, and even if we *were* to hoodwink them, the general would certainly disallow it once he discovered it – as he surely must do. No, we must admit the bridges destroyed as if by powder.'

Captain Worsley looked doubtful. 'You saw the river when we crossed at Eton, Hervey. I don't think I ever saw it worse in all the time I was there.'

Hervey nodded. He had no doubt of his brother officer's courage. 'The means of crossing is a practical question. First we must decide what the mission demands.'

Fairbrother pulled at Hervey's sleeve. 'There is a way,' he whispered.

'You have an opinion, Captain Fairbrother?' said Lord Holderness.

Hervey beckoned his friend to speak.

'My lord, I know a way to get them across – a few at least. By towing. It was a means we used in Jamaica when the bridges were swept away. A rope is tied to a tree, or something equally firm, on the far side, and the end, in a loop, goes round the horse's neck. The current takes it to midstream and then the horse is able to swim the rest of the way, like a pendulum.'

Lord Holderness looked obliged, though without the least condescension pointed out the obvious flaw in the method. 'But how, sir, is the rope to be got across the river in the first place?'

'If there are no boats to be had, my lord, then there is no alternative but to swim.'

Lord Holderness now looked incredulous. 'But if we do not believe the *horses* are able to swim . . .'

'I should gladly volunteer, my lord.'

Lord Holderness looked pained. Before him was evidently a solution, but it turned on the willingness, and capability, of a man he scarcely knew. 'Major Hervey?'

Hervey hesitated. 'I do believe it our best chance, Colonel. If we begin as soon as it is dark – otherwise we risk discovery – there will be time to try another tactic if it fails.'

The commanding officer folded his arms as he turned over the proposition in his mind. The advantages were manifest, the danger equally so. Could he take such a risk for the sake of the regiment's – and his – reputation? Could he *not* take it? At length he put his hands on his hips, and arched his back. 'I note you say "*we* risk discovery", Major Hervey, from which I infer you are content to join us in the enterprise?'

Hervey smiled. 'An honour, Colonel.'

'Very well,' said Lord Holderness, decided. 'I am obliged to you both, gentlemen. But *I* shall be the first to cross when Fairbrother has the rope secured.'

It was no coincidence that the moon was full. The general officer commanding the London District had appointed the time for the manoeuvres so that the inspecting officers might see a good deal of any movement by night. That there was no cloud this evening was another matter: luck, as ever, was a factor in war, even mock war.

Hervey had for many years counted himself a lucky officer: ill fortune may have placed him in more than his share of dire circumstances, but better fortune had always been his timely aid, whether in the form of stratagem or device . . . or a saviour (he shivered at the sudden recollection that he must count on Kat – again – in that role).

Now, however, in the lucky light of the moon, he surveyed the obstacle before them, the bend of the Thames north-east of Frogmore, and wondered how much longer he would be favoured, for although fortune might indeed favour the bold, there was a mere hair's breadth between boldness and reckless-ness (and that difference only determined by fortune). How did a man judge his course bold or reckless therefore? And it was, to no little degree, his, Hervey's, course; he had proposed it – urged it – and his friend had suggested the means by which it might be accomplished. Lord Holderness staked his own standing on the plan, it was true, but Hervey now found himself as keenly committed to the manoeuvres as he would have been were he back on the regiment's strength.

'Truly, I cannot imagine how a man might swim across,' he said, shaking his head. He considered himself to be a strong swimmer by the usual measure, but he did not see how he could challenge such a spate.

'I assure you it is possible,' replied Fairbrother, dismounting and beginning to divest himself of his uniform. 'With a little help.'

Serjeant-Major Collins dismounted alongside him, and took a coiled rope from his saddle. Collins had for many years been one of Hervey's trusted men – from his time in Spain as a young corporal – and now as F Troop serjeant-major he had been assigned by Captain Christopher Worsley, with a dozen men, for the crossing of the Thames.

'Your excellent serjeant-major here understands perfectly what is to be done,' said Fairbrother.

Hervey did not doubt it. Collins and Fairbrother had been in conclave, with the farrier-major, half the afternoon.

The farrier-major made his way forward. 'Here, Colly,' he announced grimly but with a touch of pride, handing Collins the grappling hook that he had spent the past two hours fashioning.

Hervey frowned doubtfully. The best athlete at Shrewsbury School – Henry Locke, later officer of marines, who had been his saviour at the affair of the Chintal forts – had been able to throw a cricket ball clean across the river, but the Severn at Shrewsbury was not the Thames here; and a grappling iron and rope was certainly not a cricket ball.

Serjeant-Major Collins now took his carbine from the leather sleeve on the saddle. Hervey watched with increasing dismay: he had risked his own reputation, the colonel's, and certainly that of his regiment, on a stratagem that looked as if it might tumble at the first fence. 'What the deuce will you do with that?'

But the question was unnecessary: Collins revealed the carbine's purpose as he eased the shaft of the grapple into the barrel. 'An exactly perfect fit, Smiddy. Well done!'

'You mean to fire the grapple from the carbine?'

'Ay, sir. Reckon it'll carry.'

As indeed would the noise. But Hervey was confident enough in that regard: he did not suppose the 'enemy' would so disperse his strength by picketing this far from the bridge. And as for the grapple, he had seen a musket's ramrod fired a prodigious distance on more than one occasion in the Peninsula by a panicky finger . . . 'Admirably ingenious, Sar'nt-Major.'

'Colonel on parade!' came the word from along the line as Lord Holderness made his way forward.

'Good evening, Colonel,' said Hervey when he reached the grapplers.

'Good evening, Hervey, gentlemen,' replied Holderness, breezily, dismounting. 'Is that you I see, Sar'nt-Major Collins?'

'Colonel.'

'And the farrier-major, I perceive.'

'Colonel.'

Hervey explained the plan.

' 'Pon my word – ingenious, sir, ingenious!'

'Sar'nt-Major Collins's idea.'

'Indeed, Sar'nt-Major?'

'I saw something its like once at Dover, Colonel, when the lifeboat there were in trouble.'

'I could wish for a lifeboat here.'

'The rest of the regiment has marched, Colonel?' asked Hervey.

'They have. They will engage the pickets as soon as may be, keep them alert all night, make them think we are probing the lodgement. And, should there be an unexpected opening, Worsley or Vanneck will seize it.'

Collins finished tying the rope to the grapple. 'Ready, Cap'n Fairbrother, sir.'

'Ah, Fairbrother – forgive me; I did not see you there.'

'I have that advantage at night, my lord.'

Lord Holderness rose to the jest in Fairbrother's voice. 'So you do, sir!'

Fairbrother, stripping finally to the flesh, and with but matches and candle in an oilskin tied at his neck, braced to attention. 'Permission to cross, my lord?' he asked, wholly unselfconsciously.

Lord Holderness took his flask and gave it to him. 'You may find the brandy restorative. Good luck to you,' he said nodding, and then to Collins.

Instead of firing the carbine from where they stood, however, a few yards back on the bank, as Hervey had expected, Collins remounted, gave a hand down to Fairbrother and hauled him astride behind him. 'Keep paying out the rope, Smiddy. Give me plenty of slack,' he said to the farrier, just as they had planned it. Then he pressed to the water's edge, raised the carbine above his head, and forged into the river.

146

By God, reckoned Hervey: Collins knew his horse! He could count on one hand the regiment's troopers that would take so tractably to water at night. As he recalled, Collins's had been cast as a roadster on the Bath mail, having thrown a leg over the traces on the long incline to Chippenham, stumbling and almost bringing the whole team to grief; the gelding had never taken willingly to the harness after that. The remount officer had bought him unwarranted but at a good price, thereby, and Collins had taken him on as his second trooper, remaking him, evidently, with great patience.

Hervey smiled to himself: for once, capability and patience had been richly rewarded. Collins and Armstrong were neck and neck as serjeant-majors, in his judgement; it was but Geordie Armstrong's seniority (and, he must admit, their long years' association) that to his mind placed him first in line behind the RSM. For a moment he wondered how was Armstrong, and the detached troop, in that southern autumn. Whatever their fortune, with Armstrong the troop was in good hands; of that he was sure . . .

'A really rather remarkable sort of man,' said Lord Holderness, lighting a cheroot.

Hervey snapped to in time to see Fairbrother slide from the trooper's quarters and grasp a stirrup leather as the animal began swimming freely. He held his breath as he watched the current begin taking its hold, swinging the three of them towards the middle of the river, exactly as the branch had behaved when they tried it in the afternoon. Collins lay almost prone along his trooper's neck, carbine held high, until he reckoned they were at the point when the horse would have to swim hard to make headway, the current no longer working in their favour. He raised himself in the saddle, pointed the carbine at the far bank, high, and fired.

Hervey saw the grapple arching into the darkness, and Collins turning his trooper (or rather, letting him be turned) downstream. He could not see Fairbrother, though he searched with his telescope (it amplified the light); he could only pray the grapple held fast and his friend was able to haul himself across. He could barely see Collins, now: they would, please God, be striking for the home bank, taking advantage of the slack water on the outside of the bend – but a struggle, a prodigious effort, nevertheless. How far downstream they would make their footing he did not know. Even so, he felt like cheering.

'What do you see, Hervey?' asked Lord Holderness, searching with his own glass.

Hervey could see nothing: the rope was anchored, for sure, but Fairbrother's head and shoulders were hardly a mark in such a flood. 'I can't make him out, Colonel. But—'

''E's done it, sir, the serjeant-major,' came an unmistakable voice from the shadows. Private Johnson, with a telescope of the usual provenance, was lying full length at the water's edge. ''E's just climbing out.'

'Who is that?' asked Lord Holderness (it was, to his ear, an unusual report).

Hervey cleared his throat slightly. 'Johnson, my groom, Colonel.'

'Ah, yes, Private Johnson.'

Hervey thought it better not to ponder on the reason the commanding officer might know Johnson's name. 'A good eye, he has.'

'He puts us to shame observing in silhouette,' declared Lord Holderness, now crouching to try the same perspective of Fairbrother.

'Indeed, Colonel.' Hervey took a few steps nearer the edge. 'Is the sar'nt-major out yet, Johnson?'

'Reckon 'e is, sir: can't see owt o'im now for them trees. Ah reckon Cap'n Fairbrother's gooin all right an' all cos t'rope's theer.'

'You can see the rope?'

'Ay, sir. It's 'angin from a tree.'

Hervey sighed with no little relief: if the rope were truly fast, Fairbrother would make the bank.

'Admirable *éclaircissement*,' said Lord Holderness, sounding both relieved and amused.

The sound of hoofs signalled Serjeant-Major Collins's happy approach. 'Johnson, hold that rope fast,' he barked as he cantered up, seeing the farrier was now tying the return rope to the tow. 'Drop it and you'll go in after it.'

'Right, Serjeant-Major,' replied Johnson wearily (he had no ambition for rank, but occasionally he had to bite his lip: the serjeant-major had joined the Sixth a month after he had).

'By, but there's an undertow midstream, sir,' said Collins, slipping from the saddle and rubbing his gelding's muzzle.

'How does it run, Sar'nt-Major?' asked Lord Holderness.

'It's nothing you can't make headway through, Colonel, but a nasty enough surprise. You will have to keep your charger's head at the far bank or his quarters'll swing right round, downstream.'

'Perhaps you should tie a line round yourself, Colonel, as well as Rolly's neck.'

'Too many lines, I think,' he replied, unbuckling his sabre to attach to the saddle.

'We can't use the return rope, sir, or we might not get the tow back,' explained Collins. 'There's the reins, Hervey; that'll do.'

Hervey nodded, if reluctantly. He had seen scores of upsets in the Peninsula (as indeed must have Lord Holderness too), but the memory of Chittagong, and the Karnaphuli, weighed heavily with him still. There they had lost Private Parkin, a Warminster man, one of 'the Pals', in sluggish water and broad daylight . . . 'All of the party are swimmers, Sar'nt-Major?'

'Ay, sir.'

It was as if he had never been away – the application of duty,

149

the habit of command. He searched anxiously again for Fairbrother, though in this was an element beyond mere obligation (as there had been, too, with Collins).

There was a flicker of light on the far bank – the safety match – and then the steady flame of the candle, the signal that the tow rope was secure; and, moreover, that Fairbrother was also.

'Ready, Colonel?'

'I am,' replied Lord Holderness, climbing into the saddle. His big thoroughbred, manners perfect, moved not a foot.

'Colonel, wouldn't it be better if I held your sword?' asked his groom doubtfully.

'It would, Corporal Steele, but who will hold the dragoons' swords?'

'Colonel.' Steele knew as well as the rest that the commanding officer was intent on giving a true lead.

'The tow, Johnson.'

'Right, Serjeant-Major.'

'The reply is "sir", Johnson.'

Hervey cringed, feeling somehow responsible (though he knew Johnson ought to have known): there were three officers on parade.

'Right, sir.'

'Just "sir".'

'Sir.' Johnson put the return rope over his shoulder, and handed the tow to the sergeant-major.

'Colonel, with permission,' said Collins, slipping the tow loop over the charger's neck. 'Keep his nose at yonder bank, sir, and be ready for the current to swing 'im round, about thirty yards in.'

'Thank you, Sar'nt-Major. And I should have said: that was smart work.'

'Thank you, Colonel.'

Serjeant-Major Collins counted himself especially fortunate that the commanding officer had witnessed it: in these days of peace there was little enough opportunity for distinction, and without distinction there was no alternative but the dead hand of seniority when it came to the promotion stakes.

Lord Holderness urged Rolly to the edge of the bank. The gelding paused only to take a look, curious, at the moon on the water and then slid gently into the river with scarcely a sound. As Rolly began swimming, Lord Holderness slipped his feet from the stirrups, swinging his legs up onto the horse's quarters, letting the weight off its back. As the current took hold, the tow rope tautened, and horse and rider swung midstream like the weight on the end of a pendulum, Rolly now swimming confidently. Lord Holderness, ready for the undertow, pulled hard on the right rein as soon as he felt the quarters swinging, just as Collins had told him, until slowly they began to make progress again.

Hervey, watching through his telescope, began at last to believe the scheme would work. And then he froze. Lord Holderness was struggling – upright, violently. 'What—'

He tumbled from the saddle suddenly, as if shot.

Hervey raced into the water, grabbing the return rope. 'Hold hard, Johnson! Hold hard!'

Collins remounted and put his trooper into the water. 'Keep it taut, Johno!'

'What's to do?' asked Corporal Steele anxiously, closing to Johnson's side.

'Ah don't know. T'Colonel just seemed to thrash abaht an' then tummel into t'watter.'

'Oh, no,' groaned Steele as he got hold of the rope.

'What's up wi'im then, Flashy? Is 'e poorly?'

'Just keep 'old o' this rope, Johno.'

Hervey made progress despite the weight of sodden uniform, and his left arm over the rope. But Collins bore down quicker. As he reached Rolly, held fast midstream by the tow rope, he saw Lord Holderness motionless in the water, a leg held by the reins, and knew he had but a few seconds before the current would sweep his own trooper clear. He slipped from the saddle to grasp Rolly's reins, holding on desperately to his own, until he was able to thread his arm through both sets of reins and get a hand to Lord Holderness's crossbelt.

Hervey just reached them as the drag of Collins's trooper became too much to fight against. 'I've got him!'

'Go on, then, sir; I'll cut Rolly free.'

'Hervey? Is that you? What goes there?' Fairbrother's voice came from but a dozen feet away. He had swum down the tow rope just as Hervey had along the return line.

'Hol'ness is in the water, but we have him.'

'What would you have me do?'

Serjeant-Major Collins had managed to draw his sabre. 'How close is the return line tied, sir? I've got to cut Rolly free.'

'A good six feet. Give me the sabre!'

Somehow Collins did it, before at last the drag broke Rolly's reins, and his trooper slid away with the current, Collins hanging on, exhausted. Fairbrother cut through the tow between return line and neck loop, and the commanding officer's charger drifted off downstream after them. 'Hervey, do you manage?'

Cornet Blanche, newly joined the regiment and detailed by Captain Worsley for the crossing detachment, was now in the river and closing fast to Hervey's aid. Between the two of them, Hervey reckoned they would recover the colonel. 'Yes, Fairbrother. Get back to yonder bank!'

In a few minutes more, helping hands pulled the three from the river. 'Get blankets!' gasped Hervey. 'Wrap all there are about him!'

Corporal Steele felt for a pulse – successfully. 'Thank God, sir: he's breathing.'

'I don't think he can have swallowed much water. He was not long in it. I don't know what happened; the horse, perhaps . . .'

'Sir,' said Steele, as if seeking permission to give an opinion.

'What? What is it, Corporal Steele?'

'Sir, the colonel has fits, sir. Not often, but he's had two or three bad ones since we came to Hounslow.' Lord Holderness had brought his groom with him from the 4th Dragoon Guards.

'We must get the surgeon. See to it, Mr Blanche,' he said, turning to the bedraggled new cornet.

'He'll be all right, sir, will Lord Hol'ness,' said Steele, anxiously. 'He just needs to sleep. Only half an hour or so, and then he's right as a line, sir.'

Johnson brought Hervey his brandy flask. 'Corporal White's gone off t'elp t'serjeant-major, sir.'

Hervey was relieved to hear it, and could only pray that Collins was fit to be helped. He cursed. 'A foolhardy thing, that,' he muttered – though in Johnson's hearing, not meaning to bring an answer. 'Noble, but deuced foolhardy.'

'What's tha want to do, then, sir?'

Hervey took another draw from the flask. 'Do? We do again as we just have, until we get someone other than Captain Fairbrother across!'

'Right, sir.' The disapproving resignation in Johnson's tone was too familiar to invite remark, let alone rebuke.

An age seemed to pass before Collins returned. Hervey sighed, wearied but relieved again. 'How many more times might you be able to do that, Sar'nt-Major?'

'How many times might you want me to, sir? How's the colonel?'

'He's well enough.'

Cornet Blanche came back. 'Major Hervey, sir, I have sent Corporal Beckett for the surgeon. He said he knew where to find him.'

'I told *you* to fetch him, Mr Blanche!'

'Sir, I'm sorry. I thought I would be of more use here.'

Hervey shook his head, despairing of his ill temper. 'So you would, Mr Blanche; so you would. You did right.'

'Orders, sir?' asked Collins, declining Johnson's offer of a blanket with a shrug of the shoulders.

'We carry on. Who was next to go?'

'I was, sir,' came Corporal White's voice.

'Very well ... no. Mr Blanche, you will go next, if you please, since you have your uniform waterproof already.' The ironic tone of his voice was marked.

'Thank you, sir. It can absorb no more, that is for sure.'

Spirits were restored.

'You're sure the colonel's well, Corporal Steele?' Not that there was anything they could do if the answer were in the negative.

'Ay, sir, he is.'

'Very well. Have we the tow rope back?'

'Sir,' came another voice.

'Carry on, then, Sar'nt-Major.'

Collins made a new loop in the tow and put it over Cornet Blanche's charger's neck. 'Now, remember, sir, keep his nose at yon bank and be ready for the current to swing 'im round, about thirty yards in.'

'I will, thank you, Serjeant-Major.'

Blanche sounded steady enough, thought Hervey. But if he botched it, then he did not fancy the chances of getting *anyone* across (he himself would almost certainly have to take command of the regiment, for he did not believe that Lord Holderness would be fit to do so before the morning at least, whatever Corporal Steele's assurances).

Blanche saluted sharply and urged his mare to the edge of the bank. Like the colonel's charger before her, she too took a quick, curious look at the moon on the water, and then slid willingly into the river. Blanche slipped his feet from the stirrups, swung his legs up onto the mare's quarters, and as the current took hold, and the tow rope tautened, they swung to the exact same position midstream, the mare swimming well. Blanche pulled hard on the right rein as soon as he felt her quarters swinging, and gradually they began making headway. It took no more than five minutes, although it seemed longer to Hervey, and then the mare was making her first footing in the shallows on the far side. She struggled out, blowing hard as if she had just run a fast mile, and Blanche jumped down.

Fairbrother was waiting. 'Welcome to the playing fields of Eton.'

'Welcome back, you might say, sir.'

'I should have known,' replied Fairbrother, raising his eyebrows.

'And that was as hard a game as ever I had here, I may tell you.' Blanche handed Fairbrother the water-deck bundle in which his clothes had been wrapped. 'Here's a parcel from home, as it were.'

'Good man! I confess the chill in the air is something more than I supposed.'

'A bit hotter, I imagine, where you come from, sir,' replied Blanche, affably, slipping the loop from his mare's neck.

The two following horses crossed with the same facility, albeit with as great an effort. But the third was disinclined even to enter the water. Hervey was of a mind to tell Collins to stand the dragoon down, but he decided instead to try a lead, springing into the saddle and taking hold of the reluctant trooper's reins. He pressed his spurs into his own gelding's flanks – this was no time for half measures – and pulled hard at the other's bit. 'Give him the flat of the sword if he refuses, Kelly!'

'Sir!'

But Private Kelly did not need to draw his sabre; his horse took the lead, and Hervey was able to let go while they were still treading the bottom. 'For'ard then, Kelly; keep his nose at the far bank. You'll be fine.'

'For sure, sir!' Private Kelly was an old hand; he had no wish to be disgraced in front of the others.

The moon disappeared behind the clouds as they surged forward, the gelding picking its feet up high, exaggerated like a hackney, and then the first uneasy moments of flotation, unbalanced, even floundering, until the confident action as the animal settled to a proper rhythm. Kelly loosed his feet from the stirrups and lay full length along the trooper's back, gasping at the sudden cold douche, letting the water lift him clear of the saddle, for all his sodden weight.

Hervey could no longer see them.

The current, deflected at the bend, took them exactly as the three before, but Kelly was not as ready as they for the undertow. The gelding's quarters began to swing downstream, and his rider was too slow with the correcting rein – were the horse anyway well mannered enough to respond, out of his element.

The tow-rope loop slid forward to the gelding's throat, levering his head up even more, so that he started struggling against it. Nothing that Kelly could do would get the horse to answer to the rein. He had but seconds, he reckoned. His trooper would drown, if it did not first choke. Though he knew he would be cutting himself free of his line, he reached for his sabre, groping for the hilt in its uncustomary position. He got the blade out, with difficulty, and then hauled himself by the brow-band to get within reach of the rope. Then he swung his sword arm.

The rope severed at the second cut. He let go of the brow-band and grabbed for the return line. He got but a touch – enough, though, for a desperate man – and both hands grasped it vice-like as the current swept the gelding away.

He began shouting, but against the spate it was like a whisper. Fairbrother, waiting at the point where the horses got their first footing, just had a glimpse of the loosed gelding – and thought the worst.

156

He ran back to the tether point and began pulling on the line. Resistance meant it was fouled – or there was a dragoon clinging to it. 'Give me a minute and then haul in!' he shouted to Cornet Blanche and the others, stripping off his tunic and boots. Then once more he dived into the slack water.

Blanche counted to sixty and then began hauling. In another minute it was done – the two of them dragged to the bank, Kelly exhausted, Fairbrother little better.

Corporal White was first to speak. 'Sir, if I may say so, that was a rare brave thing you did, an' we's awful thankful for it. Isn't that right, Micky me old pal?'

Private Kelly was still on his hands and knees, with Corporal White's sodden cloak about him. 'We is, sir; right thankful o' it. Can you 'ave a see for my Ben, Chalky?'

Fairbrother, gathering up his clothes and attempting to dry himself a third time, was more touched by the accolade than he might have imagined. 'Well, let us try to get the rest across without recourse to the same measures. Where's the rope? We must needs make a new loop and then get it to the other side.'

Johnson saw the candle-signal, and hauled on the return rope as fast as he could.

Back came the tow-rope; but with no moon – and no immediate prospect of it – Hervey had had enough. 'No, Sar'nt-Major. They will have to go to it with the men they have. I'll get word across in an oilskin. Have the party form up. We join the rest of the regiment.'

X

COUP DE MAIN

Later

Just after four o'clock, an hour or so before first light, Hervey arrived at the regimental contact point, a knoll half a mile to the south-east of Fifield (it was a most opportune rendezvous that Lord Holderness had fixed on before the troops had gone to their tasks).

'So ho, Hervey! Where is the colonel?'

Captain Worsley sounded unusually hale, thought Hervey as the party jingled up the hill. 'He is at the river, still. Is Vanneck here?'

'*Adsum.*'

Hervey reckoned the mood was evidently infectious: doubtless the ride through Eton High-street brought memories. 'I would speak to the two of you.'

They drew aside, remaining mounted. Hervey lowered his voice nonetheless. 'Lord Holderness was taken by a fit as he crossed the river. He damn well nearly drowned. The surgeon's with him. He says he will recover quickly, but I don't believe he'll be able to take the reins again for a good few hours.'

'What do you propose, Hervey?' asked Worsley, sounding now less hale.

'*Propose?* I propose nothing. I am damn well taking command!' Detached to the Cape though he was, Hervey could not see why Worsley should have any doubt what was to do. 'Now, I want not a word of the indisposition. If the colonel recovers in time he can be back before the general has any idea of it. Is that understood?'

'Yes.'

There was something in the tone of that shortest of replies which conveyed offence at the notion they would think otherwise. But he was taking no chances: once a general smelled blood, so to speak, he would hound the wretched quarry until it were done for – and Hervey had no desire to see Lord Holderness brought down (and even less the regiment with him). 'Where is the sar'nt-major?'

'He's checking the pickets,' said Vanneck.

'Very well, I'll tell him on return.' Mr Rennie, whom Lord Holderness had brought with him from the Fourth, already enjoyed the confidence of the officers, though Hervey himself did not know him. The RSM and the adjutant were the only two others whom he considered it necessary to inform of the colonel's true situation.

'The party otherwise crossed safely?' asked Worsley.

Hervey recovered himself. 'Yes, forgive me: they are, but only a handful. Kelly near drowned. I could not risk any others. Blanche is across. Fairbrother and he shall have to do the business.' It had been the idea that Hervey would lead the party, but Worsley and Vanneck must know that with the colonel hors de combat Hervey was obliged to take his place.

To that end he now needed the squadron leaders' reports. Lord Holderness's plan had been to send a strong scouting party an hour and a half before last light through Windsor Forest, as far as the wooded high ground overlooking Fifield (where Hervey

159

and the two squadron leaders now stood), for he had calculated that Fifield would be the southernmost extent of the Grenadiers' lodgement. He had put Myles Vanneck in command of the party, with the five remaining cornets, to picket the route through the forest, which, though hardly like the forests of India, was no place to take chances with the main body of the regiment at night, even a moonlit one (he would not give the game away to the Grenadiers' pickets by advancing in daylight), and then to discover what they could of the 'enemy' dispositions. Vanneck, as Worsley, was entirely capable, but even if the reconnaissance were detected, Lord Holderness had reckoned that it would serve his design, for the Grenadiers would stand to and reinforce their pickets, fixing their attention to the south rather than to the north and east, the other side of the Thames.

Hervey had been at one with him in this. They gambled, of course. If they had been unable to get anyone across the river, the entire adventure would have rested on a direct approach to the bridge, against the enemy's strength rather than his weakness. Hervey now had but a handful of men on the north side, and *they* had no plan but to improvise a ruse on nearing the bridge. Yet he did not doubt that they would. In what he had seen of Fairbrother at the Cape – the scrapes with the Xhosa in the night, the clash with the Zulu at the Umtata River – he concluded that he had a soldier-companion of rare facility with unpromising circumstances.

The hazard in the plan was, to his mind, the inability to communicate with Fairbrother now. All, therefore, depended on timing. Since the regiment's mission was to seize the bridge by first light, timing was in any case of the essence; but the success of a ruse, especially one with so few men, could turn on a fortuitous minute.

There was, too, the second element of the regiment's assignment: the bridge had to be *held* until the Sixth were relieved. A handful of men, in the dark and with surprise on their side, might take the bridge from the rear; but as soon as the Grenadiers had recovered themselves, they would mount a counter-attack, and easily carry the bridge. In that case it were better that the bridge was destroyed, cutting off the enemy from their own forces.

But how could the umpire at the bridge be persuaded that so few men had captured and then destroyed it? That was the material question, and one which Hervey had no option but to leave to Fairbrother. Yet even if Fairbrother were able to take the bridge, and he, Hervey, was able to get every man of the Sixth to it in time – and the artillery pieces – the general's umpire would not permit them an indefinite defence. If only he might know what were the Grenadiers' orders! He had made the most thorough appreciation of the situation – of the Grenadiers' situation, too – as they rode through the forest, but he could not be certain. That, however, was the nature of war, even mock war: *nothing* was certain.

'What is there to report of the lodgement?' he asked Vanneck.

'I think I may tell you the most effectually if we ride to the forward edge of the copse.'

They did so. And what Hervey saw in the distance both surprised and buoyed him.

'I imagine the field of the cloth of gold was no more remarkable,' said Vanneck wryly. 'They have a vast officers' tent just this side of the Thames at Dorney, and the band was playing until after midnight.'

'I don't think I ever saw so many campfires since Spain,' replied Hervey, not troubling to take out his telescope. 'What else have you discovered?'

'They have pickets within hailing of each other in an arc from a half-mile up and downstream of the bridge, almost as far as Fifield itself.'

'Worsley?' Captain Christopher Worsley's orders had been to probe the far right flank of the lodgement.

'They've assembled a dozen boats upstream towards Bray, on this side, strongly guarded,' replied F Troop Leader.

'Within the picket line?'

'Yes. I estimate there is a full company guarding them.'

'I congratulate you.' Hervey began taking out his glass.

'But why would they want boats?' added Worsley. 'Why would they be thinking of withdrawing, with the best part of a thousand men, and we but three hundred?'

'I am wondering the same,' said Hervey, searching the low-lying country below. 'And they would have the devil of a time ferrying men across, with the river in such spate. But let us presume that the Grenadiers' commanding officer knows his business. Recollect that the general has set *him* a test as well as us. Suppose he fears the general's umpire will declare that the Guards must quit the bridge – that it has been destroyed or captured by some extraordinary means – to see what he, the commanding officer, will then do?'

'You mean he might try to put men back across the river to recapture the bridge from the far side?'

'That is a possibility.'

'But with so many men, he hardly needs to make such an indirect approach – not one that would take so long to mount.'

'Supposing the umpire would by some means still deny him the bridge, even if the Grenadiers were making the most direct and violent counter-attack?'

'Is that likely?'

'I cannot say. But the Guards would then be wholly unsupported on the wrong side of the river, facing annihilation: recollect that we alone may be the "enemy", but on paper there is a division and more behind us. Might not the general wish to test the Guards' suppleness of thinking – in other words, whether they have some means of recovering themselves from a most perilous position? A prudent commanding officer would have some plan ready. What would be the general's delight if the Guards' colonel were able to re-cross the river with his entire battalion?'

'It would show an admirable capacity for improvisation.'

'Just so. And you will recall that the manoeuvres are a test not merely of the Sixth but of the Grenadiers.'

'How does this help us?'

'Think on it, Worsley: which is the more important to the Guards' colonel – the bridge or the boats?'

Worsley thought for a moment. 'It ought, I suppose, to be the bridge. If this were *real* war then it *would* be the bridge. But,' (he seemed reluctant to say it) 'I suppose, this being mock war, the boats are more important to him.'

'Exactly so. *If* the Grenadiers' commanding officer is a thinking man, and one adept at games. Do you know of him, by any chance?'

'St Aubyn. He took command last year. But I know nothing more. I think he was lately in Portugal.'

'Well, the mere fact that he has assembled those boats persuades me that Colonel St Aubyn is a thinking man.'

'Our efforts should therefore be directed towards the boats, to draw him away, I suppose?'

Hervey nodded. 'We must show him early that we know of them. That way he will have to reinforce there, at the expense of the pickets. And as soon as Fairbrother's party takes the bridge we can move a reserve rapidly to reinforce him. St Aubyn will then have to decide as rapidly what is his best option . . . and if Fairbrother can persuade him and the umpire that he has the capacity to destroy the bridge, we might just carry the day.'

Vanneck cleared his throat very slightly. 'Hervey, I do not wish to sound disobliging, but how shall Fairbrother manage that with half a dozen men and but the clothes they stand in?'

Hervey replaced his telescope in its holster, almost dismissively. 'Something will turn up.'

The first intimations of dawn towards Windsor, and the striking of Vanneck's repeating hunter – a quarter before five o'clock – were the signal to mount. Hervey was up and eager, pistols blank-primed, cloak rolled and on the saddle, though the dewy morning had a chill to it. 'Very well, Captain Vanneck: let us advance on the bridge.' He gave back the canteen of tea to Johnson.

'Sir!' Vanneck saluted and rode forward into the darkness. The glorious moon had not reappeared, and it was back to night drills.

First Squadron began throwing out scouts and flankers, to a good deal of sotto voce cursing from the NCOs. Hervey despaired at the falling away of the edge which the regiment had had in India, when to stand to and move off before first light was the merest matter of routine, accomplished with scarcely a word of command. Could they have captured the sluices at Bhurtpore in their present state of efficiency? He had better not think on it. He must hope that the Guards, devoted as they were to the parade ground in Whitehall, were likewise a blunter instrument than he had observed in Spain.

In five minutes, when Vanneck's squadron had settled to its business, there was a great eruption of noise and flame in the distance: carbines firing, bugles, whistles, rockets (always a handy device for such a show, and easily got for a few pounds in London), and then the roar of the Chestnuts' nine-pounders. Worsley's diversionary attack on the boats had begun.

'A rude reveille for the good citizens of Berkshire, Mr Rennie,' said Hervey to the RSM, who was riding on his nearside, the adjutant to his other.

'And for the Grenadiers, I hope, sir.'

'Oh, I imagine they'll be awake. I hope at this moment their light company will be double-marching to the sound of the guns.'

'There is news of Lord Holderness, sir, a message from the surgeon half an hour ago, the first I have had opportunity to inform you.'

'Go on, Sar'nt-Major.'

'The surgeon reports he has dosed the colonel with laudanum, sir. He's bedded down at a place just outside Windsor – discreet sort of place, just as you ordered.'

Hervey nodded. 'Good. We don't want a word of this outside the regiment. Nor within, if it can be helped.'

'No, sir. The colonel's had one or two turns like this before, though I never knew it to render him unfit in this way.'

The RSM's tone was of concern; Hervey was warmed by the affection and loyalty evident.

A corporal rode back up the column, turning as he reached the RSM. 'Message for Major Hervey, sir.'

'Corporal Davies, is that?' asked Hervey, there being but two Welsh voices in the regiment.

'Sir. Message from Captain Vanneck, sir. The scouts are halted at the bottom of the hill, in cover.'

'Thank you, Corporal. Wait on the reply.' Hervey reined to a halt. He had told Vanneck not to break cover until ordered, for once there was firing to their front he would not be able to hear anything from the bridge, and he could not rely on Fairbrother's signal rockets working after a swim in the Thames.

A quarter of an hour passed – anxious minutes, for it was now light enough to see the colour of the next man's coat. The diversionary attack on the boats continued, the firing mounting (Grenadiers joining the fight in growing numbers, Hervey hoped).

Another five minutes – the birdsong increasing, the sky lightening. Hervey began to lose hope.

Up went a green rocket, from exactly where he had supposed the bridge to be.

'There it is, sir!' came a helpful voice behind him.

'Thank you, Johnson. Ever obliged to you.' It amused him to see how animated now was his groom, where the day before he had been all for a quiet time with the baggage. 'Corporal Davies, my compliments to Captain Vanneck, and will he advance his squadron at once, and with all haste to the bridge.'

'Sir!'

Davies kicked furiously for the bottom of the hill.

'Well, Mr Clarke, Mr Rennie, we have had some fortune, at least. Let us go and see if the gentlemen in red will let us through.'

Hervey trotted slowly down the slope. There was no point his risking a stumble over a root he could not see, and no point in bustling upon the rear of First Squadron as they debouched from the covert. He had had an hour's sleep, no more, but Johnson's hot, sweet tea had done much to revive him; that and the thrill of . . . not battle, but the test of wits. He might almost suppose he were enjoying it. He *was* enjoying it! The regiment was under his orders, again, and he was with friends.

Minutes later came the first clash with the Grenadier pickets, Vanneck's scouts moving cautiously in the half light lest they be counted out by an umpire (ever zealous to exercise their authority). At fifty yards a fusillade greeted them, but the dense white smoke, hanging heavy in the cold dawn air, screened the scouts as well as if they had made it for themselves, and they drove in the picket – a serjeant's command – with loud whooping and the clatter of hoofs.

Vanneck took advantage of the early success by putting the advance guard into a hand-gallop.

The scouts rode on apace a mile and more down the road, unchallenged, sensing an open run to the bridge. It was daylight enough to see a good furlong, though a mist clung to the meadows on either side. Vanneck was about to order the flankers in when he saw the scouts pulling up hard ahead. Shots rang out down the road, but he couldn't see from where. He held up a hand to halt the squadron, and kicked forward with just his coverman.

Fifty yards on, and he saw the cause: a company of Grenadiers astride the road, a solid wall of red, at Vanneck's rapid estimate a hundred muskets in two ranks, bayonets fixed, with one flank on the walls of a churchyard, and the other on a spinney. And with them was a mounted umpire: there was no letting cavalry pass in the face of formed infantry.

'Skirmishers!' shouted Vanneck.

Hervey, riding close behind, hove left off the road to the cover of an orchard, and began searching the ground with his telescope. 'I must compliment the captain,' he said, as the adjutant reined up beside him and began his own observation. 'Whoever he is, he's chosen the position well, open ground to left and right, no covered approaches, and several cuts that would make it difficult to take at full stretch.'

'Shall I get the rear troop to range further left . . . or right?' suggested the adjutant (either direction seemed as likely).

'We may have to, but they're as apt to lose direction in that mist as not. Let's wait a bit longer to see if Vanneck can turn a flank. At least this is one company that can't counter-attack the bridge.' But Hervey reckoned they had half an hour at most before the company would be reinforced, and then they would never be able to shift them. If only he had the Chestnuts' guns with him! But that had been a calculated decision: he had to convince Colonel St Aubyn that his boats were under the heaviest attack . . .

Vanneck's skirmishers kept up a brisk musketry for a quarter of an hour, and made some progress, driving in the Grenadiers' own pickets (there were numerous umpires, conspicuous by their white armbands, and scrupulously fair). But short of ordering the squadron to attack on foot (and he would only be able to muster fifty or so, accounting for horse-holders) he saw no opening.

Hervey began to curse, since neither could he see a way round. If only he had kept a single gun . . .

One of the flankers galloped up to the orchard, a smart young NCO from B Troop who had taken the prizes at the horse show the year before. He jumped from the saddle and saluted. 'Major Hervey, sir . . . I'm sorry, I thought you was Captain Vanneck—'

'What is it, May?'

'They're retiring, sir – doubling off to the rear and west, down the row of alders at the back of yon spinney; you can't see them from here.'

'You're *sure* they're not heading down the road, towards the bridge?'

'Yes, sir. They're hoofing it 'cross the meadow.'

Hervey smiled, and nodded. 'Very well. Smart work, Corporal May.' He put his charger into a canter.

Vanneck saluted as Hervey pulled up beside him behind a broad elm. 'The firing's slackening, Hervey.'

'Corporal May says they're withdrawing west. They're using the smoke to mask it.'

Vanneck needed no further orders. 'Advance guard, dismount!'

'But let us not press them too hard. We don't want them turning and making a stand.' Hervey reined about to look for B Troop Leader and the main body (he would not have interfered had not Vanneck been occupied with disposing the advance guard). He saw them, halted, fifty yards or so back down the road. 'Trumpet-major!'

'Sir!'

'Call up B Troop if you please.'

'Sir!' The trumpet-major sounded the short, sharp troop call.

B Troop advanced at the canter.

Hervey cut to the road and held them up behind the reinforced skirmish line. 'Mr Margadale, at any moment the enemy will break and run. On my order we will gallop like fury to the bridge!'

Lieutenant Margadale, in temporary command of B Troop, acknowledged, and gave his own orders to the cornets.

Vanneck's skirmishers were fifty yards from the company when they let out a great cheer and raced forward. The last of the guardsmen turned and made for the alder line as fast they could, but not before the first of the dragoons could catch them. Umpires cursed foully trying to stop the brawling.

Hervey drew his sabre. 'Forward!'

They sprang into a gallop, scattering blue and red coats alike, as they made for the bridge at full tilt. Two mounted umpires joined them, but nothing short of grape could have stopped them now.

In a minute or so, through the remains of the smoke, and the mist, they gained the approaches to the bridge – and not another red coat to be seen.

'Great heavens, what a work!' exclaimed Hervey as he pulled up hard in front. There were barrels lashed to the parapet, the arches and the culverts – as many as he had seen the engineers place on the stubbornest bridge in Spain.

Fairbrother, standing dismounted in the middle, touched his cap in salute.

Hervey was as relieved as he had been at the Cape to see his friend safe and triumphant. 'So much gunpowder this close to Windsor Castle, eh, Fairbrother?' His smile was as broad as his friend's.

Lieutenant Margadale's face was all astonishment, however. 'But what . . . where did they—'

'It is an interesting illusion, Margadale, is it not? You observe a bridge with barrels lashed to it, and you perceive they must be powder kegs.'

Margadale looked no more enlightened.

'If they are not empty – which I imagine they are – those barrels contain nothing more dangerous than Dorney's best ale. That is correct, Fairbrother?'

'They are, indeed, empty. But the landlord of the Rose and Crown is well disposed to supplying a thirsty regiment at a handsome discount.'

Hervey smiled. This was not war, but it was close on the image of it – or, at least, on that heady prelude to the field battles, when wits were still superior to the butcher's knife. 'Tell me how the ruse went.'

'Exactly as you predicted it would,' said Fairbrother, serenely lighting up a cheroot. 'There was a weak picket on the bridge, which we drove in easily enough. They seemed astonished that we came from that direction, as if the possibility did not exist. Then they brought up a reserve – not much of one – but the umpire judged our shooting to be effective. Once we'd got the barrels to the bridge it was all over. The umpire agreed we had the capability to destroy the bridge if it looked as if we would lose it, and then just as suddenly they – the Guards – were intent on getting to the boats.'

Hervey nodded. 'Capital; capital!' He turned to the RSM. 'Mr Rennie, the green rocket, if you please.'

'Sir!'

Hervey now observed they had elevated company: the deputy quartermaster-general of the London District was approaching, the same who had had charge of the action at Waltham Abbey. He saluted. 'Colonel Denroche, good morning!'

Colonel Denroche returned the salute, and to Hervey's surprise, smiled. 'Major Hervey! A most thoroughgoing success. I compliment the regiment.'

'I thank you, sir. I shall convey your sentiment to the colonel at once.'

'I would do so myself. Where is he?'

A rocket streaked noisily into the sky and burst a hundred feet above the bridge, a pretty shower of green. It gave Hervey a few moments to compose a truthful but unhelpful reply. 'I cannot say for certain, Colonel: the rocket is the signal for Second Squadron to withdraw.'

'We-ell . . . I will see him presently, no doubt. He is due considerable accolade.' He turned to leave. 'The name of the officer who took the bridge?'

'Cornet Blanche, Colonel.'

'Very well. I bid you good day, sir!'

They all held the salute as Colonel Denroche put his horse into a canter in the direction of the boats. Hervey dropped his hand, and looked about. 'Well, gentlemen, I believe we may stand down and take some breakfast.'

As the order passed down the ranks, there was cheering.

Hervey was not for once minded to suppress it. Indeed, he felt like joining in.

Myles Vanneck had by now come up, looking every bit as pleased with things as the rest of his squadron. 'My God, Hervey, but that was a go!' he declared, getting down from the saddle to check his charger's feet.

'*Touch* and go, rather, don't you think?'

'A capital ruse, though.'

'And some excellent work by your squadron, I may say.'

'I will convey that sentiment to them. But tell me, Hervey: I don't understand why you ordered Worsley on no account to capture the boats. It would have been a most complete victory.'

'But it was not necessary, and it would have humiliated Colonel St Aubyn.'

Vanneck looked doubtful. 'Would not that have served?'

'My dear Myles, who has lately become colonel of the Grenadiers?'

Vanneck's face spoke of his realization. 'The Duke of Wellington.'

'Quite.'

XI

THE RED ENSIGN

The second morning at sea, 30 September 1827

Peto wiped the condensation from the eyepiece of his telescope, and took another look. 'Slow sport, a stern chase. I wonder who she is?'

Six miles or so on the starboard beam, towards the southern horizon, was what looked like a brig sailing a good two points free of the wind, and beyond, but evidently within gun range, a second, indeterminate sail chasing her.

There was another puff of smoke from the second sail's bow-chaser. Several seconds later came the muffled report. Peto did not see the fall of shot, so he had no idea whether it had struck the brig or fallen short.

'Another merchantman running from pirates?' suggested Lambe, likewise searching with his glass.

Indeed, every midshipman on or off watch was now on the quarterdeck with his telescope, the sound of a distant gun sweet music to a young man who had only ever heard it at practice.

'And the pirate has not seen us? It's possible.' None but the coolest would risk his work with a man-of-war to weather. But Peto was not convinced. 'I rather think the *chasing* sail may prove the friend. See, the brig's holding her course when it would be easier for her to bear away. It will bring her well astern of us. So perhaps she seeks to evade us too?'

Midshipman Duguid, a wiry, red-haired boy from Moray, had climbed the main mast at the first shot. He now hailed the quarterdeck with unconcealed delight. '*Frigate* chasing, sir, with a red ensign!'

Peto lowered his telescope with the satisfaction of a man who had just proved his wits. But a frigate in the Mediterranean would fly a blue ensign, the commander-in-chief's colour; red meant that she sailed under Admiralty orders. That surely meant she was cutting out slavers. 'Heave to, Mr Lambe!'

'Ay-ay, sir!' Lambe cupped a hand to his mouth. 'Heave to, Mr Shand!'

The master raised his speaking-trumpet: 'All hands, shorten sail!' There followed half a dozen more precise instructions to the captains of the tops.

The off-watch came scrambling to the upper deck – those who had not already come up at the prospect of action. The starboard watch could easily have shortened sail and trimmed the yards, but with an order to heave to within earshot of cannon (rather than merely to lower a boat), the master would lose no time where there was no need.

'Run out starboard middle- and upper-deck batteries!'

'Starboard middle- and upper-deck batteries, ay-ay, sir!'

Lambe took up his own speaking-trumpet and relayed the order.

'Mr Pelham, signal to *Archer*, "come about"!'

'*Archer* to come about, ay-ay, sir!'

Peto saw no call to beat to quarters yet, nor to clear the whole ship for action. It ought to be enough merely for *Rupert* to run out the lighter of the guns to convince a brig to strike her colours. But if the slaver did try to run astern – and she would have to be remarkably fine handled to sail so close-hauled – *Rupert* could simply turn to starboard, and with the wind comfortably abeam rake her as she bore. A single broadside would smash her to smithereens. No master, even of a slaver, would dare it. What Peto feared was that she might cast the evidence overboard. It was not unknown, as the despatches from the Preventive Squadron on the West Africa Station revealed only too well.

'Let us serve her notice. A signal gun, if you please, Mr Lambe.'

'Ay-ay, sir.' Lambe put his speaking-trumpet to his lips again. 'Middle deck, one gun to fire unshotted!'

At such a range there was nothing to choose between guns: no shot, upper-deck eighteen-pounder or middle-deck thirty-two, would reach even half-way to the slaver. It was the noise and smoke, the signal, that counted, and a thirty-two would make the most of each.

A minute and seven seconds ticked by. The aft gun fired.

Peto put his telescope to his eye again to observe for a change of course. In five minutes there was no sign of it.

'*Archer* coming about, sir!' called the officer of the watch.

Peto glanced over his shoulder. The sloop had indeed wore round quickly. 'Good man,' he said to himself (her captain was commissioned from below deck, but he was sharp enough). 'Make to *Archer*, "stand-by to intercept".'

There was no need of elaboration, for at that angle *Archer* would have a better view of the chase than did *Rupert*, and there was enough sea space for her to intercept without having to sail too close-hauled.

With a three-decker now all but motionless ahead of her, a frigate chasing astern, and *Archer* about to cut her off to leeward (the wind abeam so that she could not turn away more than a point) the slaver's only option was to strike her colours – such as *were* her colours (Peto was damned if he could see any).

But in five minutes more she still had not altered course. Peto was mystified. Did she gamble that *Rupert* would not open fire, knowing her cargo? A three-decker could certainly not give chase. He considered the propriety of his options: the Royal Navy was enjoined to suppress the slave trade, not to liberate slaves, although the latter was the usual consequence of the former; he would be perfectly justified in sinking the slaver with all hands. That offended his humane instincts, however, and although it was just, it was hardly consonant with that impulse which had animated parliament in moving the legislation in the first place.

'Make to *Archer*, "expedite", Mr Pelham.'

'"Expedite", ay-ay, sir.'

Peto thought it would now come to a fight, but could his sloop catch up the slaver and board her? Even if she could, she would have to sweep her deck first. He hoped she had the weight of carronades and small arms for the job.

The minutes passed, twenty of them before the slaver was within range of *Archer*'s long twelve-pounders – had *Archer* turned broadside to her quarry, that is (but, still making to catch her, *Archer*'s captain had to be content with warnings from the bowchaser). Still the slaver kept her course. Peto reckoned she would pass at least half a dozen cables' length astern. He thought of sending two boats' worth of marines to try to intercept her, supported by the sternchasers. He glanced at the boats in the waist and wondered if two would do it, or if he could spare a third, which might too be stove in. He had not many minutes more before he must decide . . . 'Curse her!'

The sudden discharge of one of *Archer*'s twelve-pounders made him turn – just in time to see the slaver's bowsprit carried clean away. The sloop had risked the chase for a shot by turning away from the wind, but with what effect!

'Great gods! Capital shooting! Capital!' exclaimed Peto. 'Mark you, Mr Lambe!' (Likely as not it had been a warning shot across the bows, fortuitously off its line, but that was no matter.)

'She strikes, sir!' came the cry from the maintop, Midshipman Duguid observing the pennant running down.

Peto nodded approvingly. Another minute and he would have given the order to lower three boats. 'We will keep a sharp look-out, Mr Lambe. I would not trust a slaver's crew until they were in irons. If she *is* a slaver, that is.'

'Ay-ay, sir,' replied the lieutenant, his telescope trained once more on the sloop and her captive brig. '*Archer*'s running out her launch.'

'I commend Mr Crabbe for it,' said Peto, raising his own glass. 'It doesn't do to give a crew of a striking ship time to reconsider. Yonder frigate's still a mile to run.'

Indeed, he observed, the frigate was having to beat more to windward to give herself leeway to run alongside the prize.

'Not worth a deal of money, though,' he added laconically. 'A guinea or so a man by the time it's shared out.'

Had the frigate taken the brig as prize with no other warship in sight the money would have been hers alone, but the presence of even a man-of-war's tops on the horizon meant that the prize-money must be shared (it was held that an enemy was persuaded to strike by the mere threat of a second ship engaging). And so the slaver would be claimed by sloop, frigate and first-rate; the share would be meagre indeed. If only she were a Spanish bullion, and in the glory days, twenty years before!

'Frigate's signalling, sir!' came the cry from the poop.

Peto fancied his eyes were still strong, but he strained in vain to make out the separate signal-flags.

The frigate turned another point into the wind, her signal halyards now easier to make out (it was expecting too much, per-haps, for *Archer* to be repeating them, occupied as she was). Peto turned impatiently, to see Midshipman Pelham's junior leafing through the pages of the signal codebook, while Pelham himself peered through his 'scope, calling out the flags to another, who looked about as old as Rebecca Codrington.

Where *was* Miss Rebecca Codrington? Peto had not seen her yet this morning.

'Good God!' he spluttered, realizing that the dark blue of what he had taken to be one of Pelham's afterguard assistants was in fact that of a bodice, not a jacket. 'Mr Lambe!'

'Sir?'

But he thought better of it. He had given Rebecca Codrington the freedom of the quarterdeck, and the day before, he had instructed Pelham to look after her. He could scarcely cavil now, just because there was a chase and a boarding action a mile off. 'No matter. What *does* Mr Pelham do there? Can it be so very long a signal?'

He himself had been a signal midshipman, and he knew perfectly well it could be the very devil taking down a signal in clear, let alone cipher – and *that* supposing both ships were using the same codebook. The frigate, whoever she was, would not be signalling in cipher, but did she use the same book? She was sailing under Admiralty orders, while they were Mediterranean Fleet. He took another look at her, and now saw the cause of delay – no fewer than *four* signal halyards. He could not know, of course, whether it were a long message or whether the words were not contained in the codebook, and therefore to be spelled out letter for letter. Be what may, she now appeared to be turning into the wind even more. Was she intending to tack? What *was* she intent on?

'I believe she's going about, sir,' said Lambe, sharing his captain's observation. 'I wonder—'

'From *Trincomalee*, sir,' begged Pelham, touching his hat.

Peto lowered his 'scope. *Trincomalee*: he knew her – teak-built at Bombay a dozen years ago, a fast sailer (and a savagely long name to have to spell out). 'Wear away, Mr Pelham!'

' "Request you take possession of prize. Have second out of Tangier to pursue." '

Peto huffed. He had the authority to refuse, but he had no wish to frustrate a preventive frigate in hot pursuit. Nor did he believe the Admiralty would wish it. But he could not risk putting a prize crew on board to sail her to Gibraltar – not with a hold full of slaves who, once unshackled, might fail to distinguish between captors and liberators. He would have to send aboard two dozen marines at least. And he would get back none of them, nor the crew, this side of a month if he were lucky. No, *Archer* would have to escort her. It wouldn't be plain sailing, not against the wind, but with address she could make Gibraltar and be back in five or six days. Except that it meant he would have to rely on another ship coming out of Valetta to take ashore Rebecca Codrington – and the other women. Curse it! And for a paltry fifty guineas prize-money to his own pocket!

'Very well, Mr Pelham. Make to *Trincomalee*: "Affirmative. Good hunting!" '

' "Affirmative, good hunting" – ay-ay, sir!'

'And to *Archer*: "Convoy her to Gibraltar and return".'

' "Convoy her to Gibraltar and return" – ay-ay, sir!'

'Crabbe'll ask for men if he needs to,' said Peto to his lieutenant as Pelham scuttled back to the poop.

Lambe nodded. Handling a prize-slaver would be tricky. 'Stand-by to make sail, sir?'

'As soon as *Archer* acknowledges and has possession of her.'

'Ay-ay, sir.'

'I shall walk the lower decks meanwhile.'

'Ay-ay, sir.' Lambe called to the waist for the master-at-arms and boatswain to accompany.

There were two places laid at table in the captain's steerage. Peto had asked that a dozen officers join him at dinner, and in the

179

circumstances he thought the presence of Miss Codrington not, in truth, apt. Or, seen another way, he wished his officers to behave without the inhibition that the presence of a lady, a girl – and the commander-in-chief's daughter at that – would inevitably occasion. And so he had asked Rebecca Codrington to take a late breakfast with him, which, with the diversion of the chase, was now luncheon.

'Rice b'n't so good as it were an hour ago,' said Flowerdew as he placed a bowl of salt on the table, his voice close enough to Norfolk as to make Peto feel comfortably at home.

'I'm confident that it will be most appetizing,' he replied, opening a locker under the stern lights and appearing to search.

'But the 'addock's well,' called Flowerdew, not inclined to question what it was that Peto searched for (if his captain wanted his help he would certainly ask for it).

'How many of Marsala did we bring?'

'Two cases, sir.'

'I don't see it.'

'There wasn't room, sir. It's still in the 'old. Do you want some?' He sounded doubtful. He had never known Peto to drink Marsala except of an evening, and alone with a book.

'I thought to send a bottle to Miss Codrington and her maid. She said last night she had never tasted it.'

'That's uncommon thoughtful, sir,' said Flowerdew, though sounding more doubtful still. 'I'll fetch up a case.'

'I'd be obliged.'

'I'll go an' fetch Miss Codrington, an' all.'

'If you would.'

Peto sat down in his Madeira chair and placed his hands together as if in prayer, his customary method of recollecting his thoughts. He was, indeed, fretting somewhat at the missed opportunity. He had written to Elizabeth at some length the night before, his intention being that Rebecca Codrington take the letter ashore when he put her off for Malta, whence it could travel with the next ship for England. If he had been able to pass the letter to *Archer* instead it might have been with her in Wiltshire in under a month. But now he would have to wait for a barque or something out of Valetta. It need not be any great delay, he knew, but it was a delay nonetheless. He *could* have sent the letter across to *Archer*, of course. Had there been official papers to send, too, he would not have hesitated to do so – or even a decent bag of mail from the ship's company; but two days out from Gibraltar there was next to nothing.

He warmed at the thought of communication with his betrothed, however, be it ever so distant. The night before (it was the strangest thing), he had even found himself lying awake in his cot wondering how long it might be before there was not *just* Elizabeth Hervey to think of. At first he had dismissed the idea, but then he had asked himself why he should not think thus; Elizabeth was certainly not beyond the age of bearing a child – bearing *children*. And (it was stranger still) he had found himself imagining what it would be to have a daughter like Rebecca Codrington; or a son like Mr Midshipman Pelham . . .

'Si-ir.'

Flowerdew's yap woke him. He sprang up. 'Miss Codrington, good morning! I was only . . . Forgive me, I was turning over matters in connection with *Archer*.'

'Please do not apologize on my account, Captain,' said Rebecca, with a note of surprise. 'I cannot imagine how you have the time to render me any consideration at all.'

Strangely enough, there were moments when in her manner of speaking Rebecca Codrington reminded him more of Elizabeth Hervey than of a child (he really must *not* think of her as a child: undoubtedly the midshipmen did not . . . but that was another matter). 'Miss Codrington, it is no imposition at all. A glass of . . .'

'Water, please.'

He turned to Flowerdew. 'A glass of our best water, Flowerdew.'

Flowerdew looked at him oddly (water was either potable or it wasn't). 'Mi-iss.'

'Well, well, Miss Rebecca, I trust you had a diverting morning. I saw that you were engaged in the affairs of the poop deck.'

'Oh yes, a *most* diverting morning, Captain Peto. I never saw such a thing. I think it most noble what was done. Those poor men in that slave ship.'

Women, too – but Peto was not going to be so indelicate as to correct her. Better not to imagine the situation in those holds. He had, though, thought of sending over his surgeon and mates to render what aid they could, but he was under orders to join Rebecca's father's squadron with all despatch. He consoled himself with the knowledge that, being not long out of Tangier, there would not be too great a mortality.

'The only difficulty that presents itself now, Miss Rebecca, is that *Archer* will not be rejoined when we pass Malta, so we must trust to a lighter or some such to convey you ashore.' He realized he might be alarming her. 'But be assured, you will not be permitted to hazard yourself for a moment.'

'Oh, I do not mind that in the least, Captain Peto. I am quite prepared to share the hazards of the service – just as the sailors' wives below.'

Peto looked surprised at the mention of the women; he had quite forgot them. And . . . 'How do you know of the . . . wives?'

'Mi-iss.' Flowerdew proffered Rebecca her glass of water. 'Can I serve the kej'ree now, sir?'

His cook had acquired the dish when they had been on the East Indies Station, and it was now a firm favourite. 'By all means.'

'I saw them when they came on deck yesterday,' said Rebecca, following Flowerdew to the table, perfectly at ease.

182

Peto had been content to let the women take the air during the afternoon watch. 'Ah, yes.'

'I found them very pleasant, very civil,' she continued, spooning kedgeree to her plate. 'They seem to endure a good deal on account of their husbands, I think. Do not you, Captain Peto?'

Peto almost turned red. He did not doubt that the women had been on their best behaviour, but even so ... 'Ye-es. Just so. However, I think it best, Miss Rebecca, if you do not converse with them. It ... it is ... unsettling.'

Rebecca's eyes widened. 'Oh, I am very sorry, Captain Peto, if I have offended. I would not wish for one moment to unsettle anything. I am aware that it is somewhat irregular in any case for there to be any females on board a ship of war.'

Peto nodded as in turn he helped himself to kedgeree. 'Irregular, yes, but not unknown. It is a pleasure to have you on board,' (he would change the subject) 'but after a few days at sea you will be glad of Malta. The harbour at Valetta is one of the finest sights I ever beheld.'

Her eyes lit up. 'Yes, my father said the same in his letter to me. And I have seen paintings of it too. But I assure you, Captain Peto, I shall by no means tire of being at sea – not in *your* ship. It is a revelation to me, so that I quite see now what it is that has animated my father these many years.'

Peto smiled. Any praise of the service brought him satisfaction, and praise of a ship of his the most intense pride. But more than that, this girl, this ... young woman (he must make up his mind) had such self-possession as to amaze him. He had next to no experience of those of her age and sex, and when he summoned to mind those volunteers and midshipmen of the same age he *had* known (even, he had to admit, himself) he found the comparison unfortunate. 'That is very gratifying, Miss Rebecca, though I must point out that we have unusually calm seas, a fair wind and some days in hand. It may not be so agreeable when we reach Greek waters.'

Rebecca sprinkled salt about her plate. 'I should so very much like to accompany you, Captain Peto. I should so like to see my father at sea, in his true element. And my brother, Henry: he is midshipman aboard my father's flagship.'

Peto smiled again, indulgently. 'I think it a charming idea, Miss Rebecca. Only the threat of powder and shot rather makes it less so.'

Rebecca looked a shade affronted. 'I should not mind that, Captain Peto!'

He sighed, inwardly. These girls – these *women* indeed: they had no conception of how shot transformed a deck from the most agreeable place on earth to a representation of hell. In seconds. But he could not blame her for it, nor even chide her. Besides, the matter was hardly of moment, a mere hypothetic. He would change the subject again, this time more subtly. 'You understand, of course, that in part our engagement in the Eastern Mediterranean is not unconnected with the suppression of slavery.'

'How so, Captain Peto?'

'The Turks have been abducting the citizens of the Peloponnese and taking them to Egypt.'

'I did not know that. It is perfectly dreadful.'

'Quite. I do not understand the Turk: I have met so many fine fellows, and yet they seem capable of unspeakable barbarity. Thus are all men, perhaps, but I never saw such wanton cruelty as is with the Ottomans customary.' (He rather forgot himself in the unaccustomed situation of having an interlocutor at his table who was not in the service.) 'I confess I was uncertain of this venture – compelling them to leave Greece – though delighted nevertheless to have command of *Prince Rupert*. But if it comes to a fight I shall shed no tears for them.' He now realized he had spoken in rather too sanguinary terms for a daughter whose father, and brother, would be in the thick of the fighting if it came. And, for that matter, he had spoken rather too freely about his own thoughts – as if Miss Rebecca Codrington, indeed, had been Miss Elizabeth Hervey. He cleared his throat.

'More kej'ree, miss?' asked Flowerdew, offering the bowl.

'How do you like it, Miss Rebecca? Speak plainly,' added Peto.

'I like it very much, Captain Peto. Thank you, Mr Flowerdew, I will have some more,' replied Rebecca sweetly. She helped herself to two good-size spoons full. Then her countenance turned earnest again. 'Do you truly believe it will come to a fight with the Turks, Captain Peto?'

Peto was annoyed with himself. He had dug a hole, so to speak, and now he was going to fall into it. But he could scarcely dissemble. 'I do,' he answered gravely, nodding. 'I do. But it does not follow that the fight need be . . .' (he checked himself) 'very bloody. Your father's squadron is vastly stronger, and the Caliph knows full well that the Royal Navy's habit is of unrivalled success.'

'I am relieved to hear it is so,' said Rebecca. And she *looked*, undeniably, relieved. 'I do most sincerely wish, however, that I could see my father dismay the Turks, so that those poor people of Greece might have peace.'

'Coffee, ma'am?' asked Flowerdew, in no doubt now of the real status of their guest.

XII

THE MARRIAGE KNOT

Hertfordshire, 1 May 1828

'Hervey, I am ever more delighted by your English countryside,' declared Fairbrother, looking out of the chaise window at the rippling fields of barley. 'I did not think I should see scenes more pleasing to the eye than those from the Rochester mail, and yet in whichever direction we travel there are prospects to rival those before. And such houses!'

'It is a green and pleasant land.'

Hervey still sounded . . . distracted, despite the conversation of several hours. Fairbrother thought he would tempt him one last time. 'The house of your affianced's people is, I imagine, a handsome one?'

Hervey too was gazing from the window, but not at the country. 'It is.'

Fairbrother sighed. 'You are still at Hounslow, I suppose.'

Hervey turned to him. 'I should have remained with them. At least until Lord Holderness was entirely fit. You saw him: he was not himself.'

Fairbrother had indeed seen him: he looked like a spectre. 'But the surgeon said he was recovered from the seizure, and you yourself said that the adjutant and the captains were perfectly able to carry on.'

'So they are.'

'And the manoeuvres were declared complete.'

So they had been. And Hervey had been as glad of it as he had been surprised. But, as the general had pronounced, the regiment had demonstrated its capability in spectacular measure, and his recognition of it was an early return to barracks. 'Indeed.'

Fairbrother sighed again, this time audibly. 'You know, Hervey – I will say it once more – I am at a loss to understand your thoughts in the matter. You concealed the colonel's indisposition most effectively, and that, I acknowledge, was an admirable instinct, but if in doing so you deny yourself the laurels which are rightfully yours, and a man who is incapable, however fine a fellow he is, remains in his place – and mistake me not: Lord Holderness is the finest of men – how does that serve? How does it serve the regiment? How does it serve the *King*?'

It was indeed old ground over which Fairbrother picked, and Hervey was no more moved by it than before. 'You make the case compellingly, except that you discount the injury that would be done when it were known, both inside and out, that a regiment had not remained true to its colonel. I do not wish to debate with you the theoretical limits of loyalty, my friend' (no, indeed: there was a rawness to that particular wound still – the affair of Lord Towcester) 'for if we do not admit it to be absolute, then there is no foundation to discipline but the lash.'

Fairbrother was momentarily distracted by the distant sight of rooks harrying a kite, which somehow seemed apt. He turned back to his friend. 'The lash? What? See, Hervey – and then I will speak no more of it, for the time being at least: it matters only in part that you succeed in preserving Lord Holderness's reputation with the general; there will not be a man in the regiment who is not speaking of what happened that night. And with the most decided opinions. Think on it.'

His friend turned in silence to the passing acres, and for a good while the only sound was the rumbling of the wheels.

Hervey had engaged a chaise for the journey down to St Paul's Walden, the seat of Sir Delaval Rumsey, ninth baronet, father of Kezia, and squire of extensive acres in the rich arable between Saxon St Albans and the Templars' Baldock. Only the Lankesters, he had heard say, rivalled the Rumseys in Hertfordshire antiquity.

'Lady Lankester has a daughter, you say. To whom therefore did the Lankester baronetcy pass when Sir Ivo died?'

Hervey shook his head. 'There was no male relative, I believe, so it must therefore have lapsed.'

'Would a male child of hers then succeed to it?'

Hervey laughed. 'I am uncertain, but I believe the answer to be no.' In truth, he had given no thought to the fecundity of the coming marriage, even if he had thought a good deal about the actual process. A very good deal indeed.

In a quarter of an hour more, the chaise turned into the long, metalled drive of Walden Park. Hervey looked at his watch – a little before midday. He had said in his express that he was un-certain what time precisely they would arrive, but even so, the footmen were sharp about the chaise when after five minutes at a good trot it drew up at the entrance to the great Elizabethan mansion.

The two friends alighted, adjusting their neckcloths self-consciously. Hervey paid off the coachman and arranged refreshment for him and for the horses, then led his friend up the ten impressively wide steps to the vault-arched doorway.

Inside, the only sound was of a fortepiano, and not too distant. It stopped abruptly, and a moment or so later Lady Lankester appeared. She smiled – welcomingly enough, thought Fairbrother, but without great ardour (and he wondered again if he intruded) – and Hervey and she kissed, fleetingly.

'How good you are come,' said Kezia, and turning to Fairbrother, smiled warmly: 'And this is the companion of whom you wrote so keenly.'

Hervey's companion bowed. 'Edward Fairbrother, Lady Lankester.'

Kezia did not curtsy, but held out her hand.

Hervey had marked, before, Kezia's preference in her manner of greeting. Combined with such a smile as hers it was ever the more welcoming. 'We left London betimes, but the carting traffic was savage,' he explained. 'We did not manage a trot before, I think, Edgware. The Romans would have been faster along Watling-street than we. You were practising just now?'

'You know that I practise for three hours every day.'

The manner of Kezia's reminding – almost a rebuke – told him very decidedly that he must know (truly he had no recollection of it). 'Well,' (he cleared his throat) 'Fairbrother and I returned to London only yesterday. As I said in my letter, there was urgent business to be about in Wiltshire and in Hounslow. But we are here now, and delightful it is, at last.'

They sat down near a window in the morning room. A footman brought a tray, followed by another bearing a coffee pot.

Fairbrother sensed a certain stiffness, and was inclined to ascribe it to his presence. He made to rise. 'I think perhaps I ought to see our boxes—'

'Oh no, Mr Fairbrother,' Kezia protested. 'All will be attended to, I assure you. Take your ease with some coffee, and tell me how you find London. Colonel Hervey says you have not been in England before. Did you visit the Royal Academy? There is a fine exhibition there, is there not? You have seen Mr Turner's paintings, Colonel?'

Hervey frowned. It was rather like finding his horse on the wrong leg as they turned. 'I confess I have not, yet.'

Kezia looked dismayed.

But he would make no more apology: it was true that military business did not always require his attention when he was in London, but there were other things to be about than looking at paintings, however fine. He made to change the subject. 'Where is Perdita?'

Kezia turned towards the fortepiano. Perdita lay curled on a chair next to the piano stool, silently eyeing him. 'Come, Perdi,' she said.

The little Italian greyhound slid from the chair, stretched, and stalked to her mistress's side. She sat, without taking her eyes off the interloper.

The three talked for a quarter of an hour, of this and that, inconsequential matters, until Fairbrother rose again, managing this time to beg his leave successfully. Kezia told him that in the evening they would drive to Knebworth, to a soirée which its chatelaine, General Bulwer Lytton's widow, was hosting. Fairbrother enquired whether he would be intruding, saying that he was perfectly content to remain at Walden: he had with him several books. To which Kezia protested that he was *most* welcome: Mrs Bulwer Lytton held these gatherings almost weekly during the close season, and new faces were most positively encouraged. 'The mere mention of books, Mr Fairbrother, assures me that our hostess will find your company agreeable. The soirées are of a literary and artistic bent.'

'Shall you sing,' (Hervey hesitated) 'dearest?'

Kezia rose and turned to him with an almost puzzled look. 'If I am asked to do so, yes.'

Fairbrother bowed. 'I am all eagerness, Lady Lankester,' he said, smiling confidently. And he left the promised couple to each other.

Hervey put down his coffee cup and made to embrace his betrothed. Even though he had stumbled in the preliminaries, he had been studiously admiring of Kezia's appearance. Her fair hair intrigued him more with every meeting: he had not had any proper acquaintance before with such a colour and complexion. Strange as it was, she seemed to him almost ... foreign. More so than Isabella Delgado, or even Vaneeta. Her mouth was quite perfect: any scholar of the ideal of beauty would admit it. Nothing like as full as Kat's, or Isabella's, or Vaneeta's (or Henrietta's), but appealing to him for its very ... he supposed, *distance*. Her form, a constrained grace which provoked the imagination, was powerfully pleasing, and greatly the more so for his absence these past nine months. The checked Levantine, her arms and bosom covered to throat and wrist (its being 'morning' still), only served to increase his admiration.

They kissed. She did not resist, though she did not give herself up to any passion. Hervey understood. It was not her sitting room; they might be disturbed at any moment. He caught Perdi eyeing him still – a reproachful eye, threatening, almost.

'Dearest, I am so very glad to see you. There is much to speak of.'

Kezia glanced at the fortepiano.

'Do I disturb your practice?'

She looked a shade wistful. 'In truth you do, but it was discourteous of me to reveal it.'

Hervey shook his head, smiling apologetically. 'Would you play for me?'

'Play for you, Colonel Hervey?'

He frowned. 'Is it so outrageous a suggestion? And ... *Kezia*,' (he pronounced her name – for the first time – somewhat tentatively) 'would you dispense with the formality of that manner of address?'

Kezia raised her eyebrows. 'What would you have me call you?'

191

Hervey sighed. 'Well, I have a given name, as you.' Few but his close family used it (and Kat).

She smiled a very little, but wryly, so that Hervey felt drawn to kiss her again – which she did not object to.

'You are very fond of music, I know, since you told me so at Sezincote, and we have had so little opportunity to speak of it.' She sat at the fortepiano again while Hervey resumed his place by the window. 'Did you recognize the piece I was playing as you arrived?'

Hervey had not the slightest idea. He had declared a love of music while in something of a heady state, having heard Kezia sing at the house in which they were both staying in company with Sir Eyre and Lady Somervile. He liked music – or, as Elizabeth had often chided, he liked the noise it made, especially if it were made by men in uniform.

That evening at Sezincote, he managed to recall (though how, he could not say), Kezia had sung something – *two* things – by a German called Gluck.

'Might it be by Herr Gluck?'

Kezia frowned. 'Oh, Matthew Hervey!'

Her use of his Christian name, even so-qualified, encouraged him to return a rueful half smile. '*Not* Gluck?'

'Do not you recognize *Der Erlkönig*?' She sounded dismayed.

It was time for honesty, though he would instantly regret it. 'I confess I never heard of him.'

'Oh, *Colonel* Hervey! *Erlkönig* is the name of the piece I was playing. It is by Franz Schubert. You have heard of Schubert, I take it?'

Hervey sighed. 'I was a long time in India, ma'am.'

Kezia looked at him almost studiously, and for some time. 'Of course. Forgive me,' she said softly.

There was nothing to forgive. And if there had been he would have done so readily. Kezia Lankester was a picture of scholarship, of a serious, high mind, the like of which he had not seen in a woman, certainly not one so young. Or so powerfully attractive. He thought to reply that *Erlkönig* was first a poem by Goethe, but he could not. At that moment he wished only that the nuptials were over and done with.

After a lunch of pigeon breasts, Hervey and Kezia walked in the formal gardens while Fairbrother ranged further.

'My parents will hasten back if I send word, I do assure you,' said Kezia.

Hervey had placed her arm in his. 'I would not disturb their ease. I have been to Southwold; it is very agreeable.' Sir Delaval and Lady Rumsey had left Hertfordshire but three days before for the sea air, which Sir Delaval's doctor prescribed twice yearly. 'The arrangements are easily made. You are quite sure you would not wish the wedding from here . . . or Hounslow.'

'I am quite sure. And my parents are in agreement. Quietly from my aunt's in Hanover-square, and the wedding breakfast there afterwards. I see no occasion for greater ceremony.'

Hervey was not too strongly of a contrary opinion. He understood that, her marriage to Sir Ivo having been at Walden, she would not wish to return to that church again; and he certainly appreciated the advantages of London; but he had hoped that it might be somehow a little more . . . regimental. Lord John Howard had even suggested they might avail themselves of St James's Palace.

'You would not object to my non-commissioned officers attending on us, would you?'

They strolled on a while before Kezia answered. 'I would rather they not.'

Hervey tried to put himself in her mind: would the sight of blue, and sabres, be of too painful memory?

'Besides,' she added, 'are not your non-commissioned officers at the Cape still?'

She was right. The men he would have wished to stand at the door of the church were several thousand miles away. Not all of them: there was Collins for one. But if Armstrong and Wainwright could not be there ... He cleared his throat. 'Indeed they are. And it would be a pale imitation of a guard without them. There will be no ceremony.' He squeezed her arm.

She made no move by return, but expressed herself grateful for his understanding. 'And I have asked a cousin to give the address. He is a canon of St Paul's – the cathedral, I mean.'

'Ah.'

'You object?'

He frowned, and sighed. 'I have already asked someone, a family friend. He was at Oxford with my late brother.'

'That was a *little* presumptuous, Matthew.'

She was right: it was the bride's prerogative to arrange her own wedding. 'I could, I suppose, write and tell him—'

'I should be glad of it, yes,' said Kezia, almost absently. And then more decidedly: 'My cousin is a most ardent preacher, of a very proper evangelical temper.'

Hervey groaned inwardly. He knew well the sort of clergyman. It was to counter such a possibility, in part, that he had asked John Keble to preach. 'Indeed. Of course.'

They strolled on further, Kezia stooping to pick an anemone, and twirling it between her hands as they walked. 'Did you find your people well in Wiltshire? How is Georgiana, and your sister?'

Hervey had known it must come, and he had not resolved on what he would say. He ought, he knew, to say everything, without hesitation; but he wished in some way to spare Elizabeth (the whole family indeed, and not least himself) the ignominy that would inevitably follow from the breaking off of an engagement to such a man as Peto. 'They are all in good health, thank you.'

'Is there yet a date for Elizabeth's wedding?'

He cleared his throat. 'No,' he answered, truthfully but unhelpfully.

'Perhaps I should invite her here, and Georgiana?'

'That would be very civil. My parents keep little company.'

'You surprise me; I did not think them unsocial.'

Hervey smiled. 'In this their taste and means coincide.'

'Happy thought indeed.'

'And, forgive me, I had meant to ask earlier, how is Allegra?'

'She walks very strongly since you saw her last, and she speaks much. We may see her before we leave this evening.'

He wanted to broach the question of 'arrangements', where they would live, what staff they would need, but Kezia seemed somehow preoccupied.

She stooped and picked another anemone, and gave it to him.

He threaded the stem through a button hole of the double-notched lapel of his coat, his favourite, dark green, the yellow of the anemone a felicitous match. 'I did not say, but I fancy I shall be detained in London rather, for the next month or so.'

'Oh? How so?' She sounded curious rather than disappointed.

'There's to be a court of inquiry over the affair at Waltham Abbey.'

'Ah.'

'Perhaps you will come and stay in Hanover-square the while?' he said, thinking how to make the business more agreeable.

'I fear it would be inopportune. Mrs Bulwer Lytton is giving a *grande fête* in June, and there will be much preparation.'

'And you must assist in this?'

She looked quite taken aback. 'I am to sing in the opera.'

'Oh . . . of course, the opera.'

But in truth, now that he thought more precisely of it, it might not do for Kezia to be in London during the inquiry; she might

195

learn of . . . 'I hope I may be allowed to propose myself to attend the *fête*.'

The question – if question he had made it – was to his mind rhetorical; but not to Kezia's. 'I shall ask Mrs Bulwer Lytton. I'm sure she will issue an invitation, in the circumstances,' she answered solemnly.

He wondered if she teased . . . 'Well, I hope I may propose my supporter to visit with' (he hesitated at presuming on the plural), 'us here before the event.'

'By all means. But there is a concert at Hanover-square in two weeks' time which my aunt has arranged for me to attend. Perhaps it would be convenient that we meet then?'

Hervey was beginning to wonder if Kezia thought of anything but her music, for both the months ahead seemed wholly regulated by it. 'Perhaps.'

As an afterthought (it appeared), she turned to him and added, 'I believe my aunt may be able to secure an extra ticket. Would you wish to attend?'

Hervey reeled somewhat. 'Of course I should wish to attend. I should wish to escort you!'

'And you do not wish to know first what is the music?'

He cared not in the least what was the music. He knew he would have to steel himself to it (as he had on several occasions with Elizabeth), whatever the band or the composer. He took her hand. 'Kezia, I shall be accompanying you. That is sufficient to engage me.'

She looked genuinely puzzled. 'I have known some who cannot abide Beethoven, yet call themselves musicians.'

He brightened. 'I have heard Beethoven, and liked it very much.'

It was true. He had once attended a concert by the Grenadiers' band, when they had played *Wellington's Victory*, and the duke himself had conducted the encore. But he need not burden her with such a detail.

196

Kezia brightened, too. 'Then I shall write to my aunt at once.'

They continued their stroll. The birdsong, so intense in the morning, was now diminished. A distant cuckoo called, but neither of them remarked on it.

'I have found us a very pleasant house at the Cape, and but a short walk from the Somerviles.'

Kezia said nothing for the moment, and then: 'How are the Somerviles?'

Hervey supposed the domestic details did not trouble her, that she trusted him to make what arrangements were necessary (she was, after all, in no position to make any herself). 'They are very well. I think Emma especially is glad to be in those climes again – although it is not India, for sure. Somervile himself is rather vexed at finding the administration of the colony keeps him at Cape-town, but there is a good deal for him to do. And it is the most pleasing place, the country and the climate.'

Kezia stopped suddenly, and turned. 'Matthew, I think I will return to the house. I would speak with Mrs Benn and the nurse before making ready for this evening. And I must practise a little more. We leave at six, you know.'

Hervey was a trifle disconcerted by the abrupt termination of their pleasant stroll, but he understood that Kezia had responsibilities in the absence of her parents. And, too, she had a very proper pride in her music, an admirable sense of obligation to those she would play for. 'Of course, of course. Let us walk back together.'

Hervey found the prospect of the soirée increasingly unappealing as they drove through Knebworth park. Kezia had no doubt intended the opposite in her picture of the evening, but it sounded to him an affair in which he would find little diversion. Their reception at the house was certainly warm enough: Knebworth's chatelaine was extravagantly welcoming (Fairbrother, he marked,

197

seemed entirely at his ease), but his immediate impression of the company was of a *ménage* altogether too studied.

Knebworth was, like Sezincote, a perfectly ordinary English house which had been 'decorated' to appear other than it was. Unlike Sezincote, however, which had been turned into something that would have looked entirely natural on the banks of the Hooghly, Knebworth, with its Gothic windows, battlements and turrets, looked as if it had been transported from the Rhine. Kezia explained that Mrs Bulwer Lytton had inherited a dilapidated mansion from her father, and that, in the words he, Hervey, had used, 'her taste and her means coincided': she had pulled down three sides of a most uncouth and sombre quadrangle to make a more manageable house out of the fourth. 'Old General Bulwer being now dead, too, Elizabeth is free at last of a most unhappy marriage,' she added with some asperity. 'She is finally able to pursue her true vocation, which is painting and poetry.'

It had not, therefore, been the most consoling of drives. And by the time Kezia had told him that their hostess's father had brought her up on the principles of Rousseau, which had meant her curtsying to the gardener's boy, he was in something of a mental lather. Especially since Kezia gave him to expect that there would be a good many more bluestockings than those of either sex with whom he might have easy conversation.

Mrs Bulwer Lytton greeted her guests in a voice so old-fashioned (though she was no great age) that Hervey did not quite know what startled him the more – that or her strangely medieval dress. She smiled and called him 'darling boy', then scowled and (none too teasing, he fancied) said, 'but you are naught to try to take away this jewel from among us', tapping Kezia's arm with her fan.

Try? Despite his wonder at their hostess, it was all he could do to stop himself saying that he did not *try*: it was already *accom-*

plished. But a lifetime's deference to age and rank stood in his way. 'I am a fortunate man, ma'am,' he replied, with an almost exaggerated bow. He hoped Kezia would play her part in this, but he saw that she had become preoccupied, rather in the manner he had observed that evening at Sezincote as the time for singing drew close. He must accustom himself to it, for composed though her manner invariably was, Hervey knew there was such a thing as artistic temperament – what was vulgarly called 'nerves'.

And then he was introduced, with Fairbrother, to Elizabeth Bulwer Lytton's third (and favourite, said Kezia) son. Edward Bulwer Lytton's two elder brothers had inherited estates away, and thus he lived in London and at Knebworth with his adoring mother. Hervey thought him about twenty-five, Kezia's age, rather dandified in his dress, with a long, intelligent face, and an air which suggested he might be engaging company. Except that (Hervey was certain) his cheeks were rouged.

'Edward has recently published a second novel, Colonel Hervey,' said Kezia, as the little party continued with its introductions.

Her lapse into the formality of his rank exasperated him, especially as she used their host's Christian name (and he 'Kezzy'), and looked at him with all the appearance of admiration, which Hervey had not so far been favoured with. 'Indeed, sir?' He said it a little too curtly, he knew.

Edward Bulwer Lytton maintained his pleasant countenance, however. 'I must earn a living, Colonel, as you.'

Hervey chided himself. Impatience with a man ten years his junior – and not under his orders – was neither edifying nor necessary. 'Just so. I confess I have been remiss in respect of my reading of late. I have managed only a very *few* books new-published. Might I enquire what your novel is about, sir?'

'Certainly, Colonel Hervey. It is of the intense friendship of two men, which leads the one to save the life of the other.'

Naturally Hervey was intrigued by the subject, but he judged, from the author's air, that the book would not be exactly to his taste; he would have to be nimble on his feet lest he appear an ungracious guest. 'The noblest of things,' he said, nodding.

Fairbrother's brow furrowed. 'Is it by some chance called *Pelham*, Mr Lytton? I do believe I bought it last week in London.'

'It is.'

'Then I am sorry that I did not bring it with me to Hertfordshire; I should have liked to take it back to the Cape Colony with me, inscribed.'

'There will be another occasion, I hope, Mr Fairbrother.'

Kezia took her leave of them, explaining that she must attend to the pianoforte (Knebworth, she had told them, had a concert grand), and shortly afterwards Hervey and Fairbrother bowed and left their host to his other arriving guests.

'A considerable coincidence, I should say, your buying Lytton's book,' said Hervey as they made their way into the banqueting hall.

'Ye-es.'

'What recommended it to you?'

They took glasses of champagne from a footman.

'While you were at Holland-park, before we travelled to Wiltshire, I read in a magazine called *The Examiner*, which your club most generously provided, an article which rather caught my eye under the title "The Dandy School". By Mr Hazlitt?'

Hervey nodded. He had certainly heard of Hazlitt – had read him, perhaps. Henrietta used to commend him.

'This dandy school – or "silver-fork" school it is also, apparently, called – is very much the mode, holding up for admiration, as it does, the lives of the rich and fashionable. Hazlitt was most contemptuous of it; he thought it narrow and superficial, and folly to admire a class whose characteristics were caprice and insolence. Naturally, since I expected to be moving in such society, I thought to buy several of these novels.'

Hervey pulled a face. He was used to Fairbrother's drollness, and he would not rise to the bait. 'Quite a coincidence nevertheless. But I do pray that you keep Mr Hazlitt's strictures to yourself this evening.'

Fairbrother, smiling, took a sip of his champagne as he surveyed the room. 'Oh, my dear friend, you may count on my good behaviour in such company.'

Hervey was sure of it. He held his glass to his lips as he made his own survey of the room. It scarcely seemed 'silver-fork' however. It had its share of dandies, unquestionably, but many more of an 'artistic' disposition. There were certainly no uniforms, where ten years ago at such an assembly there would have been at least half a dozen militia pleased to disport themselves. He was doubly glad to have Fairbrother at his side.

The evening passed agreeably enough, however, although Kezia was unable to spend any time with her betrothed or his friend. Hervey managed a little conversation, principally with a radical member of parliament on the question of Catholic emancipation; Fairbrother had considerably more (he was, indeed, a centre of much attention). There was an excellent cold table and some fine hock. They were bidden to take their seats at about nine, and entertainment followed for a full two hours: poetry reading, Shakespearean soliloquies – and music. The music was not, though, the popular sort with which he was familiar – no hunting songs like that the Somerviles had sung so roisteringly at Sezincote. It was the sort that delighted the serious-minded – string quartets, piano sonatas by Beethoven, lieder. Hervey sat dutifully through it all, nodding only moderately, until Kezia at last took the floor. She sang three songs by Schubert, accompanying herself. And Hervey saw – as perhaps he had sensed only distantly at Sezincote – that Kezia was more than a mere proficient. Even to his untutored and unmusical ear there was, indeed, something in her voice and playing that surely stood comparison with what he might hear in London.

And yet, as much as he might esteem her sweetness of tone, and dexterity at the keyboard, he found himself more taken by the swell of her breast in the lieder's challenging dynamics. He understood very plainly, now, that he desired her at least as much as he admired her.

The next five days passed quietly, but without any real resolution of the marriage arrangements. In this they were not helped by the absence of Kezia's father, who would, naturally, have to be consulted in the matter of the wedding and the subsequent marital establishment. Kezia largely spent the mornings practising at her fortepiano, and in the afternoons she and Hervey walked for an hour or so. Once, the three of them rode to Luton Hoo, but it was not a form of exercise that evidently delighted Kezia, and they made the journey there and back at never more than a gentle trot. In the early evening she spent half an hour in the nursery, they dined at seven-thirty, and afterwards she played for them. Twice there were guests (not greatly diverting to Hervey), and on Sunday they attended divine worship in the village. This was the least agreeable part of their stay, for although the Rumsey pew was comfortable, the sermon was interminable, a litany of the dire consequences of sin, and addressed so much to the patron's pew that Hervey began wondering if indeed the rector had some particular knowledge.

Fairbrother, throughout, was more generally at his ease than his friend had feared, which was some consolation, but Hervey found himself possessed of an increasing desire not so much to be back at the Cape as back in the purposeful saddle – anywhere. Over and over in his mind he turned the question of command. He had been all but promised the Sixth ten years ago (how he would have relished that with a young man's address!), yet now its prospect seemed only to be receding. Lord Holderness was the finest of men, though; the regiment would be well treated – cherished even – by a man with more than adequate means and the patrician's disdain of ambition. What right had he, Hervey, to wish his colonel gone, so that he himself might wear the crown? Only that he had held the reins on so many occasions now, and held them well (he would not shy from the fact with false modesty). And if the Sixth were ever to face the King's enemies, then he knew there was no one better than he to lead them. Was there no one (other than he, and Fairbrother) who recognized that – no one in a position of *authority*?

It had indeed been a pleasant stay. But glorious though he found the country thereabout, and comfortable as Walden Park was, he saw no usefulness in the life of a country squire. It was time to return to London – even to the London of his court of inquiry. He had, however, resolved on one thing: he knew with certainty, now, the present he would make to Kezia on their marriage.

XIII

AN ILL WIND

HMS Prince Rupert, 4 October 1827, the sixth morning at sea

The wind had begun freshening not long after the capture of the slaver, veering steadily the rest of the day until by morning a strong north-westerly blew, the sea heaping up, chalk-white spume trailing from the crests like streamers. By midday it was a full-blown gale, the waves prodigiously high, the crests overhanging and then tumbling with the greatest force, so that even in the seclusion of his cabin Peto could feel the shock. Not that he sought his cabin's shelter much during those days and nights: there was the example to be set by his presence on deck, his duty to discharge in the safety of his ship. And there was his curiosity to satisfy: how did *Rupert* handle in heavy weather?

He was not, however, in the least anxious. Such weather was but an exigency of the service: His Majesty's ships had been storm-tossed all about the globe for two centuries, and he himself had encountered typhoons that made a man think he was in the nether regions rather than the Indies. His only disquiet was in the delay the weather imposed, and the difficulty of transferring the women ashore.

At first he had tried to lie to in the storm, with just enough canvas set to keep her head seven points from the wind so that they could enter the Malta Channel, where he hoped the storm would have blown itself out and he could hail a tender from Valetta. But even with the helm well over, she made too much leeway; and with insufficient sea room Peto decided instead to take in canvas, and on reefed topsails to run before the gale to leeward of the island.

During those three days of the storm, Peto saw next to nothing of Rebecca, whom he had confined to her quarters. He saw even less of the sailors' women. When, the first night, he made his rounds with the carpenter, he had found their condition pitiable, and did not wish it upon his mind too much. He had never sailed with women before, in any weather, and their plight made him strangely uneasy. He wondered what the rest of the crew made of their distress. God forbid that any woman should be injured! And if ever it came to a fight . . .

When, however, on the fourth morning, the storm abated, Rebecca came onto the quarterdeck with every appearance of one who had actually enjoyed the experience. Her face showed no pallor, her hair shone, and her eyes sparkled. She blithely received the greetings of the midshipmen, who vied to have her attention, and sweetly returned hands' smiles alike, they knuckling their foreheads as if she were another officer. And not only, Peto supposed, because she was their admiral's daughter: such an appearance, after a storm of those proportions, spoke of a natural superiority that commanded, if not the obedience that was due to the youngest midshipman, a very good deal of respect nevertheless.

Rebecca glanced about with a certain surprise: nothing appeared to have been carried away in the blow. She looked skywards to see what the weather might bring next: here and there was wispy cloud, but otherwise the sun had the heavens to itself, the wind gentle in the canvas, the waves once more friendly. It was difficult to imagine how the sea could have been whipped up so malevolently.

'Whereabouts are we now, Captain Peto?' she asked when she saw he was no longer preoccupied with making sail.

'Another day and we should have been blown right through the Gulf of Surt.' He looked and sounded displeased.

Rebecca did not know where was the Gulf of Surt, but concluded that it was not convenient to their destination. 'Shall we have to turn round?'

Peto looked at her in some bewilderment, and not merely for her unnautical turn of phrase. 'Miss Codrington, with these airs it would take the better part of a week to beat back to Malta. Even as things go, we shall be altering sail every hour to tack north to the Ionian, where we suppose your father to be.'

'So you will not be able to have that lovely water you spoke of?'

He sighed. He had given up his cherished notion of taking on water from the Arethusa spring three days ago. 'No, the Portsmouth casks will have to see us through. But it is no matter.' What in fact mattered to him now was close hauling clear of the shores of Cyrenaica, otherwise he would waste even more time gaining sea room by beating due west. That, and finding a ship Malta-bound (or one that he might press to sail there). He was surprised that Rebecca herself showed no dismay at the turn of events. 'You need have no anxiety, though, Miss Codrington. There will be sloops aplenty running back and forth from your father's squadron. We are sure to intercept one in a day or so.' (He hoped he sounded convincing.) 'I trust, incidentally, you were not too shaken about by the storm?'

Rebecca brightened. 'Not in the least, Captain Peto. It was most exciting. I read three books and maintained my journal throughout.'

Peto rather wished he had made the enquiry a shade less presumptuously, recalling his own seasickness at her age. Later, indeed, he would learn from the marines that she had tended her maid throughout, who had been desperately seasick and in her cot since first *Rupert* began taking in canvas.

'Capital, capital.' He sounded almost mystified.

She smiled. 'The food was a *little* unvarying.'

'Ah, yes. I hope it was explained: there could be no galley fires in such heavy seas.'

'It was perfectly explained, Captain Peto, thank you. But you would not think me so ungracious as to complain even if I had not known?'

Peto was quite startled. 'No . . . no; of course I would not.' He cleared his throat. 'Miss Rebecca, I hope you will dine with me this evening. The food will be hot, I assure you.'

'Thank you, Captain Peto. You are ever kind.'

'I shall ask the master too, for it was he who worked the greater part these past three days.' He cleared his throat again. 'And one or two of the midshipmen.'

'I shall look forward to it, Captain Peto. And now may I ask a particular favour?'

He smiled indulgently. 'Indeed you may, and I shall be pleased to grant it if it is in my power.'

'I should like to go below and see how are the women. I should have so liked to go before, but your orders were most explicit, and the sentry always looked very fierce.'

He found himself colouring slightly at the tease. 'I am very glad to hear that my marines are capable of confining a vice admiral's daughter; it gives me great confidence they will do their duty against the Turk.'

Rebecca smiled, acknowledging the teasing on both sides. 'So I may go below, Captain?'

Peto sighed. 'Miss Rebecca, some of the women are . . . how

may I say it? Of not good character. I believe I owe it to your father, and your mother—'

'Some I know are of easy virtue, Captain Peto, but they will likely have suffered the same as the virtuous.'

He reddened very decidedly, and cleared his throat noisily. 'In that case, Miss Codrington – and you are of course right – I shall be content for you to visit the orlop ... briefly. I shall have a lieutenant accompany you.' He looked at his watch, though he did not need to know the time. 'And if you will excuse me now, I must consult my charts.' He touched his hat. 'Until dinner, then, Miss Codrington.'

After a quarter of an hour in his cabin with charts and the sailing-master, Peto settled into his Madeira chair and felt in the left pocket for the papers placed there by his clerk. There were not many, and the briefest perusal told him that they could wait. Such procrastination was not his usual practice: he had ever been raised on the imperative of dealing promptly with any matter placed before him – certainly to do the work of the day *in* the day – but the work of the previous *three* days had been essentially on the quarterdeck; and, in any case, his clerk had scarcely been able to make an entry in the ledgers, so violent had the ship's motion been. He had, too, a letter of his own to write, and if he delayed it at all he risked missing an opportunity, for they might at any moment, now that the storm was blown out, see a man-of-war or a merchantman working west for Malta.

He went to his writing table. He knew how he would begin; he had thought it over exhaustively in the long hours on the quarterdeck. He took a sheet of paper, unstopped the inkpot, picked up a pen and wrote *My Dearest Elizabeth*. Then he put down the pen and stared at the page. He smiled: he had done it! 'My Dear Miss Hervey' had been the earlier form (how could it have been other?). But now he knew different; now he was certain he could – must – write exactly as he felt. He picked up the pen again and wrote a flowing narrative of the storm, of how *Rupert* answered compared with *Nisus* and *Liffey* (*Liffey*, he informed her sadly, was being broken up even as he wrote), of how well pleased he was with his officers and warrant officers, what a spirited girl was the young Miss Rebecca Codrington, and how he was to beat upwind to find a ship to take her off, thence to sail into the Ionian to rendezvous with her father . . .

He wrote as if they were the oldest and easiest of friends. He had never written its like before. But then, as he was about to sign it, he had sudden misgivings. Did he make his true sentiments clear? He took up again where he thought he had finished:

My dearest Elizabeth, I am unused to expressing such thoughts, which fact I am joyously pleased to admit to you, and lest you should be in any doubt as to my feelings I enclose with this a page from a book of verse which I have long had in my sailing library, which I have long admired though yet been uncertain of its truth, until now when I do read it with, so to speak, the scales fallen from my eyes, though in its alluding to sword, horse and shield it is perhaps more properly the domain of your most excellent and gallant brother! For my part, it would read instead of oak and sail and gun, though these be neither so poetic nor chivalric. I would write of blustering wind or swallowing wave, and these words you will surely recognize from the poet's other work of parting – of going beyond the seas, indeed, which would be the more appropriate were it not to speak so much of the Eternal . . .

He went to the quarter gallery to fetch his razor, took the book of verse from the trough next to his cot, and cut the page very neatly from his treasured *Lucasta*:

209

TELL me not, Sweet, I am unkind,
That from the nunnery
Of thy chaste breast and quiet mind
To war and arms I fly.

True, a new mistress now I chase,
The first foe in the field;
And with a stronger faith embrace
A sword, a horse, a shield.

Yet this inconstancy is such
As thou too shalt adore;
I could not love thee, Dear, so much,
Loved I not Honour more.

He fastened it to the other sheets with blue tape, which he cut from his sea coat, and signed the letter *Your Devoted Sposino*.

Then he called for Flowerdew to chill thoroughly a case of champagne.

XIV

INFLUENCE

London, 7 May 1828

It was a warm afternoon when they returned to the United Service Club, where all the windows were thrown open and the noise of the streets intruded. Nevertheless, Hervey was able to hear well enough the discontented voices of a post-prandial knot of members at the further end of the smoking room. He and Fairbrother fell silent as they cocked their ears to the agitated conversation . . .

'The Duke of Wellington will have nothing of it, I tell you!'

'The duke will have no choice in the matter, for he's sold out to those damned Canningites!'

'He'll never have truck with Emancipation: votes for Catholics? – Ireland'd be ungovernable!'

'Ireland'll be ungovernable *without* Emancipation!'

'No need to worry about the Irish, sir! Peel and thàt constabulary of his have got them by the hip – stout-hearted fellows!'

'He'll have a constabulary here, too; you mark my words!'

'A police in London? Nonsense, sir!'

'Well I for one would cheer him in it: a police would get our men off the streets at least.'

'You'd rather see a police, and all the devil that goes with it, instead of honest men in red? Shame, sir! We fought Robespierre to have none of it, by gad!'

'*I* don't trust Huskisson. It's *he* that'll be the ruin of the country. *Free trade* – bah! He'd bankrupt every farmer on a principle.'

'The fellah's a bounder. So fat he couldn't break into double time to save his life!'

'It's that damned little Lord Cupid who'll see us ruined. Taking country seats in parliament and giving them instead to the cities! Was at Harrow with 'im, and I tell you, sir, Palmerston'd sell this country to the dogs!'

Fairbrother took a sip of his coffee, made to raise his newspaper, and leaned forward to speak confidentially. 'The Duke of Wellington, I fancy, is in for another hard pounding!'

'Oh yes, indeed,' replied Hervey, sotto voce and with a ruing smile. 'One must marvel at his sense of duty, laying aside military honours to enter into such a bear-pit!'

But Hervey's concern was more for himself than the duke: with this degree of foment in the smoking room of the United Service, what was it in the street? At the first mention of Irishmen – tantamount to 'revolution' – the gallery at the court of inquiry would be filled with the braying mob, and the pages of every broadsheet and scandal rag alike would parade his name until he might wish it changed to Smith! He wished now, indeed, that he were still in Hounslow, 'on the strength', safe behind a barrack wall. Leave of convalescence and occasional light duties with his pen were rapidly palling.

'Hervey! Well met, sir!'

He turned his head, to see Major-General Sir Francis Evans

bearing down on them. He stood, and made a brisk bow. 'Good afternoon, General.'

'No need to get up, Hervey m'boy; this aint the Horse Guards,' said Sir Francis. 'Good day to you, sir,' he added, nodding to Fairbrother, who was also on his feet.

The three sat.

'Have just come from the Commons: a regular to-do, there is, over this business of the country seats. As hot a business as they come. Palmerston may yet burn his fingers.'

Hervey was not greatly concerned – if concerned at all – with the welfare of Lord Palmerston's fingers. He only wished he would pull them from the Waltham Abbey pie. 'Indeed, General.'

Sir Francis Evans removed his monocle, polished it, and re-fixed it to his eye with a distinct sense of purpose. 'Now, Hervey, what's all this about manoeuvres at Windsor?'

Hervey supposed there must be some resentment at the headquarters of the foot guards. But that could no more be his concern than Lord Palmerston's fingers. 'The regiment acquitted itself well, I understand, Sir Francis. The GOC sent them home early.'

'Mm.'

'You heard other, Sir Francis?'

'Of course I heard other, Hervey. What do you take me for? What was the matter with Hol'ness?'

'Matter, General? His plan, dare I say it, routed the Grenadiers.'

Sir Francis screwed up his eyes. 'Hervey, do not think me feeble!'

'I trust I never have for a moment, General.'

'Colonel Denroche says Hol'ness was nowhere to be seen.'

'An admirable accomplishment in scouting cavalry, surely, General?' Hervey smiled the merest touch.

'Damn me, sir, you are the most impudent officer!'

Fairbrother shifted ever so slightly in his chair.

Hervey's countenance did not change. 'I trust, Sir Francis, that you are in no doubt whatever of the esteem in which you are held.'

'Bah! Have you had your coffee?'

'We have, General.'

'Mm. Well, since you are evidently in no mood for conversation, I shall repair to the library for mine!' Sir Francis rose. 'I see that old fool Greville's to preside at your inquiry. *The Porcupine*'ll have a field day!'

The Porcupine had been bust these twenty years, but Hervey understood full well the import of the aside. Or rather, he *thought* he did: Sir Francis could surely not have heard of . . .

The general was gone before there was any opportunity for enlightenment.

A porter came up. 'Sir, here are your letters.'

Hervey noted the postage to be charged to his account, thanked him and took the ten days' accumulation of mail. 'Permit me, Fairbrother. I would just see if there is anything urgent to be attended to.'

His friend nodded, and re-raised his *Standard*.

There were a dozen or so letters: from the regimental agents, his bank, his tailor and sundry others, from Kat, Elizabeth, Lord George Irvine, from Hounslow, from Lord John Howard, and one in a hand he did not recognize. He opened first that which he judged the most imperative.

INFLUENCE

The Horse Guards
6th May

My dear Hervey,

The U/Secrty for War and the Colonies wishes to speak with you in connection with matters raised by Sir E.S. in his despatch. Would you be so good as to call on him when you will?

I am also now reliably informed by the Adjt-Gnl's staff that the Crt of Inquiry will be convened in the middle of June, previous to which sworn statements shall be taken down. The Presidt of the Ct shall be Genl Greville, his name given by convening order, which shall appear in due course in the Gazette.

Ever your good friend &c,
John Howard

Hervey tried hard to look entirely collected. He had supposed Sir Francis Evans's information to have been simply that of the coffee room, mere speculation. To receive such confirmation from Lord John Howard . . .

He sighed deeply to himself; it could no more be helped (surely Kat could not now persuade her husband to withdraw, not now a convening order named him?). He opened a second letter, from the colonel of the Sixth, Lieutenant-General Lord George Irvine. It acknowledged his own, thanking him for his information that he was returned to London temporarily, and expressed the strongest wish to see him when Lord George returned from his tour of inspection of the northern command in June.

Hervey laid it aside, heartened, as letters from Lord George almost invariably made him, and opened a third, with the stamp of the Hounslow orderly room.

215

My dear Hervey,

I have been acquainted with the facts following from my indisposition at Windsor, of your own exemplary conduct in the matter, and indeed that of Captain Fairbrother. I would that you call on me, when your duties both military and domestic permit, so that I may properly commend your address, and also that of Captain Fairbrother.

> *Believe me &c*
> *Holderness*

A handsome communication, thought Hervey, and no easy thing for a proud man to write. What, however, did it change? What *ought* it to change? He had done his duty, just as he would expect of any man (even unto death . . .). Did he now look to reward for doing his duty? What was become of him . . .? But what manner of system was it that could not promote ability unless it were allied to interest? Why did these things have to be redressed too late, at the price of brave men's breasts? It had been so in the Peninsula; and ever since peace had come to Europe it had been even more so. He would, of course, call on the lieutenant-colonel, as bidden, but he would not do so with any haste, for it were better that more time elapsed, that sentiments be tempered.

He next read Kat's, and with some trepidation. He hoped against hope for a line that would overturn Howard's final intelligence, a sudden announcement of Sir Peregrine's 'indisposition', but the letter was merely an invitation for him and Fairbrother – whom she wished very much to meet – to dine with her as soon as they were able.

He then pondered a moment on which of the remaining letters to open next. Fancying he knew what Elizabeth's would say at last (and he would wish the time to savour it), he chose that in the unfamiliar hand.

'Hear this, Fairbrother – the deucedest thing,' he said, taking in its contents at a glance, a single sentence. *'My dear Sir, if you would call at the rooms of Sir Thomas Lawrence P.R.A. of Russell-square, you might learn something to your advantage.'* He lowered the letter. 'The stuff of theatre, eh?'

Fairbrother's brow furrowed. *'The* Sir Thomas Lawrence?'

'Just so. I wonder if Somervile did indeed sit for him before we left for the Cape. He certainly had ambitions in that direction. He said nothing of it, though.'

'Mystery indeed,' said Fairbrother, raising his *Standard* again.

Hervey was wrong in his imagining what were the contents of Elizabeth's letter, however. Indeed, he had wholly misjudged it. Far from acknowledging her fault and reaffirming her acceptance of Peto's proposal, she wrote that she was travelling to London soon in the company of Major Heinrici to attend a levee at St James's Palace, which the King was giving for the former officers of The King's German Legion. 'My God, there's no end to it,' he groaned. 'She's lost all sense of decency!'

Fairbrother lowered his paper, looking pained. 'You are not speaking of your sister?'

'I am. She's coming to London with ... with this German.'

'Well, I'm sure she will do so decorously.'

Hervey seemed not to hear. He shook his head. 'I cannot believe it. I simply cannot believe it.'

They engaged a hackney cab to Russell Square. It was Fairbrother's idea – to take his friend out of the huff and puff of the United Service's smoking room so that he might stop his most unfraternal invective against Elizabeth. The letter from Sir Thomas Lawrence's agent had admirably served his purpose.

'It really would have been better to send word that we would

217

call tomorrow,' said Hervey as they turned into Bedford Square, where the Somerviles had taken a house when Sir Eyre Somervile had been at the Company's headquarters in Leadenhall Street: was it that Sir Thomas Lawrence's rooms were so near that he had been able to prevail on the illustrious painter?

'I rather imagined you'd be detained at the Colonial Office – don't you think?'

Hervey nodded. He ought perhaps to have gone that day, but the summons had carried no particular urgency. And in any case, he did not suppose that the under secretary would be at office of a May afternoon.

When they arrived at Russell Square they were admitted promptly and received by a Mr Archibald Keightley, who had sent the note. 'I am sorry that Sir Thomas himself is not at home today, but I am his confidential agent.'

Hervey had abandoned his earlier distemper, and was now thoroughly intrigued. 'How did you learn of my address?'

The agent showed them into a sitting room, and asked the footman to bring tea. 'It has, I admit, been a considerable labour.' He went on to explain how he had consulted the Army List, had written to the Horse Guards, then the Regiment at Hounslow, and then to the Cape Colony, but had lately read in *The Times* that there was to be an inquiry into the events at Waltham Abbey and that Colonel Hervey was returned to London to give evidence to the court. 'It was then but a morning's work to locate you at the United Service Club.'

Tea was brought.

Hervey inferred that the matter could not be in connection with Somervile's aspiring commission, but could see little point in proceeding as if it were a game. 'Well, sir, perhaps you will be good enough to inform me of the reason for such a prodigious effort to find me.'

'Ah yes, indeed; forgive me.' He glanced at Fairbrother. 'It is
. . . a very *delicate* matter.'

Hervey smiled indulgently. 'I assure you Captain Fairbrother is
capable of the utmost delicacy.'

'What I meant to say was that it is of a very . . . *personal*
nature.'

Hervey had a sudden, and ghastly, premonition of an outrageous jape of Kat's. But having expressed his confidence in
Fairbrother he could hardly exclude him now. 'Proceed, sir,' he
said, cautiously.

Mr Archibald Keightley cleared his throat. 'Very well. For
some years past I have been making a catalogue of Sir Thomas's
work. You will understand that a painter of Sir Thomas's
eminence is much in demand, and has been so for two decades
and more. By the very nature of portraiture individual commissions proceed at different rates, depending as much on the
sitter's availability as the artist's. Some canvases remain only very
partially finished for years.'

'I did not know it, but I perfectly understand,' replied Hervey,
laying down his cup. 'There is, I take it, such a canvas that is of
interest to me?'

Keightley cleared his throat again. 'I believe there may be, yes.'

The footman and another returned carrying a full-length
canvas covered with a dust sheet.

'Ah, here we have it. Colonel Hervey, rather than prolong
this with explanations, I would that you first saw this un-
completed work.' He nodded to the footman, who let drop the
sheet.

Hervey gasped. He stood up, his mouth open, the colour gone
from his face. 'My God!'

Fairbrother took his arm in support, knowing instinctively who
was the artist's subject.

Keightley sighed. 'I am sorry that it should come as so great a

219

shock, Colonel; but I am gratified that my enquiries have not been in vain. It is, then, a true likeness?'

Hervey shook his head slowly. 'It is the most astonishing likeness I ever saw.'

Fairbrother saw that his eyes were filled with tears.

Hervey sat down again, still transfixed by the canvas. 'In all these years I never had her true likeness – not a miniature, not even a pencil drawing.' (The posthumous miniature he had had done in Bath had been a poor substitute.)

In a while, when he had composed himself, he asked what was known of the commission.

Keightley opened his notebook, but scarcely needed to consult it. 'Sir Thomas keeps very particular records of his work. The portrait was commissioned in 1816 – while Sir Thomas was waiting to travel to Vienna to paint the Congress – and there were four sittings, the fourth in February of 1817, which is why the face and hands are complete. For the rest of the portrait, as you see, there is a very serviceable drawing: Lady Henrietta was, apparently, most particular that it should be a blue riding habit of hers, which she was either unwilling or unable to leave with Sir Thomas. Which, I imagine, is the reason it was unfinished before . . . before . . .' He cleared his throat again.

'Just so,' said Hervey softly, nodding.

1816: it was while he was in India the first time, the year before their marriage. Henrietta intended it – evidently – as a present for him, which his return to England the following year, and the wedding, and then . . . had stood in the way of completing.

He swallowed hard. 'But I am astonished it has remained for so long thus.'

Keightley inclined his head, with a sigh that spoke of his own regret. 'Sir Thomas travelled to Vienna in 1818 and stayed there, and in Rome, two years. You may imagine the work awaiting his return.'

Indeed he could, and if the sitter were not pressing him . . . He shook his head once more. 'Well, it is the most extraordinary thing I ever knew. Tell me, Mr Keightley, what is to be done now?'

Sir Thomas's agent consulted his notebook. 'Forgive me, Colonel, but I assume you mean the pecuniary arrangements?'

Hervey was thinking more of the completion of the portrait. 'Go on.'

'The fee was four hundred pounds, and Lady Henrietta paid two hundred on account.'

'Naturally I will pay the balance. Do the terms remain the same; or is there increase? It *can* be completed, can it not?'

'There is no increase, Colonel. In the circumstances Sir Thomas would not hear of it.' (Hervey would learn later that the President of the Royal Academy's fee was now seven hundred guineas.) 'And yes, it can be completed by a pupil. I do not suppose that the particular blue riding habit is to hand, but—'

'I . . .' (he could not – or would not – bring himself to recall its whereabouts) 'I think I may be able to . . . arrange something.'

'Very well, sir.'

He recovered himself somewhat. 'And . . . I should like very much that Sir Thomas himself makes a copy of the head and shoulders.'

The agent looked doubtful. 'Sir Thomas has a great many commissions to detain him, Colonel Hervey. But a pupil could execute a very faithful copy.'

'No, I should like the hand of the man for whom my late wife sat.'

Keightley looked troubled, but recognized the powerful sentiment. 'I shall most certainly see what can be done, Colonel.'

They walked back to the United Service. Fairbrother had taken note of the route by which they had driven to Russell Square, and when Hervey, whose mind was unquestionably elsewhere, said that he would like to take a little exercise – by which Fairbrother supposed he meant air – he was perfectly able to conduct his friend to Charles Street. They exchanged scarcely a word in the best part of the hour that it took them to negotiate the pedestrians and hawkers, horses and conveyances, which at times conjoined into a solid barrier to movement. When they reached the club they ordered hot baths, agreeing that they would dine quietly, and requested two well-chilled bottles of hock to be sent upstairs.

At eight o'clock they took a table by an open window onto the street. 'I am conscious we have not had much entertainment since we came here,' said Hervey absently, seeing the line of carriages waiting to deposit their occupants at the Theatre Royal in the Haymarket.

'I'm sure there will be opportunity,' replied Fairbrother, seeking to reassure him; he was most conscious, still, of their encounter with the past in Russell Square.

A waiter brought them the menu. This was the day of the month that it changed, although there remained the staple of grills. But Hervey had little appetite for study, and when Fairbrother said he favoured the turbot and then cutlets, he was content merely to follow.

'And to drink, gentlemen?' asked the wine steward when their order was taken.

Fairbrother looked to Hervey, in part to tempt him back to the here and now. But Hervey seemed unable to make the effort. 'Continue with the hock, I think ... and a burgundy, perhaps. Might you choose for us, James?'

The wine steward made various suggestions; Hervey nodded inconclusively, until the steward saw that he must take the choice upon himself.

When he was gone, Hervey sighed and shook his head. 'You

will forgive me, Fairbrother: I do not think I may confess it to any other man ... but the painting ... it was the most thoroughgoing shock to me.'

Fairbrother smiled sympathetically. 'Of course, Hervey; of course.'

'I have her picture in my mind's eye still with easy facility; I always have had. But to see her likeness so, standing wholly independent of any effort of imagination ...'

'It is as if she were here yet.'

'Exactly so, exactly so.' Hervey shook his head slowly, emphasizing his disbelief that it could be thus. 'It is a very trite thing to speak of seeing a ghost. I have seen no ghost, Fairbrother. I saw her as if flesh and blood.'

Fairbrother showed not the least discomfort in either the intimacy or the sentiment. He nodded, gently, to reassure his friend. 'I am sure.'

They began their supper with potted shrimps and desultory conversation. Fairbrother was ever patient, however. Here was not the man he had ridden with at the Cape; here was a man fettered, almost paralysed. For his friend, it seemed to him, was bound by a notion of duty that had run too far – in the case of regiment, so far as to render him (perhaps for ever) a mere compliant; and in the case of private affairs it impelled him down a road to nowhere he could rightly wish to be (certainly not to the peace he sought). But how might these things be spoken of? He had tried, and his friend had shown scant inclination to hear. Did he, Hervey, know these things already, and yet find himself unable to do what he knew he must? Was 'duty' but a refuge? But from what (he had seen no want of courage at the Cape)?

The turbot was brought, which provoked some talk of the sea, and inevitably of Peto. Fairbrother was dismayed at the vehemence, still, with which Hervey spoke of Elizabeth's

223

intentions. Here, too, was a distortion of duty. He tried once more to moderate his friend's opinion, but with not the least success.

The cutlets, with a very good Marsala sauce, provided a quarter of an hour's respite (they spoke of what they might see at the theatre), but the savoury of smoked oysters somehow provoked mention of the court of inquiry. Another bottle of burgundy was brought.

A stew of apples partly restored Hervey's spirits, so that he began speaking with evident pleasure of the invitation to dine with Kat, assuring Fairbrother that the evening was bound to be diverting, for Lady Katherine Greville presided at the most excellent of soirées.

It had become dark outside, but for the street lamps, though it was still warm, even balmy – like an early summer's evening at the Cape. Hervey asked his friend if he would like port or more burgundy with his Stilton. Fairbrother chose port, and a bottle was decanted.

Hervey poured a little carelessly, so that he had to dab at the table cloth with his napkin. 'Damned glass too small!'

'Or the hand unsteady: I am glad you do not point a Cape rifle above my head!'

The Cape Riflemen practised by holding targets thus for their fellows to snipe. Hervey and Fairbrother had even practised the same.

'Or a bow?'

Fairbrother smiled the more. There had been archery one afternoon at Walden (Kezia was a considerable proficient), at which neither of them had distinguished themselves. 'Especially a bow!'

They dug into the Stilton with renewed appetite, replenishing their glasses, remarking on this or that, Hervey no longer so low in spirits. At length he put down his glass, and eyed his friend in some earnest. 'You found Walden agreeable, did you not?'

224

Fairbrother was at once all attention. 'Walden is, indeed, a most agreeable place.'

Hervey hesitated. 'I mean, you found ... you found my affianced ... you approve of her?'

Fairbrother was troubled by the turn of conversation. 'My dear fellow, what can possess you to ask me such a question?'

'You have made no remark on it.'

Fairbrother was momentarily in some confusion: he had indeed made no remark; it was undeniable. 'Would you expect me to?' he asked in a tone of surprise, hoping thereby to throw his friend off any scent – false or otherwise. 'Forgive me, Hervey, if I have not congratulated you.'

'I would have been glad of your good opinion,' Hervey said, a little unsteadily, the wine at length having its effect.

Fairbrother had perhaps drunk more, but he had begun the evening with his sensibility unimpaired. He sighed.

'Why do you sigh?'

'There is no good reason.'

'Is there *any* reason?'

Fairbrother studied his friend intently. They had not known each other long in the usual measure of things, but the fellowship of the veld, the common cause against Xhosa and Zulu, made for the most singular bond between them. And if he was to be true to that bond, he must speak his mind now, for there would scarce be better opportunity.

'My dear friend,' he began, reluctantly, laying down his glass. 'I have something to say which may at first give offence, but which yet I must say and trust that you will hear with every certainty that I say it only out of the very deepest affection for you.'

Hervey looked at him uncertainly. 'Why indeed might I take offence?'

Fairbrother sighed again, trying manfully, however, to keep the

225

sigh to himself. 'Hear me, Hervey. I am your good friend.
Were I to know there was another who could claim a better connection I should be glad to let him have the responsibility, but I
do not. I believe I know your mind on a great many things, and
I may say also your heart. I have observed you keenly these past
weeks, and I observed Lady Lankester too . . .'

'What is it you say? Come, man!'

'It is perfectly clear to me that this marriage is ill conceived.'

Hervey made at once to protest, but Fairbrother held up a
hand. 'Hear me, Hervey. Do me the honour – nay, courtesy – of
listening to my opinion, for you have sought it.'

Hervey sat back in his chair, his eyes narrowed.

'For Lady Lankester I cannot speak, though I am equally sure
of her feelings. For your part, I have not the slightest doubt that
you will make of her a fine commanding officer's wife, and the
equal figure of a mother for your daughter—'

He lifted a hand again to stay another protest.

'But in a few years' time – perhaps more than a few, but it must
be so eventually – you will meet another with whom your true
feelings shall be engaged, and being the man you are you will be
unable to act on them. But you will never be happy. Neither do
I believe shall she.'

Hervey rose. 'You forget yourself, sir!' he said coldly.

Several heads turned, but Fairbrother took no notice.

'I trust I do not. I trust I speak as a true friend.'

Hervey threw down his napkin. 'You have not the slightest
notion of what you speak!'

Fairbrother held the angry scowl defiantly, and then Hervey
stalked from the room like a goaded beast.

At nine the following morning, as Fairbrother lay half asleep, a
tray of tea beside his bed and *The Times* unopened, there was
a knock at the door. 'Yes,' he called wearily.

Hervey opened the door, cautiously. He was fully dressed, and with all the appearance of one who had been so for some hours.

The valet had half drawn the curtains; Fairbrother squinted in the bright sunlight, and groaned. 'What? Is the building afire? Do the Zulu attack? I did not hear "alarm".'

'I was awake before dawn, and rose early.'

'Then you're a deuced fool.' He turned away from the door.

'I had not slept well. I cannot bear to lie abed if I am awake.'

'But there's no cause to inflict your peculiar regimen on others.'

'I've been to Russell-square.'

Fairbrother at once turned, and raised himself on an arm, eyes open. 'Why?' he asked, quietly.

'I believe you know the answer.'

'Did they admit you at such an hour?'

'Yes. The housekeeper was very obliging. I did not stay long – just long enough to look at the painting again.'

Fairbrother was now sitting upright. He poured himself tea, lukewarm. 'And did you walk away from Russell-square the more composed?'

Hervey pulled up a chair and sat down. 'In a sense, yes. There was not the shock of first seeing it, naturally. But, you know, she's still there.'

'What do you mean by that exactly?'

Hervey's brow furrowed as he sought the words to explain. 'These past few years – these past five years, I suppose, the time in India principally – the memory has receded. Not so much receded, as ... Well, what I mean is that I do not think of her hour to hour as first I did, or even day to day. And there have been some weeks when I do not believe I thought of her at all, though they were exceptional – when we were in the field, or some such. And yet when I *did* think of her it was with un-diminished force. Do you understand me?'

Fairbrother nodded. 'I do,' he said, tenderly.

227

'And this painting . . . It is such a likeness that she might be there in the room.'

Fairbrother sighed. 'And so what is it that you conclude?'

Hervey shook his head. 'My dear fellow, I am most excessively sorry for what I said last night. It troubled me greatly as I lay awake, as much as did thoughts of the painting.'

Fairbrother leaned forward, as if to make a greater contact. 'Hervey, no man ought to hear such a thing as I said, any more than a man ought to say it. My disquiet can be naught to yours, however. Think nothing more of it.'

'You are very good,' said Hervey, forcing a sad smile. 'I do not believe there is a man in my own regiment with whom I could speak so freely – on any matter. Indeed, I am certain of it.'

Fairbrother smiled by return. 'Of course; it must be so. There, a man ever stands in relation to another as subordinate or superior. Except the cornets, naturally, among whom seniority is like virginity among whores. And you are no longer a cornet.'

Hervey smiled ruefully. 'No, indeed, I am no longer a cornet.'

'And so?'

He shook his head. 'That is the point, my friend: I am no longer a cornet.'

Now Fairbrother shook his head. 'I'm sorry, dear one: you lose me.'

'I am a field officer – major, with a half-colonel's brevet, and, I flatter myself, prospects of substantive promotion. I have a daughter, and no wife, but the prospect of marrying a good woman.'

Fairbrother sighed inly. A sleepless night and a brisk morning's walk had evidently done little for his friend's powers of apt intro-spection. 'Hervey, I know you to be a most honourable man, with the most honourable of intentions . . .'

Hervey held up a hand. These were deep waters – waters he had never before trodden. There were strange forces at work in

228

such depths; he did not trust himself to remain afloat, let alone make headway. But he had freely entered those waters, had he not? In truth, had he not long craved this new-found intimacy, even without knowing that he did? 'Fairbrother, I can scarce say the words, for they will, I know, dismay you the more – and why should I care about that? – but I have asked Lady Lankester to marry me, and she has accepted me. That is, truly, an end to it.'

Fairbrother shook his head. 'You do dismay me. You play the Stoic: you would beat out your brains to prove your virtue!'

'And what, precisely, do you mean by that?'

'I mean precisely what I said last night; no more, no less. Hervey, I have seen the way you look at Lady Lankester – she is an uncommonly attractive woman – but it is plain that there is insufficient love between the two of you. And it will not serve, I tell you.'

'And I repeat that I have asked for Kezia's hand, and she has accepted me. It would be unsupportable to consider otherwise now.'

Fairbrother's face was a picture of incredulity. 'You would proceed knowing that you were in error?'

'That is to distort what I said. Once we are married—'

'*Is* it to distort what you said? I cannot think so. Your sister has the wisdom and courage to recognize her error and to act on it, and yet you who have had so many years the habit of such wisdom and courage – where it touches indeed on other men's lives as well as your own – all *you* can do is be a philosopher!'

'I am resolved to make the best of things and to do my duty. Is that so very bad?'

'It is not so much very bad as improbable.'

'Perhaps in *your* philosophy.'

'And doubtless there will be "Kat of my consolation",' said Fairbrother, half beneath his breath.

'*What?*'

'Go and read your Shakespeare! He will tell you a good deal more of humanity than will *your* philosophers!'

Hervey left Fairbrother to his barber while he himself went on foot to Golden Square, to number 33 Great Pulteney Street, the premises of Mr John Broadwood and Sons, piano-makers to His Majesty King George IV &c. He had been once before, to buy a piano for Georgiana, and it had cost him twenty-eight guineas. This morning it was his intention to buy something altogether more substantial, a wedding present that would both delight his bride and express his admiration – and consideration – for her playing. He knew that the cost of such a piano – a grand, such as Herr Schubert himself would be pleased to sit at – would be rather greater, but he had no very good idea of by how much.

The demonstrator at the showroom quite understood that Hervey himself did not play, and endeavoured to tell him of the considerable improvements of late in the construction of the concert-grand pianoforte – the solid bars in combination with the fixed metal string-plate, the compressed-felt hammers, and so on and so on. And since, he explained, compositions for the pianoforte were now of greater range, it was *de rigueur* to have an instrument of six octaves, from bottom C to seventh octave F. Hervey supposed he understood that such innovations were necessary in a pianoforte to be played by someone of Kezia's proficiency. He also wished for an instrument of appropriate beauty for his wife to sit at, and recognized therefore that rosewood was the very least he could choose for the case. The demonstrator took careful note of his requirements (the pianoforte was to be portered to Hanover Square, and thence, sometime in the autumn, shipped to the Cape Colony), and retired to his desk to render a quotation for all but the cost of the shipping room.

A few minutes later, it was in Hervey's hands. He studied the figures carefully, trying to recall by how much they exceeded what he had imagined. 'A hundred and eight guineas,' he said pensively.

'We ask for a deposit of ten per cent, sir; the balance to be paid within twenty-eight days of delivery.'

Hervey nodded, then sat down at the writing desk to arrange the transaction.

He walked back from Golden Square distinctly light-headed. Within the past twenty-four hours he had committed himself to very nearly a year's pay for canvas and rosewood. But it was done, and he did not regret it. He could not, in all honour, have done other than pay the balance on the portrait of Henrietta, and arrange for its completion, for where otherwise might it have been disposed? It was only right, too, that Georgiana should know her mother thus. There had once been a very pleasing portrait of her at Longleat, head and shoulders, when she had been eighteen, but that had perished one evening when the sconce candle had guttered too much and the varnish had taken alight quicker than anyone saw.

And, in truth, he wished the portrait for himself. Where it might hang, and the copy, he had no idea, though even as he walked he began realizing that the question was not principally aesthetic.

As for the pianoforte, that was an expense of an entirely proper instinct. He could think of no better way of displaying his regard for his new wife. It was a token of that regard and, too, a means of cementing their affection. Fairbrother simply did not understand these things: intention could perfectly properly precede success in the marriage state. *No*, he had not the slightest regret in visiting Mr Broadwood's. He was, in fact, prodigiously pleased. There was almost a spring in his step as he turned purposefully into Regent Street to head for the office of the Secretary of State for War and the Colonies, whither Howard's letter had bidden him. It amused him, even, to think that he had deferred calling at Downing Street in order to visit a piano-maker, and he smiled at the memory of how far he had come in so many things since first he had visited the Horse Guards, all of a dozen years ago.

Hervey did not keep a journal except when he was in the field. There were too many things he would have to write, yet which, having neither the language nor the will, he knew he would be unable to set down. For whom would he write a journal, indeed?

He had not considered the question much when first he began writing, in Spain, as a mint-new cornet in Sir John Moore's army, for every officer had kept a journal. He had vaguely supposed that it was filial duty of some sort. And then much later, in India, the habit long established, he had vaguely supposed it some sort of testament, to be given to Georgiana in the event that he did not return.

Except that it was testament only to events: it said next to nothing of his inner life, nor indeed of that part of his external life that he considered unedifying. There was no mention of Vaneeta, who perhaps more than anyone or anything had brought him back to some measure of a full life. He occasionally found himself wishing he had her image rather than merely a lock of that shining, raven hair.

Vaneeta had been kind to him from the very first, unconditionally (the pecuniary business had soon become not a matter of obligation but of desire); she had ministered to him in his convalescence after Rangoon, fiercely protective; and then there had been the terrible parting, when he had almost lost his head, thinking to declare that he would not leave her – and it had seemed as if she might throw herself from the walls of Fort William when the day came for the regiment to leave.

There came a terrible griping, rats scrambling in his stomach. They told him what he would not otherwise hear: that things were not finished simply because he decided they were. He quickened his step, as if somehow he might leave the uncertainty behind, or advance the sooner to that day in June when all would at last be resolved and he would be a married man once more, with the simple certainties that came with his vows, and the knowledge that he did his best for a daughter he had hitherto neglected; *and*, he must admit (not admit, so much, as devoutly wish for), an end at last to the wretched, unholy desire that had so often warped and twisted him like the sapling in a gale.

18 June: this was the day that Kezia had named, a Wednesday – Waterloo Day. He understood, now, the precision with which the day of the wedding was named by a bride: he would not, as he had with Henrietta, ask that she consider another for the sake of regimental convenience. He smiled as he recalled Henrietta's exasperation, the first time he had seen her in the least discomfited, when after he had shown no understanding she had blushed and lowered her eyes and said 'Do not have me spell it out!' No, this time there would be no such callowness. Even though it would mean that not all of the officers would be able to come – Waterloo would be celebrated in some style, and by all ranks, at Hounslow – he would not raise the slightest objection.

And on Sunday next he would go to divine worship at St George's in Hanover Square, and hear the banns read for the first time: 'I publish the Banns of Marriage between Kezia . . .' (he did not know her other names) 'Lankester, widow, of the parish of All Saints, St Paul's Walden, in the diocese of London, and Matthew Paulinus Hervey, widower of the parish of St John the Baptist, Horningsham, in the diocese of Salisbury . . .'

He had given his father's as his parish, for his name was on the roll there still, and inasmuch as he thought of anywhere as home it was Horningsham. Soon, though, he would be able to think of home as the Cape Colony, and then (dare he imagine it?) Hounslow. The place did not matter: wherever Kezia was would be his home from now on. It was comfort indeed. Comfort of unconscionable measure. How *could* Fairbrother be expected to understand it?

XV

THE IMMORTAL MEMORY

The Ionian, the twentieth day at sea, 18 October 1827

Peto's launch cut through the light swell with the ease of a knife through fresh-churned butter. The same midshipman of the golden locks and fine, if boyish, features who had brought him aboard *Rupert* at Gibraltar kept the stroke sharp by the set of his jaw and the steely resolve in his blue eyes. For not only was his captain in the boat, they approached the flagship, and in all probability the admiral watched their boatwork.

Peto himself was less concerned with the crew's stroke, or for that matter with the admiral who might be watching from the quarterdeck of His Majesty's Ship *Asia*. Rather was he intrigued by *Asia*'s appearance, for he had not seen her like before, except in the Surveyor's draught. At two cables' length he was able to observe her very clearly, and what he saw, he had to admit, he did not much like. She had been teak-built three years before at Bombay to a new design, and although in many respects she looked like any other two-decker, she carried ten more guns than the 74, her stern was round, and it positively bristled with chasers. But an ugly stern, thought Peto, with unseamanlike bowed lights, and altogether too brassy a gallery: more like a gin shop, he reckoned.

Stronger, though, he had to admit, this rounded framing. And those sternchasers: no impudent frigate could rake her with impunity.

At a cable's length he lowered his telescope; he did not want to be observed scrutinizing the flagship, as if he were a boy or a landlubber. He did not know Codrington well – he had met him but half a dozen times – although he was unquestionably the better acquainted with him for the company of his youngest daughter these past three weeks. Codrington, however, had been in command of *Orion* at Trafalgar, when Peto had been a midshipman (passed for lieutenant); they were both, therefore, if not of *the* brotherhood, then of that dwindling fraternity which admitted none its equal save perhaps that of Waterloo.

Trafalgar: in three days' time they would be toasting 'The Immortal Memory'. And he would be proposing it aboard his own ship, a three-decker in the very image of *Victory*. Except, of course, the admiral would by then have transferred his flag to *Rupert*, and it would be his to propose the toast. No matter: Codrington was no Nelson, but it would be honour indeed to have his flag fly at the foremast.

Peto sighed. First, of course, there was the little question of *Miss* Codrington. It was astonishing to him that in a fortnight's beating up to the Ionian they had encountered not one of His Majesty's ships, nor even a trustworthy merchantman, to which this precious cargo could be transferred. How different it was from those great and glorious Trafalgar days when a signal might be repeated the length of the Mediterranean with speed and facility. He exaggerated, naturally; it was the way with men of war who had not yet come fully to terms with peace. Except that, to his mind, it was more the case that parliament had not come to terms with the true nature of peace. What said Thucydides? – *Peace is but a cessation of hostilities in a war that is never-ending.* And so, just as his old friend Hervey complained of the reductions in the army, parliament now resented 'ship

236

money'. It was no longer an insurance policy – keeping the wooden walls in good repair; it was like paying a chimney tax in high summer. He huffed. Well, there would be a brig or some such in Codrington's squadron by which Rebecca and the women could be conveyed to Malta; and with any luck it might be done within a day, everything ordered in a proper seamanlike fashion, so that *Rupert* might take her proper place, flying blue from the foremast, at the van of the squadron.

Asia was hove to in the lightest of airs, and the midshipman steered Peto's launch to windward, the larboard side. Peto was visiting without ceremony, and it made not a deal of difference by which entry port he came aboard. Using the weather to bring and fasten the boat alongside the more securely was exactly as he himself would have done: he would certainly appreciate it when it came to reaching for the ladder.

'Easy, oars!'

The launch's crew stopped pulling.

'Boat your oars!'

Inboard they came.

'Up!'

Up they went smartly; the midshipman put the tiller a fraction more to larboard and brought the launch scraping gently amidships. One of the crew seized the lower step, and the launch fastened limpet-like to *Asia*'s side.

Peto was on his feet in a trice, reaching confidently for the steps – narrow, weed-tangled, wooden rungs, all that stood between a dignified boarding and a watery one. The weed was cold as well as slimy. He knew to expect it; he had done it so many times, the climb was without trepidation. The trick was to think of nothing but what hands and feet were doing, step by step, rung by rung, until he got hold of the ropes – and even then to think only of climbing, without looking up, and not of the reception which awaited him.

Two mates reached out to support him into the entry port, the boatswain's pipes twittered, Peto adjusted his hat, saluted the quarterdeck, and with a few expressions of 'good morning, gentlemen', followed the first lieutenant to the apartment of Sir Edward Codrington, Vice Admiral of the Blue, Commander-in-chief Mediterranean Station.

'My dear Sir Laughton, I am much gladdened by your arrival!'

The admiral greeted him with a ready smile and a hearty handshake. Sir Edward Codrington was tall – by several inches over Peto – almost bald, and with a noble, humane face which quite belied his reputation for pugnacity in action. Peto was at once assured of his welcome. It had been many years since they had last met, and in the navy these things mattered. Since Nelson's day – even before – an admiral gathered his favourites about him, men he could trust to place themselves to advantage in battle, or to know what would be his will in some affair conducted beyond sight of the fleet. He, Peto, had never been one of Codrington's men. 'Sir Edward, I'm honoured to join your flag.'

'Then join me too in a glass of Marsala,' was the easy response. 'Sit you down. You are come most carefully upon your hour.'

Peto sat as the steward poured. 'We are come later than I had wished, Sir Edward, for we were obliged to run down into Surt before a storm as violent as any I saw here. I thought I should be blown to Alexandria.'

Codrington raised a hand to say that it was the way of things. 'No matter. You are here now. Tomorrow I shall have my captains come aboard and I shall tell you my design.'

'Ay-ay, Sir Edward. But if I may, there is a pressing matter. Your daughter, Miss Rebecca, is aboard my ship. She and her maid joined at Gibraltar, but since I was obliged to run south of Malta I was not able to transfer her to shore, and neither have I encountered any vessel since to which I could entrust her.'

238

The admiral looked as if he had not heard quite right. 'The deucedest thing!'

'She occupies your apartment, of course, Sir Edward. I wondered when you might have a sloop or other to take her to Malta. And when you yourself wish to transfer your flag.' Peto omitted to mention the other women on board: that was a detail best not troubled over now. He would simply put them aboard whatever it was the admiral detached for the duty, and no one but her master need be the wiser.

The admiral still looked distant. 'The deucedest thing indeed, for her youngest brother is midshipman with me. He stands watch as we speak. I shall send him back with you, and then, if you will, in an hour or so you may send him back in turn.'

'Sir Edward.'

'And *Firefly* will be returned tomorrow – she's taking instructions to General Church the other side of the Morea – and then she can take Rebecca to Malta along with my despatches.'

Peto nodded. 'And your flag, Sir Edward?'

The admiral shook his head. 'I intend no change – not at this late hour. You'll see my method when I have the rest of the captains aboard tomorrow.'

'Ay-ay, sir,' replied Peto, trying not to sound too dismayed. 'Shall you come aboard *Rupert* to see Miss Rebecca before then?'

The admiral shook his head again, and with something of a look which said that he was surprised. Not many months ago Peto himself would have scorned it, but now he was discomfited by the notion that Sir Edward Codrington could reject the opportunity of seeing a daughter – especially a daughter with such evident intelligence, and pride in her father. 'She will be vastly disappointed, Sir Edward.'

The admiral's mouth fell open. 'I do not doubt it, Sir Laughton. But I fear I cannot oblige her. We are about to undertake a most delicate manoeuvre at Navarin. One, indeed, which is likely to have no other outcome but a fierce exchange of shot. I cannot go calling on a daughter!'

Peto felt himself thoroughly chastened, but by no means abashed. 'I could send her to you in my launch, Sir Edward. Midshipman Codrington might escort her.'

The admiral now looked faintly indignant. 'My dear Captain Peto, I cannot disrupt a ship of war at such a time. And I have Admiral de Rigny to attend to.'

Peto saw perfectly well that having to deal with a French admiral was vexation enough without the distraction of petticoats. He concluded that he could not press his commander-in-chief further on the matter. Rebecca would, after all, be seeing her brother. 'Then I must beg pardon, Sir Edward.'

'There is no cause to do so, I assure you, Sir Laughton. My daughter is well, I trust?'

Peto smiled a shade wryly. 'She is very well indeed, Sir Edward. I believe she was almost glad to be blown south of Malta, for she expresses a great desire to see your squadron.'

The admiral nodded. 'She has spirit, but I am afraid I am unable to oblige her in that too, for I must have *Rupert* stand out well to the west. I do not wish the Turks see her before it is opportune. I shall explain my purpose tomorrow when the other captains are assembled.'

Peto noted for the first time a certain heaviness in the admiral's manner of expression. It could not have been anxiety for the outcome of any exchange of fire (there could be no doubt of the superiority of the Royal Navy's gunnery, nor indeed that of the French and the Russians, compared with the Turks and Egyptians), and he was therefore inclined to ascribe it to the uncertainty of the undertaking as a whole. From what he had learned before he sailed, Codrington's instructions were damnably equivocal.

'By your leave, then, Sir Edward, I will call on my old friend your flag captain and then rejoin my ship.'

* * *

They had no conversation in the launch. Peto wrapped his boat-cloak round himself against the freshening westerly as hands pulled for the *Rupert*. He had much to think on. He was already turning over in his mind what more could be done to put *Rupert* into best trim for Codrington's 'fierce exchange of shot'.

His old friend Captain Edward Curzon, from his closeness to the flag, had been able to tell him a good deal of what had occupied the admiral these past months. The instructions which came from London out of the embassy at Constantinople held that the Ottoman Porte would give up its claim to Greece simply because His Britannic Majesty, and the King of France, and the Tsar of All the Russias required it. Yet His Majesty's ministers would give no unequivocal expression of what should be the course if peaceful persuasion failed. His de facto deputy, de Rigny, Codrington found less than straightforward (could he *ever* trust the French? – there were even French advisors with the Turkish fleet); and Count Heiden – commanding the Russian squadron – was thoroughly spoiling for a fight, for the Tsar's own wish was to see the Turkish navy crippled.

Peto shook his head, and turned instead to observe the other midshipman in the launch. Henry Codrington was a fine-looking youth, not yet twenty, but not long for lieutenant, he supposed. What pride must the admiral have in such a son – and such a daughter indeed. He thought again of Elizabeth, and wondered . . .

The launch ran silent indeed through the heavy swell, not a word from hands or officer, conscious that the captain thought deeply on some matter.

In ten more minutes the boatswain's pipes twittered, and then it was the return scramble to the entry port.

'Convey Mr Codrington to the flag apartment, Mr Sandys,' said Peto to the lieutenant who greeted him at the top.

'Ay-ay, sir.'

'And have my launch ready to convey him back to the *Asia* in one hour, if you please.'

'Ay-ay, sir.'

Peto turned. 'Mr Codrington, be so good as to tea with me in half of one hour, along with your sister.'

'Honoured, sir.'

But Peto did not hear, for he was already taking the companion ladder two steps at a time.

'Mr Lambe!' he rasped as he came onto the quarterdeck.

The first lieutenant came up from the waist directly, and with satisfaction in his expression.

'Evidently you have something agreeable to report, Mr Lambe. Wear away, sir!'

'I have had the upper battery tackle greased again, sir. It gives us five seconds at least.'

Peto nodded approvingly.

'Very well, Mr Lambe: dry gun drills immediately after breakfast, and then divine worship.'

Lambe looked nonplussed. 'Church, sir? But tomorrow is Friday.'

'I am perfectly aware what shall be the day, Mr Lambe, but we have not held divine worship since leaving Gibraltar.' Their lordships were by no means as insistent on Sunday worship as they had been during the late war, and Peto himself had not much affection for parsons afloat, despite his filial loyalty to the profession, but they were all a mite closer to meeting their Creator, now, and on the sabbath next there might be preparations . . . or obsequies. 'A man ought to be able to listen to Scripture and say a few prayers once in a while; and wind and weather have so far conspired to prevent him.'

Lambe understood right enough. 'Ay-ay, sir,' he said, resolutely.

'Have the master-at-arms slaughter the beef. The goats he may spare.'

242

'Ay-ay, sir.'

'And join me, if you will, for dinner, with such others as you judge favourable. It will be the last occasion for Miss Codrington to dine with us. *Firefly* will take her off tomorrow – along with the rest of the women. Though her master doesn't yet know it,' he added dryly.

Lambe touched his hat before returning to the waist to see the batteries secure. Peto cast an eye aloft. He had left *Rupert* hove to with just the fore-topsail to the mast, but with a freshening westerly, Lambe had partially struck the fore and brought her a point into the wind. In a couple of hours or so, when the launch was come back from conveying young Codrington to the *Asia*, he would have the new watch make sail so that he could take station to windward, as the admiral wished. He went to his cabin.

'Tea, if you please, Flowerdew; in half an hour, for Miss Codrington and her brother.'

'Oh, tea is it,' muttered his steward, fancying that life on a line-of-battle ship was becoming a drawing room affair.

'Mr Codrington is midshipman on the *Asia*.'

'Oh, is 'e indeed. A right fam'ly going it is.'

'But the admiral will keep his flag in *Asia* for the time being.'

Flowerdew said nothing, though he was pleased, since an admiral's retinue was bound to be vexing. He began taking out a silver service from one of the lockers under the stern lights.

'And the simnel cake – I think we will have that too.'

'Oh, cake is it. Quite the tea party.'

Peto was unabashed. He would delight unashamedly in the company of sibling affection. He would observe in it, indeed, something of his own future.

Peto heard the knock. He looked at his watch: the timing was exact enough to serve for dead reckoning. He nodded approvingly as Flowerdew opened the steerage door to admit Midshipman Henry and Miss Rebecca Codrington. The brother, hat under his left arm, bowed; Rebecca curtsied. Peto returned their salutes and bid them sit, feeling suddenly awkward, which displeased him, for he was a post-captain and plenty old enough to be Miss Codrington's father.

Flowerdew came to his aid: did Miss Codrington take milk with her tea (the answer he surely knew, for he had served it to her on several occasions)?

She smiled – which Flowerdew had the greatest difficulty in not reflecting – and said that she would.

'My brother tells me that his ship is not so large as this, Captain Peto.'

Rebecca's brother coloured, rather. He himself would never have initiated conversation with a post-captain, and especially not with any comparison of ships, no matter how favourable to the hearer.

Peto saw. 'But the *Asia* is perfectly matched for any fight, Miss Rebecca. You may have no fears on that account.'

'Oh, I had no fears, Captain Peto. It is just that I had thought my father would come aboard your ship, as you suggested he would.'

'He will know his flag captain well by now. Curzon's an excellent fellow. I have known him long.'

'My brother says it is because my father intends entering the place where the Turkish fleet is anchored and compelling them to leave, and he does not wish the *Rupert* to enter.'

'Is that so, indeed?' Peto turned to Henry Codrington with the sort of enquiring look that would have made the stoutest midshipman wish he were at the maintop in a howling gale.

'I . . . That is what I have heard, sir.'

Peto had heard it too. He had deduced as much when the admiral told him he wished for *Rupert* to stand well to the west until the time was right. But he would not let Mr Codrington off the hook so easily. 'Indeed, sir? And what else might you have heard?'

Rebecca did not quite see the game. She looked at her brother enthusiastically. 'Tell Captain Peto about Lord Nelson, Henry!'

Peto turned again to the young Codrington with an air of bemusement, perfectly studied. 'Lord Nelson, Mr Codrington?'

Midshipman Codrington turned a deeper red. He swallowed hard. 'Sir, I have heard that my fa— the admiral intends entering the bay at Navarin on the eve of Lord Nelson's victory at Trafalgar.'

'Indeed?' Peto suppressed the urge to speculate aloud what effect such a celebratory manoeuvre would have on Admiral de Rigny and his French squadron. 'It is only a pity that August is past.'

'Sir?'

'The first of August, Mr Codrington – a bay, the enemy at anchor . . .'

'Oh, indeed, sir: Aboukir, the Nile.'

'Quite, Mr Codrington, *the Nile*.'

Rebecca looked to her brother for edification.

'Go on, Mr Codrington. Explain.'

'The French fleet lay in line at anchor in Aboukir Bay, the mouth of the Nile, and Lord Nelson took his ships into the bay and sailed between the French and the shore, which the French had supposed was not possible, believing it to be too shallow, because of which they had not their guns run out on that side, nor even the gunports open. It was a famous victory.' He looked at Peto for approval of his summary.

'Admirable, Mr Codrington.' He turned to Rebecca again. 'But unlike Aboukir Bay, at the bay of Navarin – your father, I note, prefers the style to "Navarino" – there will be no imperative to destroy any one of the Sultan's ships, only to compel them to leave. No admiral confronted by so great a show of force as your father may dispose, with the French and Russian squadrons, could do other than comply at once, for resistance would be as futile as it would be ruinous.' He did not add, however, that the pride of the Turkish admiral was not to be underestimated. He looked at Flowerdew. 'The cake?'

Flowerdew advanced with his tray.

Peto saw that his steward had not been able to remove quite all of the mould, which seemed always to defy his best efforts, but Midshipman Codrington was too experienced a seaman to notice, and his sister too polite. Peto himself took a hearty mouthful (he had not eaten since breakfast).

'Do I have to leave on the *Firefly* tomorrow, Captain Peto?' asked Rebecca, sounding suddenly rather younger than before. 'I should so like to see our fleet sail into the bay, and the Turkish ships sailing away.'

Peto had taken rather too hearty a mouthful: the request induced a sudden, and somewhat messy, fit of coughing. 'Miss Rebecca, greatly though I – we all – have prized your company these past weeks, I have to tell you that nothing would induce me to prolong that pleasure into a place of active operations. The *Firefly*, though I do not know her, will convey you with considerable speed to Malta.' He spoke decidedly but kindly. 'Is that not so, Mr Codrington?' he added, turning to her brother for assurance, as if his was an opinion of equal rank.

Midshipman Codrington cleared his throat in turn. 'Yes, sir; yes indeed.' He turned to his sister. 'The *Firefly* is a ship-sloop. She is a very good sailer, and Mr Hanson is a very able and gentlemanlike master.'

Peto now smiled, and with some wryness. 'Your quarters, I'm afraid, will be a little more cramped than you have been used to of late. And you shall have to put up with the babbling of the ... wives, that I am also obliged to put off.'

Rebecca brightened. 'Oh, I have no concern for my comfort,

Captain Peto. And I shall be only too glad to make closer acquaintance with the sailors' wives.'

Peto now felt himself turning a little red under what he supposed might be the scrutiny of a brother who knew perfectly well the status of the women below deck, and who must therefore have some instinct to shelter a sister from such coarseness. 'Yes . . . quite . . . Now, when you go aboard *Firefly*, Miss Rebecca, I would have you take letters for me, if you will.'

'Yes, of course, Captain Peto. For Miss Hervey, I imagine?'

Peto felt his face now thoroughly reddening. The enquiry was entirely innocent, for all that it might have been precocious. He cleared his throat noisily. 'Letters to the Admiralty . . . And yes, to . . . Miss Hervey.'

XVI

CLEAR FOR ACTION

Late afternoon the following day, 19 October 1827,
off Navarino Bay

Captain Sir Laughton Peto, second-senior post-captain of the British squadron in the Ionian, clambered up the ladder to *Rupert*'s entry port for the second time in twenty-four hours. The pipes trilled, the marine sentry presented arms, and the boatswain barked 'off hats' as the master of their wooden world, at once weary and yet animated, came inboard, touching his hat to the quarterdeck and nodding his acknowledgement to the first lieutenant's salute.

'Assemble all sea and warrant officers in the admiral's steerage in one half of one hour, Mr Lambe, if you please.'

Lambe walked with him as Peto made for the companion ladder. 'Miss Codrington shall have to wait in your cabin, then, sir. There has been no sign of *Firefly*.'

Peto broke his step momentarily. 'Damnation!'

'I've sent word to the flagship.'

Peto huffed.

'Perhaps we shall have to put the ladies in the boats, sir, instead of the hen coops.'

It was a gallant attempt at humour in the circumstances. Peto turned, to see his lieutenant's ironic half smile. 'I would that I were not made to choose, Mr Lambe.'

'Ay-ay, sir!'

At a quarter to six, Peto entered the admiral's apartments. 'Good evening, sir,' chorused the assembled officers. He returned the courtesy heartily and with a smile. His signal midshipman unrolled a chart on the dining table and weighted down its corners with pieces of lead.

'Gentlemen,' began *Rupert*'s captain, with just the merest expression of drollery, 'a good many of you – perhaps the majority – saw action in the late, "never-ending" war. Well, I tell you, we are about to undertake a *smokeless* action in what our fellow-countrymen touchingly believe is never-ending peace.'

There was a buzz among the officers – a puzzled applause, as well as lively. How might an action be smokeless? Between two ships, with surprise on one side, perhaps; but between *fleets*?

'Gentlemen, your disbelief does you credit. The pertinent word, however, is "undertake". I am myself convinced that an action such as this is bound to precipitate a fight; and I believe that that too is the admiral's opinion, at heart. I wish you therefore to hear the design for tomorrow's endeavour with that possibility – nay, let us not mince our words, *probability* – firmly in mind. For only thus shall you perceive the part which *Rupert* plays in it. Otherwise we might appear to be mere spectators at a fleet review.'

Faces spoke of enthusiasm.

He pointed to the chart. 'Now, see the set of the coast, and the bay of Navarino . . .'

For a full five minutes Peto spoke the language of the sea, so that a midshipman of the most elementary schooling might consider himself able to assume the position of sailing-master – or even pilot. 'You will thus appreciate, gentlemen, why with such prevailing winds the admiral concludes it would be nigh impossible to maintain a blockade through the coming season.'

Heads nodded. It was long years since the Royal Navy had practised blockade, especially winter blockade – storm-tossed ships, ever watchful. Nor, indeed, would blockade prevent a Turkish *army* from marauding in the Morea itself.

'The admiral has therefore concluded, in concert with the French and Russian commanders-in-chief, that the combined squadrons shall enter the bay of Navarino tomorrow – *la mèche à la main*, so to speak – and dispose themselves in such a way as to make clear to the Turkish admiral that he must at once comply with the terms of the ceasefire, and sail his ships to whence they came, Constantinople or Alexandria.'

There was general approbation. Peto nodded to his signal midshipman, who then unrolled another chart, on which was drawn large in charcoal the bay and the dispositions of the Ottoman fleet.

'Gentlemen, you perceive that the admiral's intelligence is most particular.'

They did indeed, for the dispositions were in the greatest detail: every man-of-war by name.

'The Ottoman fleet consists in all of three ships of the Line, each of seventy-four guns, some twenty frigates, thirty or so corvettes, half a dozen brigs or sloops and five fireships. They are arranged in what might be called a horseshoe in the space enclosed by the citadel, the small island, and Sphacteria – which on some charts is rendered "Sphagia".' He indicated each with his finger. 'In the front line, at a distance of about two cables apart, they have moored their battle-ships and most powerful frigates.

In the second line, covering the intervals of the first line, they have placed the rest of the frigates and the most powerful corvettes, these latter being reinforced by a third line of corvettes. There are fireships placed at the two ends of the arc – two of them on the side of New Navarin, and three under the island of Sphacteria, protected by its battery.'

There was much nodding of heads. The Ottoman fleet did not possess so many ships of the Line as the French at the Nile, but the dispositions here were altogether stronger.

'You will perceive, however, that the right wing is rather less powerful than the left. This we may suppose is because the Turks imagine that since the right wing faces the entrance of the bay, the main weight of any attack, taking advantage of the wind, will be directed to the left wing.'

They all nodded.

'Now, gentlemen, Sir Edward Codrington's design . . .'

Peto spoke for a quarter of an hour. He told them that the French admiral would place his squadron abreast of the Egyptian ships to the south-east. These, he said, were the ones on which the French advisors were still embarked. Codrington's own squadron would anchor abreast of the Turkish ships to the west, and the Russian squadron next in succession, the Ottoman 74s each being matched by an allied two-decker. The allies were to moor – supposing there was no hostility committed against them – with spring anchors, just as had the Turks. 'No gun is to be fired from the combined fleet without a signal being made for that purpose,' he added gravely, taking his finger from the chart at last, as if he had come to the end of his orders. 'Unless, that is, shot be fired by a Turk . . . in which case the ships so firing are to be destroyed immediately.'

There was a deal more acclamation, until it dawned on each of the officers that Peto had said nothing of *Rupert*'s place in the enterprise. The quizzical looks returned.

'And so, gentlemen, to our own part. Once the combined fleet has entered the bay, we shall take station at the entrance in such a manner as to suggest that a further squadron of first-rates is disposed ready for action: there'll be sloops showing their tops on the horizon. The Turkish admiral shall therefore be obliged to put from his mind any thoughts of resistance which his mere numerical superiority might tempt.'

The stratagem met with approval.

Peto stepped back from the table. 'I trust thereby that the design is entirely clear, gentlemen?'

Heads nodded.

'Very well. Now, it is possible that these Turks will attempt to quit the bay under cover of darkness, without obligation to leave Greek waters. Lookouts are therefore to be doubled. All hands shall be piped to stations at first light. If there is no signal from the flagship within one hour, I shall have them piped down again, to breakfast. After breakfast we shall clear for action.'

The words 'clear for action' struck home, with relish and apprehension in equal measure on the assembled faces.

'And an extra tot of rum for each man to toast the Immortal Memory!'

'Ay-ay, sir!' they chorused, with a will; there was nothing like an increase in grog to signal fighting intent.

'Carry on, Mr Lambe.'

The lieutenant replaced his hat and touched the point as the captain took his leave accompanied by the signal mid-shipman.

Back in his cabin, Peto sat in the Madeira chair, and began rubbing his chin. 'What say you, Mr Pelham?'

'Sir?'

'What say you the Turks might do to confound this manoeuvre?'

'Sir, I . . .'

'Come, Mr Pelham. You are entitled to your own thoughts on the business, and I would know how you think.'

The midshipman stood rigid.

'Easy, man!'

'Well, sir, it seems to me that in a place of such little sea room, a fireship could do horrible destruction. Is there not a danger the Turk might make a pretence of parleying all day, making ready their fireships the while; then they could set loose a deal of confusion when night came?'

Peto nodded. 'Your thinking does you credit, Mr Pelham. They are precisely my thoughts. The admiral gave no indication of how long he would allow the Turks to quit the bay. He will be aware of the destruction that might follow if the fireships are loosed. But, as you intimate, if the Turks appear to want to parley, it will be devilish hard to call them out.'

'Sir.'

Peto rose, and turned to look out of the stern lights. 'My compliments to Mr Lambe, and have him inform me the instant there is sight of the *Firefly*.'

'Ay-ay, sir.'

'As soon as she comes alongside I wish you to escort Miss Codrington aboard.'

'Ay-ay, sir.'

Peto cleared his throat. 'That is all, Mr Pelham. You may dismiss.'

When he was gone, Peto poured himself a glass of Marsala, and took his copy of Thucydides from the rack. He leafed through it to Book Four, to the events at Pylus – Navarino as now was. The Athenians had been tempted to bring to battle the Lacedaemonians – the Spartans – by landing and erecting defensive works. The historian of the war described the bay in some detail; Peto did not suppose it had changed much in its essentials in the intervening centuries.

Demosthenes, before the coming up of the Peloponnesian fleet, had timely despatched two vessels to Eurymedon, and the Athenians on board that fleet now lying at Zacynthus, pressing them to return as the place was in danger of being lost; which vessels made the best of their way, in pursuance of the earnest commands of Demosthenes. But Lacedaemonians were now preparing to attack the fortress both by land and sea: presuming it would be easily destroyed, as the work had been raised with so much precipitation, and was defended by so small a number of hands. But, as they also expected the return of the Athenian ships from Zacynthus, they designed, in case they took not the place before, to bar up the mouths of the harbour, so as to render the entrance impracticable to the Athenians, for an isle that is called Sphacteria, lying before and at a small distance, locks it up and renders the mouths of the harbour narrow; that near the fortress of the Athenians and Pylus a passage for two ships only abreast, and that between the other points of land for eight or nine. The whole of it, as desert, was overgrown with wood, and quite untrod, and the compass of it at most is about fifteen stadia. They were therefore intent on shutting up these entrances with ships moored close together, and their heads towards the sea. And to prevent the molestation apprehended, should the enemy take possession of this island, they threw into it a body of their heavy-armed, and posted another body on the opposite shore: for by these dispositions the Athenians would be incommoded from the island, and excluded from landing on the main-land: and, as on the opposite coast of Pylus without the harbour there is no road where ships can lie, they would be deprived of a station from whence to succour the besieged: and thus, without the hazard of a naval engagement, it was probable

254

they should get possession of the place, as the quantity of provi-
sions in it could be but small, since the seizure had been executed
with slender preparation . . .

Peto closed the book, thoughtful. The Turks might have occupied the place with slender preparation, and their quantity of provisions might be small, but they had fireships and forts to block up the entrance, not merely the prows of ships placed close together. He began wondering how, if Codrington had to shoot his way into the bay, he could best bring *Rupert*'s superiority in gunnery to bear.

By nightfall, *Rupert* was hove to five leagues to the west and north of the entrance to Navarino Bay. She had beat back to windward during the last two hours of daylight so that if she made leeway during the night her hull would be below the horizon to observers on Sphacteria. There was no sign of *Firefly*.

'The weather's set fair for tomorrow, by the look of it, Mr Lambe,' said Peto, as the first watch came on.

'The glass is high and steady, sir. I believe we might get the women away in the cutter.'

Peto shook his head. 'I cannot put the women in the cutter, Mr Lambe. I wouldn't trust the Greeks, even if I trusted the Turks. There'd be little to choose between a Greek pirate and a mussulman faced with such a catch.'

The appearance of Rebecca Codrington at the companion ladder cut short the discussion.

Lambe touched his hat to her, and Peto a moment later. 'Good evening, Miss Codrington,' they said as one.

Rebecca was smiling, with not the faintest trace of anxiety. 'The *Firefly* must have very important business, Captain Peto. Mr Pelham has told me my father's intentions for tomorrow. I imagine not a ship can be spared, no matter how small.' She sounded delighted.

Peto nodded awkwardly. He had two objections to her other-wise charming company. First, he had no desire to be deflected from any course of action, should battle be joined, by consider-ations for the safety of the commander-in-chief's daughter. Secondly, a ship of the Line in action was so infernal a place as to be unfit for any but the strongest of stomachs (which in truth were not to be found in every man, let alone a female). 'There will be something in the morning, Miss Rebecca, have no fear.'

'Oh, I have no fear, Captain Peto. You need not trouble on my account.'

He had made that mistake before, of using an everyday phrase that might be interpreted literally, and which then was – to disarming effect. He cleared his throat. 'Just so, just so.' He turned to the lieutenant, making a great effort to keep a com-manding countenance. 'Well, Mr Lambe, I believe I shall repair to my log. We dine in one half of one hour.' He turned back to Rebecca, almost reluctantly. 'You will join us, I hope, Miss Codrington?'

'Oh, Captain Peto, I should be most honoured.' Her delight was evident. 'You are to toast the memory of Lord Nelson: I do not suppose there is another of my sex who has observed it on the eve of battle!'

Peto groaned inwardly.

It was the finest of new mornings, even by the standards of the heavenly Ionian. Peto had come on deck shortly after the middle watch stood down, searching for signal lights or some other sign in the moonless early hours before the sun served its first notice of intent – the faintest marbling of the otherwise black wall of the eastern sky. He could see the stern lantern of *Calpe*, sloop, a league and a half east-south-east, standing ready to relay the flagship's signals. He wondered if he might yet transfer the women to her, for there could be no imperative need of her in Navarino Bay ... But, Peto's seniority notwithstanding, *Calpe*'s master would never heed him in this. Not without the flagship's express authority.

Hands had come on deck cheerily, despite being turned from their hammocks early, bantering and capering as if pay were to be had, and shore leave, the prospect of action (for most of them, the first time) a powerful animator to fellowship. They stood lively at their stations, guns or shrouds. Here and there a man mock-flinched at a belay pin which a boatswain's mate pretend-threatened, exchanging the crack with the officers, mouthing ribald encouragement to the marines.

Peto marked it all with satisfaction. It took months as a rule to drill a crew well enough for the fight, and yet in less than one, *Rupert*'s was handy enough. Perhaps if they had met a Frenchman in the glory days, before Trafalgar, or even before Lissa, they would have been hard-pressed to overmatch her in broadsiding, but these were not the glory days – thank God – and the Turk was no Frenchman when it came to admiralty. This was the future: willing volunteers who did their duty ... willingly.

The sun, full clear of the horizon now, was already warm on his face, even on a day when in Norfolk (in the house he would soon truly be able to call home) there would be a fire burning in the grate. Happiest of thoughts! – Miss Elizabeth Hervey before that fire, Lady Peto. For Elizabeth he would be glad to give up all flag ambition, to live peacefully and companionably on half pay in that incomparable county. There too, in due course, he might steal away before first light, as he had as a boy, to behold the sea, what the day brought of wind and wave and sail, never the same sea picture, daily the

257

new in the familiar guise of the old. But those breaks of day (dare he imagine it?) would not be, as before, in his own company alone – nor even in that of Elizabeth – but in the company of one who shared their name, who would grow to maturity in the love of a good mother and the encouragement of a proud father, so that he too in due season might know the wonderful prospect of life that came with a midshipman's collar-patch. *And*, in his turn, that glorious thing which was a post command.

Rebecca came on deck. Peto, standing below the poop on the weather side, braced involuntarily: the crew were at their fighting stations, ready in an instant to clear for action; it was not seemly for a female to be on the quarterdeck. *Nor* on a gun-deck – as now he saw *Rupert*'s women, coming up for their allowance of air. He had given no orders to the contrary, however, and Lambe had evidently not seen fit to cancel their privileges. It was the very devil! Where *was* that sloop?

Peto acknowledged Rebecca's curtsy – no more now than a pause and a bow, in deference to his asking that she did not bend the knee, yet acquitting herself in what she felt most strongly was her obligation as a female, and a subordinate.

He could not quite bring himself to smile, but his intention was warm enough. He so much admired this . . . girl, with her pleas-ing self-possession, intelligence, pluck – and her pride in her father. He thought it the greatest pity that father and daughter could not have met, though he perfectly understood the very proper instincts of a commander-in-chief. Indeed, he trusted that his own would have been no less dutiful; except that – he would freely admit it – since his betrothal to Elizabeth, his judgement in certain matters was not as it had once been. Perhaps he gave way to sentiment, but could he have denied himself the pleasure of an encounter with his own daughter, especially before action? He could not but reflect on how his old friend –

soon to be his brother-in-law – was so happily obligated to *his* daughter.

He raised his telescope again and swept the sunny eastern horizon, and to north and south, stern to bow, in another vain search for the sloop that would take *Rupert*'s women off. He called for his signal midshipman.

Pelham fairly flew down the ladder.

'Make to *Calpe*, "For *Asia*. Where is *Firefly*?"' He said it briskly, trying to conceal his chagrin at having to signal the flagship on a domestic matter when action loomed.

Midshipman Pelham now had the squadron's additional codebook, with each ship allotted a number, so that the signal was a matter of but half a dozen flags and a couple of minutes' work in the hoisting. Nevertheless it was a full quarter of an hour before any reply came, and then it was 'Not understood'.

Peto fumed. 'In God's name, man, what did you make to the flag?'

But Pelham did not flinch. ' "For *Asia*. Where is *Firefly*?", sir.'

Peto glowered. 'I grant you may have a perfect memory, Mr Pelham, but what *flags* did you hoist?'

Lambe was already bounding up the poop deck ladder to prove the reserve codebook for himself. Before Pelham was even halfway to verifying the signal, the lieutenant had Peto's answer. 'Signal is accurate, sir.'

Peto cursed again. 'What in God's name is *Asia*'s flag-lieutenant thinking, then?' Or was it – surely not? – *Calpe* seeking clarification rather than simply repeating? It was her duty, after all, if she could not see the flags clearly enough. But they flew well in this breeze . . . 'Repeat, and make: "For *Asia*, urgent, lady still aboard." '

It was possible, of course, that the flag-lieutenant did not know what the *Firefly*'s special duty was, and therefore had not appreciated the urgency of the enquiry. But unless he believed the signal to be corrupted it was his business to put it to the admiral at once.

It took Pelham rather longer this time, for he had to spell out 'lady' and 'still'. Nevertheless, he managed to get it hoist inside of seven minutes.

The reply, however, was half an hour in the coming, and in the meantime the crew were piped down to breakfast. Peto himself remained on deck the while, determined as he was to have the business concluded before battle was joined – *powderless* battle as may be.

Flowerdew brought him chocolate in a silver pot, on a tray with two other cups and saucers.

'Ask Miss Codrington to join me,' he said gruffly. 'And Mr Lambe.'

Rebecca came at once. 'It is a beautiful morning, is it not, Captain Peto?'

Peto cleared his throat. 'It is indeed, Miss Codrington. I fancy your father will be well pleased with the weather: light airs, just enough to make easy headway without too much sail set – just the thing to enter Navarino Bay.'

'Shall we be able to see it, Captain Peto? We are not so very far away, are we?'

Peto cleared his throat again, and consciously. 'We are some dozen and more miles out. Yon brig, the *Calpe*, stands between us and the fleet, to relay your father's signals. We do not close until we have his order.'

Rebecca nodded. 'And there is still no sign of the ship that will take us off?' She said it quite matter-of-fact.

'There is not,' replied Peto, gravely. 'I am waiting on a signal telling me where is the *Firefly*, and what's to do.' Only then did he think about the activity that would follow breakfast. 'Your belongings, Miss Rebecca, and your maid's – they are ready to be taken off?'

'They are. Mr Pelham has been most kind. And Mr Flowerdew.'

His steward, standing by, looked sheepish as Peto turned to him, and then back to Rebecca.

But both were spared any remark by Midshipman Pelham's hailing from the poop. '*Calpe* signalling, sir!'

Peto put his glass to his eye. He could not read a signal without the codebook, but he might judge the length of it well enough.

It was mercifully, and encouragingly, brief. Pelham had it out in no time. ' "From flag, *Hind* to take off lady".'

'*Hind*?'

Pelham was already rifling through his Admiralty progress book and the Navy List. 'Ex-Revenue-cutter, sir.'

'*Cutter*?' rasped Peto. There was scarcely decent room in a cutter for one woman, let alone ... There again, he had said nothing of *Rupert*'s total complement of that sex. He cursed himself.

'Yes, sir, cutter,' Pelham confirmed, mistaking the captain's exasperation. 'Mr Robb, sir.'

Peto huffed. He considered it were no consolation had its captain been called Nelson. But, if a cutter was all the admiral could spare ... 'Very well, Mr Lambe: have the officer of the watch report as soon as *Hind* hoves in sight. Have you breakfasted?'

'No, sir.'

'Then join me at mine, if you will.' He turned to Rebecca. 'Miss Codrington?'

'I have not, Captain Peto.'

'Then you may well have your last egg this side of Malta.'

While he was perfectly capable – indeed, inclined – to interpret liberally (some said flout) the Admiralty's fighting instructions, in matters of routine Captain Sir Laughton Peto observed to the letter the customs of the service. The practices he had learned in the midshipmen's berth, the aptness of which he had witnessed time and again, were to him as the rubrics of divine worship were to his father: to be followed without variation, lest a greater error ensue. And so at breakfast this morning he wore his best linen, shirt-points white as chalk, cuffs unchafed. His sea coat was sponged clean, its formerly invisible nap teased back to life with a steaming bowl, comb and a score years of Flowerdew's know-how, and the gold braid restored by the application of soap and water with ancient tooth brush to a glister that would do justice to a Portuguese high altar.

Rebecca wanted to say something – 'How smart is your appearance, Captain Peto' – but she sensed she ought not to: Lieutenant Lambe's turnout was no less to be remarked on, and she could hardly favour the one without the other. Instead she made seamanlike conversation (the captain did indeed seem rather distracted in his thoughts), but not once did she enquire of the *Hind*.

As Flowerdew poured his captain a third cup of coffee, there was a sharp knock at the steerage door. Lambe made to rise, but Peto shook his head. 'In good time,' he said, as Flowerdew shuffled off to answer (now that, evidently, *Hind* was sighted, and thereby the means of relieving him of the safeguard of the commander-in-chief's daughter, he was in no hurry to be discharged of it).

Flowerdew opened the inner door to admit the officer of the watch.

'Yes, Mr Wilsey?' said Peto, airily, as one who knew what was to follow.

'Signal from the flagship, sir. "Close up to signal distance."'

The admiral's intention had been to enter the anchorage just after midday. Why order him up now when he had sent him to windward for the night?

Lambe was already on his feet as Peto rose. 'Make sail, Mr Lambe . . . And clear for action.'

'Ay-ay, sir!' The glint in his lieutenant's eye scarcely made the acknowledgement necessary.

Flowerdew brought hat and sword.

'Miss Codrington, you will accompany me to the quarterdeck until such time as *Hind* comes alongside,' said Peto, buckling on his swordbelt. 'It may well be that at that time I shall be engaged elsewhere, and so I will bid you farewell now, and thank you, most sincerely, for your company.' He held out a hand.

Rebecca took it. She knew not to detain him with any speech, though she was dismayed rather by the suddenness of their parting. She began fumbling in her workbag. 'Wait, a moment, if you will, Captain Peto,' she begged, anxiously, until she was able to produce what she sought. 'I should like you to have this.'

She held out a folded square of dark blue silk.

Peto took it, colouring a little, and clearing his throat once more. No woman had ever given him anything, except his mother (so many necessaries when first he had gone to sea) – *and*, of course, Elizabeth, her consent to be his wife. 'Miss Codrington, I . . .' He unfolded the square, a sampler, worked in gold-coloured thread. In the middle was an anchor, with 'HMS Prince Rupert' stitched below, and in each corner an initial: L, P, E, H.

'It is not quite finished, Captain Peto. I had intended embroidering the date, but—'

Peto cleared his throat most determinedly. 'Quite. Just so. It is most handsomely done, Miss Codrington. A very proper memento. I thank you.' He folded it very carefully, and placed it in the inner pocket of his coat.

* * *

As they left the cabin, the marine drummer was already beating to quarters, and the first of the carpenter's mates had begun knocking the dowels from the bulkheads of the steerage. Peto had seen the work so many times, yet still the business of clearing for action thrilled every nerve-ending in his body. Banging, shouting, cursing, crashing . . . the order midst chaos, reason midst bedlam: it spoke of the umpteen-hundred men working to a single noble purpose, of his reliance on them, and of theirs on him. And he delighted in it.

He looked down into the waist to see men hauling with a will on the gun tackle, and boys bringing up powder as if coals to a fire. His breast swelled with pride, and his mind cleared itself of every triviality in the knowledge that he was responsible for everything – *everything* – in the wooden world about him. What comfort there was in that knowledge: his responsibility – his alone.

'No sign of *Hind*, sir,' said the officer of the watch.

Peto cast his eyes to the tops. 'There is no need to inform me of a negative, Mr Wilsey.' He said it kindly enough, but there was no use his beating about the bush with a lieutenant wanting promotion.

Nevertheless, Wilsey's 'Ay-ay, sir' was a half-swallowed affair.

By now the topgallants were set, and *Rupert* was picking up speed. In this breeze she ought to run a good nine knots, he reckoned, and he was content enough with that. Had the signal been 'immediate: close up' he would have told the master to set the royals too, but he saw no cause to have the ship pitch over-much as the crew were running out the guns.

Yet while Lieutenant Wilsey's negative observation had been both unwelcome and unnecessary, *Hind*'s whereabouts was beginning to exercise him. And he would have to heave to for the cutter or her long boat to come alongside: *more* work for the topmen, not without hazard, and less speed for *Rupert*.

It was time for him to see how things were below . . . He turned to his signal midshipman. 'Make to *Calpe*: "Hasten *Hind*".'

'Ay-ay, sir.'

'Mr Lambe, bear a point more to larboard: bring her up on the flagship to nor'west.' When the time came he intended running down into the mouth of Navarino Bay unseen from within, masked as he would be by the island of Sphacteria.

'Ay-ay, sir.'

He glanced at Rebecca. She stood with her hand shielding her eyes, eager for sight of her father's ship, her cloak billowing. He thought of Elizabeth: how he wished she were here at this moment . . .

No! What in heaven's name was he thinking of? He clenched a fist. 'Mr Durcan! Your company below, if you please!'

'Ay-ay, sir,' sang the third lieutenant, happy to be given the honour.

An hour passed, *Rupert* running hushed, only the sound of wind and waves, the comfortably creaking timber and softly groaning rigging, and the occasional bark from a petty officer, the sotto voce crack among the crew, the measured reporting of the quartermaster, and the stilted conversation of the officers. From orlop to forecastle, Peto, with the third lieutenant, the boatswain and several mates, made his rounds, congratulating, warning, encouraging; but never reproving (that, he knew, he could leave to the boatswain in his wake), for now was the time that men must give their hearts to him. On *Nisus* some of the older hands would have tried a larking word or two, and he would have bantered, with an amusing put-down of a retort. But *Rupert*'s captain and crew had been together not nearly long enough. Such a state could only come, in a ship of the Line especially, after a long cruise, a year and more. Or after a sharp (and successful) action. *Then* the crew would have earned a little licence.

He spoke briefly to the women, shepherded now into the surgeon's realm, where already the loblolly boys had enlisted their willing help making tourniquets and pledgets. He spoke softly to them, yet with authority, for he wanted both to reassure them while at the same time dissuading any from adverse comment. He apologized for confining them so, explaining the necessity of having the decks clear of everything that might impair the fighting of the ship – even, as he was quick to explain, though they were some hours from such an event. He assured them that the admiral was sending a ship to take them off (he almost coughed at the deception in describing the *Hind* thus), and rather to his surprise there was no voice in protest at his course. Indeed, as he touched his hat to them and turned, one of them called out 'Good luck to 'ee, Captain.' It made him swallow unaccountably hard.

Back on the quarterdeck, Peto found Lambe berating a midshipman for what he evidently considered was a lubberly getting away of the pinnace, but having dismissed him with a heartening 'only get your shot away sharper!', Lambe reported that *Rupert* was cleared for action.

Peto had seen the effort for himself, but until the officers of the quarters had sent their word to the quarterdeck there was no knowing the end of it. 'Very good, Mr Lambe,' he replied, turning his attention to the sail. There was not a sign of shiver, the wind dead aft, the yards braced square, and the helm five degrees to starboard: the master had her trimmed perfectly (though Peto would not own it tricky sailing).

Lambe motioned the officers to dismiss to their fighting quarters.

Peto checked himself; he had been minded to ask Lambe if there was any sign of *Hind*, but since it was inconceivable that her sighting would not be reported to him at once, his enquiry would only indicate anxiety. He took his telescope instead and searched east for the fleet. *Rupert* had made little leeway in the night: he reckoned there was an hour and more's sailing before they closed on the flagship. 'Very well, Mr Lambe,' he said at length, lowering his glass: 'you may beat retreat.' He saw no purpose in keeping men on their feet who might otherwise catch forty winks between the guns.

'Ay-ay, sir.'

'Sail ahoy, two points off the starboard bow!' The lookout's easygoing call, the voice of a seasoned topman, nevertheless animated the upper decks.

Peto looked at his watch – a quarter after nine – and then at the main mast, seeing the midshipman climbing purposefully to the cap. He fancied he himself might do it as nimbly still after all these years if . . .

'*Calpe* signalling, sir!' hailed Pelham.

'And about time, too,' muttered Peto (he supposed inaudibly to all but the quartermaster not six feet away).

But the maintop midshipman beat Pelham to the next call. 'Two frigates direct ahead, sir, English!'

Nothing surprising in that, reckoned Peto, frigates to windward. Codrington intended entering the bay with the line-of-battle ships leading – his own first, the French and then the Russians – and his frigates, more manoeuvrable, taking station last. Peto calculated another half-hour's running with this canvas, and then he would take in the courses, heave to and await the admiral's pleasure. That would be the time for *Hind* to come alongside. He smiled to himself wryly: Rebecca Codrington would see her father's ship after all. Likely as not she would see the man himself if she could screw her eye to a glass.

'*Calpe* signals: "From flag", sir,' called Pelham resolutely. With the maintop midshipman now in distinct competition, he was eager to have his captain's attention. '"*Hind* making way from Kalamata."'

Peto frowned. What was Codrington trying to tell him? Evidently the admiral had no true idea when the cutter would return.

He had a sudden and alarming thought. Would Codrington keep *Rupert* out of action until *Hind* had taken off his daughter? Good God! It would be a very proper paternal instinct, but . . .

He forced himself to look aft at the weather. There was no cloud to speak of now. If anything, the wind was lightening. Could he not rig the launch and put the women in it; and a couple of lieutenants, and conduct them clear and safe to . . . *where?* That was the rub.

'Acknowledge!' he rasped.

Twenty more minutes passed, the quarterdeck silent throughout save for the quartermaster and the midshipman marking the speed on the half-hour (eight knots).

The maintop midshipman's strengthening voice broke the peace. 'Sail ahoy, three points on the starboard bow!'

Peto quickened, keen for confirmation he was making contact with the flag. If it were so, then he flattered himself he had come down on her exactly as intended.

Five more minutes, and then, 'Blue at the foremast, sir!'

Lambe hastened to Peto's side.

'Helm two points a-larboard, Mr Lambe.'

'Two points a-larboard, ay-ay, sir. D'ye hear that, Mr Veitch?'

'Two points a-larboard, ay-ay, sir,' intoned the quartermaster, nodding to the mates to begin heaving on the wheel.

Peto watched the main course slacken momentarily as the bows turned through the direction of the wind, until *Rupert* was sailing large once more, her canvas filled again. Such a turn as that in a lightening breeze with just the topsails full – she answered well in these airs, no doubt of it: he would order the courses reefed as they went into action.

He took his glass to the starboard shrouds and searched for the distant sail, but it was a full minute before he was sure it was the *Asia* (by heaven, that maintop midshipman had good eyes!). A quarter of an hour more, a league's running, at most, and he would heave to within easy sight of the flagship's signals.

Rupert ran before the wind for the best part of that league until Peto judged he need approach the flag no closer. The admiral had for some reason changed his mind and called her up sooner, showing his heaviest guns early to Sphacteria (the lookouts there, even the most laggard Turkish sentry, could not fail to see she was a three-decker). What was the cause of Codrington's second thoughts, he wondered. Had he received intelligence that the Turks would offer resistance, or try to sortie?

No explanation came. For the rest of the morning *Rupert* lay all but motionless in the water, courses furled and fore-topsail backed to the mast, as perfectly balanced as a windhover spying its prey. Peto was close to fretting for the liveliness of the crew, for the ship had been cleared for action now these four hours, and the men at their stations. With the galley fire doused there was no prospect of a good trencher of beef come midday (it would have to be biscuit and slushy), but he had ordered a generous issue of bacon at breakfast, and half a ration again of rum, so he was not too exercised on that account. Besides, there would be feast enough at the day's end – 'when the smoke had cleared'. That was what the crew were promising themselves.

He thought of going about the decks again, but it would have looked strange, perhaps making him appear uneasy. No, he would have to leave it to the lieutenants to keep the crew from torpor. Doubtless some of them would be thinking he had cleared for action too soon; and with four hours' inactivity, and no enemy ship within sight, they had some cause. But he was ever of the opinion that it was not possible to clear too soon for action: there was a sort of superiority that came with taking the initiative, rather than having the enemy drive the business. What was an early rouse and cold food compared with knowing all was ready when the enemy hove in view?

'Cutter ahoy, sir!'

Peto sighed with relief.

Lambe, coming up the companion ladder from yet another inspection below, barked the order without missing a step: 'Mr Corbishley, the gangway if you please!'

'Ay-ay, sir!' The midshipman sounded pleased to have something to do at last.

They had not taken the gangway to the hold when they cleared for action, anticipating its imminent need. Midshipman Corbishley and the boatswain's mates could have it rigged in ten minutes or so, lashing the frame to the ship's side at the entry port on the middle deck, and then lowering the end to the waterline. Peto would have the women descend quickly and with all modesty to the cutter (rather than have them clamber down the side-ladder). It was something of an irony, as the whole crew knew: modesty had not been a mark of their time on board.

Except for Rebecca Codrington (and her maid). There was not a midshipman – and a good many lieutenants – who had not in some measure lost his heart to her. Indeed, she had somehow endeared herself to those before the mast too, for one of the hands was sent to the foot of the quarterdeck ladder with a present of a brightly coloured parrot in a cage, and a sentiment carved on a wooden tag: 'Health to our Admiral's Daughter'.

Peto made a mental note for his log, and with considerable relief: *Two bells of the Afternoon Watch, Miss Codrington and ship's women transferred to cutter Hind.*

Rebecca stood in her brown cloak taking the sun, exchanging quiet words with her maid, understanding that the usual pleasantries with the occupants of the quarterdeck were necessarily curtailed in a ship cleared for action. She marvelled at *Rupert*'s transformation. The captain's cabin, in which she had enjoyed the most attentive of company, where she had been extended every courtesy, as if she had been a grown woman, which to her own mind she was in all respects but that which she could not yet know (which did not in truth disbar her from that claim, for such knowledge was by no means given to all), was no more: it was now but a fighting station, as the rest of the ship, with rude-looking men gathered about the guns, where before there had been gentler faces, gold lace, and quiet-spoken servants. These men by no means repelled her; quite the opposite, indeed, for she saw in them the very safeguard of the nation, and of the ship and the fine officers she had come to know (and the finest of men that was the captain) – and most particularly of her father's reputation. How, therefore, could she not admire – love, even – these men who held their life at his disposal? The thought made her blood run fast. And when Peto bid her farewell a final time her face was suffused with a colour he had never before seen in a female.

'Miss Codrington, you are unwell?'

She smiled at him with the satisfaction of one who knew something her superior did not. 'I am very well indeed, Captain Peto. Only that I have no desire to leave your ship.'

Peto returned the smile, indulgently. 'Nor would any of us wish your leaving, Miss Codrington, but as you will understand, it will be no place for a female heart, erelong.'

Rebecca smiled once more. Had not a female once denied she had the heart of a woman, but of a prince of England – and declared it so on the fighting deck of an English ship? But Captain Peto was so admirable a man that she could not fence

271

with him thus – not at least in the hearing of his own officers. 'You are very good, sir.'

Hind was turning in to starboard. Midshipman Pelham, whom Peto had detailed to see Rebecca safely down, stepped forward smartly and saluted.

But that had been earlier; there was nothing pressing on the captain's attention now. 'I shall accompany Miss Codrington myself, Mr Pelham.'

'Ay-ay, sir.' The voice betrayed only as much disappointment as the midshipman dared – which was but a very little.

Hind ran in alongside with exemplary ease. It was, after all, a fleet cutter's purpose to dart from ship to ship thus. She had been built to overhaul smugglers, and rigged to outmanoeuvre the handiest of them. Her master, a stocky man, a lieutenant perhaps not yet thirty, but with a wide, honest face – a man who might look useful in a boarding party – leapt for the gangway and came up briskly to the entry port. Seeing *Rupert*'s captain waiting for him at the top, rather than the midshipman he had expected, he saluted him, rather than the quarterdeck, just in time (for Peto's humour was sorely tried by the business). He quickly regained his poise, however, smiling with such manifest cheer that Peto was at once deflected from any rebuke over the tardiness of his arrival. Indeed, having watched him handle the cutter, Peto was at once assured that he could perfectly entrust the admiral's daughter – and the ship's women – to such an active and engaging man as he.

'Robb, sir. The admiral's compliments, and would you be so good as to read these supplementary orders.' The lieutenant held out an oilskin package.

As Peto took it, there was a single cannon shot from the *Asia*. He stepped out onto the gangway for a better look. The flagship firing thus meant but one thing: she drew attention to an imperative flag signal. He cursed, thinking that his lookouts had not seen it.

Lieutenant Robb at once had his telescope to his eye. Peto's was on the quarterdeck, which made him crosser still – not that he could have been expected to read the commander-in-chief's signals without a codebook.

Robb could, however (as commander of *Asia*'s tender he had a thorough acquaintance with the codes; cutting about the fleet, he lived by them, indeed). ' "Prepare to enter"!'

The next second, Robb was saluting again and taking his leave.

Peto's mouth fell open. 'Avast there, Mr Robb!' he spluttered. 'Where do you go? Take the women down, sir! I'll read my orders first, damn it! They may require an answer!' (though what answer was needed when the admiral signalled 'prepare to enter' he would have been hard put to suggest).

Robb looked puzzled. 'Sir, with respect, I cannot now take off anyone with the flag signalling action. I am the flagship's tender. My place in action is alongside her.'

'Mr Robb, your orders were – were they not? – to take off the admiral's daughter!'

'Sir, with the very *greatest* respect, my orders were to give such assistance as I might, but the admiral's signal is general to the fleet. As tender I must return at once.'

Peto's face turned as red as the marine sentry's jacket next to him, as if he would explode with all the violence of a carronade.

But he did not explode – just as if the gunner had stopped the flint with his hand. For he knew he would do the same as Robb were *he* master of the flagship's tender. *Hind* was Codrington's Mercury after all. The admiral would have need of this young officer and his cutter almost as much as he would have need of his flag lieutenant.

From the corner of his eye he could see the line of women, Rebecca and her maid at the head, for all the world like passengers on a packet come into Dover harbour. He sighed, but to himself (he would reveal nothing more of his dismay). 'Very well, Mr Robb, but you will wait until I read through my orders!'

'Ay-ay, sir!' Robb was astute enough to know that a minute or so would make little difference to him, but in the circumstances a very great deal to a post-captain's pride.

Peto opened his orders and read them rapidly. 'No reply necessary,' he growled, refolding them. 'Good luck to you, Mr Robb. You may dismiss.'

Robb looked relieved. 'Ay-ay, sir. And good luck to your ship too.' He saluted again, adding cheerfully, 'We shall next meet in the bay, I imagine, sir.'

Peto nodded, then watched him scuttle down the gangway, recollecting his own youthful, even carefree commands, before resolutely turning inboard.

'Miss Codrington, ladies,' he began, gravely but with every appearance of easy confidence, 'I am obliged to offer you the continuing hospitality of my ship. Mr Corbishley, you are to escort Miss Codrington to the purser's quarters; and,' glancing at the boatswain, 'Mr Mills, have the ladies conducted to the surgeon's.' He would have them all safely confined to the orlop deck, below the waterline, but at different quarters: if he could not get Rebecca Codrington off, he could at least keep her from the company of the ship's women – whose conduct was certain now to be the ruder.

'Ay-ay, sir.'

He turned once more to Rebecca. 'Miss Codrington, you will be perfectly safe, no matter what the action on deck.' Which was without doubt true unless there was a catastrophic explosion. He cleared his throat once more, as if something did genuinely inhibit what he would say. He bowed. 'Until . . . until we are anchored at Navarino, then.'

Rebecca curtsied, but before she could reply, Peto had turned.

'Make sail!' he boomed, striding for the companion ladder as if with no thought in his mind but to close with the Turk.

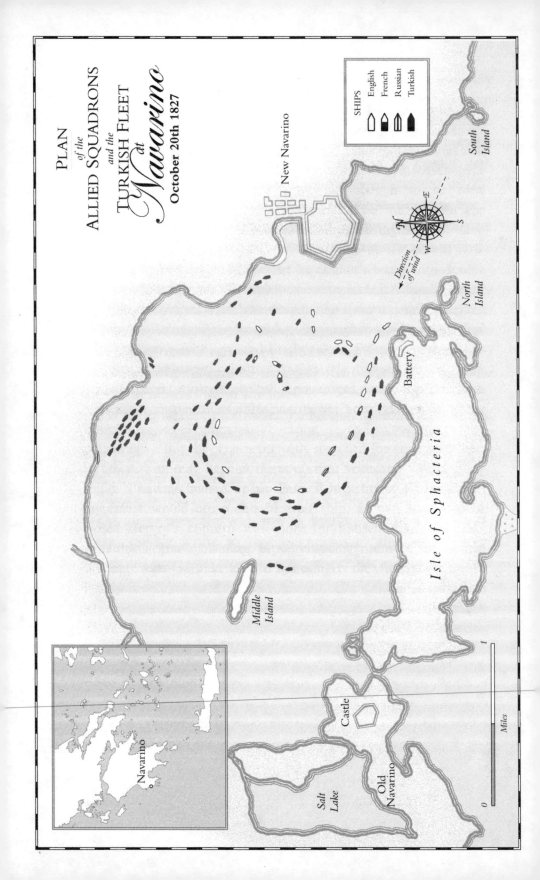

PLAN
of the
ALLIED SQUADRONS
and the
TURKISH FLEET
at
Navarino
October 20th 1827

SHIPS
English
French
Russian
Turkish

New Navarino

Direction of wind

Battery

North Island

South Island

Isle of Sphacteria

Middle Island

Castle

Salt Lake

Old Navarino

Navarino

Miles

0   1

XVII

THE UNTOWARD EVENT

A quarter of an hour later

'Full and by, Mr Lambe.'

'Ay-ay, sir,' replied the lieutenant. 'Full and by, Mr Veitch.'

'Full and by, ay-ay, sir!' replied the quartermaster, through teeth clenched on unlit pipe.

With a full course set, and studding-sails low and aloft, he would have his work cut out.

'Very well, Mr Lambe, the admiral's orders . . .' Peto turned and advanced to the weather rail, more symbolic of privacy, now, with so many men at the quarterdeck guns. 'Codrington intends entering the bay, *Asia* leading, then the French and after them the Russians. You will recall that the Turks – and when I say Turks I mean also the Egyptians – are drawn up in a horseshoe.'

Lambe nodded.

'The fleet will anchor alongside the Turks exactly as I described. As you perceive, Codrington no longer wishes *Rupert* to stand off but to take station in the entrance to the bay to suppress the shore batteries on either side if they open fire. I can only conclude thereby that he believes it will assuredly come to a fight.'

Lambe nodded again, gravely. The entrance to the bay was not a mile wide: *Rupert*'s guns would play very well with the forts, but any half decent shore battery would have their range with the first shot.

'Codrington's advice is that the fort at New Navarin, to starboard, is the stronger. There's a small, rocky islet to larboard which masks the fort on Sphacteria. If there were time we might first deal with Navarin and then Sphacteria, but I suspect we shall have no choice but to engage both at once, since the admiral will wish to close with the Turkish ships without delay if the forts signal any resistance. There are fireships, too.'

Lambe looked even more grave. 'A regular powder keg, sir.'

'Just so. We will take station now behind the flag, with *Genoa* abaft of us.'

'Ay-ay, sir.'

Peto put his glass to his eye to see if *Asia* was signalling anew, but her main-mast halyard bore the same as before. Codrington was evidently standing well out to give the French and Russian squadrons time to catch up before turning for the bay.

The marine sentry struck the half hour – six bells.

'Very well, Mr Lambe: secure guns, and have the boatswain pipe hands to dinner.'

'Ay-ay, sir!'

Flowerdew advanced with a silver tray and coffee. There were two cups, as always (except when Rebecca had been on deck, when there were three), in case the captain wished to take his coffee with another. But Peto chose not to be sociable at this moment.

'Might you procure me an apple?' Admiral Collingwood had munched on an apple as his line ran in at Trafalgar, a fine tradition of sang-froid in which to follow.

'They're a deal wormy,' Flowerdew protested.

'Even so.'

Peto took the cup, and extra sugar, stirring it for a minute and more without speaking. He drained it in one, and held it for Flowerdew to refill. 'And I would have you attend on Miss Codrington in the purser's quarters. Stay with her until the action is finished.'

He expected the usual protests.

Flowerdew surprised him, however. 'I was going to ask.'

'She will need reassurance if it comes to a fight.'

Flowerdew merely nodded.

Peto cleared his throat slightly. 'Miss Codrington has letters . . . you'll see to it that she is . . . able to get them away.'

'I will.'

He cleared his throat again. 'Good, good. Capital. Now, the apple if you please, and then you will go below.'

'Ay-ay, sir.'

He would make a little more of it when the apple came – no sentiment or the like, but Flowerdew had been with him a good many years.

Left alone again, he reached into his pocket and took out Elizabeth's letter (it might be his last opportunity to read it for some time). He unwrapped the oilskin package with a reverence some might accord a relic, and held the folded sheet for several minutes without opening it.

'Flagship signalling, sir!' Midshipman Pelham's voice revealed the pride with which he alerted his captain.

Peto carefully returned the letter to its oilskin, and his pocket, and took out his watch: it was just gone one-thirty after noon. It was a slower affair by far than Trafalgar, but at Trafalgar they could see the enemy, unlike here. Until now, when the bay opened up before them . . .

'It can be but the one signal, I imagine, Mr Lambe,' he said (*Asia* was a mere couple of cables ahead, and with no room to go about even had Codrington wished it).

'From flag, sir: "prepare for action"!'

Peto quickened as if by an electric shock. 'Run out all guns, double-shotted, Mr Lambe!'

'Ay-ay, sir!'

He had drummed hands back to quarters after dinner with 'Hearts of Oak'. They had stood or crouched by gun and hatch since, awaiting the order. The entire crew now sprang to frenzied life as if they too had been charged with electricity.

Peto closed to the quartermaster's side. It was time to take the con directly. 'One point a-larboard, Mr Veitch!'

'One point a-larboard, ay-ay, sir!'

He put his glass to his eye again: the Turk forts would see the guns run out; might he see some activity by reply?

'Captain Antrobus!'

The captain of marines crossed the quarterdeck briskly, and saluted.

'Yonder fort,' said Peto, pointing to Sphacteria. 'Should we need to carry it, it may fall to you and a landing party.'

'There is nothing I should like better, sir.'

'We might spare, say, fifty men, perhaps sixty.' The complement of marines was 138, of whom half had fixed fighting stations; the rest deployed as sharpshooters in the tops and upperworks.

'Thirty of my men, I suggest, sir, and the same from the afterguard.'

Peto nodded. 'Very well. Make ready.' He turned to hail Lambe. 'Lower two boats, in anticipation, and detail thirty of the afterguard to Captain Antrobus.'

Lambe rattled off the executives to the boatswain and the captain of the afterguard.

The guns running out sounded like distant thunder, noise enough to alert the dullest lookout. Which of the forts would be first to fire? Or would it be the Turk flagship?

280

Fifteen long minutes passed in silence but for the voice of timber and rigging, and the occasional yap of a petty officer. *Asia* was now within pistol shot of the entrance, but still the forts were unmoved.

'I can scarcely credit it,' declared Peto, spying out every detail of Sphacteria with his scope. 'They're lounging on the walls, smoking!' He swung round towards New Navarin. It was the same. 'Nothing, nothing at all! Not a flag flying or the like. Extraordinary!' He recalled Ava, when they had sailed up the Rangoon River, the wooden fort sullenly silent, until too late, when the Burmans had fired a futile, suicidal shot at his flotilla. Was the Turk just going to allow them to sail into the bay and take possession of the fleet?

A cannon boomed on Sphacteria. Peto swung round.

'Unshotted, sir,' said Lambe. 'I wonder they're signalling: the whole Turk fleet must be able to see *Asia* now.'

Peto nodded. 'How do you judge the current, Mr Veitch?'

'Little or none, sir.'

He had thought as much. He would have to bring *Rupert* round a point or two into the wind to heave to; dropping anchor, even with a spring attached, was out of the question under those guns – and he wanted to have his broadsides as square-on as might be. 'Prepare to heave to.'

Lambe hailed the sailing-master: 'Prepare to back main-topsail, Mr Shand.'

Veitch brought *Rupert* into the wind.

Peto judged it the moment. 'Heave to!'

The topmen did their work fast and sure. Shand barely needed his trumpet.

'Boat ahoy!'

Peto looked up, cupping a hand to his mouth. 'More advice if you please, Mr Simpson!'

'Pinnace, sir, I believe from the Turkish flagship, heading straight for *Asia*!'

'Indeed,' said Peto to himself, though clearly audible to Lambe. 'The Turks submitting, sir? The only reasonable course.'

'The only reasonable course, Mr Lambe, as you say. But what Turkish admiral could present himself in Constantinople in consequence? No, I think there's a deal of joukery yet ahead.'

'And a deal of powder for the Turk to hoist himself with.'

Peto looked at the horseshoe of men-of-war. There were no three-deckers, but if it came to a fight they would be closer engaged than ever Nelson managed at Trafalgar. 'Have the fo'c's'le lookouts keep a sharp eye on those *brûlots* yonder,' he said, pointing ahead and to starboard. 'It'll be like the burning fiery furnace if they're loosed.'

Lambe sent a midshipman forward with the word.

Peto was now intent on the pinnace. What terms did the Turkish admiral propose? *Rupert*'s crew – the crew of every one of Codrington's ships, indeed – would be disappointed if he struck without a fight. But the cost would be high if he did otherwise. Peto did not doubt that every Turkish ship would end at the bottom, but the lack of sea space would mean a good number of allied ships might go down with them. He turned to the forts again: the guns commanded the entrance rather than the bay itself; once the squadrons were in there would be no need of *Rupert*'s fire. Where might he then place himself to advantage?

A quarter of an hour went by in the same silence. *Genoa* and then *Albion* passed him, their captains acknowledging his quarter-deck, but no cheering as at Trafalgar. 'Recollect, gentlemen,' Codrington had insisted, 'that no act of hostility is to be attempted by us on any account.' Neither were they to provoke a fire, and cheering was bound to inflame a proud Turk.

Asia dropped anchor alongside the Turkish flag.

Lambe, intent for the moment only on the trim of *Rupert*'s sails, acknowledged the report without looking.

'And the pinnace makes for the shore,' added Peto. He checked his watch. 'Ten minutes past two o'clock. Make note of that, Treves,' he said to his clerk, touching his hat now to *Dartmouth*, the first of the frigates, passing so close on the starboard beam that he could have exchanged words with his old friend Captain Fellowes without much raising his voice. He rather envied him: a frigate would be a veritable cat among the pigeons in such an affair, able to manoeuvre with far greater facility than *Rupert*. And, at forty-four guns, by no means incapable of crippling a two-decker with raking fire.

He turned back to the pinnace. What did she do thence to New Navarin? But *Asia* made no fresh signal: there was no change in Codrington's design.

Dartmouth bore to starboard as she entered the bay, making for the fireships to the south-east, while the rest of the squadron advanced steadily, line-ahead. The pinnace reached the south shore. Peto observed an officer jump out, throw off his turban and race up the hill to the gate of the fort, where others had assembled. There was a hurried conference, and then a red flag was run up on the walls. A gun fired, again unshotted. But still Peto could detect no activity on Sphacteria: the gunners remained entirely at ease (and in spite of the flag and the signal gun, New Navarin looked no more lively). Was it a ruse? Did the Turks *want* them to enter the bay?

'Boat ahoy!'

This time Peto would wait for Midshipman Simpson to gather his advice, since evidently his eye was to be trusted.

In a couple of minutes he had it: 'Barge from the Turkish flag to the Egyptian flag, sir!'

Ten minutes passed as silently as before.

'Boat ahoy!'

Peto imagined it too would now be making for New Navarin. 'Deuced queer business, this, Mr Lambe. You might suppose we'd taken them by surprise.'

'Indeed, sir.'

He contemplated going forward for a better look, but checked the instinct. His place was on the quarterdeck. And besides, it mattered little what he saw: he could take no action until they were fired on.

'Barge making for fireships, sir!'

This was it! He put his telescope under his arm, clasped his hands behind his back and concentrated hard on giving no appearance of agitation.

The captain of marines came up. 'Sir, might I get the landing party into the boats, ready? It will be tricky otherwise once firing begins.'

Peto shook his head. 'I can't help it, Captain Antrobus. This is politics. The Turks will deem it a hostile act. I fear it must be "*Tirez les premiers*".'

Antrobus looked disappointed, put out, even, as he saluted and took his leave. Peto wished he had been a little less peremptory with him. He had the highest regard for the marines' offensive spirit.

But then, the entire ship's complement was possessed of nothing but desire for a battle. The quarterdeck, lately a place for sunny recreation, swarmed with gun-crew; jollies, bristling for some sharpshooting, lined the gangways; and hands danced impatiently about the forecastle carronades. Here was death in twenty different calibres, and every man eager for its issue.

A pigeon walked along the strings of the *sauve-tête* above the waist. Peto recalled he had not seen netting on a three-decker since Trafalgar . . .

Another quarter of an hour, and then: '*Dartmouth* lowering a boat, sir!'

Was there ever occasion when the quarterdeck listened so intently on a midshipman? Peto shook his head: *politics*.

Five more minutes: 'Pinnace sir, from *Dartmouth*, pulling for the fireship.'

Peto saluted Admiral de Rigny's flag in the frigate *Sirène*. As he turned to speak to his signal midshipman, a shot rang out from towards *Dartmouth* – a musket, perhaps a pistol, but a crack like fork lightning in the silent auditorium of the bay. And then a whole fusillade.

'Shots from the fireship, sir! She's firing on *Dartmouth*'s pinnace,' called Midshipman Simpson.

Peto leaned out over the weather rail to see how close was the first of the French line-of-battle ships, what support he could expect: but they had fallen well astern of *Sirène*. 'Damn me if they haven't reduced sail too soon!'

He made for the poop for a better view. 'Who is she, Mr Pelham?'

'*Scipion*, sir. And *Trident*, I think, astern of her.'

'She is either *Trident* or *Breslau*, Mr Pelham,' replied Peto brusquely. 'There is no good in being uncertain which.'

'Ay-ay, sir.'

'Fireship alight, sir!' came the voice from the tops again.

Codrington had not said if firing a *brûlot* was to be taken as *the* hostile act.

'*Dartmouth* lowering her cutter, sir.' Midshipman Simpson's voice was becoming hoarse, but decidedly less reedy. 'I believe the shots have struck the pinnace's crew.'

Peto cursed beneath his breath. He had to admire Codrington's nerve, but it was like chipping flints atop a powder keg.

Ten minutes crept by. *Scipion* drifted past, and *Trident* a hundred yards astern of her, as if pulled by plodding barge horses. Peto, back on the quarterdeck, shook his head. 'A little bolder, our French friends might be, think you not, Mr Lambe? Our Russian friends press them hard.' He nodded to the third column of sail fast approaching.

'I do, sir. T'gallants *and* royals, at least.'

Peto lowered his telescope, resolved. 'We are too inactive, Mr

Lambe. Lower the cutter. *Dartmouth* may require assistance towing the *brûlot* clear.'

'Ay-ay, sir!'

Captain Antrobus came up. 'Permission to embark my landing party, sir?'

Peto scowled. He did not require prompting to give his orders. Yet from the marines' narrow perspective, Antrobus was right. He hated evasion – '*Tirez les premiers*'. It was a damned muddle-headed business, this: the government took sides in a war without taking any responsibility for action ...

He had an idea. 'Wait for the cutter to get away and then get your men into the boats. The Turks will think you're to make for *Dartmouth*, too. Have your men take off their jackets. God knows I detest such skulking, but if the devil drives ...'

'Ay-ay, sir,' said Antrobus, keenly.

'And show yourself well to us, mind, if you do land. I want no men killed by our guns.' (He had seen it often enough in the French war, even if Antrobus had not.)

'Ay-ay, sir.'

'The recall signal – yellow at the stern. Go to it. And good luck.'

Antrobus saluted, and bustled away.

There was a sudden welter of shots.

'Shots at *Dartmouth*'s boats from the fireship, sir!'

The firing increased – an exchange of musketry for several minutes.

'This may yet begin in a tuppenny-ha'penny fashion,' said Peto. 'Fellowes is showing admirable restraint, I would say.'

'Indeed, sir,' replied Lambe, his glass trained on Sphacteria, however. 'And, most curious, still no sign of activity at the fort.'

Peto shook his head. 'Why would the shore batteries stay idle while the fireships are primed ready? It reeks of a ploy.'

Lambe had no opportunity to answer: two cannon spoke – like the crack of doom.

'Turk frigate firing a-weather, sir, hard inshore!' screeched Simpson.

Cannon now roared a good deal closer.

'*Dartmouth* answering, sir. And *Sirène*!'

Smoke and flame suddenly erupted from New Navarin, and a second later came the thunder of her guns.

'Starboard batteries, open fire!' snapped Peto.

Fountains of shot from New Navarin played ahead of *Trident*, before she was obscured by the smoke of *Rupert*'s broadside.

Sphacteria now belched into life. Shot whistled through *Rupert*'s rigging, carrying away a spar from the mizzen, and one of the topmen. The captain of the forecastle threw a float over the side, but the man was dead in the water, his neck broken.

'Mr Lambe, larboard battery, if you please!'

Lambe raised his speaking-trumpet again. 'Larboard battery, *Fire!*'

The upper-deck battery roared as one gun, the middle- and lower- a split second later. Pulverized stone thickened the smoke which already wreathed the walls of the fort.

Peto gave but one other order for the moment (the captains of the batteries knew their business, and their targets were obligingly immobile). 'My compliments to Captain Antrobus, Mr Lambe, and bid him away to the shore.'

'Ay-ay, sir.'

'Turkish flagship firing on *Asia*, sir!'

Peto was strangely relieved: *Asia* was engaged at last. There could be no doubt about the issue now.

The action spread like a flame along a powder trail. Soon there was continuous cannonading, and smoke enough to fill the anchorage. A ball from Sphacteria struck *Rupert* by the break of the forecastle, scattering hammocks and showering the waist with splinters. Two marines fell, writhing terribly.

'Sail, if you please, Mr Lambe. Let us give the Turks a harder mark still.'

The starboard watch hauled up the main-topsail by the clew-lines rather than sending more men aloft to furl. In a minute or so, with no wind in the (backed) sail to counter the fore and mizzen, *Rupert* began to make headway.

'Bring her up into the wind a point, Mr Veitch.' It would mean putting half of each broadside off its line, Peto knew, but that should be of no matter now that each gun captain had the range.

The landing party was nearing the shore. He had a mind to recall them, for his guns would have the better of the fort soon enough if the Turks continued to fire so ill, one true hit in all of ten minutes.

Midshipman Simpson called again, even more hoarsely: 'Two more fireships ablaze, sir!'

Peto made for the poop deck once more: with *Rupert* turning into the wind he ought to be able to see nearly as well as from the tops.

He felt the roundshot tear the air just above his head, saw it graze the flag lockers and carry away the stern lantern before plunging into the sea, aft. He raised an eyebrow: as well he had not taken the ladder a moment earlier. But it was the way of a fight at sea, and he did not dwell on near misses. 'Stand up, Mr Hart,' he said briskly to one of the midshipmen, flat on his back and with an expression of astonishment.

'I'm sorry, sir. I—'

'Nothing from the flag, Mr Pelham?'

'No, sir,' replied the signal midshipman, surveying the wreckage of his flag locker in dismay.

Peto took up his telescope to observe for himself. There was so much smoke it was a while before he could find the flagship.

'Codrington has hot work of it, I see.' *Asia* was engaged at close quarters with one, perhaps two, of the Turkish Line. Peto shook his head: that decided it (their lordships did not send a three-decker to the Mediterranean to pound at shore batteries on the edge of a general action).

He slid back down the ladder without a word (he had no time for signals now), before thinking better of leaving Pelham with nothing but carpentry. He turned and hailed him in a voice that would carry above the gunfire yet conveyed indifference to it. 'Mr Pelham. I may have need of you on the quarterdeck!'

He was surprised by how agreeable he found the young man's 'ay-ay, sir!'.

'Make straight for the flagship, Mr Durcan!' The third lieutenant had resumed the watch as soon as the captain had turned for the ladder.

'Straight for her, sir!'

The last of Admiral de Rigny's frigates was nearing. Peto took Lambe's speaking-trumpet to the starboard side. 'Ahoy, monsieur!' It ought to have felt strange: the only time he had ever hailed a Frenchman was to invite him to strike his colours.

The reply came at once, and heartily. '*Je suis l'*Armide, *capitaine! C'est une vraie bataille, n'est pas?*'

'*Oui, capitaine, c'est ça.*' Peto was confident of his French, though he knew his accent to be that of an Englishman: 'I have put ashore a party of marines to take the fort. They will have need of support but I must join the action. Will you take my place here?' He prayed the Frenchman would not choose *la gloire* rather than the course of military reason.

He need have had no concern. '*Oui, capitaine, bien sûr . . .*'

The detail was dealt with briskly, so that Peto could thank his (to his mind still) unlikely *allié* with true gratitude, and assurance, before turning back to the helm.

A ball crashed into the main mast just above the netting, and ricocheted into the waist. He closed his ears to the screaming of the wounded, as he had too often before.

'More sail, Mr Lambe!'

Another ball from Sphacteria crashed into *Rupert*'s hull – impenetrable save by one path. It struck the edge of a gunport aft on the middle deck just as its huge thirty-two-pounder fired, carrying away the retarder tackle, sending splinters the width of the ship. The gun itself reared up and over, killing outright a midshipman and two hands, and rendering eleven more for the orlop.

An arching, heated shot from New Navarin plunged to the quarterdeck, taking off the head of a corporal of marines, which followed the hissy ball into the sea. Several men threw up as two older hands heaved what remained of the NCO over the side.

Another ball from Sphacteria carried away the main-topmast cap, which flew half-way to *Armide*. A man fell headlong from the yard into the *sauve-tête*. Blood trickled to the quarterdeck like water from a faulty tap as hands tried to get the lifeless body to the side, and thence to its watery grave.

Meanwhile the afterguard and marines were straining every muscle to extend the mainsail (all they wanted to do was get back to the contest of broadsides), while the topmen calmly overhauled the clewlines along the yard – those not trying to cut loose the now useless topgallant.

But the fire from Sphacteria had slackened, even if its accuracy had increased. A three-decker might be an easy mark, but there was no doubting that three decks wrought heavy damage on the fort, and faster than any 74 could have done it. Peto reckoned that *Armide* with her single deck of eighteen-pounders would keep the Turks occupied until Captain Antrobus and his party decided the matter with the bayonet. As for New Navarin, the battery there was already under cannonade from the French *Magicienne*, who had found herself with otherwise little to do, since the fireships masked her allotted station at the eastern point of the horseshoe.

He checked his instinct to see for himself the damage in the waist. *Rupert* was not a frigate: if the entire upper deck were out of action, there were two more. He fixed his gaze instead – as best he could in all the smoke – on *Asia*.

Rupert made good headway. Peto thought to steer between *Asia* and the Turkish two-decker to her starboard, firing as they bore. If that did not silence her he would at least have bought *Asia*'s starboard battery a little respite. He would then turn hard across her bow to rake the other Turk from astern with the larboard battery. 'Damage report, if you please, Mr Lambe,' he barked as they left the traverse of Sphacteria's remaining guns.

A boy was swilling the quarterdeck, but no one spoke. They had been blooded, just as had the deck, and it was a powerful concoction, at once sobering and yet invigorating. The antidote was rum or more blood.

Not long and he had his damage report: the main-topsail was gone, but sail and rigging were otherwise intact; two guns of the middle-deck batteries, one each side, were disabled. And – it had never been the practice in the French wars to report the human damage – one midshipman and six seamen dead, seventeen taken below.

Peto nodded – no damage to trouble them, though a considerable surgeon's bill for the opening of an action. 'Thank you, Mr Lambe. Guns double-shotted again, if you please.' He looked at his watch: a little after three o'clock. He had not thought it so late.

Rupert bore down silently on *Asia*'s besiegers like some giant predator. She might use her bowchasers to some effect, but Peto reckoned on the greater shock of the broadsides. Whether the Turks saw or not, they made no move. It was the mark of the novice to be mesmerized by the fight at hand, when the mortal danger lay often in what threatened. Peto intended teaching a lesson that those who survived it would never forget.

'Larboard batteries to hold their fire, Mr Lambe. Remind them that it is the flagship they see. Starboard batteries will fire as they bear.'

Lambe had his midshipmen-repeaters relay the order to the larboard lower deck, and then back up again to be sure, before giving the discretionary order for the starboard guns to fire as they bore.

'Mr Shand, we shall go about across *Asia*'s bows. Be ready if you please.'

'Ay-ay, sir.'

There was resolution in the master's voice: tacking with so little sail would be the very devil; *Rupert* might be pushed a good way astern before gathering headway.

Peto looked at his watch again: a quarter after three, and a hundred yards to run. *Asia*'s fire was slackening. He prayed she had not been too severely mauled.

He clasped his hands behind his back. It was time for kind words. 'An admirable course, Mr Veitch.'

'Thankee, sir.'

'Capital trim, Mr Lambe.'

'Sir.'

The smoke thinned a little. Peto peered disbelievingly, then raised his telescope. 'That deuced cutter is alongside the flagship!'

'Sir?'

'Robb – the deuced fool has put his boat between the flag and yon Turk. I do believe he's firing! He must be sorely in want of promotion!'

Lambe lifted his own glass. 'He'll be raised up one way or another,' he said drily.

Peto growled. *Hind* would likely catch a good deal of metal when they began raking the Turk. But it could not be helped.

Rupert's marines fired first as they ran in – sharpshooters and the fore carronade, sweeping the Turk's quarterdeck, though half blind with the smoke, breaking every piece of glass in the stern. And then the starboard battery, gun by gun, simultaneously on each deck, regular enough to sound like the mechanism of a monstrous clock. The Turk – the *Souriya* – fired but two guns in reply, neither doing the slightest damage. Carronades swept her upperworks so completely that Peto thought there was not a man left standing to strike the colours. Below, the work of *Rupert*'s gun-decks had made of her nothing but a bloody mangle. The Asias cheered the Ruperts heartily. The larboard gunners returned the cheer, leaning out of the ports for three lusty 'hoorahs' before bracing for their own action.

'Hard a-starboard, Mr Veitch!' snapped Peto as the aftmost gun fired.

The mates heaved mightily to put the rudder full to larboard.

With her mainsail filling the more, *Rupert* answered well, rounding *Asia*'s bows with a graceful ease indeed – and to the great dismay of the second Turk, whose crew only now realized their fate.

Rupert's leading guns fired. At fifty yards, aim was nothing and the effect devastating. By the time the fourth bank fired, the Turk's stern was shot right away above the counter. But Peto could not have checked *Rupert*'s firing even if he had wanted to. Shot upon shot tore the length of the dying ship, turning over her guns as if they were balsa. Flames were soon lighting the smoky darkness of her gun-decks, and she fell silent but for the agonies of her shattered crew, whose cries the Ruperts could now hear quite clearly.

'Let go!' The master's speaking-trumpet recalled the topmen to their work – stretching the weather braces ready, hauling the lee tacks, weather sheets and bowlines through the slack ... 'Off tacks and sheets!'

Rupert came into the wind. Peto gasped as he saw the Turk's starboard guns were not run out. She had not had the crew to man both sides at once; and now she had not the crew to man a single gun. He had thought to sink her, but it was not worth the effort. The Ruperts began cheering again as flames took hold and the mizzen toppled. 'Cease firing!'

In the silence which followed, a single voice piped clear. 'Fireships close on *Dartmouth*, sir, and corvettes engaging!'

Peto made mental note to commend Midshipman Simpson in front of the crew when it was all done. 'Let us hasten back to her, then, Mr Lambe.'

Twenty backbreaking minutes' labour, the sailing-master barely drawing breath, Veitch himself taking the helm to feel with his own hands how close he could sail to the wind, and the gun-crews working like machines to have the batteries ready once more. *Dartmouth*'s perilous position compelled the Ruperts as no lash could: fire ringed her, and two corvettes off the lee beam plagued her with shot and grape.

'Damnable,' muttered Peto, several times. How had Fellowes allowed himself to be pressed so? And somewhere in that fog of smoke and flame was *Rupert*'s own cutter ...

The bowchasers opened up. The range was too great and the motion of the ship too uneven, however. Nevertheless the corvettes recognized the approaching danger. One of them began bearing away into the smoke; the other made a clumsy attempt to wear, and ended making unwelcome leeway instead. Peto smiled, ironically: the wind, such as it was, now worked to his advantage.

There was a convention that a ship of the Line did not fire on a single-decker unless that ship herself opened fire. Doubtless the corvette would prefer to drift by, guns silent. But it was too late. 'Larboard guns fire as they bear!' said Peto, coldly.

The Turk's crew began abandoning her even before *Rupert*'s first gun bore. When the third bank fired, the corvette blew up, her yards soaring into the sky like rockets, debris falling across half a mile, the sea about her like a puddle in a hailstorm. Most of the Ruperts had never seen an explosion; they stood gaping, until the boatswain's curses recollected them. Peto nodded grimly; he only wished he had caught the other on the hop so. Now he must sink the fireships.

Midshipman Simpson's voice was suddenly urgent. 'Two-decker dead ahead!'

Peto could see nothing ahead but smoke. There should have been no Turk battle-ship in this quarter; had Simpson seen the *Genoa*?

The white smoke was suddenly flame. Shot smashed into *Rupert*'s prow, bowled along the gangways, ricocheted into waist or quarterdeck, bringing down the netting. Splinters swept the upperworks like grapeshot. Men fell like skittles at a fair, mashed to a bloody pulp. Others were carried off as if by hurricane.

'Hard a-starboard!' bellowed Peto, though he was but five paces from the helm. He turned, to see two of the quartermaster's mates now corpses, and Veitch himself covered in blood.

By the taffrail lay Midshipman Simpson writhing crazily, his entrails on the deck like offal at a slaughterhouse. Peto motioned to the third lieutenant, who looked at him with an expression of hopelessness. He angered. 'Mr Durcan, do your duty, sir!'

Durcan sprang to horrified life. With two marines, he carried Simpson to the side and cast him into the water – a ghastly, merciful end to his torment.

Peto swallowed hard. 'Mr Pelham!'

There was no answer.

Lambe was now at his side. 'No option but to fight it out, Mr Lambe.'

'Ay-ay, sir,' he replied doggedly, raising the speaking-trumpet. The upper- and quarterdeck batteries had suffered sorely: 'All hands to starboard!'

Peto turned to the poop. 'Mr Pelham!'

A faltering voice answered. 'Mr Pelham is killed, sir.'

Peto turned back, biting his lip. 'Mr . . . Bullivant!'

The Turk followed with grape. A hail of iron scythed across the quarterdeck as *Rupert* got off a ragged broadside.

'Sir?'

'Mr Lambe?'

'I asked if—'

Peto fell back, staggering, then to the deck, his face all astonishment. His right shoulder was cleaved in two, his chest was a sea of blood, his right leg looked as if it were all but torn from the hip.

'Mr Durcan, two marines, at the double!' Lambe knelt beside his captain, in utter dismay. He had not known him a full month, and yet . . . 'Get a hammock to bear the captain below!'

Peto struggled to support himself on his left arm, despite Lambe's entreaties. He knew from long years' observation that he had but a minute or so before the pain would bear upon him too greatly, and he had always known what he must do in that minute's grace. 'My signal midshipman, Mr Lambe. He must come with me below.' He would have his orders properly recorded, for there would be periodic bouts of lucidity in the cockpit.

'Of course, sir.' He turned to Durcan. 'Mr Pelham, hurry.'

'Pelham is dead, sir.'

'Then Bullivant.'

'Ay-ay, sir.'

Peto's face was now ashen. 'Mr Lambe, see that the landing party is properly supported.'

'Ay-ay, sir.'

'And there is the cutter.'

Lambe nodded. In the din of continual firing it was as certain an acknowledgement as 'ay-ay'.

Peto's strength began to fail. 'Keep close on the flag, Mr Lambe; that way you will not do much wrong.'

'We shall do our duty, sir. Have no fear of it.'

The marines laid the hammock beside him. Two more, themselves bloody, joined them. 'Take him up gently, men. Mr Bullivant, stay by the captain's side. Make careful note of his instructions.'

Peto breathed deeply as they bore him up, as he knew he must (though the pain of doing so increased with each breath). To close his eyes, to give in to the pain, would be to risk not opening them again. He had seen it time and oft. Until he was in the surgeon's charge he must look to himself. And he would leave the quarter-deck – *his* quarterdeck, committed in temporary charge only to Lambe – with his eyes open, for he was captain still.

But he could not turn his head in the hammock, and he lay deep. All he could see was masts, and rigging, and sail . . . exactly as they would have been on *Nisus* . . . first post command . . . as if it had been yesterday . . . simpler days . . . harder days . . . happier days? They were taking him to the orlop: he had never been carried below . . . he must tell Pelham to make a note . . . Elizabeth . . .

His eyes closed.

By diminishing light, down ladders, along decks, under tarpaulins, over wreckage, they brought him to the cockpit, as hot and airless a place as an oven. A handful of purser's dips lit the wretched scene, dimly. Peto's eyes opened and closed, but he said nothing. Midshipman Bullivant's eyes streamed. He did not in the least know his captain, but he knew the service.

The marines bore the hammock as if they bore the bones of a saint, for the captain embodied their own sense of worth. They laid him at the surgeon's feet, and wiped the sweat from their brows. 'The captain, sir,' said the corporal, softly.

Peto opened his eyes. He felt numbness rather than pain. He knew it boded ill, yet he was thankful for it. 'Mr Morrissey, I—' He blinked in the sudden light of the mate's lantern. 'Miss Codrington! What do you do here, girl? I said you were to—'

'*Easy*, sir,' said the surgeon. 'Miss Codrington has been working in the cockpit since we began the action, and admirably so.'

Rebecca said nothing, aghast at the sight before her . . . yet determined to continue, *admirably*.

Peto could not find the breath to protest. A searing pain in his neck required all his powers of self-mastery.

A loblolly boy began cutting away his coat, while Rebecca sponged his brow.

'Miss Codrington,' he managed, barely audible: 'in my pocket, a letter . . . from Miss Hervey; take it . . . keep it safe.'

Rebecca stayed the loblolly boy's work by the gentlest of glances, then edged her hand inside the torn and bloody coat, not daring to blink lest the tears fall from her eyes. She found the precious relic, the little oilskin package, and took it from the pocket, tenderly, as the nurse takes up the newborn. And, struggling to breathe the words, she gave him her pledge: 'I will keep it safe, Captain Peto. I will keep it safe.'

XVIII

THE BANNS OF MARRIAGE

London, 8 May 1828

After spending the better part of the day in the War and Colonial Office, elaborating (unnecessarily in his opinion, for Eyre Somervile's despatches and estimates of expenditure were admirably clear), Hervey went to the Horse Guards. Soon the comfortable thoughts that had accompanied him from Golden Square to Downing Street – the resolution of his unhappy status, and the prospect of returning to the Cape in the company of wife and child – were, if not dashed, then considerably spoiled.

Lord John Howard took him to a small ante-room on the other side of the building rather than see him in his office as before.

'I'm afraid matters appear to have taken a turn for the worse, Hervey. I saw the depositions yesterday which the Sixtieth's commanding officer and the superintendent of the mills have made: Lauderdale from the adjutant-general's office let me have sight of them, at some risk to himself I might add, and I fear they may be construed as suggesting you acted hastily.'

'Hastily?' Hervey looked at him in utter disbelief. 'When there were riflemen firing as if it were . . . ?' He shook his head. 'No, I shall not go down that road. There's no blame to be attached to that corps, any more than to mine.'

Howard raised his eyebrows. 'I should not be too reluctant to defend yourself were I you. There may be – how can I put it? – some predisposition on the part of others, in and out of uniform, to lay the blame on men on horses.'

'Oh, great God! Silly, petty jealousies . . .'

'No doubt they play their part. It is enough to wear a pelisse and carry a sabre to enrage some. The trouble is, since the Peter's Fields affair—'

'Spare me, Howard. The home secretary wanted resolute action at Waltham Abbey, and now he appears to be shrinking from it on account of . . . what? Not on any humane principle, as far as I can see, but over a rotten borough in Sherwood Forest!'

'Something of a simplification—'

'And why, might I add, was "Peterloo" so wretched an affair? Because the butchers and bakers of the Manchester Yeomanry were called on, rather than regular troops. How so? Because there were not enough regulars, because the selfsame parliament that howled so much then, and continues to, has disbanded so many regiments of cavalry since Waterloo. Indeed, three more *since* the Peter's Fields affair!'

Lord John Howard smiled ruefully. 'My dear friend, your vehemence – I may say eloquence – is wasted on me, as well you should know. You will have many supporters in parliament if the inquiry goes ill: that much I may say with certainty. I think you might count on the prime minister himself for one!'

Hervey looked suddenly less sure. 'You think it will become such a business – taken up in parliament?'

Howard shrugged. 'That may have been Lord Palmerston's very design in demanding an inquiry of the Horse Guards. Let me put it this way: there's such suspicion of the Duke of Wellington in some quarters, his turning coat and favouring the Catholics on

Emancipation – the Test and Corporation Acts will be voted tomorrow – and on Reform, too, *and* the Corn Laws. Anything that might serve as a whipping board.'

Hervey groaned. 'I had rather thought Palmerston could not be a mover in such a thing – so many years at the War Office and all.'

'He is by no means the only uneasy bedfellow in the duke's cabinet, though it is true that it was he who pressed for the inquiry. He is a most diligent Secretary at War, of that there is no doubt.' Howard raised his eyebrows again, and the rueful smile returned. 'But, Hervey, he is first and foremost a politician!'

Hervey bridled. His friend had been too long in the proximity of placemen: how dare he sport so! 'I think I am better out of this viperous nest.' He rose.

Howard, cut to the quick, angered at what he perceived was his friend's growing inclination to see insult and injury where none was intended. 'Hervey, if you will permit me to say so, your attitude is offensive. Do not presume that your distinguished service gives you licence to sneer at this place.' By which he also meant at himself.

Hervey hovered between defiance and remorse. He took three steps towards the door before turning. He sighed and shook his head.

But his friend spared him the discomfort of an explanation, or even apology. 'My dear Hervey, if my manner led you to believe I did not – that any here did not – regard your conduct at Waltham as admirable in the extreme, then I am at fault and I am sorry of it. Bear up, my friend. If the worst comes to the worst there will be idle speculation in the press; but what harm can that do when the commander-in-chief himself is so strongly disposed towards you?'

Hervey felt like saying that he had his aged parents to think of, which was true, although it did not very greatly exercise him, for they were stalwart enough, even if his mother was somewhat inclined to the vapours; but what was more true was that he could not be at all sure how it would go with Kezia, and her father. Until the banns were read . . .

Lord John Howard now sought to change the subject to something more palatable. 'Why did not you tell me that your sister was coming up? I saw her name yesterday on the levee list for the King's Germans!'

Next morning, Hervey received a letter from Kat asking him to call at Holland Park that afternoon. She was to dine at Apsley House, and she had 'information that will be of the greatest reassurance to you'.

He arrived at three, and was admitted at once to Kat's sitting room. They kissed, on the lips, though briefly, and sat down cosily together in a fauteuil by the French doors to her little, private rose garden.

Kat wore a dark blue day dress, tight-bodiced and full-sleeved, with a yellow muslin tucker – Hervey's favourite colours. She was a year or so past forty, he understood, but she was undeniably (this afternoon especially) one of the handsomest women in London.

'I hear you are the King's new favourite,' she began, playfully.

Hervey screwed up his face. 'What is the game?'

She smiled. 'I heard that you humbugged the Guards at Windsor.'

Hervey looked uneasy. 'Where did you hear? From whom?'

Kat raised an eyebrow. 'From Captain Darbishire.'

'Mm. Captain Darbishire.' He sounded faintly vexed.

'Poor Hol'ness. Such an agreeable man.'

Hervey sat up a little, as if to distance himself. 'Kat, you did not summon me to relay tattle.'

'*Matthew*,' she said, sounding hurt. 'Be not unkind!'

He sighed. 'I'm sorry.' He took her hand. 'It has been the very devil of a time. And yesterday Howard told me the depositions from two senior officers at Waltham Abbey do not augur well.'

'Ah,' she exclaimed, brightening. 'It is that of which I have good news. Sir Peregrine is *not* to be president of the inquiry.'

'What? But only the other day—'

'I made it quite plain to him that it would require his presence here wholly unreasonably, and that we would not be able to spend August in Alderney . . . or Sark, or wherever it is, if he were to preside. I told him, too, that it was all Harry Palmerston's doing, and that the commander-in-chief disapproved of it, and no good could come of it – that Lord Hill might even be minded to recall him from the Channel Islands.'

Hervey was wholly taken aback, quite overcome with admiration, indeed; for Kat's imaginative use of 'fact' was masterly. 'Kat, I—'

She lowered her eyes, modestly.

His relief was prodigious. He kissed her.

She smiled, happy to have made him content.

He put his arms around her, and kissed her more.

She rose, left the sitting room for a minute or so, and returned looking uncommonly demure. 'I must leave for Apsley House at eight. I have dismissed the servants for the afternoon.' She held out a hand. 'Come.'

After breakfast the following morning, while Fairbrother took a hansom cab to Mill Hill (where he had an appointment to meet with Mr Wilberforce, who lived there quietly in retirement, but active yet in his interest in the fortunes of the West India slaves), Hervey took to his feet for Berkeley Square, where (he could not bear to put a name to the man) Major-Baron Heinrici kept a house. Fairbrother had offered to abandon his interview, though it was one he had looked to keenly, for he would have liked to see Elizabeth again. And not merely for the pleasure of spirited company: he knew very well that his friend was in ill humour at the prospect of their meeting this morning, disapproving still of his sister's proposed course, and especially her accompanying to St James's a man to whom she was most unofficially attached; and he believed that his attendance might do something to ameliorate matters. But Hervey had prevailed upon him: it was unhappy family business to which he would not wish to expose an outsider, even one whose friendship he valued so much.

When he arrived at No. 27, Berkeley Square, he trusted that it was at an hour when Heinrici would not be at home, having sent word to Elizabeth the evening before that he would call on her. His sister received him warmly, happily indeed, yet with just the suggestion of unease that derived from knowing her brother's disapproval. She showed him into a small sitting room and asked Major Heinrici's man to have coffee brought to them. She did it so sweetly, and Heinrici's man was so pleased to be obliging (evidence, he rued, of his sister's being entirely at home with her lamentable decision) that Hervey had to remind himself not to be beguiled into complicity.

'A handsome house,' he said, with a note of accusation.

Elizabeth ignored the note. 'It is, is it not? Major Heinrici, I find, has the most felicitous taste.'

That did not sound entirely like his sister. There was a note of irreverence, of defiance even. He would not mince his words (what point did it serve?): 'And you are resolved on this . . . course?'

A footman brought coffee. '*Schönen Dank, Hartmut. Und eine Bissen Kuchen, vielleicht?*'

Hervey's expression was now undisguised: he had never known her possess a word of German. 'You have wasted no time in that regard, I see.'

But again Elizabeth would not give battle: if her brother

304

wanted to test her defences, he was going to have to do so more resolutely than mere tilting. 'Indeed I have. All Major Heinrici's servants speak the most excellent English, but I have a mind that they like to hear me try at least.'

'So you see a good deal of them, then?'

'Daily – when I am permitted by my obligations at Horningsham, and the workhouse.'

One of those obligations, he knew full well, ought wholly to be his own, and the other – their parents – he rightly shared with Elizabeth, though in absentia. Was she trying to wrong-foot him by such a remark? He would not be shaken, however. He cleared his throat determinedly, and moved to the edge of his chair. 'So you refuse to give up this scheme?'

'Scheme, Matthew?'

'Your . . . renouncing Peto, and taking instead this . . . German. You refuse to change your course?'

'Who asks me to?'

Hervey was astonished. 'I cannot believe I am speaking to my own sister!'

'And *I* cannot believe it too!'

Hervey stood up. 'You give a man your word to marry him, and then renounce him to take another: is that right conduct? Is that what people would consider right conduct?'

Elizabeth rose, and threw up her chin. 'Do not you judge me, Matthew! Do not you presume that because I have lived quietly all my life – ay, and obligingly – that I have no feeling!'

Hervey's mouth fell open in utter incomprehension. Then his voice began to rise. 'I might understand it – though heaven knows how – if you were simply to say that you did not wish any longer to marry Peto. But to take up with another while still promised—'

'I have written to Captain Peto . . .' There was just a note of imploring.

'Written? *Written?*'

305

'Matthew, it is our only means of communication. His proposal to me was in writing, and my acceptance too.'

'It is not decent, Elizabeth. You cannot marry this man!'

Elizabeth stiffened. 'Ah, for the sake of appearance you would have me die an old maid!'

'I can't believe what I hear!'

She breathed deeply, her face red with anger and dismay. 'Well, Matthew, I may tell you that I am incapable of obliging you in that regard any longer.'

'What do you mean?'

She held his stare, though with the greatest difficulty. 'I have lain with Major Heinrici!'

Hervey looked as if he would explode. 'Good God!'

Elizabeth's jaw now positively jutted. 'How dare you, Matthew! How dare you condemn me when you do as you do!'

Hervey's face returned to incomprehension. 'What do you mean, "do as I do"?'

'Hah! You think me so provincial that I do not know what takes place between you and Lady Katherine Greville? And she a married woman, Matthew – *a married woman*! Do you want to debate the degree to which we both individually break the seventh commandment?'

Hervey reeled. 'This is unsupportable! I cannot believe what I hear. We can have no more to say to each other. Goodbye, Elizabeth!' And he turned and stalked from the room as if he would knock down the first man who ill-crossed his path.

He ate no lunch. He walked instead for mile upon mile, at turns angry and despairing, yet not knowing precisely what was the true root of the anger, nor of the despair, which did not help his recovering the composure he considered necessary for returning to the United Service Club. Until at about six o'clock, in St James's Park, a Guards band playing gentle Irish tunes he

306

recalled from the Peninsula began to calm his savage breast.

He sat on a bench listening, observing two ducks from the lake making affectionate display, until he started wondering at his own judgement, which he knew, in his wholly rational moments, to be distorted still by the image of Henrietta and that short but perfect consummation of all his childhood longing (and that of his cornet years – the uncomplicated time, the *honest* years). He was doing his very best, was he not, to recover the simplicity of those years? And was he not merely, and rightly, alarmed for Elizabeth's sake, anxious that she too did not fall into the sort of maze in which he had stumbled for so long?

He rose, replaced his hat, dusted off his coat, and, suppressing a sigh that might have been deep enough to make the ducks give flight, strode peaceably at last towards the Horse Guards Parade, and thence to the United Service.

There he found Fairbrother in the coffee room, looking more uneasy than ever he had seen him. 'My dear fellow, are you quite well?'

Fairbrother, holding a large measure of whiskey and soda, which looked as if it might already have been replenished at least once, shook his head, as if doubting his ability to give an answer.

'I am sorry I was not returned at our usual hour,' continued Hervey. 'I imagined, though, that your interview with Mr Wilberforce might become an extended affair.'

His friend nodded, and then shook his head again, seeming to correct himself. 'No, it was of no very great length.'

'What is the matter?' Hervey sat down opposite him and nodded to the steward.

Fairbrother scratched his forehead. 'How was your sister?'

Hervey looked away and cleared his throat. 'I think the least said the better on that account.'

'Why? What transpired between the two of you?' Fairbrother was now sitting upright.

Hervey was first inclined to think it was no business of his friend's, but . . . 'She is adamant she will not marry Peto, and that she will marry instead this German.'

Fairbrother frowned. 'He has a name, has he not?'

'Heinrici.'

'Yes, I know it is Heinrici. If you would use it rather than "this German" you might become better disposed towards him. In any case, I rather thought you approved of Germans.'

'Of course I approve.'

'The most faithful fellows, by all accounts.'

'Yes, indeed, though—'

'Well perhaps you might admit that Elizabeth may admire that quality too.'

Hervey took the glass from the steward, and a long sip of it to gain a little time: his friend was distracting him with superficially reasonable propositions. 'Why were you looking so discomposed when I returned? And still do.'

Fairbrother stifled a sigh, biting his lip and fair rolling his eyes. Hervey knew at once he was steeling himself to something.

'I went to Mr Wilberforce's this morning, and he received me very civilly, but abed. He had a severe chill. I had not thought that he was such an age, which was remiss of me of course. I stayed only a little while; we resolved to meet again when he was better. And then I went to Greenwich, instead of tomorrow. I told you that I'd learned that Admiral Holmes's papers were there, and I wished to see them.'

Hervey nodded: he recalled the intention well.

Fairbrother breathed in deep before resuming. 'Well, in the course of that visit I was shown the hospital – I never saw such a noble place – and on the door of one of the officers' rooms was the name of your friend, Peto.'

Hervey's face at once betrayed alarm.

Fairbrother's changed from resolution to sadness. 'It was

pitiful, Hervey. So active a man as I heard you so often describe, yet reduced to . . .' He fell silent.

Hervey, gathering his own strength for the question, was some time before he could reply. 'What is it? Are you able to say precisely? He is wounded, is he, or is it an infection – something from the east?'

Fairbrother nodded. 'He is wounded, really very grievously. He has lost an arm, and the left is still badly shattered. And he has not the use of his legs. The surgeons do not know why.'

Hervey groaned – a long, hopeless sigh of despair. He made to rise. 'I must go at once.'

'No, Hervey,' said Fairbrother, reaching out a hand to grasp his friend's knee. 'He was dosed with morphium as I left. The surgeon said to give him a peaceful night.'

Hervey sat back and emptied his glass. 'Was the surgeon able to say what had happened? Why have we not known before now?'

Fairbrother sat back, too, and beckoned to the steward for more whiskey. 'It seems he made his lieutenant keep his name from the casualty returns until the following day, by which time Codrington had sent his despatch. The ship's surgeon thought he would not live more than a day or so. He removed the arm and filled him with laudanum, and after ten days or so, though he was still very fevered, he was transferred to a brig and taken to Malta. He was brought to Greenwich not ten days ago.'

'Were you able to speak with him?'

'I was, yes. I told him of our acquaintance . . . and Elizabeth.'

Hervey groaned. 'What did he say of her?'

Fairbrother's voice almost broke in the reply. 'He asked to see you, so that he might tell you he wished to release Elizabeth from the engagement.'

Hervey sighed, loud, and shook his head. 'Was there ever such decency as in that man? Oh, God!'

'The very greatest nobility.'

Hervey gritted his teeth. 'I *shall* see him – tomorrow; and so shall Elizabeth. Let her see for herself what duty calls a man to do – and judge for herself what a woman's response should be!'

Fairbrother looked troubled. 'Hervey, I don't think—'

'No, Fairbrother: I am utterly determined on it!'

XIX

RAIN ON SAIL

Next day

Hervey engaged a chaise for Greenwich, which proved a longer and more trying journey than he had imagined. Scarcely a word was spoken between brother and sister in the two hours that it took to drive there. Even Fairbrother fell quiet after his attempts at generating conversation failed, so that he resolved instead to be their good supporter, though as a silent buttress.

Hervey looked severe but composed. Fairbrother perfectly understood: he knew that his friend had scarcely slept for thinking of the consequences both of Peto's wounds and of the reunion. Elizabeth, on the other hand, looked as gentle a woman as ever she was, but most ill at ease. Fairbrother wondered that her certainty in her new-found love (he hoped very much to be able to meet Heinrici soon) did not arm her more for the ordeal that was to come. But he had not been privy to the meeting of brother and sister the morning before, and certainly not in the evening, when Hervey had taken her the news. He could only imagine what effect his friend's commanding assurance had on a sister who deferred to him as, in most respects, paterfamilias.

When they arrived, he conducted them to Peto's quarters.

There was a rank smell to the place this morning – stale urine, faeces, and something Fairbrother fancied was suppuration. Perhaps it was because the presence of the gentler sex made him more sensible of such things, though had he but known that the Warminster workhouse could smell ranker still, he would not have troubled on Elizabeth's behalf.

Hervey hesitated as they neared Peto's room, second thoughts crowding in on him. Should he not permit his sister to enter first (they were officially engaged, after all) or should it be he, as older friend? Or perhaps they should enter together? Was it truly why he hesitated? He looked at Elizabeth, hoping for the answer, as so often. She took a deep breath, slipped her arm round his, and led him through the door, leaving Fairbrother sentinel outside.

Peto's eyes remained closed. He sat upright, strapped in a high-back chair, his left arm free but in a splint, a scar across his forehead, and another to his neck, his legs bound, and his right sleeve empty.

Hervey's eyes at once filled with tears.

Elizabeth took three silent steps to his side, and bent to kiss his forehead. Peto woke, with a look that spoke of both happiness and dismay. 'Miss Hervey—' he sighed, as if wearied beyond measure. He saw Hervey, and his look became a kind of relief: 'My dear friend.'

Hervey, fighting hard to keep his own anguish in check, took hold of his old friend's hand. 'I had no idea—'

Peto seemed to brace himself, though restrained by the fastenings. 'We sank five, and saved the flagship, likely as not. The deucedest ill luck, this . . .'

Elizabeth, managing for the most part to conceal her own distress, looked at him anxiously nevertheless. 'We received no letters; we had no word, or of course we would have come.'

Peto shook his head, as if to bid her not to distress herself on that account. 'I wrote a good many, but getting them away was—' He began coughing, motioning to the water glass on a side table. Hervey tried to put it to his mouth, but Peto shook his head and took it for himself by the splinted arm. 'It's nothing,' he said, giving back the empty glass; 'a chill caught on the passage home.'

Elizabeth looked more anxious still: the coughing was not wholly unlike the rattling hacks she heard of a winter night in the Warminster union. 'Shall I ask a doctor to come? Is there a powder I may get for you?'

Peto tried to smile, though the effort looked painful. 'No, Miss Hervey, there is no need of either. Only a chill . . .' He closed his eyes momentarily. 'The letters: getting them away from a man-of-war is ever a business.'

'But no word in the fleet returns of your . . . your *situation*,' said Hervey, looking deeply troubled. 'I read Codrington's despatch.'

Peto closed his eyes again, as if fighting something unseen (he would not ask his friend to send for more of the morphium). 'My dear Hervey, you of all men should know that a general's first despatch can be but an incomplete account – a notice of victory, and the bare bones of a narrative.'

'Yes, but I hazard – and from what you have said I am certain – that your ship was in the thick of it.'

'She was, and many a good man we lost, too. But . . . See you, I may as well tell: when I was hit and taken below,' (he began coughing again) 'I gave a most positive order to my lieutenant that he was not to report my injury to the flag . . . which I am pleased to say he obeyed without question for a full day and a half, until I lapsed into . . . sleep, and was not in any degree able to exercise command.'

'But why, in God's name, did you do that?' Before him was a man barely capable of speaking, months after the event: how had

313

he imagined he might command a ship? What spirit was this that animated his friend?

Peto raised his hand, with no little effort, to say 'enough'.

They drew up chairs.

The conversation was no less halting for its being seated, however, and after a quarter of an hour Peto appeared to tire quite markedly. He asked if Hervey would leave him for the moment so that he could speak with Elizabeth.

When her brother was gone, and the door was closed, Elizabeth made to begin, but Peto stayed her. 'I must speak first,' he insisted, and with patent effort, '. . . if you will permit me, Miss Hervey.'

She smiled. 'Of course.'

'It was never my wish that you should learn of things in this way, but you now see what is my condition, and,' (he swallowed, as if to suppress his own reluctance to say it) 'I am resolved upon releasing you from your acceptance of marriage,' (Elizabeth tried to speak, but again he stayed her) 'for you see – and must know when I tell you – that I am unable to be that which you had every right to expect.'

Elizabeth was silent, stunned by both the nobility of the concession and by the gentlemanlike manner of its delivery. There were no tears, though she felt the profoundest sadness. Her countenance was transformed instead by the evident goodness of the man with whom she had once thought she would be contentedly married. And then, after what seemed an age of contemplation, she lowered her eyes, gathering some sort of strength or resolve, and, taking his hand, began her reply.

'My dear Captain Peto, I scarce know how to form any response, for you are in such . . . discomfort, and I in perfect health. I thank you for so noble a thing, and it is for that nobility as much as anything that I believe I must tell you in absolute truth that your release is welcome to me. Not because of your

314

injuries, for they would have been nothing to me were it not for the discovery of my own true heart, which I confess is engaged with another, by a means I could scarcely have thought possible and in a manner I had never imagined could be. Forgive me, my dear Captain Peto, if this is painful to you, but I could never be dishonest with a man such as you, and wish fervently to remain your friend . . . come what may.'

Peto sighed deeply. His own regard for Elizabeth Hervey was now complete. He did not suppose that any man, let alone woman, might be so truthful – not merely in the candour of her confession, when there was no need, and when it was at some discomfort to herself, but in first acknowledging, and then following, her own heart. He knew nothing of women, but this much he did know: there could be no contentment in dutiful attachment alone, not when there was someone else who truly engaged the heart of one party or the other. He sat regarding her, with loving admiration, for a full, silent minute. And then he smiled. 'I think, then, my dear Elizabeth, that we may summon your brother to hear the happy news – the *truly* happy news.'

Hervey received the news with utter incomprehension; neither could he account for the sudden lightness of his old friend's mien, nor his sister's composure. All he could do was reply to Peto's several diversions as if they had been entirely sincere. They took tea, for all the world as if they were at a country drawing room, except (as Hervey perceived, in all its terrible consequence) that Peto could barely lift the cup to his mouth – was incapable of being the man he once was. Would there be *any* restoration? What was he, Hervey, to do?

In a half-hour more, he and Elizabeth began taking their leave. 'Well, my dear old friend,' he attempted, breezily, gathering up his hat and cane, 'I will bid you goodbye for the time being. And be assured that I will return just as soon as my duties permit.' He took Peto's hand and shook it firmly.

'And I, too, Captain Peto,' said Elizabeth, to her brother's further incomprehension. 'Whatever there is I might do, I trust you will ask it.' She bent and kissed him on the cheek.

'I only ask for time,' said Peto, stoutly. 'And a good carpenter to knock me up some contraption whereby I can propel myself to useful purpose!'

Hervey smiled, for his friend's fortitude. He knew full well what must be the dismay of a post-captain deprived of his command thus – and of the woman who was to have been his companion in wedded life. 'I am sure there are many good carpenters in the fleet. Until our next encounter, then.' He bowed, and they left Peto's handsome but land-bound cabin to its doughty tenant.

When the door had closed, and the footsteps receded, Peto reached painfully into the pocket of his coat, and took out the little oilskin package. It was no longer rightfully his; yet he had not been able to give it up, return it to Elizabeth, as honour truly required. Could he summon the strength to do so – if not the next time, then sometime in the future, before the . . . marriage with this other man made it something improper? His head sank to his chest, he let go the moorings that had held fast his countenance while she had been there, and salty tears trickled down his cheeks like the first drizzles of rain on sail.

The chaise returned with but two occupants. Hervey had asked Fairbrother to take Elizabeth back to Berkeley Square, while he stayed behind to satisfy himself with the arrangements for his old friend. Elizabeth had objected very firmly, claiming both a right and a proficiency to be of help, and the unseemliest of quarrels looked like breaking out in the very corridors of the naval hospital, until Fairbrother stepped decisively between them and took his friend into the disciplined sanctity of the magnificent Stuart chapel. Then he had spoken with Elizabeth, and a peace had prevailed in which she agreed to return to Berkeley Square

316

on condition that her brother did not attempt to visit with Peto again that evening.

Fairbrother sat beside her (at Elizabeth's insistence, for the occasional seat facing rear was not a comfortable one). He remained silent, however, allowing her to recollect herself. What thoughts he imagined there must be: the relief of speaking face-to-face at last with the man to whom she was formally betrothed; the compassion which any of her sex and upbringing must have for a man whose body was sacrificed in the service of his country; above all, though, the freedom now to follow her heart. How he envied her! How he wished he could tell her of the object of *his* longing. But it would not do: his friend's sister, whom he admired more each day, did not merit the burden of another's sorrows.

'Mr Fairbrother,' said Elizabeth at length, still gazing out of the window at the crowded Thames. 'You must not judge my brother harshly, if that is your inclination. Forgive me, but I could not but notice your manner this morning and at the hospital. He means nothing but well. It is only that he sees his course, and others', in terms of duty. He was ever thus, even as a boy, though he was not then so . . . unbending. I believe that came later, on account of the death of his wife. I believe he is convinced there can be no contentment on this earth for him; hence his embrace of duty – duty as he perceives it. And I believe he has extended that conviction to me, without in truth thinking on it deeply, only that by some strange device we are conjoined in the natural affections of the mind. I care for him very much, but I am entirely resolved now upon my own happiness. I love Major Heinrici in a way I had never before understood, and I wish Matthew, who has known what I now know, would simply yield to that.'

Fairbrother had to clear his throat, such was his surprise (if not quite embarrassment) at being admitted to such sentiment. 'Miss

317

Hervey ... your expression ... I have never heard its like.'

She turned to him, and smiled. 'Have you not, Mr Fairbrother? I had understood you to have moved in far more elevated and cultured society than mine!'

'Evidently not, madam.'

Elizabeth smiled the more, and turned back to the Thames. 'You know,' she resumed, 'I am quite certain that if my brother were to shake hands with Major Heinrici they could be friends within a very short time.'

Fairbrother almost laughed. 'I don't doubt it for a moment, Miss Hervey. I am certain your brother is incapable of disliking any who answers to the description of good soldier, and I am disposed to thinking, from my study in the matter, that any officer of the King's German Legion would serve in that description!'

Elizabeth smiled and nodded.

'I feel bound to say, however, that I doubt he will leave Greenwich with that intention.'

She sighed. 'I am certain of it.'

The wheels growled over a particularly rough stretch of cobble. After a few minutes, when they were back again on metalled going, Fairbrother brightened. 'Your brother goes to his regiment at Hounslow the day after tomorrow. That is sure to restore his spirits, and his good sense. I go with him too.'

Elizabeth was encouraged by this modest glimmer of hope. She would pray with all her heart that she and her brother might be restored to their former happy state. Did she not deserve, now, some happiness for herself, after all these years of ... (no, she could not scorn familial duty thus). If only he knew, if only he could understand, he would surely not deny her a contentment she had long ceased to have any expectation of?

The chaise rolled on. Her eyes filled with tears. 'But poor Captain Peto: it should never be so!'

* * *

Hervey returned to the United Service Club a little before eight o'clock, having taken a steam-paddle as far as London Bridge and then a hansom cab which had made slow progress on account of the May fairs in the City.

'Lord John Howard is here to see you, sir,' said the hall porter as he collected the key to his room. 'He came half an hour ago. He is in the coffee room, sir.'

Hervey went at once to find him, curious – a shade anxious, indeed – as to why he should visit without prior notice. He found him talking to a man in his late fifties, a tall, handsome, vigorous-looking man whom he did not recognize, and he hesitated for the moment to intrude, until Howard saw him, and rose.

'My dear Hervey, you have come at last!' He turned to his interlocutor. 'Sir George, may I present Colonel Hervey,' and then back to his friend: 'Hervey, the First Sea Lord.'

Hervey bowed. But the First Sea Lord rose and took his hand. 'I am honoured to make your acquaintance, sir. You are become quite celebrated.'

Hervey groaned inwardly. It was a celebrity he could well do without. 'The honour is mine, sir.'

The admiral sat down. 'Will you take a little wine with us, Colonel?'

Admiral Sir George Cockburn was not long appointed. Indeed, it was only this very year that the senior naval member of the Board of Admiralty had been designated 'First Sea Lord'. Until then, the distinction had been the Duke of Clarence's, as Lord High Admiral. Hervey, though not entirely certain of these facts, was content nevertheless to be in the company again of his old Guardee friend, and an admiral of no little fighting reputation.

'I should be honoured to take wine, Sir George, if you will forgive my appearance. I have been out all day. Indeed, I have been to Greenwich.'

'To Greenwich? How so?'

'To see a very particular friend, recovering from his wounds.'

The First Sea Lord looked intrigued. 'Do I know his name?'

'Laughton Peto, Sir George.'

'Indeed, of course. I was myself at his bedside not two days ago, though he was so dosed with laudanum he little knew it.'

Lord John Howard looked perplexed. 'Peto ... wounded? But—'

The First Sea Lord knew the story well. 'The stubborn devil refused to let his lieutenant report him hors de combat, insisting he was as capable of commanding from the orlop as any other was from the quarterdeck. He was probably right, too. His lieutenant risked court martial, damn him, though I have this very week promoted him commander. These frigate men!'

The three smiled knowingly, if each for his own reason.

'What shall happen to Peto, Sir George?' asked Hervey, sombrely.

The First Sea Lord shook his head. 'I'm not at all sure. You will know well enough the trouble the so-called "untoward event" at Navarino has brought: the government – Goderich's government, at least – got in highest dudgeon. The King himself was all of a dither.'

Hervey was intrigued that the First Sea Lord made no attempt to lower his voice at this latter charge.

'And now that the Russians have declared war on the Turks, there'll be no end of it.'

'I did not know that, Sir George.'

'The news is lately come,' explained Howard.

'But what was Codrington meant to do? He had to winkle out the Turks from Navarino, and once there was shooting ... I tell you, frankly, I have the greatest difficulty keeping Codrington in his command, let alone look after his officers.'

'I understand, Sir George. But if—'

'If Peto can get himself to his feet, or even whole and into a wheelchair, I might find him something. Scarcely a week goes by without the same request from Codrington – and not least his daughter!'

Hervey looked puzzled.

'Ah, you would not know of course. Codrington's daughter, his younger daughter, girl of fourteen, she was aboard the *Rupert*. Did sterling service with the surgeon. She nursed Peto back to Malta. Then wrote the most astonishing letter to Clarence! Told him everything he'd done in the fighting.'

Hervey felt like saying 'we are ever grateful for the intervention of female supporters', but thought the better of it. He nodded instead.

The First Sea Lord smiled ruefully. 'And not just to Clarence. She wrote to the French ambassador, and the Russian too. Did you see all the ribbons at Greenwich? Most fetching. He'll have something from the King, too, without a doubt.'

'I saw the ribbons, yes, but Peto made no mention of Miss Codrington.'

The First Sea Lord shook his head. 'I doubt he recalls much of those weeks. And certainly no one would have told him of her intervention on his behalf.' He rose. 'But Codrington himself has the very devil of it still, the affair being picked over as if it were a game of cricket! And by men who'd quake at the first discharge of a musket.'

Hervey and Howard rose to acknowledge the First Sea Lord's leaving, but Fairbrother had by now come in. He bowed, and Hervey made the introductions.

'I am most particularly honoured to make your acquaintance, Sir George.'

The First Sea Lord smiled indulgently. 'Indeed, sir? Upon what account? You do not, I trust, hold against me the burning of Washington still?'

Fairbrother returned the smile. 'No, indeed not, Sir George. I am not an American. But I have long admired your action there in recruiting a corps of marines.'

The First Sea Lord's face became rather tired. 'Oh, the marines.' He shook his head, and turned to Hervey and Howard. 'From the emigrant slaves. That was Cochrane's idea. *Another* of his outlandish schemes!'

'Outlandish, Sir George? How so?' asked Fairbrother, looking disappointed.

'Oh, mistake me not: they were fine men we took in service. Excellent men, for the most part. But the Americans exacted a heavy penalty from their relatives, poor devils. And those they took prisoner they shot out of hand. You're not by any chance a descendant of one of these, Mr Fairbrother? No, of course you cannot be; are you related in some way?'

Fairbrother shook his head. 'No, Sir George. My father was – is – a planter in Jamaica.'

The First Sea Lord had served on the West India station; he understood at once.

Hervey thought he must declare his friend's naval credentials. 'Fairbrother's father's godfather was Admiral Holmes, Sir George.'

'Indeed? They still spoke of him when I was there. Well, I must go back down the hill for an hour or so. I am pleased to have met you, Captain Fairbrother; and you, Colonel Hervey. Do not trouble yourself too much in the matter of Peto. He will have a pension at least. He shan't be forgotten.' He turned to Howard. 'Well, Lord John, thank you for your intelligence of the War Office. We were favourably met this evening. It's as well to know Hardinge's thoughts so soon.'

'A pleasure, Sir George.'

The First Sea Lord left for evening office (the Russian news was occasioning some dismay).

'May we sit once more?' asked Howard, observing the

courtesies punctiliously (the United Service was not his club).

'Of course, of course,' replied Hervey, absently, thinking still of Greenwich. And then he recalled himself wholly to the coffee room. 'Wine?'

Fairbrother, sensing that Howard had business with his friend, declined. He wished, he said, to consult with some periodicals in the library, and so took his leave.

Hervey leaned back in his chair, the exertions of the day finally telling. 'Did I hear you rightly? Sir Henry Hardinge?'

Howard smiled. 'Palmerston's resigned over Retford, and the duke has appointed Hardinge in his place.'

Hervey nodded. 'Then the War Office will be in the greatest state of efficiency – if it was not already.' Sir Henry Hardinge's reputation in the Peninsula was matchless.

'Oh, great efficiency indeed. He went there yesterday morning, by all accounts, and worked without interruption until he rose for dinner not two hours ago. He took all his meals at his desk, and they had to send out for more ink and paper.'

'Hill and Hardinge: the army is fortunate in the extreme.'

Howard smiled the more. 'As are you, my friend. He has rescinded the order for the court of inquiry!'

Hervey sat bolt upright. 'You mean ... into Waltham Abbey?'

'I do.'

Hervey sank back into the deep comfort of the leather chair, to savour the sense of total release, to be free of that feeling that others were in command of the future, in a way that he could not influence by any meritorious service. It was sweet indeed. There could be no last-minute objection now to a marriage to which (he was well aware) some believed him impertinent to aspire. At one stroke of the Hardinge pen he had been liberated.

In a month he would have a fine wife, and his daughter a proper mother. These were blessings of a degree he had scarcely been able to imagine these late years. Only the Sixth's lieutenant-colonelcy eluded him now. But his fortunes were in large measure restored to his own hands: his happiness and professional fulfilment ought now to be but a matter of the correct application of manifold advantages.

XX

PORTRAIT OF A LADY

London, two days later

Hervey stared at the canvas with scarcely less wonder than the first time. The studio pupil had followed his directions admirably, and with great despatch: the blue riding habit had long been lost (it was still, for all he knew, in some press in the snowy wastes of North America) but he had remembered it well enough. The effect, indeed, was of seeing his sweetheart, his wife, as if she stood at Longleat, and he an observer unobserved. He said nothing for some time, until, turning to Sir Thomas Lawrence's agent, he smiled. 'I am most content. The likeness is in every detail perfect.'

'I am greatly pleased, Colonel Hervey,' replied the agent, and with every appearance of it. 'Sir Thomas has been vastly busy these many months, and though he desired to complete it himself he would not have been able in the time you specified.'

It was the greatest irony. The painting had lain unfinished, anonymous, for a dozen years, and now he perceived he had need of it within weeks. But if Georgiana was to see her mother thus, he judged it imperative, for a reason he could not, or did not want to, put form to, that she did so before she acquired a step-mother. 'I understand, Mr Keightley.'

'The usual procedure is to allow one month in order that the paint should dry thoroughly, and we should be pleased thereafter to have it delivered to whichever address you choose. It should then be varnished, of course, but in a year's time.'

Hervey nodded. 'I will let you have a note of the address directly. And in the meantime, if you would let me have an invoice, at the United Service Club . . .'

'Of course, Colonel.'

The address to which the portrait (and in due course, the copy) was to be despatched was indeed something that had occupied him a good deal. As he took his leave of Russell Square, he began once more to cast his mind over the options. In his heart, however, he knew there was none that recommended itself above the others, save perhaps Longleat; but then that would be to consign the image to a place with which yearly his connection diminished. The parsonage at Horningsham did not have walls for such a portrait; and his new wife could not be expected to welcome to their home the presence, even in likeness, of his former wife as well as daughter. In fact, he was already beginning to think his conduct somehow improper: was it not an act of infidelity to be engaged with Henrietta's memory in this way? He could not convince himself that he did it for Georgiana alone; and Kezia might not therefore herself be convinced.

He quickened his pace, as he did, one way or another, when an intractable problem touched him. He began wondering if he should go to Golden Square, to see how were the arrangements for the pianoforte. So that he might salve his conscience a little? He shook his head. He must not deceive himself, no matter who else he might. Not that he wished to deceive anyone at all, except that he was ever uncertain who had title to a man's inner thoughts. *The secret things belong unto the Lord our God*: he troubled over that verse of Scripture as much as he did over any other.

His thoughts returned to Peto, however. His friend had no family – none to speak of: if he did not recover sufficiently for the Admiralty to employ him, in however sedentary an appointment, how was he to be attended? He had wealth enough, Hervey was sure: he would be able to engage such help as was necessary. But how might his *mind* be occupied? That was the material question. How might such a man as Peto, whose life had been spent at sea and in the habit of command – and, it had to be said, who had received the cruellest rejection from the woman who would have been his wife – how might such a man be kept from despair? Did his old friend, as did he, harbour hopes that Elizabeth, even at this hour, would have a change of heart?

He had not seen his sister since putting her into the chaise at Greenwich; she had not written to him, or communicated with him in any way. Nor he with her. Neither would he, indeed. It was unthinkable now. And yet in not many weeks' time she would bring Georgiana to Hanover Square and see her brother married to the woman who would thereafter supplant her in the role of guardian.

In this, too, there lay a concern: he had not spoken with Georgiana of his intentions, where they would live, how things were to be arranged. He had left the explanations to Elizabeth, as he had so much, and yet he had given his sister little enough information with which to allay the anxiety that Georgiana might have – must have, indeed, at least in some small measure. Why did he see these things only now? He had not, in truth, discussed any arrangements with Kezia. He had thought vaguely of engaging a governess to accompany them to the Cape, but more he had not been able to turn his mind to.

That evening he and Fairbrother dined at Holland Park. Kat had pressed him hard to do so before the week was out, pleading imminent necessity of leaving for Warwickshire to visit with her sister. And she was – she insisted – determined to meet Fairbrother properly, 'for he is evidently of singular virtue to have secured your friendship'.

The only other guest was a dowager Irish countess, a near-neighbour in Connaught, who had known Kat's mother since childhood, and who now lived in semi-seclusion at Portland Place. She greeted Fairbrother with a most quizzical look, Hervey too, until after a while she appeared suddenly at ease. 'So *you* are Captain Hervey.'

Hervey was puzzled; they had been introduced, and for some time – for a whole glass of champagne indeed (and Kat had distinctly pronounced his rank). 'I am, Lady Ballindine, though in point of fact it is "Colonel".'

'But you were "Captain", were you not, these many years past, when you wrote to Lady Katherine from India?'

Hervey stopped himself from clearing his throat; the Countess of Ballindine evidently knew something of their acquaintance, and he hoped she did not intend revealing all of it. 'Yes, I was, your ladyship. I received my majority but a year ago, and acting rank at the Cape Colony.'

'Whither he returns in but a few months, Aunt,' explained Kat, raising her voice very slightly.

Hervey had surmised that Lady Ballindine's hearing was faulty, but it did not entirely explain her expression of surprise. He was certain she must know of their . . . friendship.

'And with a new wife!' added Kat (and with exaggerated pleasure, thought Hervey).

Lady Ballindine eyed him most particularly. Hervey braced himself for an infelicitous question, but, having imperilled him in the first instant, Kat came to his aid. 'When is the happy event to be, Colonel Hervey? Is a date resolved upon?'

Hervey swallowed hard, and hoped no one – Fairbrother especially – noticed. 'The eighteenth of next month,' he near-stammered, adding, for no reason he would be able to recall, 'a Wednesday.'

'In London?'

'Yes.'

'Are you able to be more *particular*?'

He cleared his throat. 'Hanover-square.'

'Oh, that is most agreeable – think you not, Aunt?' She turned to Lady Ballindine with a distinctly conspiratorial smile, and then back to Hervey. 'I shall be returned from Warwickshire then;' (she paused) 'I may take it that I *shall* be invited?'

Hervey now saw the net into which he had so obligingly stepped. In the company of an 'aunt', and Fairbrother, and the conversation heavy with overtone, like a huge rain-bearing cloud threatening to burst, there was not a thing he could do but concede the game. 'Yes, indeed, of course . . . I would deem it a true blessing were you to attend, though it will be a very small wedding.'

'Then I shall suspend all other engagements, my *dear* Colonel Hervey.'

He could not but admire, even as he despaired of it, Kat's consummate skill in persuading a man of a course he would otherwise not choose to take, yet in a way that appeared his free choice alone. And so swiftly, so deftly, before even they were sat down to dine. It was, of course, the same skill that she had exercised so well to his advantage these several years; but he had never seen it played to Kat's own advantage at his expense. A very little expense, it was true, for Kat's presence at Hanover Square would be no occasion for concern (except, of course, that his sister believed she knew of their association), though it might be considered faintly distasteful – Kat's sharing a 'secret' with the bridegroom. He sighed inwardly: these were the consequences of the life, the unwholesome life, he had drifted into – *descended* into, indeed.

But it would soon be put to rights by Holy Matrimony. For, as the Prayer Book proclaimed, was it not 'ordained as a remedy against sin, and to avoid fornication; that such persons as may not have the gift of continency might marry, and keep themselves undefiled members of Christ's body'? And if he was not entirely certain any longer of the claims of the Church, there were some practices which were proven by time. Of course, there were other causes for which Matrimony was ordained, said the Prayer Book, and these were by no means disagreeable to him; quite the contrary, indeed – in due season. But chiefly he sought, and confidently, the promises of the remedy, not so much against sin as its wretched consequences. He sought a simpler life in 'the honourable estate', and a better one for the child he neglected.

And he had no doubts, none at all, that Kezia Lankester was that remedy. A delightful remedy too, in the wait for which he could barely contain himself.

XXI

THE EYE OF THE BEHOLDER

London, 17 June 1828

Fairbrother stood winding his new hunter in the United Service's hall. On the inside of the cover was engraved *EF from MH*, and he was still relishing the sentiment with which his friend had presented it to him the evening before. Hervey had spoken of the Cape, the Xhosa and the Zulu, of his gratitude for Fairbrother's 'singularly faithful and adroit service in the most dangerous of circumstances'; and most of all for his 'companionship these latter months ... forbearance and good counsel, support and ... friendship' which he confessed he had not imagined he would see so manifest again in any but Peto or Somervile. And now he, Fairbrother, waited, unusually, on his friend, who was invariably in advance of him. He was, however, early upon his hour; but he had business with Hervey's tailor – a new coat, the final fitting for which had been most promising. He wished it done before midday, after which the two were to dine early with Hervey's parents, and with Elizabeth and Georgiana, at Grillon's Hotel in Piccadilly, where they were lodging, having arrived in the afternoon of the day before in a glass landau lent by the Marquess of Bath.

'Forgive me; I had a letter for the agents,' said Hervey, come at last.

'It was an agreeable wait; I saw Lord Hill.'

'Indeed?'

'Was presented to him.'

'How so?'

'Your friend Howard. They are breakfasting now.'

Hervey hoped that whatever the deliberations were, they would not inconvenience Lord John Howard, who was to stand supporter at Hanover Square in the morning. 'Well and good. Let us go to Gieve's together, then.' It was but the shortest of walks: he would in truth have preferred to take a turn about the park, but he had arranged to call at Russell Square with Georgiana at ten-thirty, and it was already twenty after nine. 'You are certain there is nothing more I can do regarding Devon?'

Fairbrother had written to his father before leaving the Cape, informing him of his sojourn in England, and his father had secured an invitation to visit the relicts of his family in the West Country. He was at once delighted and apprehensive, but he had been determined to detach himself from his friend – and his friend's new wife – for a decent period following the wedding. 'Everything is arranged: the mail to Exeter, and from there I shall be conveyed to Crediton by my aunt's carriage.'

'I must hope you will not be *too* pleasantly detained there: I shall count on your arriving at Walden on the fifteenth.'

'On the ides proximo: depend upon it.'

'I shall. And ... may I say again, my good friend, how prodigiously grateful I am that you will escort my people tomorrow.'

'There is no cause for gratitude. I am honoured.'

But there was most particular cause. Hervey knew full well that Elizabeth wished Baron Heinrici to be invited, for, as she had insisted 'he is soon to be your brother in law, Matthew'. The idea was, however, unsupportable. He had no clear notion of what had passed between Elizabeth and Peto at Greenwich, but he was certain yet that she would come to her senses before it was too late. Which was why he must make sure there was no impediment to her doing so, and Heinrici's attending at Hanover Square would undoubtedly be such an impediment. Fairbrother had, without doubt, been the very model of tact in this: Hervey knew that he owed much to the good offices of his friend in ensuring sufficient harmony for the wedding to be celebrated with all due decorum . . . and happiness. He squeezed Fairbrother's arm.

The Hervey family was, indeed, much engaged this morning. The archdeacon was to call on his old Oxford friend (and as sometime vicar of Bradford Peverell, fellow Sarum priest), the Bishop of London. Dr Howley was soon to be translated to Canterbury, and Archdeacon Hervey wished to present him with a copy of his new-published (at last) monograph on Laudian decorum, as well as his felicitations. Mrs Hervey was still of a mind that such a thing was perilous: ten years before, her husband had been threatened with the consistory court on account of 'popish practices', and she saw no occasion for raising suspicions once more. She had decided to forgo accompanying the archdeacon to Aldersgate on account of the necessity of finding a milliner selling ribbon appropriate to her needs, for which neither Warminster nor even Bath had apparently been satisfactory. Elizabeth had her own calls to pay. And so Hervey was able to take his daughter from their charge with universal contentment.

'I thought that we would walk,' he said as they left Grillon's. 'It's a fine morning, and but a mile or so to our destination.'

'Oh yes, Papa,' replied Georgiana, taking his hand. 'I would see all there is to see!' It was her first time in London proper. 'Where do we go?'

He had thought carefully how he might broach the matter. He

did not know quite why he was so determined that she should see the painting *before* the wedding, before she would have a new mother (have a mother, indeed, for she had never known one). It was, he supposed, some sort of desire for – as Kezia herself might put it – an appropriate 'cadence'.

They crossed Piccadilly at a brisk walk, Hervey tipping the sweeper a penny, thence propelling Georgiana to his left, inside, hand. 'We are going to see a portrait of your late mama. It was begun before you were born, and I learned of it but a month ago. It is by Sir Thomas Lawrence, who is a very great painter.'

'Oh Papa! Have you seen it? Is it like her?'

He felt Georgiana's hand squeeze his, and knew the keenest relief at her evident joy. 'I have, and it is the very image of her, just as she was before . . . before we were wed.'

Georgiana bubbled with questions – how large was the portrait, where had it been all these years, what did her mother wear, did she stand or sit? And then, as if the thought came suddenly to her, she paused for a moment, and her voice changed. 'But Papa, does it make *you* sad to see her?'

He had never imagined such a question of her, for he had never imagined her grown to such sensibility. It fair took him aback, and he was momentarily at a loss to make any reply. 'I am very glad that it is discovered,' he said, resolutely.

Georgiana knew that her father's answer was an evasion of sorts, but she would not press him, for the evasion answered for itself.

When they arrived at Russell Square – it took them all of three-quarters of an hour to get there through the throng of pedestrians, drovers and carriages in Soho – they were received by a footman with whom Hervey had become almost familiar. He took them at once to the viewing room, where the canvas stood upon an easel, and then withdrew.

Georgiana advanced on the portrait in silence, and cautiously, as if she were to be presented. She gazed only at the face, and for a long while. Hervey stood back, not wishing in any way to influence her reaction, hoping, indeed, that she might forget he were there, so that he might see her true opinion, and not merely of the portraitist but of his subject.

'She has a very kind face,' said Georgiana at length, admiringly. 'And she looks very happy.'

Hervey had observed the same: all was revealed in the eyes, which sparkled exactly as he remembered. 'Indeed. We were engaged to be married.'

'And she is very beautiful.'

'She is.' He caught himself echoing Georgiana's present tense, and resolved to correct it as he elaborated: 'She was as beautiful as any I ever saw.'

Another long silence followed, in which Georgiana examined every aspect of the painting. And then she stepped back, as if to take in the whole once more. 'But Lady Lankester is very beautiful too.'

Hervey swallowed. Georgiana's capacity to surprise was disconcerting. 'Indeed.'

She took two more paces back, and towards him. 'And Lady Lankester is now to take Mama's place. Aunt Elizabeth says that I am very fortunate to have such a mother.'

Hervey cleared his throat. 'Fortunate ... yes. But deserving also.'

'What does Aunt Elizabeth think of the painting, Papa?'

Hervey's insides twisted in the peculiar way they did when he was suddenly confronted with some dereliction: he had not even thought to tell Elizabeth of it, let alone to have her see it – and Henrietta had been her best friend. 'I ... I believe I wanted you to know of it first,' he said, hopefully.

'And Lady Lankester, does she know of it? Shall it come with us to Africa?'

'I'm not yet resolved on that, my dear. It is, as I said, barely a month since I myself was first acquainted with the painting.'

'I hope it does *not* make you sad, Papa. I know, of course, that I cannot feel the same as do you, because I never knew Mama, but we are now to begin a new life, are we not? We shall be together for the first time! I wish Aunt Elizabeth could be with us, but she will have her own family, new, just as ours. I hope she will be as happy as we shall be.'

Hervey was rendered speechless once more: he could not have spoken even if he had known what to say. 'This is eloquence', he marvelled, somewhere in his mind, echo of something he had read years ago and had forgotten what or where. *This is eloquence*. For Henrietta could be no more, and neither could their love, for ever now unrequited. Never could there *be* such love again. Yet be some sort of love there must – ay, and with it its compensations. For his family's sake; for his own. Else he would find himself again as he was in that cell at Badajoz . . .

Presently, seeing Georgiana looking at him and not the painting, he took her hand, smiled at her, and led her from the room, unhurriedly but without speaking. Perhaps, now, the ghost was laid to rest. He could not quite tell what or how, but there was a change . . . Curiously, and possibly for the first time, he felt altogether composed for what the morning – the rest of his life – promised. He was, indeed, at peace.

XXII
AN HONOURABLE ESTATE

Next morning, Waterloo Day, 1828

The wedding was an altogether smaller affair than had been the first nuptials of either Hervey or Kezia.

Eleven years earlier, in May 1817, Captain Matthew Hervey and Lady Henrietta Lindsay, ward of the Marquess of Bath, had been joined in stately matrimony at Longleat House amid resplendent uniforms, the regimental band and a guard of honour formed by the non-commissioned officers. And but three years ago, Kezia, only daughter of Sir Delaval Rumsey, Bart, and of Lady Rumsey, and Lieutenant-Colonel Sir Ivo Lankester, Bart, had been joined in very county matrimony at Walden in Hertfordshire, the families of that and the neighbouring shires joining in the grandest of wedding breakfasts at Walden Park.

This morning, however, at St George's church in Hanover Square, there was not a uniform to be seen, and the music was the organ's, though a rather grand instrument on which Handel himself had played (the organist this morning played sober glees). Indeed, to Hervey's taste, the whole church was rather too austere, singularly lacking in ornament except for the gilded names of rectors and churchwardens on the panels of the gallery, and a reredos-painting of the Last Supper, which he thought very dull compared with those he had seen in Rome. It was, however, not an unhappy interior: the late-morning sun streamed through the brilliant plain glass of the Venetian window above, and there were flowers, fashionable hats and silks.

There was an equal number, a dozen or so, on either side of the nave, some standing, some sitting in the high box pews – Hervey's immediate family and brother officers, including Lord Holderness, and some of Kezia's family and friends, from both town and country. Georgiana wore dark blue, and yellow ribbons, the only touch of regimental colour among the congregation (Elizabeth had taken some pains with the millinery), for even Private Johnson wore plain clothes. And there was Kat, in a turban and a magnificent pelisse of green silk, a beauty to turn every head, male and female.

If only Peto had been there – whole or in his invalid state, and Elizabeth at his side ... Hervey, standing with Lord John Howard between the soaring Corinthian columns at the top of St George's elegant steps, greeting the guests as they arrived, could not give up the idea of a reconciliation, even now. The thought of his friend's lonely return to Norfolk, the inevitable if gradual rejection by society (for a man with such disfigurement, even with a Bath Star at his breast, could be no adornment to their pretty world) ... this saddest of thoughts exercised him more each day. Indeed there were moments when he did not think he could return to the Cape, leaving his old friend thus.

As the appointed hour approached, Hervey and Lord John Howard took their places at the front of the nave. And soon after eleven o'clock, Kezia, on the arm of her father, with her attendant, a married cousin, began her decorous procession towards the chancel, the organ accompanying them with something Hervey did not recognize, nor hardly even notice. They had

338

spoken little of the arrangements, for he had understood the difficulty, perhaps, of the undertaking: his own wedding, notwithstanding its bitter-sweet memories, was some time past, whereas Kezia's must yet be vivid in her mind's eye, and that of her family (although it had lately occurred to him how similar were their circumstances, each having lost a marriage partner, violently and within a year of being wed, and each with a child made at once unknowledgeable of a parent). He turned to glimpse his bride.

Kezia's appearance was indeed arresting. She wore a dress of levantine, narrow coral stripes on cream, low-waisted as was the fashion, the skirt spread full at the hem; and in her hair were flowers and ribbons above a lace cap. If he had been capable of admitting it, he would have owned that her appearance was in truth as pleasing to him as that of his first bride. And a curious triumphing sense overcame him, a strange notion that there advanced on him Lady Lankester, the widowed wife of a regimental hero, himself the brother of a fallen paragon, and that she would retire as Mrs Matthew Hervey . . . He could not explain it (or if he could he would not wish to), but it was as if he crossed a threshold, perhaps one that he had not before even recognized. It thrilled and invigorated him to a remarkable degree. And he wished devoutly – *no*, irreverently – for its consummation.

As the bridal procession reached the east end of the nave, Kezia turned to acknowledge her husband-to-be. It was with a look more of composure than of joy, but, he was sure, it was a look of the surest beginnings.

'Dearly beloved,' began the rector, the Reverend Mr Hodgson, whose ministration Kezia had been at some pains to secure since his plurality of livings made his attendance variable and by no means consistent.

Hervey now forced himself to listen with due attention to the solemn words. He had heard them many a time, and always with due regard, for as the Prayer Book said, they were gathered together in the sight of God.

The Reverend Mr Hodgson read the words with compelling weight: they were come, he announced, 'to join together this Man and this Woman in holy Matrimony; which is an honourable estate, instituted of God in the time of man's innocency, signifying unto us the mystical union that is betwixt Christ and his Church ... and therefore is not by any to be enterprised, nor taken in hand, unadvisedly' (Hervey was sure in his own advice) 'lightly, or wantonly, to satisfy men's carnal lusts and appetites, like brute beasts that have no understanding' (he was certain that, whatever instincts were awakened, he did not marry like a brute beast without understanding); 'but reverently, discreetly, advisedly, soberly, and in the fear of God; duly considering the causes for which Matrimony was ordained.'

Hervey looked again at his bride, but she maintained her strictly forward gaze.

The rector reminded his congregants of the purposes of the married state: 'First, It was ordained for the procreation of children ...'

Hervey had not considered this in any particular, but in the natural consequence of events he imagined there would be issue.

'Secondly, It was ordained for a remedy against sin, and to avoid fornication; that such persons as have not the gift of continency ...'

This he knew to be so, and was heartily resolved upon it.

'Thirdly, It was ordained for the mutual society, help, and comfort, that the one ought to have of the other, both in prosperity and adversity.'

This was indeed his design, the remedy he had resolved on in Badajoz, yet which he had never imagined was to be had so quickly or so favourably.

And so the ceremony proceeded. Hervey's thoughts flitted from past to present in a dizzy tableau of his life – its joys, reverses and errors, the people who had been kind to him and those who had not, the people on whom he depended and who in their turn depended on him. What did the sacred poet say?

> *Freely we serve,*
> *Because we freely love, as in our will*
> *To love or not; in this we stand or fall.*

Yes, he had lost a paradise in the white wastes of America; now he would in the largest measure possible regain it: 'I, Matthew Paulinus, take thee . . .'

And with these words, Hervey plighted his troth.

'I, Kezia Charlotte Marjoribanks, take thee . . .'

And thereto Lady Lankester gave him her troth.

At the wedding breakfast, at the house of Kezia's aunt in Hanover Street, the families became acquainted in a more or less agreeable way, although Hervey's mother – as she had feared – imagined herself addressed a deal too highly by the bride's mother (and she some years Lady Rumsey's senior, too), but the presence of so many of Hervey's brother officers, and Lord Holderness, gave the happy event a more appropriate liveliness.

Hervey had eyes not only for his bride, however, but for Georgiana – somewhat anxious eyes to begin with, until by degrees he assured himself that she was as happy with the day as was he.

Even Kat appeared happy – and greatly to his joy (and no little relief). When he spoke to her in the garden she was all smiles and felicitations. 'An adorable creature, Matthew. I perfectly see now your attachment. She will make you the finest colonel's lady. I am certain of it!'

Hervey smiled by return (he hoped not awkwardly).

'I have sent you both a little present. I hope it will please you.'

'Kat, I—'

'And I have news – received this very morning, else of course I would have told you of it before. It will delight you, I'm sure.'

Hervey looked suddenly doubtful.

'After you told me of poor Captain Peto's misfortune I wrote at once to my good friend George Cholmondeley at Houghton – do you know him?'

Hervey shook his head.

'He is Marquess,' she explained. 'But he succeeded only last year,' she added, as if this somehow excused her former beau his not knowing.

'Kat, what can this possibly—'

'He is the dearest boy – your age, I would think. He married very young, and lost his wife not long after.'

'Kat, this is too—'

'I told him of your old friend's circumstances, and he replies that he will take it upon himself to receive Captain Peto at Houghton, to give him quarters there – I think it very near where you said he had taken the lease on a house, and near where he was born? – and indeed to attend to all his material and spiritual needs until such time as he is able to return to his own. Such is dear George's patriotic admiration of his service. You need have no further anxiety on your friend's behalf!'

Hervey was for the moment quite speechless. He recovered only with the most conscious effort. 'Kat, the marquess does this on your recommendation alone? He does not know him?'

'Ye-es, Matthew,' she replied, sounding perhaps surprised at Hervey's own surprise.

'Kat . . . Truly, I am all astonishment. It is the most perfect thing imaginable. And come at such a time, on this day: it makes me so very happy. How shall I ever thank you? I am ever in your debt.' He kissed her hand, smiled with such gratitude as he never imagined to possess, and took his leave of her utterly content.

*   *   *

At the Horse Guards, the windows full open to admit the music of the band of the Grenadiers on the parade ground, crescendo and decrescendo as they marched and counter-marched, Lord Hill was considering the military secretary's memorandum of the bi-annual Board of General Officers. From the list marked 'Majors certified willing and qualified to purchase', the board had selected seventeen of the forty-three names, a process in the main derived from seniority, but some by recommendation of especial merit. The commander-in-chief nodded as he saw and approved each one, and the regiment of which they were to purchase the lieutenant-colonelcy.

Now came the happy strains of 'Shrewsbury Lasses', Lord Hill's favourite (as the bandmaster knew full well). He rose and went to the window, his eyes becoming quite misty at the thought of his Shropshire childhood, of his fifteen siblings, five of whom had fought, as he, throughout the French wars. 'Daddy' Hill, as the army knew him (his paternal regard for the men under his command had been proverbial in the Peninsula), was now fifty-six years old, though by his round face and ungainly frame he might have been a country squire of seventy and more. But his mind was still active, young.

He returned to his desk. 'The Cape Mounted Rifles: that is the decided opinion, is it, that they be reconstituted as separate companies, and no regimental staff?'

'It is, my lord: the express recommendation of the War Office. The lieutenant-governor at the Cape accepts it as a retrenchment measure, and that the penalty is bearable.'

'And Hervey thereby relinquishes lieutenant-colonel's rank.'

'Just so. With effect from the first of January proximo. The appointment was always to be provisional, though I understand that Colonel Hervey was originally gazetted to the following December.'

'And so the board recommends he has a brevet.'

'Yes, my lord. The general officer commanding the London District has made a very particular recommendation, as too has the lieutenant-governor at the Cape.'

Lord Hill frowned. 'Why has the GOC made a recommendation?'

'In part because he believes Hervey to have been ill used over the affair at Waltham Abbey, in which, after all, the regiment under his orders acted in the most trying circumstances, and to advantage. And also on account of a letter he received from Lord Holderness.'

'How old is Hervey now?' (Lord Hill searched for the detail.) 'Thirty . . .'

'Thirty-seven, my lord.'

Lord Hill shook his head. 'And the board recommends that he has a brevet and not substantive promotion.'

The military secretary nodded.

The commander-in-chief shook his head once more. 'I was major general near five years when I was his age. It won't serve, I tell you. I know Hervey from the Peninsula – he galloped for me at Talavera – and I differ from the board's recommendation.' Lord Hill recollected young Cornet Hervey's service very well indeed, and with a warmth that his present frown utterly belied.

The military secretary saw only a disapproving look, and heard only dissent at the recommendation of promotion. He made to speak, but then thought better of it. It was, after all, the commander-in-chief's prerogative to countermand the board's findings.

Lord Hill continued studying the list for another minute or so, before laying it down and taking up a pen. He dipped it in the silver inkwell in the middle of his desk, and struck through the nomination to a brevet.

'Sir, may I beg you to give a reason for disallowing Major Hervey's brevet?'

'You may. It is insufficient.'

'My lord?'

'He is to have command, Harry. *And* he is to advance without purchase.'

NAVARINO

Le vieux colosse turc sur l'Orient retombe.
La Grèce est libre et dans la tombe
Byron applaudit Navarin.

Victor Hugo

Not everyone applauded the battle of Navarino. The Anglo-French-Russian statesmen who signed the Paris treaty had not envisaged a battle at all, believing that a strong show of force would somehow compel the Turks to give up their sovereignty of the Hellenes. Such a vain hope is not unknown to the military today, although at least at Navarino there was more than enough force to do the job once the politicians' hopes had been confounded. The Tsar was pleased, certainly, for Russia's great eastern rival was reduced (Nicholas I offered Codrington a ship to carry his flag while the *Asia* was being repaired); the French, too, were delighted with the news, for it was a most welcome restoration of *la gloire*. In England, however, although the victory was greeted with the usual popular acclaim which Britannia's soldiers and sailors rightfully expect, the official reaction was far from joyous. The Duke of Clarence, Lord High Admiral and a

347

naval enthusiast of almost childlike conviction, was, not surprisingly, delighted: without reference to his brother the King, he awarded Codrington the Grand Cross of the Order of the Bath. But the King acquiesced only with reluctance: 'I have sent him a ribband,' he is reputed to have said, 'but it ought to be a halter.' Indeed, in his speech at the opening of parliament in January the following year, he declared: 'Notwithstanding the valour displayed by the combined fleet, His Majesty laments the conflict should have occurred with the naval force of an ancient ally: but he still entertains a hope that this untoward event will not be followed by further hostilities . . .' And so the recriminations began. They would not abate in the best part of ten years, and never to Codrington's satisfaction, although he was reinstated to command, and promoted Admiral of the Red in 1837 (under a Whig, not a Tory, government).

The casualty returns in Codrington's despatch of 21 October 1827, published in *The London Gazette Extraordinary* of 10 November, were as follows:

British: *Killed 75, Wounded 197*

French: *Killed 43, Wounded 144*

Russian: Returns had not been received at the time of the despatch, but were later given as *Killed 59, Wounded 137*. Of these, *24* and *67* respectively were from Count Heiden's flagship *Azov*, 74 guns, which came valiantly to the aid of the *Asia* in her peril, and which might therefore have been the model for *Prince Rupert*.

Turkish-Egyptian: *Killed 2,400. Losses: three line-of-battle ships, nineteen frigates, twenty-six corvettes, twelve brigs, five fire-vessels*

In fact, Codrington's later estimate put the Turkish–Egyptian figures at *Killed 6,000* (swelled by the primitive or non-existent provisions for first-aid; indeed, some men were chained to their posts), *Wounded 4,000*. Among these were captured British and American sailors, as well as Slavs and Greeks. At least sixty Turkish–Egyptian ships were totally destroyed. Many that could have been repaired were blown up or fired during the night 'in a spirit of wanton fatalism', says one historian of the battle. According to another, French, account, the only fighting ships still afloat the following day were one dismasted frigate, four corvettes, six brigs and four schooners.

This scale of loss is not surprising considering the expenditure of ammunition: from *Asia*, 9,289 lb of powder and 40 tons of shot (1 ton = 2,240 lb); from *Genoa* 7,089 lb and 30 tons respectively; and from *Albion* a staggering 11,092 lb and 52 tons respectively. Readers of *An Act of Courage* will be interested in the comparable effect on land: the expenditure of *Genoa* alone was calculated to be enough to open a breach 65 feet wide in the ramparts of Badajoz at a range of 600–700 yards. Needless to say, the expenditure was considered excessive in the counting houses of Whitehall.

The Allies lost not a single vessel, although many of the small ships suffered proportionately more casualties than those of the Line. The gallant little *Hind*, having no place assigned to her, deliberately took up position alongside Codrington's flagship *Asia*, under the guns of the Egyptian *Warrior*, which tried in vain to sink or capture her. The action earned her the fleet's accolade of 'His Majesty's Cutter of the Line'. She lost three killed and ten wounded out of a crew of thirty, though among the dead was not, I am pleased to say, her gallant commander, Lieutenant John Robb, else my younger daughter would not today be married to the man she is.

MATTHEW PAULINUS HERVEY

BORN: 1791, second son of the Reverend Thomas Hervey, Vicar of Horningsham in Wiltshire, and of Mrs Hervey; one sister, Elizabeth.

EDUCATED: Shrewsbury School (praepostor)

MARRIED: 1817 to Lady Henrietta Lindsay, ward of the Marquess of Bath (deceased 1818).

CHILDREN: a daughter, Georgiana, born 1818.

MILITARY HISTORY:

1808: commissioned cornet by purchase in His Majesty's 6th Light Dragoons (Princess Caroline's Own).

1809~14: served Portugal and Spain; evacuated with army at ✗Corunna, 1809, returned with regiment to Lisbon that year: Present at numerous battles and actions including ✗Talavera, ✗Badajoz, ✗Salamanca, ✗Vitoria.

1814: present at ✗Toulouse; wounded. Lieutenant.

1814~15: served Ireland, present at ✗Waterloo, and in Paris with army of occupation.

1815: Additional ADC to the Duke of Wellington (acting captain); despatched for special duty in Bengal.

1816: saw service against Pindarees and Nizam of Hyderabad's forces; returned to regimental duty. Brevet captain; brevet major.

1818: saw service in Canada; briefly seconded to US forces, Michigan Territory; resigned commission.

1819: reinstated, 6th Light Dragoons; captain.

1820~26: served Bengal; saw active service in ✗Ava (wounded severely); present at ✗Siege of Bhurtpore; brevet major.

1826~27: detached service in Portugal.

1827: in temporary command of 6th Light Dragoons, major; in command of detachment of 6th Light Dragoons at the Cape Colony; seconded to raise Corps of Cape Mounted Rifles; acting lieutenant~colonel.

Main mast

15

16

Mizzen mast

22

23

19

24

17

13

20

18

25

21

14

Poop deck

Captain's cabin

Quarter deck

Admiral's apartment

Upper gun deck

Ward room

Middle gun deck

Gun room

Lower gun deck

Orlop deck

Bread room

Spirit room

After hold (water storage)

Main hold (store room)